JAKE OATS

First Year in The Big Time

Mark L. Williams

Brilliant Books Literary
137 Forest Park Lane Thomasville
North Carolina 27360 USA

For
the players and coaches
of an exciting if defunct era

DISCLAIMER

Many anecdotes related herein are based upon the author's eyewitness observations. Many characters are loosely based on real people. Others are purely imaginary.

This is a work of fiction, *not* history.

The liberties taken with actual chronology will confound the fastidious and amuse others.

A Friend Indeed

Jakob Ots sat behind a large polished mahogany desk. He'd inherited it two years before and was proud of it. Had he more power and authority, he'd insist it be shipped to his new office—soon-to-be new office. The eight-hundred-pound work of art, alas, belonged to the college. It was not the only thing he'd regret leaving behind.

The players and coaches—well, that was always tough. He always regretted leaving people behind. When one works, argues, sweats, and toils for the common good with a dedicated group, it becomes one's family. Once established, a familial bond never breaks. Frequently, one finds oneself squaring off against a family member. Neither expects quarter; neither extends quarter. Nevertheless, the family remains intact. Reunions take place, usually over adult beverages. Those things that were so important once upon a time are discussed impartially. You smile and laugh over the memories, and the familial bond grows stronger.

Damn! It's so difficult to leave those you love and respect. It's one thing when you're kicked out. Jake had yet to experience that humiliation, but the event is made worse when you leave for a better position. Your fellow coaches and players gush over you and wish you good luck and good fortune. Sometimes, your paths cross again, and friendship is discarded; you attempt to knock the "stuffing" out of your "former" family members. When the dust settles, however, you shake hands and are comrades again.

Jim Agee, a "family member," all muscle and sinew crowned by an astronaut-style crew cut, ambled in without ceremony and helped himself to one of the two armchairs canted toward Jake's desk.

"I ain't talkin' to you, Jim," Oats announced with a growl.

Jim swatted away the comment with the back of one hand. "Boss, had I any idea. Well, I'm not *exactly* honest, I guess."

Oats leaned back in his plush reclining chair. "I don't blame you, Jim. You're headed for the big time."

"So are you, Coach."

Oats rocked for a few moments. "Close that door, Jim," he commanded.

As his friend and subordinate rose to obey, Jake moved to the door nearest his desk and closed it gently.

"I'm not sure it *is* the big time, Jim."

He made space on the edge of his desk and perched.

"I've been having second thoughts. Why me? They're trying to dodge a suspension—or worse. I think they hired me until they can find someone with more experience. If they're sentenced to go two or three seasons with a reduced number of scholarships, I'll just be holding the fort until they can find somebody to rebuild their program."

Agee opted to keep the conversation light. "Maybe by then, I can hire you."

Jake was *not* amused. However, it was worth serious thought.

Jim Agee, no fool, realized his error in judgement. The offer to join the staff at Iowa was completely unexpected. He'd been loyal to Jake since their time together as assistant coaches. When Oats climbed the ladder, Agee followed. Had their football fortunes been reversed, Oats would have followed him. Unfortunately, Iowa wanted Agee. They might have agreed to take Oats as well, but there was an unwritten rule: you don't offer an assistant's job to a head coach before he's been fired.

"Fontes is at Iowa," Jim offered, eager to change the subject.

"I know," Jake replied. "I was hoping I could get you to lobby for me. I could use him."

"You know Wayne?"

"I've heard good things about him. You two were together at Dayton, right?"

"Yeah. Before I met you. Jake, if you want…I mean, I could pull out."

Jake shook his head emphatically. "Iowa is a great opportunity, Jim. I'd never forgive you if you pass on this."

Jim crossed his legs and, a moment later, uncrossed them. "Buck up, Jake. You're acting as if you're taking over a sinking ship. Maybe they do want you to fill in while they serve probation. No one knows if there'll be penalties. You're a damned good coach, Jake. If they don't want you for real now, they sure as hell will when they see you in action."

Jake took a deep breath and abandoned his perch. He crossed around behind his desk, gently dragging one hand over the polished service.

They hired Jake to take over a team without a winning season since the war. He skippered them to a 5-5-1 record his first season and 7-4 his second. The small town and its small campus were still celebrating. He'd been offered a new contract for more money. By moving up to Division I, he'd have more prestige and slightly better pay than were offered under the "new and improved" contract.

"It isn't my time, Jim." He sighed. "I haven't the experience to move up yet. If I could keep you *and* if I could get Fontes or someone like him…Hell! Even then, it would be guts for garters. These guys are expected to be conference cellar dwellers this year. Their glory days are over—have been for some time. They had one of the best coaches in the country for a decade, but he couldn't compete with the recruiting of the other conference schools. Now, he's been snapped up by a perennial power. Good for him, but I'm getting stuck with the leftovers."

"Just like you did here," Agee reminded.

Jake Oats shook his head and stared at nothing. "This is way different, Jim. I'm going to a conference where they have three or four teams playing in bowl games every year. I don't know if I have what it takes."

Jim Agee stood up and slapped his former boss on the upper arm to get his attention. "I'm going to walk out of here and pretend this conversation never happened, boss."

The muscular coach shook Oats none too gently for a moment.

"A George freaking Patton you ain't, Jake. You're the Bradly type. You surround yourself with the best coaches possible, point 'em in the right direction, and let them do their jobs. Stay on top of your staff, Jake, and good things will happen."

"Thanks, Jim. I'll remember that."

"Well, remember this too: I been looking at the schedule. We play you the second game of the season. We're going to kick your sorry ass!"

Jake laughed. He couldn't help himself. A fiercer competitor than James Agee did not exist. He'd been a great player; he'd become a great coach. Additionally, he was a true friend.

"When you get to Iowa City, Jim, I want you to march into the AD's office and tell Evy for me that he's a sorry bastard for copping the best coach I've ever worked with."

Jim responded with a tight-lipped smile. He accepted Jake's hand and shook it with fervor. "I'm rooting for you, big guy. I hope you can hire me back before too long."

Jake smiled. He hoped so too. More importantly, however, he felt better than he had for several days.

Jake never cared for the town or the school or the house he and his family shared. Tami, their precocious twelve-year-old daughter, didn't like her school; by default, neither did her papa. He even changed his name upon arrival. The publicity department thought Jake's Estonian moniker was too abrupt for a head coach. They suggested he change to Oats—more American and more Midwestern. Maybe, but for a man who was proud of his grandfather's heritage, it grated to be called Coach Oats—not that Mr. Oats was any better. Betsy, however, got a kick out of being Mrs. Oats. She chuckled whenever she heard it. More often, however, she was Mrs. Coach. She didn't mind that, but it wasn't as "jolly" as Betsy Oats. Tami was teased at school. Tami Oats and, worse, *Little Coach* really got her pants in a bunch (a phrase her father frequently used).

Tami was as proud of her Estonian roots as her father. She insisted on being known around the neighborhood as "the Last of the Estonians," a pretentious title she created for herself. She frequently changed her name to something "more Estonian" and planned to take this habit to college. For one so young, she was a long-range planner.

Jake was not a long-range planner. He was forced, by circumstances, to be a day-or-two-ahead planner. That did not, however, prohibit him from looking ahead in a purely professional capacity.

He felt the warmth of friendship as he chatted on the phone with a former friend and teammate. For a few brief minutes, he recalled those glory days when he and Evy were blocking a path for Tom Harman in his sprint to the Heisman. It was bold, bloody iron man football, but lord, it was fun!

Well, it was still fun, but not nearly so often as in the old days.

<hr>

Oats hung up the phone gently and looked across his desk into the probing eyes of Brice Churchill, the sable-skinned assistant coach who had played for him six years before. Brice lived football, ate football, breathed football, dreamed of football, and drank football. His loyalty was to the game *and* to his former coach and mentor. They were close friends.

"Bastard," Oats said in his gravel baritone voice. "Evy calls me up to congratulate me. He yanks an assistant from my staff and congratulates me on my new job."

"You didn't tear him a strip?" the former running back/receiver asked.

"I know he wanted me to, but—to hell with them both."

Churchill grinned. His polished white teeth sparkled. "A kid from State tells me that Forest Evashevski is a stand of timber in Russia."

Oats laughed. "Next time I talk to Evy, I'll pass that on."

They stared at each other for several seconds. Brice was used to the stare. He'd seen it often enough during his playing days. Coach always assumed an ominous glare prior to delivering devastating news. When he yanked a scholarship or disciplined a player (or a coach), he put on his thunder face. He didn't like hurting people. Even when others hurt him, Coach didn't like taking appropriate action. He was not vindictive. He'd turn and look away only so long. In the end, when action was required, he'd step up. He didn't like it. His thunder look was not intended as a terror device; it was Coach's way of summoning the nerve to "drop the bomb."

Brice was no coward. He wasn't afraid, even if his boss was. "Lay down your cards, Jake," he dared. "What's your problem?"

Oats drew in a deep breath and held it for several seconds. "Church, you've been my friend since you first put your cleats on for me," he began. "You've been a rock, as a player and as a coach."

Brice leaned forward. "Coach, you don't need the gloves. There is nothing you can say or do that will dampen my loyalty. You made me what I am, both as a player and a coach. Just give it to me, warts and all."

"I'm counting on your friendship, Church. I'd never ask another person on this planet to do what I'm about to ask you."

Brice didn't hesitate. "I'll do it."

"Church, you don't know what I'm asking."

"I'll do it," Churchill repeated. "I owe you a debt I can never repay. We're friends, Coach. Nothing's going to change that."

Oats nodded and took in another deep breath. "These freshmen, Church. I didn't recruit them. I don't know a thing about them. We've got to take whatever we get and turn them into fanatics. We're playing in the big leagues now. We're going into one of the toughest conferences in the country. We cannot use our system out there—offense or defense. I need you to take those kids, Church, and make them into monsters."

"You want me to coach the frosh squad," Brice deduced. "I can do that, Coach. I'll be proud to."

"Well, that's the easy part. Church, there are only five games. You'll have only twenty-four practices before the first game—"

"I can do it, sir."

"I need daily reports in writing. Who is best at drills, who is best at system knowledge, who has the best techniques, who looks the best in scrimmage, their forty times, their endurance, the whole pizza. You got to let me know everything. If someone is claustrophobic or has diarrhea of the mouth or hates his mother or has a fruit allergy—I gotta have it all, Church. I can't watch films or spend time with those kids, but I must know them as well as I know you."

"I can do it, sir."

"I know you can, Church, but I can't get you the money you deserve. Next spring, of course, I'll need you on staff, but it's going to be pretty thin this first season."

"I don't have a family," Churchill reminded. "I can hold out for a few months."

"I appreciate this, Church. There's just one more thing."

"*Just* one more?"

Oats nodded. He scowled. "If I fall on my face, I expect you to get a head job and hire *me*."

He intended it as gallows humor. Churchill would have none of it. "If you fall on your face, it's because I let you down."

Oats forced a smile. Churchill, as a player, never let him down. Unfortunately, his best was not always on par with the competition. Well, Oats had crossed the Rubicon. If he gathered a loyal staff of the highest quality, it still mightn't be enough. Players, injuries, team pride and spirit—these were the intangibles. Even the great Tom Harman was just another ball-lugging joe without people like Evy and Jake to make space for him.

Oats was faced with creating a team. If he had a coherent team, he had a good chance—not a great chance, but a *good* chance. He could draw up the Xs and Os and bring in great experienced teachers to drill them and train them, but you win or lose as a *team*.

Who once said, "*Once the game starts, the coach is just another spectator*"? Only a few hundred people—most of them coaches. Oats himself said it *often*. However, he did *not* want to be a spectator at the sinking of the *Titanic*. That would be tragic and sad, and not only for him; he'd take many fine men down with him.

A Friend in Need

Oats returned to his office shortly after lunch. He'd met with the AD and a few boosters who wished him luck. It was all very jolly, but there was an undercurrent of sadness. Jake had enjoyed a successful two-season stint. It was crammed with fond memories and proud young men who made him proud of them and himself. He'd left programs before, but this one was particularly difficult.

He said he wanted to "check" his office one last time to search for anything he'd inadvertently left. That was a lie. He wanted to sit behind that polished mahogany desk one last time. He wanted to say goodbye to the secretaries—again. The following morning, he'd fly on ahead to find a house and conference with his new employers.

Damn! It was exciting to be headed for the "big time." Other than Evy, none of his teammates ever took charge of a major program. It was within his grasp to make a mark on the game he loved. However, it was tough to leave.

It hurt!

He was sitting at his former desk and thinking of nothing and everything. The door was open, and he heard Lois typing out a letter, one of thousands she'd dispatched at his command. This one—who knew?

Perhaps his successor was getting a jump on recruiting. He wasn't due in until the next week, but he was likely as nervous as Jake himself.

Bev rapped on the door frame. He swiveled in his chair rather than turn his head. She stood, businesslike and prim, in a greenish suit. She held a slip of paper with both hands. It was probably a memo to self. The matronly woman's hair had turned gray in the service of the athletic department. She'd seen many coaches come and go. One of them was her husband, who, despite his years, remained, for two decades, the school's most successful track coach.

"Mr. Manning would like to see you," she announced.

For Bev, everyone was *mister*. Well, not Tami, of course. She often came by to see Papa on her way home from school. Bev always announced her.

Miss Tami would like to see you.

How many times had he put her off because of a meeting? How many times did Tami grow tired of waiting and set off for home? That hurt him. It hurt him even more because Tami never scolded him or made him think she felt slighted.

Another school kid was asking to see him. Jake could not keep him waiting.

"Send him in," Jake said, hefting himself out of his chair.

Bev made a gesture and disappeared. A moment later, Mel walked in.

He was *almost* sixty-eight inches tall, but he was built like a cement truck. His handsome features were enhanced by his chocolate-toned skin. He bounded into the room and shook the coach's hand, showing off his patented take-charge attitude.

"Great to see you, Mel. Sit down. I'm happy you came to say goodbye."

The young man grinned. He was in no hurry to release Jake's hand. When he did, he charged to the nearest armchair as if intending to tackle it.

"Coach, I wanna tell ya how happy I am that you gonna take that job! I wanna come witch ya."

Jake was dumbfounded. He thought this was a friendly goodbye. Realizing there was an issue, he returned to his chair. "Son, you've got to think of your education," he warned.

"I got a *ed-jucation*," he announced. "My mom and pap both worked they asses off ta see we had a place to live. Pap, back in the day, worked three jobs, and Mom had one too, jus' to make sure there was food on table and clothes on my back. He never sat at the mailbox waitin' for a gov'ment check. He was too busy. That's my ed-jucation, Coach. Don't sit and wait. Make things happen!"

"This is making things happen?"

"Yes, sir!"

There was no reserve in Mel Manning. It was full speed ahead.

"My pap, he wanted me ta play ball because I wanted ta play ball. I was ready to work and be a provider, like Pap always been. He say, 'Na, boy. Ya got yer whole life ta work. Treat yourself ta some fun.' An' I did. An' I was damn good. But you're the only coach ta give me a look. I wanna go with you."

"Mel, I can't do in the big leagues what I planned on doing here. They're sumo wrestlers out there. I was just going through some of the rosters the other day. There's a team out there that has a 215-pound safety. In my day, he'd be a lineman. Out here, speed and agility count for a lot. Out there, it's size! Not to be disrespectful, son, but you don't have size."

"You're the only coach in these U-nited States that give me a look," he reminded.

Guilty, Oats thought. *I got the kid's hopes up.* "You still want to go to college?"

"Yeah, man. They's ways to do it, work-study and all that jazz. A scholarship would be cool. Pap wants me to go, but he'll have ta start workin' other jobs. It ain't gonna be 'nuf. I says, 'Pap, I can join the Marines like Coach Oats.' It will take longer, but Uncle Sugar will pay me to go to school."

Oats cleared his throat. "When I joined, there was a war—"

"Hell, Coach, they's always a war! They's one goin' on now. I ain't afraid of takin' my chances. You wasn't afraid. You won the Silver Star, man!"

Oats held the young athlete's eyes for several seconds. Finally, he stood up and quietly closed the door. He returned to his place. For some reason, he wanted a barrier between them and the outside world.

"I want you to understand something," he began softly. "There was nobody *ever, ever* more scared than I."

"Coach!" Mel exclaimed incredulously.

"That Silver Star…thing. I was so scared, I don't remember anything. There were several people who saw me, but I don't remember doing any of those things they said I did. I remember waiting and waiting and waiting in that damned jungle. When the shooting started, I remember shitting my pants. That's all I remember of that night."

Mel Manning's eyes grew large and protuberant.

Truthfully, Jake did not remember soiling his pants, but it was doubtful anyone else could be blamed.

He was a college grad when he enlisted. They wanted him to be an officer, but he was anxious. If he went to officer training, he'd ship out long after his friends. He got through basic training with gusto, qualified with his rifle, and was one of the leaders of his training platoon. There was a brief time at home, then a long train ride. Before he was fully aware of what he'd voluntarily got himself into, he was on a crowded transport headed for New Zealand.

Where was the fighting in New Zealand?

Once ashore, he participated in additional training. The brass told them they'd see action in January or February at the earliest. Meanwhile, there were marches, speed marches, rifle requalification, bayonet practice, and lots of saluting, scrubbing, swabbing, boot polishing, lousy chow, bossing, and bulling.

In August, they shipped out. Hell, it wasn't even Christmas. They'd go out, land on a beach, play in the dirt for a few days, and back to New Zealand for more monotonous damned training.

The Marines hit the beach. It was a screw-up from start to finish. Indeed, Jake never got into the landing craft. The brass called off the exercise with less than half the unit on the beach. The brass decided it was too dangerous for the "cluster f———" to proceed.

Jake sat on deck, leaning up against the railing. He listened to the ship slicing through the water. They'd go back to New Zealand and another two or three months' training before they'd dare take another shot at a practice landing.

A stoop-shouldered pimple-faced Marine shuffled up. He sported no visible rank insignia. Jake resented his presence. There was precious little room on the rust-bucket transport, and Jake resented being crowded.

"We ain't goin' sou'-west for double damn sure," the kid muttered.

A few moments later, the sickly Marine shuffled aft from whence he came.

Stupid punk kid! He probably didn't know port from starboard.

The sun hit Jake on the right side of his face. It was nearing the horizon. Startled, he turned his head and squinted into the blazing light. For certain, the ship was not headed back to New Zealand. They were on a westerly heading.

"Oh shit," he muttered to himself.

Mel was leaning forward in the chair. Jake feared he'd drop to his knees and beg. He didn't want that. He'd only known the kid for a few weeks. He liked him. He was not a product of "the hood"; there was no inner-city slum in his fairly new and relatively unpopulated city. Mel had grown up in a small frontier town. Black people were rare, but not uncommon. Mel played with three other blacks, but he was the standout. His team went 6 and 3 Mel's senior year, but the little runt ate up yards like a demon. He gained a mountain of yards rushing and caught more passes than any receiver, save one. He averaged eleven yards a carry. He'd never been thrown for a loss. He was difficult to hit and impossible to wrap up. Somehow, he gained the attention of only one college coach—Jake.

Jake liked Mel. He liked him a lot. He was eager and determined. He wanted to play ball. He wanted to be a college running back in the worst way. If Jake ordered him to climb a nearby mountain in his bare feet, Mel would be off in an instant. He reminded Jake of another eager young lad who was too small and frail to play with the big boys.

That other "young lad" was Jake Ots.

"Let me tell you something I do remember, Mel. Just between us, okay?"

"Sure, Coach," the boy assured eagerly.

If it was "just between us," Mel was the kind of person who would take it to the grave.

"I was sleeping—kind of. It wasn't easy on that damned island with mud and bugs and other pests buzzing and crawling everywhere. Explosions woke me. When I opened my eyes, the sky was red. There was a hell of a naval battle going on out there. Someone started cheering. Soon, we all were. We just knew the Navy was giving the Japs hell! When it was over, we were feeling pretty good. I slept like a baby."

There was a prolonged pause. Coach studied the shine of his (former) mahogany desk.

"When I woke up, the Navy was gone. Gone! The Japs sank much of our fleet. The rest ran away—to include our supply ships. We were alone on an island nobody ever heard of. The Navy was gone, and so was our food and ammunition. I knew we were going to die. We were going to die on that freaking island. Nobody would ever know what happened to us. Our bodies would rot in that jungle. No one would ever know we'd been there. That, son, was as scared as I ever was. Whenever my wife or daughter get sick, I feel that same helplessness. I'm scared because I can't do anything—not a damned thing."

They sat together in silence for a very long while.

"You'll make a good Marine, Mel," he concluded.

Manning leaned back in the chair and threw his right leg over his left thigh and let it rest there. He smoothed out the pant leg of his jeans. "Coach," he announced at last, "I want to go with you. If I prove myself, I'd earn a scholarship, right?"

"I'm sure there might be work-study options," Oats suggested. "You might be able to get a part-time job to help you out. What do you want to study?"

The young man didn't hesitate. "Math and engineering."

Coach had to digest that for a moment. "You're serious?"

"Yes, sir. I want to be a surveyor or someone who does surveying. That's how George Washington got started. I'd like to be like him. Well, I ain't much interested in being president, but the surveying part, well, I'd enjoy that."

"Well, son, you don't have to go to college to learn surveying. You should think about a good trade school."

"Oh, I can't done that, sir."

"Why not?"

"Trade schools don' have football teams."

"I'm sure the new coach will make good use of your talents."

"I ain' goin' ta school here, sir."

"Get a better offer?"

"No, sir. I'm going where you're goin'."

Oats took a deep breath and let it out slowly. "Son, I told you. I don't think I can use you."

For the second time, Mel Manning responded instantly. "Then I'll be the best damned bench sitter you ever seen. You came to me, sir—you and nobody else. You had faith in me. I have faith in you. It yo fault!"

Achilles

Jake had two days to hunt for a house. The Booster Club, of course, was eager to assist. He needed them, but he was wary. It was Booster Club shenanigans that were instrumental in encouraging his predecessor to move on after a long stint. The NCAA was monitoring the program very closely.

He spent two days on the road talking to prospects his predecessor recruited. They were solid players. Jake didn't want them to follow the departed coach rather than commit to Jake's program. He got to meet parents, a key to his style of recruiting. There was a difference between proud parents and stage mothers. In Jake's experience, young men brought up in the right environment are more dependable than those raised as ballplayers.

Jake didn't bother with a motel. He camped in his office. He slept on the leather upholstered couch under a blanket with a bright school logo. He'd retire late and rise early. He missed his family and was eager to have them join him. Betsy vowed to stay until Tami finished the school year. Until then, his ritual six o'clock phone calls would have to do.

He met the team doctor. He was a balding man of retirement age, but he'd been the team physician for seven years. He stood ramrod straight, sat and walked ramrod straight. He wore glasses, and perched as they were six feet from the ground, he could see a considerable patch. If he must examine an injury, he bent at the waist. Jake learned that some players called him a horse doctor. Perhaps he was. However, he was a cracker-jack diagnostician and no slouch with knees and knee operations. When he spoke, his eyes locked on Jake's. His voice was resonant and his grammar perfect. In truth, his posture and demeanor unsettled Jake. Nevertheless, Dr. Richmond was venerated by the athletic director.

Jake watched a lot of film. He wanted to grade as many returning players as possible.

Jake was watching defensive films, rerunning and rerunning and rerunning every play to watch individual players. He studied the goal line technique. In the game he selected, the defense spent way too much time near the goal line. It wasn't a defensive formation Jake would use, but that did not disguise player techniques and abilities.

The year prior, the team used the "brownie" technique inside the five. The linemen squatted like toads, head down, tail up. They were to move under the blockers and make a pile *behind* the line of scrimmage. It was the job of the linebackers to find the ball and stop the play. When the ball was snapped, the offensive lineman aimed for the *V* of the neck of the defensive lineman. That was a standard coaching technique. However, one toad did *not* drive. Instead, he *hopped* like a toad onto the back of the would-be blocker and created havoc in the backfield. It was for naught. The power play went to the opposite side; six points for the bad guys.

Jake reached for the game program. The leaping toad was a junior; he'd be back. He was listed at 215 pounds, big enough to play safety for one of opposing teams. Regardless, the kid was agile and quick—he moved the same instant the center snapped the ball, and he made a hell of a mess.

"I can use you," he muttered.

The phone rang.

He consulted his watch. It was nearly nine o'clock.

"Jake Oats here," he growled.

"Jake! Last I heard, you were in prison!"

"Gus! I was beginning to think you'd been deported."

Gus Avery, a southern boy who hitchhiked north to play for the only school who'd have him. Jake never saw him play, but they served on the same staff a dozen years before. He was hands-on. He could coach a T. rex to tap dance. He'd also forgotten more about defensive football than Jake would ever know. Jake called for him the moment he knew of his new job. Gus was difficult to get hold of. Apparently, one of his messages got through.

"You still in Winnipeg?"

"I'm in Montgomery. I'm coaching in Calgary this next season."

"You didn't get that job at Wake?"

"Nah."

"Good. How'd you like to be my defensive coordinator?"

"Couldn't get anybody good, huh?"

"When can you get up here?"

"I can leave tomorrow."

"No hitchhiking, Gus. I need you as soon as possible."

"See ya soon, you old fraud."

Click.

Jake was amazed that Gus didn't throw open the office door and walk right in. Too bad he didn't. He could use an extra pair of eyes to go over all those damned films.

Jake enjoyed a shower and shave in the coach's locker room. He kept three suits and a set of street clothes in his capacious locker. He opted for his dark blue getup, plus a tie in the school colors. The tie clashed with his togs, but he hadn't yet budgeted time to be measured for a dress uniform in the colors of his new environment.

He spent the morning chatting with some of the recruits his predecessor left him. He spent a few minutes getting acquainted with the secretaries.

Barbara Hicks made it a point to dress well. She was a blondish woman and very attractive. She enjoyed a good *clean* joke and was quick to share those she collected. She was pushing forty very hard if, indeed, she hadn't broken the barrier. She looked as trim and vivacious as a woman in her late twenties. Indeed, Jake thought of her as *too* young until he learned she had a daughter graduating from high school that coming spring.

Holly Baker was content to be banished to a desk farthest from the office door and nearest the wide outside window. She monitored the venetian blinds. More correctly, she was in sole command of them. Once adjusted to her liking, it was dangerous to tamper with them or even suggest they might require readjustment.

She was full figured with shoulder-length black hair. Her skin had a darkish tone suggesting an ethnic background—Mexican? Indian? Basque? Jake was curious, but not enough to snoop.

Holly was a workaholic. She must keep busy. She typed up all *official* documents, filed any stray item she came across, and kept the office "neatenized" (her word). She opened all incoming missives and promptly delivered them to the proper people. She'd leave all coaches and player mail with Barbara, who, in turn, left them with Jake for proper dispersal. When she had nothing to do, a rare occasion, she'd amble down to the break room and brew a fresh pot of coffee. If the coffee she found was freshly brewed, she'd dump it out and start another. Jake heard she once scrubbed down the ladies' room when the cleaning crew's efforts didn't match her exacting standards.

Holly seldom took a coffee break. She'd have a mug sitting on her desk as she worked. Frequently, she'd toss out half a cup or more after it became stone cold. She'd listen to Barbara's jokes and laugh politely. The two women got on well but seldom associated beyond the athletic department.

Barbara for looks, Holly for precision, Jake concluded.

"Coach Oats," Barbara hailed the moment he entered the office.

Jake watched her abandon her typewriter for a moment to reach across her desk. She captured two slips of paper and held them out.

"Two messages for you."

Jake accepted them with thanks and ducked into his office. He left the door open, the universal symbol that he was available.

One was a list of eight players who could not attend the "all hands" meeting that afternoon. They might be attending class or skylarking. Until he knew, they'd get the benefit of doubt. He'd filed this list against the day when he'd know them better.

The other message was from Joe Epps.

Jake and Joe had crossed paths several times as adversaries. At coaching clinics, they tended to sit together and discuss presentations (*dissect* would be more accurate) over coffee in the evenings. Joe was an

All-American guard in the early fifties. He was too small for the position, but as Joe himself often reminded, "Nitro comes in small packages." From Joe, Jake learned more about line play and techniques than he and Evy ever learned during their playing days. Joe liked strong cigars and coaching. Joe also liked Jake.

"Joe," Jake blurted into his phone. "Great to hear from you. What can I do for you?"

"They canned us," he announced. "Could you help a fellow Armenian who's down on his luck?"

"You're kidding!"

"Nope, Marion, Little Joe, and I are living on the street."

Jake doubted that.

"What the hell happened?"

"Hell, like I know! There were some dirty goings on in the department, and the board of regents sacked the entire staff to duck litigation, and so and so and so. Pisses me off! If I'm accused of something, I think I have the right to know what the charge is so I can defend myself."

There were two things Jake knew about Coach Epps: he was one hell of a coach, and he was a friend.

"Oxford, Ohio, called me," Epps continued. "They want me to interview for the top job."

"Obviously, they think you're clean," Jake deduced. "There's a legion of great coaches who started in Oxford."

"I appreciate their confidence, of course, but I don't want the job. Too much ass-kissing for my blood."

Jake sucked in a lungful of air. "Thanks for that, Joe."

"Jake, I'll crawl over broken glass for a job. I mean, we're okay for a while. I can go back to selling houses. I'd probably make more money, but, Jake, it's only been a few days, and I miss it."

"I've got an o-line coach, Joe, but I can't afford to pass up your expertise. How'd you feel about coaching running backs?"

"I'll coach the yell squad if that'll get me on the payroll."

"I'll have to clear this with the prez and his boys."

If they didn't want scandal in the Beehive State, they certainly didn't want it imported into Jake's domain.

"It's called ass-kissing, Jake," Joe reminded.

"Level with me, Joe. Were you involved in anything?"

"Scout's honor, Jake. The first I knew that something was cracked was when I get the pink slip."

"Okay, Joe. As far as I'm concerned, you're in the club. I'll talk to the man first chance."

"I'll be sitting by the phone, Jake. I got no place to be."

Damn!

Jake got up from his larger desk (though not nearly as nice as the one he'd left behind). He sauntered over to his office door. "Can one of you ladies get me an appointment with the president?"

"Nature of business?" Holly asked, not bothering to look up from the papers she was collating.

"Staffing."

Without a moment's hesitation, the phone was in her hand. She dialed.

He picked the hour because it was the normal practice time during the football season. There were, however, eight players "missing." Presumably, they had a class or a lab. That was not a problem. This was not a formal meeting. However, the players had a right to see the newbie.

He entered the meeting room at the exact time he announced. A mob of students in eclectic attire lounged in the theater seats. They rose to their feet without command. Many swiveled to catch their first glimpse of the *big guy*. Jake said not a word until he got to the podium.

"I'm not here to lay down the law, gentlemen," he began, projecting his rich baritone across the room. "I'm up to my armpits in alligators. I'm getting acquainted with people and facilities, collecting a staff, watching you men on film, house hunting, and scoping out the coeds."

This got a modest chuckle.

"If you were a starter last season, you're a starter this spring—until someone shows me they're better. In that case, adjustments will be made. I want to speak with all of you individually. When I get settled, I'll have a sign-up form in the main office. Sign up for a time. If you sign up, I expect you to be there *and* on time. If you miss the date and time *you* selected, you will drop on the depth chart. Don't be surprised if I show up at one of your classes. You're here to play ball, but I'm a stickler for discipline, gentlemen. If you skip classes or slack up on assignments, you're more likely to dog it on the field. You skip class without a damn good reason, we will have words—guaranteed!"

The door opened. In came a latecomer. Jake recognized him. He was the Italian import, a running back.

Damn all running backs.

Jake, and everyone else, watched the senior-to-be enter. He was visibly flustered at the attention. He was very concerned about Jake. He wilted under the mentor's frown. He quickly and awkwardly moved to an empty seat.

No one spoke. No one moved.

Beads of sweat gathered on the young man's brow. Figuratively and from his point of view, several hours crawled past under the heat of Coach's frowning glare. Further, his teammates appeared to be committing his every move to memory.

Once seated, his eyes locked onto Jake's.

Jake waited an additional several seconds before clearing his throat. "Being early is to be on time," he announced, looking squarely at the running back. "Being on time is to be late. Being late is to be...*forgotten*!"

The running back squirmed. In this activity, several of his teammates joined him.

"Offense, you go on the snap count. Defense, you go on the movement of the ball. Everyone in this room will be where you're required to be and ready to work as directed. That's a part, an important part, of what we do."

Jake let it sink in. He let it sink in for a *long* while. Every moment of that long while, the tardy running back was the recipient of Jake's undivided attention. It must have seemed an eternity before Jake cleared his throat again and expanded his view to include the rest of the squad.

"Gentlemen, I told you I'm not here to lay down the law, but I am a troubled man. When I walked in here today, I found a group of young men relaxing, picking their noses, scratching their asses, chatting with teammates, chewing gum, and various other things one has a right to expect of college students. Well, everyone, that is, except for Gino Della Corte over there."

Every eye widened. Not only did he know the offender's name, Jake pronounced it correctly, without the American corruption. That earned him a pile of oomph!

"The problem is simple: you are *not* just college students. You are a football team. *Casual* doesn't fit in that context. I'm a Marine, for those of you who don't know. That does *not* mean that I want to turn you into killers. It does mean, however, that you must be alert and ready. I appreciate your standing up when I made myself known. That's good. It's a small part of good discipline. Even during the off season, keep your hair clean and neat. During spring drills and during the season, I will not allow hair hanging out of your helmet. No jewelry on the field. Rings and things can get caught too easily on too much. If you lose a finger or the necklace a rich uncle left you, we ain't calling time out or wasting practice time to look for it. At practice, you do not lope or jog to your next drill or station. You sprint. Practice time is precious. Get there fast, and be ready. If you need a break, take it while your position coach, or me, get our fat asses over there. When I call a meeting, I expect everyone, including coaches, to arrive before I do. That includes you, Gino."

There was a subdued expression of mirth over this.

"Hit that weight room. Keep in shape. When spring practice begins, I expect you to be ready to hit and scrimmage and drill and sprint like it's the third week of practice rather than the first. When my office door is open, you may enter without permission. If you have problems with your classes, or if you don't have heat or hot water, or if you have problems at home, we can talk. Do *not* come to me with wife or girlfriend problems— see a chaplain or somebody else about that stuff. My wife thinks she can handle those things. Be warned, though, she will always side with the woman."

He knew who the married men were by the way the other players smirked while turning heads in their direction.

Jake looked at his watch. "Next time we meet, we will talk football. Now, I must get out of here, or *I'll* be forgotten. Gentlemen, make certain Gino is the last to leave. Gino, you turn out the lights."

That got a laugh. It also ensured that Gino would, indeed, be the last out the door.

Questing

Three days on the recruiting road were welcome. He slept in a real bed and had plenty of time in the evening for phone conversations with Betsy and Tami. He even got to help Tami with her math homework, something he had no time for when at home.

Restful though his afternoons and evenings were, he was restless and worried. There were ten thousand things requiring his attention. He made a note whenever he thought of one, but the list grew longer; few of the items were getting checked off. Whenever he called the office, Barbara answered. He gave instructions; she knew in whose lap each item should rest.

When he returned, she jumped up from her desk. After greeting him, she handed him a page from her notepad (in shorthand). Each item he'd phoned in was recorded and, subsequently, lined through.

"Good work," he congratulated.

Of course, he would have to spot-check. Barbara knew that. He trusted her enough to delay his snooping until the morrow. There was a stack of messages on his desk that required attention. He noticed his framed picture of Forest Evashevski was mounted on the wall, as per his instructions. There was a thin black strip of tape running diagonally across the lower left corner. Evy was his friend and mentor; it was he who talked Jake into coaching. Subsequently, he'd provided invaluable advice over the years. However, he'd "stolen" a coach from his staff, a man Jake sorely needed. Someday, he'd tell Evy about the black mark. They'd laugh about it. Currently, however, Jake was not in a laughing mood.

———•———

Mike Miller was seated in one of the fancy leather-upholstered chairs. He was the second person, after Evy, to catch his attention. The buzzer on his phone console rang.

"Right with you, Mike," Jake assured, picking up his phone. "Coach Avery wants to come by before he leaves."

It was Barbara. He'd left her only five seconds prior. Well, bigger school, faster game.

"Send him in the moment he gets here."

"Ten-four."

Click.

A woman of few numbers. He wanted to get to know her better. He'd sized up Holly quickly. Barbara, however, was harder to read. There was something beyond her efficiency that was, well, *alluring* for want of a better word. Meanwhile, he was here to do a job, and that job did not include investigating the office staff.

He looked directly into Miller's youthful face. He wasn't very big, but a blind man could tell he was athletic. Not too many years before, he played quarterback and safety behind an all-American. He didn't get much playing time. Instead, he got the coaching bug. His career goal was to become a head coach. Toward that end, he studied every facet of the game, attended every possible clinic, and coached every possible skill. Jake hired him as offensive line coach. He was knowledgeable and eager.

So what the hell did he want?

"You hired Epps."

"The big boys wanna check him out first, but I think it's likely," Jake explained.

"He's the best damned line coach in the country," Miller assured. "I'd be a fool to keep him from what he does best. It wouldn't be fair to any of us."

"You got a solution?"

"Let me take the D-line. I'll be working with Gus. What he don't know about defense ain't worth knowing."

That was big of Mike. Damn big!

"Only if Joe comes," Jake insisted.

"Understood."

"Good. Now, get out of here and get me a linebacker."

Mike stood and nodded. "Speaking of linebackers…"

It was Gus, all six-two, 150 pounds of him. He was scrappy. He hitchhiked from the deep south to the northwest to play for the only team that would have him. He was good, not great. However, competitive juices flowed through his body. He'd coached high school, college, pro (in the CFL). He could have been (*should* have been) a head coach years before, but he, like Joe Epps, was too focused. Neither of them wanted to be diverted from the game for a second.

"Hey, Gus," Miller greeted.

"Hey, yourself. Go get us a linebacker."

"I'm leaving in an hour," Miller informed.

Gus threw himself into the chair Miller vacated. Before the new D-line coach exited the room, Gus got down to business. "I've studied so much film in the past two days, my dreams are running in reverse."

"And?" Jake urged.

"We got two backers. That's it."

Jake frowned. Counting the sophomores-to-be, there were five on the roster. One or two might impress during spring practice, but they'd remain cyphers until trial by combat. Jake did not want to consider the consequences. Wisely, Gus would not place bets on the unknown.

"We'll have to run a fifty-two," Jake grumbled.

He tried to like the fifty-two. All the coaches he'd worked for used the fifty-two, but he was never comfortable with it.

"I don't want to cover the center," Gus announced. "The center is three of my initial keys."

"Well, hell, Gus! Ya just told me we can't use the forty-three."

"Who said anything about that?" Gus demanded.

Jake leaned back in his chair. He looked at his watch and at his desk calendar. "You got ten minutes, Gus."

The man with the southern drawl leaned forward and rubbed his hands. "I've watched a lot of films. I've looked at the stats of every conference team for the past three years. Here's the poop: five conference backs have broken school rushing records during those three years. Most have quality passing games, but the run is the bread and butter of every conference team. Suppose we have a modified forty-four. Two studs on guards, two studs on the outside shoulders of the tackles, and two backers on the outside of the formation—"

Jake opened his mouth, only to be stilled by a cautionary finger.

"We've got linemen for the middle. We're good there. Instead of outside linebackers, we use the ends. It's the same position they play in the fifty-two. Have them right up on the line for outside contain."

Jake couldn't help but smile. "It's the old 6-2-2-1," he reminded. "That went out with leather helmets."

"Because every coach in this country is paranoid of the pass. I ain't. If it's a run—and odds are it will be—we have eight men on it. If it's a pass, we've got four rushing and seven defending."

"You interest me, Gus," Jake said without hesitation. "Draw it up for me. I have Wednesday morning free. I'll meet you in the conference room. I'll make certain Holly has the coffee cookin' before we get there."

Next was the trainer, Tom "Lacey" Brian. He got his nickname because he could tape a tight ankle in less time than it took Jake to tie his shoes. He'd been taping ankles, tending booboos, and cinching up leg and arm braces for longer than the collective athletic department's memory. His physique betrayed his fondness for food, and his face was slightly bloated. Jake's first impression was that Lacey was a poster child for the gout. There was nothing wrong with the man's brain, however. He liked to speak in doggerel whenever he had more than a dozen words to say. He was witty without being vulgar.

"The boss wants me to run something by you."

"It can't be too important," Jake grumbled, anxious to get to the paper blizzard off his desk.

"It ain't, but he's the money man." Lacey snorted. "I gotta young feller takin' a few classes here. He wants to work with animals, but he hasn't the aptitude to be a vet. I want him as an assistant."

"And I have to give the green light?"

Lacey shrugged his meaty shoulders. "I never said it made sense. I just follow orders."

"Why would the AD want me to put my oar in? Is this kid a Russian spy or something?"

"He's got a game leg. Elephantiasis."

"This is a problem?"

"Not for me. He can tape as good as me. He can't run, but he can move as fast as I can."

"Is there any reason why we shouldn't hire him?"

Lacey shook his head and sighed.

"If he can do the job, if he has your endorsement, that's good enough for me."

Lacey slapped his thighs and proceeded to lift himself up. "Thanks, Chief," he said with enthusiasm. "The kid needs the money 'cause his family ain't got none."

"Hold up there!" Jake snapped.

Lacey was caught in midstride.

"We're not running a charity ward here," Jake reminded.

Lacey looked the coach dead in the eye. "This kid can handle the job as my assistant," he insisted. "What's more, he *wants* to be my assistant. Don't you see? He can't work for free!"

There it was. Jake had been warned. At the end of a serious exchange, Lacey worked in a couplet.

"I'll get a memo on the AD's desk within the hour," Jake promised.

Lacey nodded and took his leave.

Jake followed him out to find Barbara typing away on a department yellow memo form.

"Consider it done," she said to Jake.

He nodded and turned about to battle the clutter on his desk.

"Chief," Barbara added belatedly.

He was tempted to say something, but that would only waste more time.

Don't dig a rut, he said silently to himself. *Keep your mouth shut!*

Lacey wasn't the only po 8 in the department.

Questing II

Jake attended the Booster Club luncheon in his rented car. He stood behind the podium and presented the multitude the standard hip-hip-boom-bah bit. In return he got a rousing ovation. Half the members held a grudge against—well, whoever they held a grudge against for "allowing" the previous coach to secure a "better" job. The other half welcomed the man they'd turn on at the drop of a hat—or the loss of a game. On that afternoon, however, they were pleased with Jake's fire and brimstone.

Jake hoped the word would circulate.

Prior to the welcome wagon bit at a local Chinese eatery, Jake sequestered himself with the president of the organization.

"I welcome your support," he began solemnly. "I don't have time to be cute, so I'll lay it on the line. We are on the NCAA radar—don't interrupt please. Just listen. I don't know if there is any substance to the rumors, but we better keep our heads down. If I see a player driving a car I know he can't afford, I'll call the Association myself. If any of these men get paid for jobs where they don't show up, you and me and all the players and everybody in the Booster Club will be up to our asses in sharks out for blood. Help a player find a job—fine! Pay for a team banquet once or twice a year—fine! Support my program—super fine!

Know this: anything that sounds or feels as if it's *at* or *over* the line, I insist you shut it down. If in doubt, call me.

"If the NCAA sniffs blood in the water before I do, I'll interpret it as disrespect for the program, the school, and me personally."

"Read you loud and clear, Coach."

The president was a balding car dealer. He listened closely. He nodded his head in the appropriate places. If he was a grifter, he disguised it well.

"I don't mean to accuse you or the Booster Club of doing anything wrong," Oats added quickly.

"Understood, Coach."

Quickly, Jake filled him in about hiring Joe Epps.

"The NCAA has investigated. Joe's got a clean bill of health. Still, I won't bring him in until the president and the board give me the okay. Understand, if there are Association snoops in this town now, they're certain to be more if Joe comes here. We must be squeaky clean."

The man nodded. "I'll make sure our members understand the situation," he assured.

"Good enough!"

The two shook hands to seal their understanding.

<hr>

As Jake walked into the office, Barbara waved him over to her desk. She handed him a small page from her memo pad. It took him only a moment to read it. She then handed him a formal letter. He read it through twice.

"Should I keep this?" he asked.

"Sure," she replied. "We have a copy in the files here. We sent another to the AD."

"Thanks, Barbara. Good work."

He entered his office and placed the letter in his top right drawer. That, habitually, was his *hot spot*. Anything demanding attention was stowed there until the matter was dispatched.

He picked up the phone and dialed the number taped to his desktop. Amazingly, the man himself answered in record time.

"Joe, I just got the high sign. Pack your bags."

"Thanks, Jake. I'll be there in a couple days."

As if on cue, Barbara buzzed. She was only a few feet away from Jake's open door. She could speak in a normal voice, but she opted to use the interphone. Jake guessed she wanted to give the appearance of official business.

"The team captains are here."

Jake felt like a fool, but he'd play the game.

"Send them in." He hung up the phone and stood. In walked two burly young men. Stan Zwetschke (6'1" and 220) and Steve Ogle (6'1" and 185) marched in shoulder to shoulder. Stan had light brown hair with a definite reddish tint that he combed with a neat part above the left ear. He had a boyish, impish face and a thick neck. His chest swelled impressively.

Steve had light hair, cut short. He was Jake's notion of Joe College, trim, neatly dressed, and armed with an infectious grin.

It was unusual for an offensive lineman to be elected captain. Jake had watched enough film to consider Stan competent and effusive, but he was hardly a *star*. Steve was a sure tackler and adroit at man coverage—*tight* man coverage. He was a sure tackler and not afraid of man nor beast. However, if his time in the forty-yard dash was ever made public, Steve would be reduced to waving goodbye to speedy receivers. Their choice as cocaptains provided insight. These were not stand-up-and-take-notice players. Obviously, they brought important intangibles to the team.

Jake loved intangibles. Properly utilized, they were motivational. Additionally, they encouraged everyone to up their play a notch—or two.

They shook hands, and Jake ushered them over to the couch against the far wall. He fetched a chair from the back of the office and parked it across the coffee table from them. It was a highly polished armchair, but hardly attractive. Jake planned to use it as a "hot seat." When he called in someone for a dressing down, they'd have to squirm in the least attractive, least comfortable furnishing in his office.

There was five minutes of chitchat. Jake learned that Stan wanted to be an architect. Once his eligibility was spent, he'd transfer to a school better suited to his career choice. Similarly, Steve was aiming for law school to follow in his father's footsteps. He was not aiming for the high-stakes stuff. He hoped to settle down in a small rural community and deal with local problems and squabbles; he didn't want to get *stuck* in a specialty.

"Men," Jake began at last, "I've been so busy with the newcomer bit that I haven't had any face time with the players. I'm not here to be your pal or do the Dear Abby bit, but I like to know with whom I'm working. Yes, gentlemen, *with*. We go down this road together. If somebody has problems with classes or profs, I can lend a hand. I'm interested to know what they're doing here beyond football. Beginning Tuesday of next week, I'll begin meeting every man on the squad, starting with the seniors. I'll meet three in the morning and three in the afternoon. Thirty-minute blocks. If I need more time or if a player wants more time, I'll schedule additional meetings. It's my goal to talk with everyone before Christmas break. Sound okay?"

"Yes, sir," the replied in unison.

"It goes without saying that I'm depending on you to help the staff and myself. If I call you in, don't assume that you're in for an ass chewing. I'll be checking with you on gripes and mutterings. No names. You aren't spies. You're the heart of this team. If there's something, anything, that might impact team performance, I want to know. Together, we'll work it out."

Steve looked at Stan for a moment. "We understand," he concluded.

"I mean it, men. We work *together*, but I'll take the lead. I can't cope with something I don't know about. Meantime, hit the weights and keep up with your conditioning. You set the example. Your teammates look up to you."

After they departed, Jake took a deep breath and returned the chair to its proper place.

Finally. Finally, finally, finally he was getting to the important business of doing what he was hired to do.

Fighting for a Coach

It began as any conspiracy should. There was a secret meeting. The president of the university, two members of the board of regents, the athletic director, a school lawyer, and Jake. The meeting place was set for the most innocuous of the school's conference rooms in the main hall of the Union. The time was set for the dead of dark. They were instructed to arrive severally.

Jake, a not-quite-identified figure, walked through the bookstore just before closing. He wore an old work shirt and a pair of jeans under a seasonal jacket. He paused to examine some of the items embossed with the school seal and logos before not buying anything. He exited through the door leading into the Union proper. He shuddered when he passed the school's newspaper office. The lights were on and the door ajar, but he saw no one. Presumably, no one saw him.

He climbed a flight of stairs and accessed the main hall. Spaced at uniform intervals on both sides of the long hall were display flags of every nation. He might have enjoyed a survey, but he didn't want to be conspicuous. There were few people in the main part of the building. The offices were closed. Several students studied, read, or gathered in small groups for a chat, but they were in the main lounge or the attached recess where people could listen to one of several LP records called up, jukebox style, by entering three digits on the rotating dial. Most of the music was instrumental; a few selections were classical. Jake heard no music. He hadn't expected to. The room was virtually soundproof. Unless an occupant could see around two corners, he'd remain undetected from the music room. There were two young people on a couch in the lounge. They might have seen him, but one was frowning at a very thick biology text, and the other was rapidly scribbling on a notepad.

Was the scribbler a snoop?

There was nothing for it. Jake suggested they gather at someone's house; there were plenty to choose from. His proposal was vetoed. Too many cars in the same neighborhood might tip their hand. Around the Union were a plethora of parking spaces. Further, the extremely cautious could park off campus and walk to the Union, as Jake himself had.

He found the assigned conference room. It was the second one in from the end of the hall of flags. He tried the knob. It was unlocked.

Quickly, but not so quickly as to appear suspicious, he entered the room. It was dark. He closed the door behind him before turning on the lights. He went to the far end of the table and sat at its head. He was the first to arrive. He'd "pretend" to chair this silly meeting.

The big shots didn't want to leave footprints. It was "de-riculous" (Tami's diction) to play cloak-and-dagger, but Jake was common clay. The potters turned the wheel.

Over the course of the next twenty minutes, the jury assembled. They were dressed casually; no suits or blazers and no ties, but their expensive overcoats were anything but inconspicuous. Further, the president's white shirt, dress slacks, expensive overcoat, and calfskin gloves were about as subtle as a flashing neon sign.

"Is everyone here?" Jake asked. He would play the guise of chairman to the hilt.

The assembly examined each other silently.

"Joe is a hell of a coach," Jake continued. "I wouldn't have nerve enough to ask him to be on the staff, but *he* called *me*. I thought this thing was settled, and I'm pretty upset to discover it isn't. Not accepting him is criminal. I'm not exaggerating. Having Joe here is the closest thing to having two head coaches. He has as much experience as anyone in the country. He's probably the best offensive line coach ever to come down the pike. He was an academic All-American in his playing days. He's smart, diligent, and reliable. I want him."

"There was his firing," a grizzled, curmudgeonly, lean-and-hungry, chinless, gray-haired loon across from Jake muttered.

Jake assumed he was the lawyer.

Jake had had his say. He sat and waited for someone else to speak.

"The entire staff was sent walking," one of the regents announced.

"Was he implicated?" the lawyer demanded.

"I spoke with the president down there," the president *up here* reported. "They had the goods on three or four of the staff. However, he assured me that there was no evidence against Epps."

"How do we know that?" the lawyer growled.

"I have the president's word, and the NCAA is pressing nothing against him—specifically, that is. The legal case, if there is one, is centered on three of the other coaches, but it is largely circumstantial. In any case, it's guilt through association."

"So far," the lawyer warned.

"If we hire this guy and something comes out—"

"We fire him," Jake interrupted. "Am I right, Mr. Athletic Director?"

Jake and the AD had met only formally. They hadn't any chance to know one another.

"I'm certain the president would insist. Is that right, sir?"

"Correct," the big man seconded. "However, that would leave the university with one huge black eye."

Silence descended.

"I was looking through the latest alumni magazine yesterday," Jake said finally. "The publicity people did a good job with our research programs. Hell, if we believe the propaganda, much of what we are doing here is cutting edge—especially the oceanography school. At the risk of sticking my foot in my own mouth, how much of a black eye will the football program give you? If we go zero and eleven, people will laugh their asses off, and we will be the butt of a thousand jokes. Maybe instead of hiring me, you should shut down the department completely. Not to put too fine a point on it, but doing that would make this university an object of national derision."

"Nobody is suggesting any such thing!" someone thundered.

"In that case, gentlemen, I move we hire Joe Epps and take the chance."

Everyone looked squarely at Jake. They looked for a long while.

"Do you trust this man?" The president threw down this gauntlet.

"Implicitly," Jake replied.

"You could be betting your job here," the lawyer reminded.

"If those are the terms, I agree to them."

Jake's announcement obviously impressed them.

The president cleared his throat. "This is an informal meeting," he reminded. "I trust no one is taking notes or will write up a synopsis after we leave. I allow no *terms.* They'd be useless in any case. All I want is an agreement. Do we agree to allow Joe Epps to join Coach Oats here on his staff?"

"Objection, Your Honor," Jake interrupted, hoping he didn't sound too sarcastic. "The question is not one of *allowance.* I was hired to coach. Any coach should have the power to create his own staff. I want Joe. If there is any tangible evidence of his unfitness, show it me. It's my place to renege on this offer. If—and I say again *if*—I'm made privy to information I don't yet have."

There was a palpable tension in the room.

"With all respect, Mr. President, I'm the only person in this room with the authority to decide the issue. I'm in charge of my staff. I want the best. Joe Epps is the best. If he embarrasses this institution, I am sorry. However, unless someone can produce damning evidence against the man, I presume him innocent. A document exists, a document I trust we all know and have read. It guarantees *presumed* innocence until one is *proven* guilty. I stand on that sentiment."

He looked directly at the AD. The others in the room joined him. For a very uncomfortable while, no one moved or spoke.

The president cleared his throat again. "I will schedule a meeting Wednesday afternoon," he declared. "We will review the matter, *formally,* at that time. Coach Oats, unless you hear from us by Thursday morning, you may assume we have no tangible evidence against this man. Satisfactory?"

"Satisfactory," Jake echoed.

He saw no need to inform the group that Joe Epps was arriving the following afternoon.

They left as they arrived, singly and at different times. Jake was the last to leave. He turned out the lights and closed the door.

He was too old to play secret agent. This silly meeting was kid stuff. He had serious matters to address.

There was a part of him that hoped he'd see a feature story in the student newspaper, *The Spectator*, the following morning. That members of a major university were slinking around after dark like common thieves would make exciting copy. It would also embarrass the pants of those people who refuse to act like adults.

Friend or Foe...and Joe

This is *de*-riculous.

True, Jake arrived on the hop, but he should have been ushered directly into the AD's office. There should have been a "welcome wagon" thing. Perhaps a banquet at a local feed bag or a get-acquainted meal at the big man's house to meet the wife, at least, if not other dignitaries.

The AD was away when Jake first arrived. They had two hurried conferences, but no chance for them to get to know each other. Jake learned, through Betsy, that the big man didn't want Jake. The school lost an established coach and hired a "level 2" coach who'd only had two years as the head man.

Scuttlebutt!

Jake hadn't been in the Corps for two weeks before learning that "scuttlebutt" is as unreliable as a cheap flashlight. Still, there was that once-in-a-thousand moment when the scuttlebutt was spot-on.

Jake was blind.

Ralph Preston was the athletic director. He'd been at the Junior G-Man meeting in the Union. He hadn't said much. He let the shyster do the talking. Either he was very cautious, or he was yellow.

"Morning, Coach," Barbara hailed cheerily.

"Could you put the AD through to my office please?"

"Roger Dodger," she chirped, reaching for her phone.

Was she prodding him? She didn't seem the type. He'd give her the benefit of the doubt. In truth, what else could he do?

He sat at his desk and scanned the items left on his desk—by Barbara, no doubt.

"Preston on 4," Barbara reported without leaving her desk.

"Thanks."

He picked up the phone.

"Mr. Preston?"

"Ralph," the voice corrected.

"I need to talk with you—not in your office and not in the break room. Too public."

If Preston wanted to play Junior G-Man, they'd play Junior G-Man. It was silly and distasteful, but when in Rome…

There was a pause. Jake heard the squeak of a chair.

"Still raining," Preston deduced after looking out his window. "Let's see if they finished putting the new carpet down in the coaches' locker room. Ten minutes?"

"Fine."

Jake got up and returned to the women typing, filing, collating, and phoning. He knew the routine. Barbara and Holly would work like furies for an hour and slack off leading up to the lunch hour. Neither woman liked a backlog on the desk. Neither liked leaving anything unaddressed prior to leaving work. Mysteriously, however, they were unfailingly deluged by every petty, trifling thing Jake and the others created for them.

"If anyone asks, I'm on a secret mission," he instructed Barbara.

"If the CIA calls while you're out?"

It was only a guess, but Jake sensed that Mrs. Hicks was not a fan of silly games. That made him feel more comfortable. It also added to his appreciation of her.

"I'll be thirty minutes, tops."

"Roger Dodger."

The sign and countersign for the day?

He had a master key, allowing him access to every lock in the arena. He wasn't certain about the "every" part. Jake doubted he could access the AD's office. If the Junior G-Man routine continued for much longer, he might be tempted to find out.

He entered the spacious area roughly under his office. The door was locked, as expected, and the smell of epoxy prickled. It was under construction when Jake first arrived at the facility. He'd used his locker as his wardrobe, showered and shaved there until he found the house. This was his first homecoming, and he feared the improvements might prove worse than the drab and dreary chamber he'd first experienced.

The newly installed pile carpet was battleship gray.

"Thank you, Jesus," he muttered.

He feared the carpet would feature the school colors. White carpet would prove a disaster. Blue carpet would force Jake to change attire in his office.

There were banks of lockers on three of the walls. They were larger than those Jake enjoyed as a Marine. Moreover, these had neatly stenciled names. He recognized the basketball coach's name and that of the baseball and track coaches. Judging from his designation, the head coaches were awarded bright red stenciled letters; assistant coaches rated flat black.

He examined the shower area. It was recessed and featured six shower heads, much as he had seen in fraternity houses. However, to reach the showers, one passed through stainless steel basins and mirrors. Four people could shave simultaneously. He couldn't imagine such a scenario, but it was nice to know he had a bathroom should Betsy ever throw him out of the house.

The heads were on the opposite side of the room. Jake used them during his earliest days. They were standard: two urinals and three stalls. Unless a coach was homeless, as was Jake at first, the coaches preferred to take care of their "Johnny dos" elsewhere.

Save for the potty room, the place resembled the changing room one would find in an upscale country club. There were few towels and partially filled soap dispensers. Save for the basketball crew, there was little need. Jake assumed that there would be supplies enough on game days.

Preston pushed through the oversized door as if he owned the place. In a manner of speaking, he did. He paused to inspect the carpeting.

Ralph Preston was tall and svelte. He'd never been an athlete, at least not at the collegiate level. His neck was too fragile and his hands smallish. His fingers were long and slender and hadn't been subjected to physical punishment. His styled hair and cologne suggested he was something of a dandy. His suits were tailor-made, his shoes imported.

Preston started his career as an assistant information director. Twenty years on, he was made the school's AD. The people in charge wanted the former football coach to take the job. He refused. They offered him the job again with the assurance that he could continue to coach. He refused again. Next, "they" made Preston the interim AD for two years before relenting and letting him have the job outright. He was a paper pusher. He was good at it. However, Jake maintained a saturnine view of the man. He wasn't an athlete, and he didn't reverberate much with players and coaches. He was a glad hander and cash bar kind of guy.

"Looks like they did a pretty good job."

Jake retired to one of the benches near his locker and sat.

"Ralph," began boldly, "we haven't an opportunity to get to know each other very well. You interviewed me. We've talked on the phone several times. I don't know you well enough to judge if you'll have my back on this thing."

Preston sighed and took up a bench nearer the door. They faced each other. "This is about Joe Epps."

"Yes."

A silence ensued. Jake was uncomfortable, but he refused to show it.

"You hired me despite the fact I had only two years' experience as top man. I appreciate your sticking your neck out. Maybe you think you've cashed in all your chips to get me, but I need Joe. This program needs Joe."

Preston sighed and looked away. "The guys upstairs are pretty timid, Jake. They don't like bad press."

Jake took a breath. "I've done my homework, Ralph. The NCAA had nothing on this guy. The university, well, they're mad as hell—still! But they don't have anything on him. They sacked the entire crew to make certain all the bad apples were gone. I understand a couple people have charges pending, but make sure you hear this, Ralph, no one has pointed a finger at Joe. He's clean. They can't dig up anything on him."

Preston made a gesture. Jake hadn't the slightest idea what the gesture meant.

"Ralph, in the country I live in, people are innocent until proven guilty—judicially! The papers and the pundits must not be allowed to hand down judgement. Only a legal authority can do that. That damned lawyer doesn't have the authority. The president and the members of the board don't either."

Jake stood up.

"There are two NFL teams that are after Joe. If we wait too long…"

He was getting angry. That would not serve.

"Let me put it this way: if I can't have the staff I want, I can't deliver. If I can't deliver, I don't want to coach here. Do you want me to write that up?"

Ralph shook his head. "No, Jake. Don't do that. Let me…get back to you."

"I hope it's soon. Those NFL guys have a hell of a lot of money to throw around."

⬥

That evening, Jake phoned Betsy and asked her to type out a letter of resignation. He wouldn't sign it or date it. However, if the paper pusher couldn't grow a spine by the end of the week, he'd show him the letter after another day. If that didn't get the job done, he'd give it to Barbara to type up and make it official.

He sent Churchill and the others out recruiting. They were to touch base with those who had signed, but they must concentrate on those who had yet to commit. He wanted to get on the road as well, but he was forced to stay close. He had to get a playbook together, but that was a staff project. He didn't have a complete staff.

Jake busied himself watching film—miles and miles and miles and miles of film. It was something to do. Despite taking copious notes on the returning players, he was bothered by the fact that he might *not* be coaching. Betsy was supportive. She was willing to go to work while Jake went job hunting. He might get lucky and become an assistant someplace. If he didn't get lucky, well, he'd sold vehicles and tires before. They'd get by—somewhere.

No one told Tami. That would create tumult over something that, hopefully, wouldn't arise.

He cringed over line blocking he saw in the films. He didn't understand the blocking rules. Someone likely had a copy of the previous coach's playbook. He wanted to understand the blocking rules. That would take time. Additionally, it would keep him from film study.

Jake learned one thing: the returning linemen may not be big or particularly talented, but they were scrappy and resourceful. They didn't look fluid or pretty, but they created space for their backs to run. Unfortunately, that space was seldom where it was supposed to be.

He thought of Mel. That little scooter could change course at full speed. He was exactly the kind of back to take advantage of spotty blocking. Unfortunately, he was too frail; one good hit, and he'd be in traction for the rest of the season. Fortunately, as a freshman, he couldn't play with the varsity.

What kind of backs would he inherit? Those who started most of the games the previous season were gone. The single exception was Billy Morris. He was an elusive runner, a determined (if undersized) blocker, and could catch the ball. Three of the team's opponents keyed on him. One team put a spy on him.

When he'd seen enough film for his vision to blur, he took a break. He'd return to the office and pretend he was doing something.

"Ralph wants you to call him, like, yesterday," Barbara informed while she surveyed a fresh stack of papers in the in tray.

This was it!

He pulled out his right top drawer and extracted his resignation letter. Either he'd tear it up and pitch it, or he'd hand it to Barbara.

He picked up the phone, punched the intercom button, and dialed.

"Jake?"

"Yes, sir."

"You've got a green light."

Rome Is Where Christmas Is

Betsy and Tami arrived the day after school let out for Christmas break. Tami missed that last school day to catch the flight.

Several hours later, the family was whole.

They enjoyed a reunion dinner at a no-name hash house several miles from the airport. It was quiet. The staff was congenial and friendly. The food was better than expected. Fortunately, no one fingered Jake as the new head coach. That added considerably to their enjoyment.

Tami loved travelling. She enjoyed frequently changing houses and schools. She was eager to see her new environment. She babbled so enthusiastically that Jake and Betsy managed only occasional exchanges.

Tami wasn't supposed to happen. There was something awry with Betsy's plumbing. They were informed by experts that their union would be devoid of offspring. Once Betsy's pregnancy was confirmed, the same "experts" advised her to abort. The risks were too great.

Betsy refused to cooperate.

There were many nervous, dangerous moments during her term, but she exercised supreme courage. She was eighteen hours in labor, and Tami, as stubborn as her mother, created as many difficulties as possible. When she finally arrived, Betsy's reproductive capacity was ruined. To be sure, the doctors made certain "necessary adjustments."

Tami was the miracle baby. There'd be no more. As a result, her parents indulged her. The sound of her incessant chatter was music to parental ears, and they refused to discourage or inhibit her vocal proclivity.

Everyone, including mater and pater, expected Tami to be spoiled rotten. Somehow, familial harmony (another miracle) abounded. Tami realized she was special, but she set her sights on ordinary. She made a concerted effort to be just one of the neighborhood kids and merely one of many schoolgirls. She made friends easily and often.

Tami was thrilled by the move. She'd miss those left behind, but she was excited about a new school and making new friends. If Jake announced they were moving to the Gobi Desert, Tami would pack instantly and without qualms. Doubtless, she'd insist that Betsy tutor her in Mongolian so she'd fit in.

Tami was proud of her father and grew morose when anyone expressed a negative opinion of him. Her sullenness, however, was momentary. She didn't cry or throw things when Dad lost a game—any game. It baffled her why her father and others mourned over a loss as if there'd been a death in the family. They could wear long faces and complain all they liked; Tami was too in love with life to give it any thought.

Betsy often recounted one precious moment when Tami authored a memorable third grade homily. She always treated her father's arrival with joy and thanksgiving. Papa was home, and dinner would soon follow. Yum!

She bounded out of her room to give her father a hug of welcome, only to balk when noticing the storm on his face.

"Papa! What's wrong?" she asked in childish innocence.

"We had a lousy practice," he growled.

"I wasn't practicing, Papa," she reminded. "Give me a hug."

Who could remain a dedicated curmudgeon in the face of such solicitations?

From that day forward, whenever Jake returned from work in a foul mood, Betsy was quick to whisper, "I wasn't practicing."

That reminder of a precious family moment of bygone days never failed to bring Jake around. He did his best to keep work and home separate. However, he required periodic reminding.

Betsy Ross was the only daughter of five siblings. Betsy is *not* a diminutive. One of her brothers served in the Navy during Jake's war, though he never saw action. Another brother served in Korea and saw more action than was anyone's due. Both brothers earned a GI Bill education. Her remaining two brothers eschewed college; otherwise, Betsy might never have had the opportunity.

The Ross family was well-to-do in the context of post-war America, but hardly affluent enough to send five children to college. There were lengthy discussions about which would be sent off. When her remaining brothers declined, that was the proverbial *that*.

Betsy possessed ambition and gall. Possibly, there was a hint of revenge. Betsy was plagued by much hazing during her early school years. She was bullied and chided by a gang of brothers. Further, she thought her parents were either cruel or fatuous to burden her with the name of a national celebrity. Her family owed her recompense.

"You don't need college to learn home ec," her father insisted. "Work in the house with your mother for four years."

Betsy didn't think that was funny. In the end, her father realized that the high-spirited young woman rated a chance to prove herself.

She studied business at a time when women didn't study business. She was one of three coeds so inclined. Betsy didn't party—well, not much. She spent the bulk of her free time studying and working part-time jobs. She was on her father's dime, and Betsy vowed he'd get his money's worth.

During her junior year, she haunted the library armed with snippets of family documents and lore. After several months, she established that her family's name was originally *Rus* or *Russ*. It was either Norse or Ukrainian. The family acquired the name *Ross* through some Ellis Island bureaucratic fumble. Her ancestors, apparently, arrived prior to the Civil War with a gaggle of Irish and Swiss.

Betsy vowed to hire archivists to check her work when she earned enough to afford it. This was a long-range plan, however. First, she would pay back her family's college loan.

Her entry into the business world was modest. She began as a secretary for the dean of men. After a year, she was invited to help the registrar. She jumped at the chance since the job included more than secretarial drudgery. Additionally, her duties allowed her to meet and work with people from many university offices and departments. It was during one of her inter-office forays that she met a young newly hired assistant football coach.

He was soft-spoken and personable. She liked him from the moment they met. A tall girl, she could—and did—look him in the eyes. Unlike most people, he wasn't intimidated. He invited her for coffee at the union. Soon, they were making dinner dates. One spring morning, Betsy invited the Estonian to her tiny apartment for a spaghetti feed.

As a cook, Betsy was no slouch, but she offered something simple and safe. If she planned a more elaborate meal, circumstances might thwart her. She'd not take the chance. Her tossed salad and improvised garlic bread added a certain flair to an otherwise mundane menu. Her theme of simplicity continued with a dainty fruit salad with heavy cream for afters.

Jake did not eat like a Marine; he ate like a young gentleman. Their conversation was light and uninhibited. However, Jake felt obligated. He invited Betsy to his apartment the following week.

Had Betsy's family known, there'd have been fireworks. A young lady does not go to a bachelor pad! However, what her family didn't know wouldn't hurt her.

She didn't expect much. Visions of canned hash and ice cream sandwiches for afters haunted her for days, but Betsy was, as ever, brave.

Meat loaf!

This was not so far removed from canned hash, but it was much more labor-intensive. Further, the mashed potatoes were *not* from a box. The greatest surprise, however, was *fresh* peas. Jake put in a long day with the coaching staff, but he managed to stop by a greengrocer before starting dinner.

Betsy was impressed.

She couldn't recall what they talked about. She once asked Jake. He couldn't remember either. Romance was certainly in the air, but it did not bloom until football season.

The team lost a lopsided game. The coach tore into Jake during the game and on Sunday when the coaches graded the film.

"Your linemen weren't ready, Jake!" the coach roared. "This is humiliating! If you can't do any better, I'll coach the line, and you can be head manager!"

They watched several more plays from the first half. A pass play collapsed due to three missed blocks. These blocks weren't *muffed*, they were *missed*!

"Assistant manager," the head coach amended.

Jake was hardly good company that evening. Being with Betsy soothed him. She knew he was disappointed at the previous day's performance, but she'd no inkling of his fear of being fired. They talked of many things. The many things did not include football.

They kissed good night when Betsy left. They each felt that they had crested an emotional wave.

Jake coached at a school on the big prairie for two seasons. His coaching improved greatly. When he was offered a job for larger pay, he was eager to accept.

They discussed it. To that point, the relationship between Jake and Betsy was more innocuous than anyone had a right to expect. Betsy, however, had made up her mind. She was in love. She wanted to lure Jake up the aisle. Being a Ross, however, she'd inherited the family tradition of deviousness. She said not a word, but she was suddenly a very, very busy young woman.

Jake hugged and kissed Betsy when he left campus. He promised to write.

He spent two weeks with his family before reporting in.

The first person he met at his new school was Betsy Ross.

"Aren't you supposed to be at work?" he asked suspiciously.

"I don't start until next week," she replied.

Betsy secured work as an assistant business manager in the athletic department. She landed the position through pure luck.

They each interpreted this as a sign.

Their first Christmas in a new residence was the latest in a quartet. Even Tami, who was very young during the first transplanting, realized being together was more important than the usual trimmings. Indeed, the three-bedroom house was sparsely furnished. What spartan furnishings they enjoyed were supplied gratis by a local outlet.

Betsy brought basic cooking accoutrements with her. She borrowed from Holly, Barbara, and other eager AD employees to take up the slack. Tami's contribution was buying a set of dishes.

The young girl enjoyed the first "big" adventure of her life. She stuffed a wad of bills in the pocket of her jeans, hired a taxi, and set off for a superstore. Tami was budget conscious. In fact, she was Scrooge. She returned with plastic plates, salad bowls, saucers, and mugs. She was delighted to find four chimney glasses. They were also plastic; however, she thought they were cute.

The meal was simple but plentiful. The tree was small and decorated with esoteric lights and bobbles.

"It will be better next year," Jake promised.

This was the expected platitude repeated every Christmas in a new venue. Thus far, his assurances proved true.

The department worked mornings during the Christmas-New Year break. Jake, however, often worked until midafternoon. Sometimes, he conferenced with members of his staff. Most of the time, he worked alone. There were tons of minutia that were routinely shunted aside until "later." Christmas break, Jake judged, was *later*.

Additionally, there was planning. Gus and Jake sketched out the sixty-two defense. Much of the fine-tuning must wait for spring drills, but the overall details were set. Jake, however, was a fuss budget about matching tactics to personnel.

"We have a quarterback who can run the forty in good time," Joe Epps announced. "This freshman kid is a question mark."

Jake grunted. *What the hell do you expect* me *to do about it?*

"Coach, we've got to attack the edges, or they'll stack their defenses," Joe began, answering an implicit question. "I want to roll out. The quarterback gets depth as he's rolling, twelve to fifteen yards—"

Jake whistled. "That much?"

Joe ignored this. "He comes to run, Coach. If they don't challenge him, he squares his shoulders and gets what he can."

"Um. With Foote's speed, it will pressure the defense." Jake held up one hand to gain attention.

"Foote is pretty fast, but I've been watching the films. He commits late, run or pass. He'll be a senior. I don't want to bench him, but he's not going to change. This kid, Peck, he doesn't have the speed, but he was All-State two years ago and red-shirted last season. I've seen his audition tape. The kid can throw, he can run, and he isn't afraid to take a hit."

The air left the room quickly.

"Start a new program with a sophomore quarterback?" Miller asked.

"It's a different offense," Joe pondered. "Everyone's starting on the same page."

Jake nodded. "As you said, we take whatever we can get," he replied.

"This is Foote's fifth year," Churchill reminded.

"I need a safety," Gus announced. "I can use his speed. If he's as tentative on defense, we'll have to bench him, but I doubt it. He is so afraid of making a mistake with the ball that he waits until he's out of options. He won't have that problem on defense. He isn't afraid of getting hit. I assume he's not shy about hitting others. Let's start him at safety and dare him to fail. I'll put my money on his making the grade. He wants to play."

"I'll think on it, Gus," Jake promised. "If we do go with Peck, a twelve-yard drop...boy, that makes me nervous."

"On a rollout," Churchill reminded. "He can throw on the run, I bet. If he keeps and just runs to the sideline, he'll get something."

"Gus wins balls games," Joe emphasized. "We help him by keeping the ball away from the other team. If we gain three or four yards every play, we're stealing time from their offense."

Jake grunted. Joe Epps knew his business. He knew it long before Jake ever became a head coach.

"Blocking schemes? This rollout business is tricky."

"I'll have something tomorrow morning, Coach."

Jake gave him a confident pat on the shoulder and left. He must take care of a few "laters."

Betsy and Jake chuckled after Tami went to *her room.*

"That stuff Tami bought, I won't be able to eat off that without either laughing or crying."

Betsy smiled in agreement. As always, however, she looked beyond the obvious.

"She was so excited to buy them on her own. That makes them priceless. I won't take a million dollars for them."

Jake agreed—with reservation. "I won't give two cents for any more."

Betsy nodded and joined in his mirth.

In the early days of their married life, Betsy and Jake played a game: "Can I have this when we get divorced?"

Over the years, they'd divided up nearly everything for an event neither expected. After Tami, the miracle child, their relationship was cemented. They would do nothing to harm their little girl.

"When we get our divorce," Betsy jibbed, "you get to keep Tami's dishes."

Jake chuckled. "Some of your threats terrify me," he replied.

Christmas Eve and Christmas Day were sacrosanct. Jake made it clear that he'd honor no appointments and tolerate no interruptions. He promised not to answer the phone. These two days were family time.

It was a relief to lounge the morning away, though Jake spent most of his time mentally reviewing Gus's defense and Joe's offense. He didn't let on, but Betsy and Tami knew. They let him sit quietly on the couch, pretending to read. Betsy tuned to a music station; Christmas music wafted through the house.

The evening meal was, as expected, perfection. Tami eagerly assisted her mother in the preparation. She took great pride in the cranberry salad. It was little more than opening four cans, adding pecan pieces, whipped cream, and marshmallows, but she accomplished it unaided.

Betsy opted for roast lamb with potatoes and as many vegetables as she could procure. She was a fanatic about fresh vegetables, which, considering the season, must be imported from other regions at extortion-level prices. Because linen napkins would make a mockery of Tami's dinnerware, Betsy utilized red paper napkins featuring a snowman with a broom (?) and a black top hat.

After the feast, residuals were stowed and the plastic dishes washed. They gathered around their tiny tree and sang three carols, each person selecting one. Then they opened the gifts.

Tami went first, of course. She was giddy over getting a set of Nancy Drew books. Her hugs were enthusiastic and unreserved.

Betsy was astonished by an expensive winter coat Jake picked out. She was both surprised and appreciative. She'd had her eye on such a coat for months, but the family budget wouldn't stretch far enough. It still couldn't, despite Jake's increase in salary. He'd have to cut back on cigars during the coming year.

The entire family roared over Jake's gift. Betsy bought a polo shirt, windbreaker, cap, and a pair of athletic shoes with the new school colors and logos. Predictably, Tami was responsible for picking out a stuffed toy of the team mascot, also in school colors.

Jake, as head coach, would get a ton of school apparel gratis. It came from his employers as part of the standard publicity schtick. Betsy and Tami selected these nonessential items as a sign of pride and approval of Jake's new position.

Later, they attended a ten o'clock "midnight" service. Betsy was Methodist; Jake was raised Episcopalian. Somewhere in their travels, Tami went to a Lutheran church with a girlfriend. They attended Vacation Bible School together one summer. That, more than any scriptural or family tradition, made them (de facto) Lutherans.

Jake was well known, but his visage was not yet widely recognized. Few if any worshipers knew him by sight. That was satisfactory with the Oats trio. Christmas is a private time.

A few people addressed Jake as "Coach" during the dismissal. He was recognized by a few. Thankfully, no one made an issue. It was Christmas, not a pep rally—or a lynch party.

Spring Forward

The playbooks were issued. There were three plenary meetings. Two covered the plays and playbooks; one was devoted to specialist drills. Jake oversaw the agenda for each, but the individual coaches drew up their own. He conferenced with Miller about D-line drills. A few appeared questionable. Miller had a chance to justify them. He failed. Jake suggested the replacements.

"You're the boss," Miller conceded.

"Wrong, Mike! You're coaching the line because I can't. If you find something that will improve skills and make a better defense, it's your job to get in my face about it. You failed this time at bat. That does *not* mean that you nod like some bobblehead doll."

"I understand, Coach."

"Do you? Both our jobs are on the line, Mike. It's up to us to make these kids damned good players. Let's make certain we do that."

"Yes, sir."

Mike Miller knew the boss was keeping him under a microscope, but Jake was soon convinced that the young man was dedicated to his job. There was no sign of animosity. More importantly, Jake was satisfied he hadn't stoked resentment.

The first two practices were in sweats and helmets. They practiced the kicking game, mostly against handheld shields. The place kicker was the starting right guard, Lee Smith. He had limited range, but he was accurate. For kickoffs, they had an anemic senior who got good distance but no touch and one wide receiver who kicked low trajectory (worm burners) to the goal line. At least they had a choice. Game situations might favor one over the others.

The punter was a former high school quarterback. He never did master the offense of the previous coach and hadn't played a down in that position. His punts were moderate in range, but his hang time was unbelievable. Jake wanted to get him some practice snaps as QB, but his future with the team rested on his punts.

These first two practices demonstrated his men reported in with strong bodies and good wind. There may have been a few slackers, but strapping on the pads the third day would weed them out. One player experienced back problems from the previous season. The doctors treated him; he reported in with the proviso that he avoid contact until fall. Jake assigned him a distinctive white jersey. He could run plays with the team, but he was hands off, even against the handheld shields. During contact drills and scrimmages, the wounded duck would run laps, stadium steps, or pass routes.

The first day in pads went much smoother than Jake expected. The assistant coaches handled separate contact drills, which shook loose the spiderwebs of winter.

The offense came together to practice rushing plays. They started with the simplest plays and graduated to powers, options, counter options, and traps. After the first-team offense worked on timing and execution, it took over the shields and let the second team practice against them. The last fifteen minutes was spent on Joe's rollout passes.

The defense did reaction and pursuit drills. Those supernumeraries who were lower on the offensive depth chart provided a skeleton offense to give the defense a picture.

Gino Della Corte gained the nickname Mr. Hustle the previous year. Under Jake's tutelage, he was known by his teammates as Lights

Out. He didn't mind. He was a year older and a year better, and he continued to hustle. He was the first back to the huddle after every play.

Jake stepped in only once. "Gino! You gotta sell that fake! I want eleven men busting ass to tackle you!"

"I'm supposed to block to the offside," he protested.

"Sell the fake, Gino. If you're good enough, the offside will come to *you*. If you *don't* get tackled, you block. Sell it, Gino. Sell it!"

"Yes, sir."

A few plays later…

"That's it, Gino! Hell, you even fooled me—and I *knew* the play. Good job, son."

The university did not have a tower for the head coach as had many other schools. Jake would not insist on one. He strolled around from specialty area to specialty area, watched and heard both coaches and players as they drilled. Normally, he kept his oar out. If he saw something he didn't like, he'd have words later with the assistant in charge. If he needed to chew out a player, he did so in the privacy of his office.

Of course, there were times when he couldn't keep his mouth shut. When he stepped on someone's toes, he forced himself to make amends.

Coach Ostrander was an All-American honorable mention running back nearly three decades prior to joining Jake. The fifty-year-old did not look a day over thirty-five. He was sleek and agile. His reddish hair was kept short and neat. During his playing days, he preferred a Sinatra style slick back. Hair oil and poor artificial light combined to earn the team moniker "Pink." He'd dropped twenty pounds from his playing days, but he kept fit; he was as strong as an ox. His only vice was annoying: he smoked cigarettes incessantly (not on the field however).

After practice, Jake joined Ostrander at his locker in the coaches' room. He was in his briefs with a towel draped around his neck and reaching for a cancer stick and lighter. He took a long drag before resuming dressing.

"Stew," Jake said, "I apologize for getting on Gino out there. I'll try to do better."

"No offense taken, Coach," Pink replied, setting his cig down on the wooded bench behind him.

"It doesn't matter if you're offended or not. It isn't my place to mind your business for you, Stew. Still, your backs must sell every fake. Ninety-nine times out of a hundred, it don't mean a damn. One time out of a hundred, it pays off."

"Leave no turn unstoned." Stewart smiled. "Read you loud and clear, Coach. We will work on carrying out our fakes."

Jake nodded appreciatively. "Thanks, Stew."

It wasn't always that simple.

———•◦•———

Joe, Churchill, and Jake spent an hour reviewing a game from a previous season. The starting quarterback and team leader was injured and left the game early in the second quarter. Jeff Foote, then a sophomore, played the remainder of the game. He didn't make any major mistakes, but his performance, even for a sophomore, was flat.

"Inexperience can only cover your ass so much," Jake grunted. "This guy isn't selling out."

"Hard to fire him," Joe Epps reminded. "He's on scholarship. His brother played here two years ago. He was a good utility back."

"I know all that," Jake announced. "We all do. That's why Gus grabbed him. What's that red shirt's name?"

"Peck," Churchill reminded. "Dave Peck."

"I should know them by now," Jake scolded himself. "He looked impressive on the frosh squad. Then we have Murray. He's a junior, some experience. He can run, he can throw. The kid gets the ink, but Murray has fire. He'll push the kid—make him better. From what I've seen, he isn't as smart as the kid."

"He ain't stupid," Churchill reported. "He pushes. He's pushy. He tries to make a big play when it isn't there."

They watched and reran three more plays.

"Let's put Parks on the orange team and Foote on the purple for a couple days. Let's see if that doesn't light a fire. If Foote doesn't show us something by the end of spring drills, we'll see if Stew can make something of him."

The group silence was a sign of tacit approval.

"Make certain Foote doesn't know what we're thinking. He might get discouraged."

That would be bad. It could also get worse. If players started looking over their shoulders instead of charging full speed ahead…

⸻ •⸺

Jake went to his office and called Betsy. They talked for fifteen minutes. Then he talked to Tami for fifteen minutes.

Must stick to the schedule.

He'd rather call after work, but the time difference made that unwise.

He dictated three letters into a machine and left them for Barbara to type and send out in the morning. He scribbled a few notes on items he'd discuss at the coaches' meeting the following morning. He went through his mail and set aside those missives requiring a response. He scribbled three memos, one to the equipment manager concerning practice pants. Holly would type them and dispatch them in the morning.

His stomach protested.

It would be so nice to go home to one of Betsy's meals. She was a balanced diet freak, but he never had to force himself to eat her food. However, when she wasn't around, Jake ate only to keep his stomach quiet.

The campus parking sticker on his leased vehicle came in handy. The campus was between his office and the rented house. Because of the stickers, the sentry waved him onto campus, saving him an eight-minute loop around the sprawling school. There was little traffic after dark. Jake opted to save a few extra minutes by getting something at the Union.

The kitchen shut down at six, but a cashier remained on duty until nine. There was a bowling alley below; people fetched soft drinks and packaged snacks. Additionally, there were a few hot food items baking under the warming lights until closing. Any residuals were thrown into a plastic bin and trucked over to the school of agriculture. There, they'd be processed and fed to livestock.

Jake bought a mug of freshly brewed coffee and grabbed the foot-long hot dog that appeared the least aged. There were few students distributed about the voluminous cafeteria at that hour. Most lounged over coffee and sodas to conference. A few apparently recognized him, but he had yet to rate serious attention.

The dog quieted his stomach, and the fresh coffee was an unexpected burst of flavor. He could get a refill for half price, but that might interfere with his sleep. As a Marine, Jake learned to sleep under the most appalling conditions. He also learned to sleep for brief periods. This proved a vocational enhancement; he could go for eighteen hours on three or four hours sleep *if* he could steal slumber in quarter-hour bursts.

"You are Coach Oats."

The voice was soft and well modulated. The syntax and pronunciation betrayed non-English language heritage.

Jake found a diminutive woman with black-rimmed glasses wearing a casual cream-colored shift. She had slant eyes and a huge winning smile. Her hands rested gently on her thighs.

"I am."

There was no need to be rude.

"Ah, excuse me. I am graduate student for two year. My English is not so good as I wish, but I learn more every day."

During her oration, she initiated a bow, but terminated it before it ostentation kicked in.

Jake forced himself to stand. He wasn't in the mood for chitchat. His mind was awash in Xs and Os. However, he was in a public venue, and people recognized him. The last thing he needed was some undergraduate bonehead to noise it around that the new coach was a rude son of a bitch.

"I think your English is very good," he said without perjuring himself much.

This was a conversational dead end. Jake was no champion at small talk, so he shut down. The young woman had come up to him; let her play or punt.

"Ah, excuse. I am to have job in athletic department next school year. I begin this term to learn how to do. Work-study job. I am, they tell me, to work in business and ticket office. Ah, um, I am Mieko Takada from Kyushu, Japan."

He shuddered and froze. It took him a moment to thaw out. He must have appeared a motionless simpleton. There was no way to explain his sudden epileptic fit. He didn't try. "I am pleased to meet you," he said, extending his hand.

She accepted it with a second abbreviated bow.

Her hand was gentle and warm in his suddenly icy hand. His head and the back of his neck was anything but cold; he felt beads of sweat forming. He could not see, but he was certain his face was beet red.

"Mieko—may I call you Mieko?"

"Please, yes."

"I am happy to meet you, but I shouldn't be here. A coach must work, even at night, and I'm a little behind. Excuse me. I look forward to seeing you again soon."

Lying bastard!

"Please," she replied, apparently intending a word that eluded her.

———•—•———

He drove slowly. He was a nervous wreck; he didn't want to make matters worse by bashing a streetlight or a pedestrian. By the time he reached the house, his clothes were wet. He closed the garage door and fumbled with the keys until he opened the side door.

It was going to be one of those nights!

With Betsy's help, he'd come to grips with his war memories. They visited him periodically, but he managed to ride them through without undue stress, though his gag reflex often got a workout.

He may have killed a couple hundred Japs, but when thousands of bullets are tearing the air, no one was certain if they hit an enemy. There was that nightmare on the creek and the nightmare on the ridge where the Japs came in waves. It was impossible to fire into hundreds of screaming troops and *not* hit someone, but there was no way of knowing. Save for the stark terror that climbed up his throat whenever he relived these scenes, Jake felt guilt-free.

However…

He killed three Japs.

He picked off a sniper on the Canal. There could be no doubt; he alone had fired.

He killed two on New Britain in incidents weeks apart. Both times, he was part of a patrol that crept silently through jungle foliage during never-ending rain. Both times a Jap soldier appeared from behind a green curtain. Both times, the Jap was as startled and surprised as Jake. Both times, he got off the first round.

It's difficult to miss a target five feet away, even with a hip shot.

The second time, he was so angry, he emptied his magazine. The first shot likely killed the soldier, but Jake was enraged—at the Jap, at the Marines, at the war, at the rain, at the jungle, at the hunger and cold, at the heat and the bugs, at the lousy chow, at the filthy clothes that turned to rags in the heat and humidity, at the inability to take a decent crap, at the know-nothing officers and NCOs who lorded over him, and at anything that ever irritated him in his life.

That Japanese soldier received every ounce of Jake's stored-up hatred.

He was forever haunted by the men he killed. There were truckloads of justification for his actions, but nothing could satiate the horror of killing someone.

Now, it all returned. He'd met a not-very-attractive woman in the union. She was…what? Maybe twenty-four. Hell, she could be thirty. He could never accurately estimate the age of an oriental.

It was possible Jake killed her father.

Possible but not likely.

The odds were a million to one—three million to one. However, a very real possibility remained.

"What did your father do in the war?"

The odds were ten million to one he'd never ask Mieko.

Jake took off his jacket and tossed it onto the couch. He kicked off his shoes. He didn't bother to brush his teeth or undress. He plopped down on his back and stared at the darkness. He tried to think about football, but the faces of Japanese soldiers made it impossible.

He slept fitfully and got little rest. He woke a few minutes before the alarm clock sounded reveille. His hands were shaking, so he used the electric razor. He preferred a blade, but unsteady hands promised disaster, so he suffered the muted buzz of the machine. The images of his nocturnal visitations were fresh in his mind.

"Settle down, Jake," he muttered to himself. "You have to make decisions today."

Should he call on the AD? He could *suggest* that Mieko Takada be "redeployed." There were several work-study billets scattered across campus. Surely a few remained vacant.

He grunted.

This wasn't Mieko's fault. Jake was the one with the problem. Maybe this was the time to face his dragons. It was doubtful that he'd see her more than three or four times a month. He could give a friendly nod and say a kind word or two. That mightn't squelch his nightmares or his memories, but it wouldn't do to go into seizures at the sight of her.

He bid Holly and Barbara good morning and crossed their zone to enter his office. Holly set a schedule on his desk every morning. Those meetings and activities pertaining to his job were highlighted as per his instructions. Other concerns were entered in ten-minute blocks.

Jake sighed with relief when he noticed there were no short meetings that day. They were mostly PR and glad-handing jobs. If a player or a parent desired a meeting, they were granted thirty minutes, though few required the entire time.

Barbara placed a neat stack in his upper right corner of memos and letters requiring his attention. He reached for these and glanced through them. Most could be dismissed. Those requiring action were generally assigned to others; the assistant coaches were assigned specific recruiting areas and duties. This arrangement took a lot of weight off Jake's shoulders.

Today, politics!

"Shit!"

He kept his voice down, but he suspected Barbara heard it.

Jake picked up his phone and punched Churchill's button. He heard the buzz from a doorless office several yards distant.

"Yeah."

Great! He was in.

"Church, let's powwow."

The reply was a click of the phone returning to its cradle. Jake moved to the door separating his office from the secretarial bay. As he was closing it, Churchill came through the door leading to the assistant cubicles.

"Close it," Jake requested.

Churchill closed the door behind him and settled into one of the overstuffed chairs canted toward Jake's desk.

"I got the threat notice this morning."

Churchill nodded. They'd spoken of the issue briefly a few days before.

"How many black students are enrolled here?"

Churchill shrugged. "Only a couple hundred, maybe three hundred."

"Well, this student group is upset that we have only five black players on the roster."

"It ain't our fault, Coach. We're the new kids on the block."

"Yeah. Try telling the brainiacs that. Get in touch with the registrar's office and get me a count. Let's see if five players reflect the same percentage of black students. That will give me a little ammo. Not that it matters. You can't discuss with these holier-than-thou people. You can only listen and nod your head."

"Not many black athletes want to come here, Coach."

Yeah, the backwater school surrounded by farmland and forested areas wasn't appealing to many white players, never mind black, inner city. Of course, Jake knew problems existed when he signed on the dotted line.

"You know my position on this," Jake challenged.

"Yes, sir. You want to recruit the best damned players we can hook."

Jake nodded. "That's what I want. *Players*. I ain't gonna start recruiting skin colors—"

Churchill held up his hands defensively. "Coach, you don't have to chew my butt. If you're looking for an argument, you'll have to change the subject."

Jake nodded. "Thanks, Church. I appreciate that. Still, if we have any black prospects, well…"

"Loud and clear, Coach. I'll be sure to pay a visit."

Jake grunted. "I'll noise it around to the others so they won't think you're horning in on their turf."

Churchill raised his hand. "Coach, sir. Can I go back to work now?"

Jake chuckled. It was the first slice of mirth he'd enjoyed in days. "Get outta my office." He smiled.

Churchill slapped his knees and stood up. He left the door open when he retired. Jake got up and opened the other.

"Politics," he muttered. "A pox on your house."

Sure enough!

The following morning, Churchill came into the office unannounced. Jake did not encourage this, but he was the head coach; it wouldn't do to require his assistants to make an appointment. Still, he had a desk full of minutia to wade through and a coaches' meeting in the offing to put together the afternoon practice schedule.

"The registrar won't release the numbers," he reported. "They claim that sort of information is not available to outside interests."

Jake took a deep breath. "So race information is gathered for *statistical purposes only.* Why do I not believe that? If I'm not allowed to see the statistics, who is? What's the point?"

Churchill shrugged.

Okay, Jake thought, *that's a declaration of war.* He had no desire to cause a ruckus. He was, after all, the new kid. However, he wouldn't be bullied.

"Church, have you filled out any university forms?"

"A couple."

"Did they ask for your race?"

"One did."

"As a personal favor to me, leave that blank in the future—or put *decline to state* if there's room. Obviously, this data is *not* for statistical use. There's something more sinister going on. I won't volunteer my race. I'll encourage the entire staff to decline as well. I cannot, however, order you. I can't order anyone."

"As a personal favor to you, Coach, I'd sign up for the Girl Scouts."

Jake appreciated the sentiment, but he would never hold his youngest coach to it.

"I'll put the word out to the team," Jake announced. "I think we will create a new race: *football*. Let them crunch those numbers."

Churchill chuckled. He liked the idea.

Spring Back

There were perhaps three hundred "fans" in the stadium for the intra-squad game marking the end of spring drills. The crowd consisted mostly of family members, girlfriends, and the odd passerby taking advantage of free entertainment. Jake's predecessor kept the time and date of the scrimmage a secret. Jake didn't need to. He and his staff had no secrets. It was sink or swim with the system they'd introduced. The scrimmage would be filmed. Players would be graded. The offense and defense playbooks would be fine-tuned over the summer in preparation for summer camp.

Brice Churchill would be on the sidelines with the blue team in home uniforms. Pink would handle the white team in visitor uniforms. The team doctor, the trainers, and managers would perform their duties just as they would on game day. The referees were local hires. They were selected from the association that officiated the area high school games. Jake insisted that they be strict unless penalties slowed the game over much. He wanted his players to shed any sloppy techniques they'd accrued during practices. Gus and Joe didn't put up with sloppy or dirty play, but they each had only two eyes. The officials provided several pairs, and each pair looked for specifics.

Jake sat in the press box with Gus on his left and Joe on his right. The rest of the staff roamed the sidelines to assist (advise) Churchill and Ostrander.

The teams were selected from the latest depth chart. Joe tossed a coin. It was heads, so the first team split end went to the blue squad, the second team weak tackle, the first team weak guard, etc. Those farther down the depth chart were evenly distributed between squads.

Jake insisted that every player participate. The coaches would rotate personnel in the second half to ensure his dictum was observed.

Foote played safety. He also dropped back to receive punts. He was a novice but showed well for his first contest in a new position. He could cover a zone surprisingly well. Twice he broke up a pass. He tackled well and pursued expertly. His man coverage was not impressive. After a receiver beat Foote a second time, Coach Avery didn't wait for Jake to comment.

"He learns fast, Coach," Gus assured. "He'll be better this fall."

The opposing quarterbacks did well. Peck could throw accurately, and he was not afraid to tuck and run on the rollout. Unfortunately, his lack of speed and that twelve-yard drop didn't threaten the corners as effectively as envisioned. Murray had a lot more experience and was a step quicker than the young former All-Stater. Neither did well enough to secure the starting job, but they played with brains and determination.

The fullback and halfback traps looked good.

"Joe, I want to put some kind of stripe on our helmets," Jake announced. "It will be easier to see in the films. The quarterback's head must come all the way around to sell the power play fake. I'm not certain Murray's doing that."

Joe made a note on his yellow legal pad.

"Our ends aren't reacting fast enough to the pass," Gus complained.

Joe made a note.

"Roberts keeps ducking his head," Jake noted. "You can't block what you can't see."

Joe made a note.

"Forty-one pass," Gus recognized practically from the snap of the ball.

The trio watched as Murray lofted the ball far down field to a very lonely end.

"I ain't even gonna mention this to Eberhardt," Gus said. "He bit on the fake and got caught flat-footed. His brains, not my yelling, will fix it."

Jake grunted.

"I'll take a thirty-eight-yard TD pass any day," he announced.

"The middle traps have been our money play today," Joe observed. No wonder the defensive back got caught looking.

"Come fall, we'll work on stuffing trap plays." Gus nodded.

Joe made a note.

***

The staff began viewing the film at eight o'clock the following morning. They broke for lunch at twelve and resumed at one. They completed work shortly after seven and departed the building severally. Jake gathered all the staff's notes and each player's grade Monday morning. He'd review them carefully while his coaches hit the recruiting trail.

***

The Black Student Union struggled to make a mountain out of its pet issue. Jake conferenced with other varsity coaches: basketball, baseball, tennis, track, swimming, and the ROTC drill teams. They weren't being hounded. Only the football program was under optics.

Well, that's discrimination, Jake thought.

He dared not say it aloud. He knew enough about politics to know that hypocrisy was a defining characteristic. Pointing out the obvious only inflamed issues. It was tempting to let the matter slide and hope it would dissipate of its own accord. Unfortunately, that might prove a major mistake.

Jake drafted a letter explaining his philosophy of recruiting. He included his inability to determine if his football team reflected the ethnic diversity of the university since the university refused to provide enrollment numbers by race. He encouraged the Black Student Union to request such information on the grounds that an organization of *students* would have more clout than university employees. He expressed his desire to comply with BSU concerns (he daren't use that abbreviation, however, for *very* obvious reasons). However, he reiterated his recruiting philosophy, which was the basis of any athletic program worthy of the name.

He filed a copy for public release if needed.

It wasn't easy to get the letter into the proper hands. The BSU had no organizational home and no known officers. It appeared to be more of an idea than an organization. Even the university authorities had no contact information. The black players were aware of both the complaint and the complainants, but they knew nothing more of the union than could be found in the student newspaper.

He called Wes Jordan to his office.

Wes was a two-year starter as an outside linebacker. In Gus's system, he was the "swing" linebacker, assigned to line up over the opponent's tight end. This ensured both defensive ends were stationed outside the enemy's formation and difficult to hook on wide plays. The end and the swing linebacker would maintain leverage and force a runner back into the heart of the defense.

Wes was a human fire plug. His neck was as thick as a tree trunk, his chest was one Superman would envy, and his thighs were pistons powerful enough to propel an ocean liner.

He maintained a 3.38 GPA in business administration and knew more about defense than many coaches. He possessed phenomenal instincts.

Wes's body demanded respect. Jake, however, respected him because he'd earned it during spring drills.

"You wanted to see me, Coach?"

There was nothing timorous in his voice. He knew he was not there for a dressing down. He also knew that Coach was not one for chitchat. Jake wanted to know his players and conversed openly with any and all. However, a summons to the office was strictly business.

"Sit down, Wes." Jake motioned.

The hulky linebacker filled every inch of the leather upholstered armchair.

"I need your help."

Wes shifted uneasily. "Sure, Coach. What do you need?"

"I'm trying to reach out to the Black Student Union. They seem to be top secret. Do you know anything about them?"

"A couple people have talked to me around campus now and then."

"Are you a member?"

"That's a tough question, Coach," he replied, clearing his throat. "The way they talk, they assume anyone who is black is a member. The only union I belong to is me and my teammates. Not the answer you're looking for, is it?"

"Wes, your team loyalty is not in question—never has been. The union is kicking up a fuss, and I feel entitled to communicate with it— and them—freely. That's a chore. No one seems to know how to contact them. If anyone talks to you again, see if you can get names. It would be great if I had the names of the leaders."

"Sure, Coach. Not a problem."

"Let them know I'm not looking to stir the pot. I just want to talk. I want them to address their concerns to my face. I'd rather respond to them in person than through the student paper."

Wes nodded. "I will do exactly that, sir."

"There is one other thing."

Wes went from relief to caution. His body language made the transition clear. "Sir?"

"Someone told me your father visited you a couple weeks ago."

"Yes, sir."

"What's he do?"

"He drives trucks—big rigs."

"Got his million miles yet?"

Wes's eyes sparkled. "Years ago, sir. He started with Red Ball Express during the war."

"I'd like to meet him, Wes. Whenever your parents are here, please bring them in."

"I'll do that, sir. They come to all the home games—I mean when Pop isn't on the road. He tries to arrange it so he can be here."

Typical, Jake thought.

He liked families. He liked good young men who came from good families. Wes seemed to fit into that category quite comfortably.

***

Jake kept an eye on the *Spectator*. It was the university's bold attempt to emulate the major propaganda press. It began as reporting on student affairs and state policies and legislation impacting education. In the turbulent period of Viet Nam, it became a document of social and political concerns. The Black Student Union was, of course, grist for the mill. He hoped the rag would provide a name or contact information. The nearest Jake came to legitimate information was student reactions to the periodic demands issued by the BSU.

He habitually scanned the paper. His interest was piqued by the sports section. There was some mention of the new football coach and three column inches about spring football. Track and field, golf, and tennis were the mainstays of spring. Jake was surprised and irked that baseball got very little attention.

One day, however, he noted a feature of the university's "oldest freshman." Ordinarily, he'd not have paid attention. He'd met the oldest freshman at the president's spring reception. She was a sixty-four-year-old grandmother who initiated her retirement by signing up for a degree program. Hers was a dream deferred.

The article, however, was not about the grandmother. Instead, it featured a twenty-four-year-old man. He was a former Marine. He'd fought in Nam and earned a medal. He'd rescued wounded men from a helicopter crash. His enlistment up, he sought to get his life back on track. His ambition was to be a forester.

Interesting, but hardly what Jake sought. He was about to deposit the paper in his round file when he caught sight of the magic word: *football.*

Before he became a Marine, Mark Davidson was a football standout at a high school less than fifty miles from campus.

"Do we have a copy of *Hall's Guide?*" he asked Barbara.

"Nooooooo. Not here. I'm sure there's one in the building somewhere."

He didn't need to instruct her to find it. If Jake didn't want it, he'd never have asked.

Jake was planning to spend the following day and the weekend getting the house ready for the arrival of Betsy and Tami. They couldn't arrive until school let out, but he could replace the fixtures in the bathroom and recarpet Tami's room. He could have, and should have, hired professionals. Time, however, dragged. He could fill that time better by keeping busy.

"Here we go, Coach."

It was Barbara. She'd hurried down the long hall to the athletic director's office and found a copy of *Hall's Guide*. She placed it in Jake's inbox and hurried back to her desk.

Jake picked up the document. It was professionally bound and featured an aerial view of the sprawling campus. Inside the cover was an alphabetical listing of each student, residence, hometown, major, and phone number.

Mark Davidson lived in Maxwell Hall, one of the newer dorms. He called the number. He left a message for the former Marine.

He wandered into the coaches' cubicles, not expecting to find anyone. However, Gus was sitting over a playbook. His right leg was bouncing, as was his habit when contemplating.

Jake knocked on the doorframe. He would have knocked at the door, but there was none.

Gus leaned back and greeted him.

"Thought you were on the recruiting trail," Jake said. He was not scolding.

"I head out Monday," Gus replied. "I'm trying to plug some holes."

The greatest benefit to the spring game was the intelligence the coaches gained. If something was wrong, the spring game brought it into focus. If something was obvious, it must be addressed.

"I'm satisfied this *will* work, Coach."

"I agree, Gus. It's as clear as anything can be that we don't have the linebacking corps we need. My concern is that once we work the kinks out of the sixty-two, we might not be able to retool once we have the players we need."

"First things first, Coach," Gus reminded. "How many teams face a sixty-two? Every opponent will burn meeting time and practice time preparing for something they seldom see. It's a small advantage, but we gotta take what we can get."

"True. You seen the write-ups? The press has Georgia ranked in the top ten."

"Another advantage," Gus insisted. "They'll be looking right past us to their conference games."

Jake hesitated a moment. "Do you really think that will make a difference?"

Gus turned to look directly at him. "Not one chance in a million," he sighed.

Jake had a fry pan meal at home.

The house was his—well, the bank held the paper, but…

It was probably a mistake. The life span of a college head coach was short. Still, the rentals he'd examined were either too small or outside the school district they felt best for Tami.

Jake considered his current job a mere preface to whatever came next. He'd had job offers before he stepped up to the big leagues. He kept in touch with key people. It was part of his insurance plan.

He'd made an informal survey of Georgia, his first opponent. It was a perennial power in the nation and had a coach many Georgians considered a god. Jake examined the scholarship athletes of the past three years. The list was impressive. If Jake were a betting man, he'd put a bundle down against his own team. Well, he wasn't a betting man. However, he was a realist.

Joe Epps had an infallible formula for victory.

"If you block better and tackle better and get good field position more often, you win."

Judging from the spring scrimmage, the defenders of the Alamo stood a better chance than Jake's squad against a juggernaut on its home turf. The best he and his staff could do was get the team ready.

He dialed Maxwell Hall again and left his number.

He had a nice chat with Betsy and Tami. When he hung up, the walls closed in. Spring drills were done, his staff was scattered to the four winds, Betsy was a million miles away, and Tami's relentless chatter and singing were denied him. The only company he had was the nightmare of a top-ten team tap-dancing on his motley collection of also-rans.

He turned on the radio and found a station featuring mellow music. It wasn't to his liking, but it was far better than listening to…whatever the college kids listened to.

Jake tried to read. He began with a book he soon set aside. He picked up a sports magazine, but he quickly tired of that. He scanned the newspaper on the off chance he'd missed something earlier. He found himself reading the announcements in a dated church bulletin.

He checked his watch. Was it too late to catch a movie?

He considered calling Evy. They could swap anecdotes of the "good old days," and he could scold him for "stealing" one of his coaches. It was tempting, but it was too late in Iowa for social calls.

Finally, he stretched out on the couch and studied the ceiling. He allowed his thoughts to wander where they would.

The phone rang.

"Davidson returning your call."

"Mark Davidson? This is Coach Oats."

"Who are you? I've got better things to do than return prank calls."

"Jake Oats, and this ain't no prank. I'd like to talk to you."

"About what?"

"Let's try this. Do you have a class in the morning?"

"I've got a nine o'clock and an eleven o'clock."

"Ten fifteen? In the Ag. Building. You know where the milk bar is?"

"Yes."

"Okay. If you show up and I don't, you know it's a prank. That should settle it. What do you have to lose other than a few minutes?"

"Not much, I guess."

"If you don't show, I come to your dorm and make a scene."

"Okay."

"Semper Fi."

"Sem—hey! Who the hell are you, really?"

"I'll show you my ID in the Ag. Building. Ten fifteen."

———•———

Nothing ventured, Jake thought.

He reported to his office shortly after seven. Barbara and Holly arrived promptly at eight. Jake pondered about their punctuality. If he broke his habit of coming in early, would the ladies arrive at eight, or would they follow the dominant campus norm and begin work "around" eight?

There was nothing new on his desk, but Barbara added an unnecessary punctuation mark.

"No messages and no mail," she reported.

"Mrs. Hicks, I trust you implicitly," he responded. "If there's nothing on my desk, I'm satisfied there is nothing pending."

"Okay."

Her delivery was less than congenial.

"Sorry. Did I come across as brusque? That was not my intention."

She paused for a moment and glanced his way. The expression on her face told a story. "I'm sorry too," she began meekly. "My daughter and I…um, well, problems."

Jake sighed. "I understand. In a way, I envy you. My daughter may as well be on the moon."

It was Barbara's turn to sigh. "Sometimes, I wish mine was on the moon."

It was as funny as a broken rib, but it was a stab at humor. She regained her poise and began working as efficiently as ever.

———•———

He called the parents of a couple prospects. He inquired after their (the parents') health and their son's grades. The mothers were quite chatty. They seemed to like Jake. That mightn't count for much when the player made his commitment, but it certainly couldn't damage his chances.

He ambled down to the equipment room and had a chat with the equipment manager.

Steve Thompson was a gray-headed loon who kept an unlit cigar in his mouth. He appeared to be a nervous wreck. If he wasn't busy with something, he became moody and contentious. He'd survived the Battle of the Bulge. The scent of pine upset him mightily. He returned from the war a basket case. He couldn't hold a job—until someone put him in the basement. The equipment room was far removed from the scent of pine, snow, and the heat of battle.

Steve cared about players. He sweated blood in an uncompromising effort to make certain he outfitted each man with the proper equipment. He kept the helmets polished to the same degree as a barracks floor on the general's inspection day. He issued fresh clothing and towels every practice day and collected them after. He, or the managers, gathered up any stray towels and segregated them from the regular laundry.

The man took a month off during the summer to hike and fish or build anything that kept his hands busy. Must keep busy!

Neither the player nor the coaches would survive without Steve. During the games, he paced the sidelines like a nervous sentry. Should something need repair, he was on it like syrup on a stack of wheat cakes.

"Kicking pad ready?" he'd bark at the nearest manager.

"Kicking tee. We need the kicking tee!"

Never mind that the kicking tee was already on the field in the competent hands of the player who'd put it to use.

Despite his vital position, Steve eschewed self-promotion. Similarly, he, brushed off plaudits. Whenever he was introduced as the university's equipment manager, people were eager to hear some "inside baseball" anecdotes. Steve had collected a thousand stories over the years, many of them hilarious. However, he wouldn't be baited.

"I just sock, jock, and T 'em," he'd announce.

The only time he imparted a thigh slapper, it was to a player, a coach, or a manager. That is, he shared his mirth with insiders only.

His favorite word was *Jesus*. Jake could not make up his mind if Steve used it as an invective or as a plea for divine assistance.

When Jake caught up with him, Steve was drilling holes and affixing face guards on newly arrived helmets. He continued work as they talked, his cigar dancing in front of his face.

"Write it down, Coach. *Jesus*."

Jake printed items on Steve's ubiquitous yellow pad. It was littered with scribbles and hieroglyphics only the cigar chomper could decipher. After each entry, Jake would introduce the next topic.

"*Jesus.* Write it down."

Jake was sorely tempted to remind Steve that he was the football coach and *not* Jesus. He hung fire. Steve appreciated the lamest humor, but only when not working.

Jake noticed an autographed picture hanging on the wall over Steve's workbench. It was an eight-by-ten glossy mounted on a made-to-order plaque. It was of a cheerleader in full regalia. It was an action shot of her and her pom-poms. It must have been taken during a basketball game because she was indoors. The autograph looked genuine enough for a young college student, but her name *Joe Del Lessing* didn't ring true. Well, campus names were often amended for purposes of vanity or as part of a trend, so he asked no questions.

After he recorded his list of items on Steve's yellow pad, he bid him goodbye and returned to the land of the living. On his way, something fatuous flashed across his busy brain.

Tam Mee.

He shivered. He loved his little girl, but he hoped she wouldn't fall into the trend trap. It was acceptable whenever she wanted to wear an Estonian moniker, but Shady Blue, Moon Shadow, Tam Mee, or Tamm Tamm might push Jake over the precipice into the depth of despair.

He walked into the AD's office. A thin blonde (thin enough to look anemic) and a dark-haired woman were on display. The blonde, Jake knew, was the assistant ticket manager. The husky woman, all six feet of her, was very attractive.

She rose when he entered. "He's not in just now."

"Why do you stand?" he asked. "Downstairs I'm *Jesus.* In here, I'm treated like the King of Pomerania. I'm here on a whim. Do you have a copy of last year's football program?"

The athletic woman thought for a moment. She may have been scanning her memory bank, or she may have been evaluating Jake's sanity.

"I'm sure we do," she mused. A moment later, she marched to the counter. She bent down and searched through, what Jake assumed, was a cardboard box. Seconds passed before she produced a glossy booklet. "Will this do?"

He took it and paged through. The photo of the rally squad, four men and six women, was featured above a three-quarter-page ad for a big-city TV station that carried highlights of each game.

Jo Dell Lessing.

He closed the program and returned it with thanks. "Coffee fresh?"

The woman with the short black hair and the penetrating eyes nodded. "Maybe ten minutes old," she informed.

He nodded and made his was across the hall to the lounge.

Steve, he thought, *you're full of crap.*

Nevertheless, he understood.

———•———

Jake put to bed letters, phone calls (made and received), authorized signatures, and a myriad of items unconnected with anything Jake Oats was hired to do. He kept a close eye on his watch.

"I'm going to the Ag. Building for a milkshake," he announced.

"Okay."

It sounded normal, but Jake noticed how one of Barbara's eyebrows arched upward. She'd never mention it, but she thought Jake had slipped a cog.

The milk bar was recommended by a player. The products served there (except for the coffee) came from university crops and livestock. Moreover, they were processed in university facilities.

Jake changed his mind. Rather than a milkshake, he opted for a vanilla cone.

"I'll wager the cone comes from a commercial vendor," he said for no purpose.

The young man in the old-fashioned soda-jerk cap never batted an eye or cracked a smile. "You lose," he replied, handing over his order.

There were only two small tables and four chairs across from the counter and next to the exterior wall. All were vacant. Jake settled in and enjoyed his first taste of university ice cream. It was worth the trip, but he didn't really expect Mark Davidson to appear. Too bad. This was the perfect venue. It wasn't as crowded as the Union or as public as the library or the dorm. Mieko, against all odds, had recognized him. That was a bitter tonic for a man who preferred anonymity. Unfortunately, the head coach of a major university program would experience precious little privacy.

A young man clutching two thick textbooks sauntered through the main entrance and turned right. He didn't look very happy as he approached the milk bar. Suddenly, he stopped in his tracks. "It really *is* you!" he choked.

"I've been me ever since I can remember," Jake replied.

The man stood stock-still and gulped.

"The ice cream is good. I'll buy you a cone."

Cautiously, the barrel-chested ex-Marine approached. "You want to talk with me?"

"Why should I not?"

The poor guy was flummoxed. He approached slowly and placed his textbooks on the table across from Jake. Thereupon, he imitated a statue.

"Get yourself a cone." Jake motioned. "Maybe you'd like a milkshake. I'm buying."

Davidson decided he should do something other than stare. He shuffled over to the counter and ordered a strawberry shake. It would take the attendant several seconds to get it ready. Rather than remain unoccupied, he returned to the table and sat down as if he wasn't certain it was proper behavior.

"What position did you play in school?" Jake asked.

"Um, offensive guard and defensive end."

"Would you consider turning out in the fall?"

There was a long pause. "I never even thought about it."

"You're on GI Bill, correct?"

"Yes, sir."

Jake struggled momentarily with his snack. "Please, don't call me *sir*. I was an enlisted man, just as you were."

"Marine?"

Jake nodded.

The shake arrived.

Jake, reaching for a napkin, was caught unprepared. "Can you trust me until I'm finished?"

"That's cool," the barman said.

Jake frowned. He didn't approve of glib, nonsense slang.

"If you turn out this fall, you'll eat at the training table once a day. That will cut your personal expenses. I need linebackers. You might not play much. If somebody gets hurt, you might play a lot. Dave Thorne will be your position coach. He's young, but he knows his stuff. I know how you miss being yelled at by your NCOs. Dave can yell to match any DI. You'd feel right at home."

Davidson swallowed hard. "I'm not certain I'm good enough to play here. I considered going to a smaller school and playing."

"Why didn't you?"

"My degree program is here."

Jake nodded. "Look at the academy schools, Mark. Many of those players are better suited to smaller schools. They manage to keep up with the big boys. Army and Navy both play Notre Dame regularly. You can't get bigger than that. You could be a real asset to this team, Mark."

Mark looked away and pondered. His left leg started to bounce.

Jake let him think for a minute.

"You need to work out. Distance running, sprints, weight room— not just now, but through the summer. You'll have to pass the physical. You didn't get shot up in Nam, did you?"

"A little. The Corps took care of me and my rehab. I got a clean bill on my discharge physical."

"Then that shouldn't be a problem. Think it over, Mark."

"I'm kinda old," he reminded.

"My first coaching job was after the war—the second one. I was coaching ex-service people almost exclusively. Believe me, you're a baby compared to some players I've coached. Then there's this: your age gives you an edge in leadership. If you work as hard as everyone else, the men will look up to you. A Marine knows what that can do for a unit."

There was a lingering oppressive silence.

Jake got to his feet. "I need you, Mark. Think it over. You know where to find me." He reached for his wallet and returned to the bar.

Banana Boat

First and second floor, east wing of Maxwell Hall.

Jake jotted down the information on his to-do pad. He double-checked the information. He'd inform Barbara though, likely, Holly would oversee the summer and welcome-back packets. Despite gleaning the pertinent information, Jake forced himself to read to the end. He was the big boss. Part of his job was to ensure he knew *all* the details.

There it was!

The memo was prepared by Mieko Takada and signed by the AD himself.

It came back instantly. The abandoned water where once a veritable armada sprawled from horizon to horizon. Then Jake's terrifying aloneness. The following instant, he saw the surprised, hopeless, resigned expression on the face of a Japanese soldier as Jake fired eight rounds into his body. Then the climax: the recent horrible, terrifying, gut-wrenching feeling that he'd murdered Mieko's father.

He must have made some peculiar sound. Jake didn't hear it; he wasn't even aware.

"Coach, are you okay?"

It was Barbara framed in his doorway with a concerned expression on her face.

Embarrassed, he cleared his throat.

"I was thinking of a stupid last-minute fumble that cost us a game some years ago," he reported.

She didn't believe it. Her expression announced as much. Before the workday ended, she'd put out the word that it might be wise to keep the emergency call list handy. Jake must be extra careful. If people in the department got the idea that Jake Oats was a prime candidate for Coconut Grove, his tenure would be brief.

He spent several minutes with inconsequential silliness before ambling down the hall. Ostensibly, he was refilling his coffee mug. His real objective, however, was across the hall.

The Amazon secretary snapped to attention once more. He made a mental note to obtain the draft rights to her children. During a later conference, he dropped a comment in front of Steve Thompson.

"Oh, *Jesus*, Denise Davenport, that's her name. Ain't married—not yet. Too good-looking to be single for long. She's probably waiting for some basketball player to come along. She's got a sister going to school here. Vikki—two *ks*—plays softball. *Jesus*, I think she's taller than Denise! Nice looking, the both of them, but I wouldn't want to get on their bad side. If you got any sense, you don't want to either. The AD thinks she walks on water. Denise replaced two secretaries. After she was here for a couple weeks, the Big Guy decided he didn't need that second hire. He says to me once, 'If I ain't careful, Denise will have my job!' Yeah, *Jesus*, she gets praise from everybody—not just a pretty face for sure, for sure!"

"The athletic director said *ain't*?"

"*Jesus*, Coach, you know what I mean."

Jake made two decisions in the same instant. First, he'd not complain about Steve saying *Jesus* every few seconds. Second, he would be certain to walk cautiously when Denise Davenport was in the area. If he did anything that might encourage her to quit, the AD might not be gracious.

"Miss Davenport," he began softly, "if you must stand every time I come in here, I'll refuse to come in here."

Deb, the anemic-looking blonde sorting tickets, smiled and produced a subdued chuckle. "There are two jack-in-the-boxes now," she offered sotto voce.

"Pardon?"

Deb squirmed visibly in her chair. She reserved tickets, sold tickets, procured group bookings, and a dozen additional duties. She was good at her job. Though she could placate Attila, she became extremely curt if pushed too far. Jake didn't like her—not because of her demeanor or bleached hair, but because she looked like a graduate of Auschwitz. Should someone open a door abruptly and create a draft, it might knock the woman over.

"Mieko stands when anyone, man or woman, comes in," she explained.

"Is the chief in?" he asked of Denise.

What a poor way to change the subject! Jake needed polish. If Betsy were available, she could coach him. Well, she was hundreds of miles away. He was on his own.

"Conference AD meeting. He won't be back until late Friday."

A meeting of conference athletic directors to sign off on agreements already decided via phone and mail. It was a boondoggle. Afternoons spent sightseeing, evening spent…well, it depended upon whether wives came along. The mornings spent swapping lies and throwing off the odd suggestion. The afternoons, of course, featured cash bar.

"Are you real busy at the moment?"

"Not *real* busy," Denise replied.

"Well, as long as you're on your feet, would you come down the hall? Barbara has a memo from the old man that…well, we disagree over what action the AD expects."

Denise eyed him suspiciously. She wasn't stupid. Deb probably wasn't stupid either. Well, there was nothing for it.

"I'd have brought the memo down here, but Barbara, well, she's very protective about what's on her desk. It shouldn't take more than a few seconds."

Denise looked at Deb, who acted coy. She was as suspicious as Denise, but she pretended to be unconcerned. Finally, the tall dark secretary made a command decision.

She vacated her desk and crossed to the hall in long strides. Once out of the office and away from prying ears, Jake spoke quietly. "I have nightmares about the war. Mieko triggered one. I've nothing against her.

I like her, but can you help me get some sleep? I want to know if Mieko's father is living."

"I can't divulge personal information," she quoted from a university or department regulation.

"I'm not asking personal information—no names, no dates, no visa stamps. I just want to know if her father is alive. Yes or no? I won't noise it around."

"You could ask her," she suggested.

"Someday, I promise, I'll tell you why I prefer not to."

She considered the proposition for two more lengthy strides. "It might take me a while," she said. "I don't have access to files, but I can find out from someone who does."

"I'd appreciate it. This is a personal favor, understand? I can't buy you dinner or retile your kitchen. This is on the QT. Understand?"

"Yes, sir. I'll be in touch."

She turned and retraced her steps. Deb would require some explanation. He doubted Denise would lie. If she reported that Coach Oats is whack-a-doodle, that wouldn't bother him in the least. He'd been whack-a-doodle since the day Evy talked him into coaching.

He took comfort in knowing that much without requiring professional help.

Jake settled behind his desk and examined the outline of offensive line drills Joe and Pink left for him. While he examined the comments, sketches, and diagrams, Jake's mind wandered.

The Japanese soldiers marched with a bit of home in their packs. Jake was never tempted to rifle through the enemy's gear, but several of his platoon mates weren't as fastidious. They frequently boasted about their finds. There were, of course, family photos or snaps of children. However, there were banners, tiny effigies, small plaques, rings, things, and in one case, a child's toy.

Jake eschewed souvenirs. Knowing of the American propensity to loot the dead, the Japanese booby-trapped bodies of former comrades whenever possible. Jake had no ambition to be a booby.

The two Japs Jake dispatched on New Britain were left with personal items intact. First, the patrol was in no mood to tarry; where there was one Jap, there were bound to be several more—unseen but deadly. Second, Jake had no interest in learning anything about the man he killed. He did wonder, while examining Thorne's notes, if one of his victims may have carried a small photo of baby Mieko.

His scalp crawled at the thought.

He pushed away from his desk and stood. He waited a moment for the creepy crawlies to cease before moving to the rear entrance. He turned through the small conference room to find Coach Ostrander in his cubicle examining the playbook Joe Epps had distributed.

"Your drills are top hole, Stew," Jake began.

"Thanks, Coach. I think we can really sharpen key skills if we work hard."

"Always the case, Stew. Can I sit down for a sec?"

"Of course." Quickly, Pink swept up the debris on the second cubicle chair and placed it in the upper left corner of his desk.

Jake sat down and planted an elbow on the same desk. "Dave, we're in a bind here," he began. "Except for a couple trick plays, we've got to run and pass the ball. Our passing game is hobbled by available personnel. I'm looking at a short game, eight to twelve yards a go. We must rely on fullback and halfback powers. That means your backs have to block like guards."

Stew leaned back. He didn't have a reclining chair, so he tipped back on the rear two legs of the one he had. He picked up a pencil and bedded the eraser end against his cheek before studying his boss.

"Your men must do a number on the backers, Stew. Every practice, pads or no pads, you must work your crew like men possessed on power blocking. It don't need to look pretty. Moving a linebacker out of the hole is ideal, but our backs won't have the size or strength to do that. They must throw themselves at a cement truck hard enough to give the ball carrier some space to run—no matter how small. They ain't gonna like it. They especially ain't gonna like having to beat their heads against a stone wall for four quarters, but they must do it. Remember, that kid who is running to daylight on one play will have to block like hell for his teammate on the next play."

Stew rapped the eraser portion of his pencil against his front teeth thoughtfully for a few seconds. He'd been with his players through spring practice. He knew what he had. He knew what he needed. "I guess things do look a little desperate," he concluded.

"*A little?* We open against a team with a winning pedigree. Some polls have them ranked as high as number 3. They can outrun us and outpass us on offense and outquick us on defense. If we're going to stay with them, we gotta make it an alley fight. Our lead blockers have to throw their bodies around and make space where there ain't any."

"The ol' *three-yards-in-a-cloud-of-dust*, eh?" he pondered. "*Throw their bodies around.* I like that, Coach. Mind if I use it?"

"Use any damned thing you want, Stew. Just know we are not big enough or fast enough to outfinesse anybody on our schedule. Until we get more and better people, we gotta fight like hell and hope we can make something happen."

Ostrander tossed his pencil onto the desk and slammed his chair down on all four legs. "Read you loud and clear, Coach," he said. "Save the pep talk for the men. I'll dream up some drill for throwing bodies around."

"Talk to Dave," Jake suggested. "You two could run a drill or two against each other."

Stewart was intrigued. "Blocking backs against linebackers…and ends."

The wheels were turning.

"Don't forget this," Jake said, pointing to Stewart's proposed drills.

"I won't," Pink promised. "Still, it looks like the bulk of our specialty time will be lead blocking."

"I appreciate it, Stew. Keep in mind, three yards in a cloud of dust will leave us with a fourth and one. We've got to do better."

Stewart grinned. "On one of three plays, at least."

The Golf War

Jake agreed with Mark Twain: "Golf is a good walk spoiled."

He never cottoned to the game. He despised basketball because in his view, the rules did not allow for aggressive defense. Were he the head basketball coach, the only people to drive the lane against his team would be out for the season. In tennis, the best defense is leaping over the net and getting nose to nose with the opposing player. In swimming, the best defense is crossing the lane and driving an opponent into the wall. In golf, the surest way to win is to eliminate the other players. However, his golf aptitude and skills tallied several touchdowns, field goals, and extra points. If only he could score as much against Georgia.

Jake tried to beg off, but the athletic director, Ralph Preston, invited him. When the AD issued an invitation, declining was tantamount to insubordination. The foursome included Harry Bower the business manager and Charles Morgan the publicity director. Bower obtained a membership in the country club for Jake and his family. This was one of the traditional perks offered to all head coaches. The athletic budget didn't allow the university to compete with other major institutions. Therefore, a coach's modest pay was augmented by certain community-driven "fringe benefits."

Jake could do without club membership, but Betsy and Tami were certain to make ample use of the pool. They could also enjoy lunch in the club restaurant and enjoy gourmet birthday dinners there. He owned a set of clubs, inherited from another coach years before, but they were parked in the garage of his soon-to-be *former* home. Ralph, however, had an extra set "for emergencies."

It was a *friendly* match, no stakes up front and no side bets. In truth, however, it was a grilling session. Had Jake been bold, he'd insist they skip the game and go right to the nineteenth hole. They could chat over beer and snacks without expending energy and unnecessary swear words. However, golf was the preferred interrogation technique of most colleges and universities.

Sure enough, they wanted to know about players, assistant coaches, facilities, equipment changes and modifications, and team's travel apparel. They were less interested in offensive and defensive strategy.

"Your first game is going to be a big challenge," Charles, aka Chas, announced needlessly. "How do you feel about going head-to-head with Georgia?"

Chas was fishing for a quote.

"I'm underpaid," Jake replied.

That got the obligatory laugh, but no one was satisfied.

"We must play harder and better," he added. "That's true of any game. I can't be more specific than that. Ask again after two-a-days. I'll have a better idea of our strengths."

It wasn't what they wanted to hear, but they couldn't argue. Only a fool would write a postdated check he mightn't cover.

"The conference athletic directors issued a travel ruling," Ralph announced on the eighth hole. "No air travel for any game within 250 miles. Every cross-state rivalry is covered by that, of course. In our case, we have two additional opponents within that radius."

Jake took this with a grain of salt. He'd been around long enough to know that pre-season conference agreements weren't worth much. Moreover, he had a player who didn't handle flying well. There could be others, but he knew of one for certain. He might require a mild sedative. If one were administered, the NCAA would require notification.

Bus travel was fine. Jake preferred the bus. It reminded him of the train travel back in the day when he and Evy were escorting Harman up and down the field. Bus travel for three games would be less stressful for him personally. He hoped it would prove more relaxing than the chaos of airports and transportation to and from.

On the way to the fourteenth tee, Jake got an opening.

"Where's the team bunking this year during twice-a-days?" Ralph asked Jake.

He thought it queer since Harry Bower was less than a yard away. Still, it was an opportunity. "Maxwell," he replied. "I got the letter a few days ago. I saw Mieko's name. Did she handle that?"

"She did it all," Harry responded. "You know Mieko?"

Jake explained how they met. "I thought she wasn't on board until fall," Jake announced.

"She's a good kid," Bower replied. "She's been haunting my office for days wanting to know how things work and where things are. We decided to give her the job of finding a dorm. She cut her teeth on it. In truth, we just wanted her out from under foot for a while."

"She a bother?"

"Not really. She's very go-ahead. Anxious. So we handed her the ball and let her run with it. There wasn't much to it. A few phone calls and a modicum of leg work. She has a knack for not rubbing people the wrong way."

Ralph opted to add his endorsement. "I'd go further, Harry. She has a knack for rubbing people the *right* way."

"Agreed." Harry nodded. "I'm going to let her handle the charters. That's a lot of fuss and bother, but she'll shine."

"So if the team and I find ourselves in Mexico City for our first game, I can't complain to you."

Harry laughed. Until then, he hadn't been in a laughing mood. He was one walk spoiler who feels he must be as good as Arnold Palmer, or his time is wasted. "We'll check her work, Coach," he assured.

Jake didn't say, though he could have, that he might prefer being in Mexico rather in Athens. "Know anything about her family?"

Harry looked at Jake as if he caught him cheating on his score card. It was a momentary glance, but it reeked of suspicion. "She was born and raised in Japan," he replied. "She's all the time inviting us to visit her there. She promises to take us for dinner at a fugu fish place."

Ralph whistled. "Isn't that the poison fish? No antidote."

Harry didn't know. He didn't care. The chances of his going to Japan were only slightly greater than his chances of eating fugu fish.

"Maybe she'll invite me too."

Jake's remark was superfluous. However, his mind was racing. If he did kill her father, Mieko might *insist* on having him to dinner.

He'd dismissed the notion that he'd killed the young woman's father. However, there remained a possibility, however unlikely. When hundreds of men launched thousands of bullets on the Canal and New Britain, who is omniscient enough to know which were kill shots? If Mieko's father died on either island, well, she'd have an excellent reason to rub Jake the *wrong* way.

The war was over, but to Jake, it was a part of him still. He didn't want it, but there was no way to rid himself of it.

Dead week was only ten days distant. It was so called because by university rules, no projects were due nor tests administered in the week preceding final exams.

Jake's workload lessened slightly. He devoted more time to getting the house ready to receive his family. Betsy supervised the loading of furniture and household items; the van was on the road. Wife and daughter enjoyed a week in a motel room prior to flying out. Household goods could be easily dispatched, but friendships and financial obligations were different.

Dr. Linus Pauling was slated to speak in the indoor arena, aka the basketball pavilion. Jake wanted to attend. It was only a few steps from his office to the venue, but there was always something requiring his attention. Joe Epps, for example, had a young recruit on the hook and suggested Jake chat with him. The appointment, of course, coincided with Dr. Pauling's appearance.

Denise Davenport was not similarly obligated. She did not ask her boss if she could attend the double Nobel laureate's shindig. Instead, she announced her intention to be absent from the office for the duration of his public appearance. Ralph Preston prized his secretary. Indeed, she was an aesthetic enhancement to the department in addition to her skill and efficiency. If she opted for a little time off, Preston was certain the athletic department could bumble on without her for ninety minutes or so.

By the time Jake's meeting ended, Dr. Pauling's pep rally (for want of a better phrase) was nearing an end. As much as he wanted to see the great man, he had other priorities.

He was behind in his correspondence due to his recruiting spiel. As he dictated into his machine, he heard a commotion in the outer office.

Barbara shot up out of her chair much as Jake once had whenever an officer was on deck. To his perplexed amazement, Holly was on her feet. They were offering praise and congratulations. The object of the disturbance was Denise Davenport. Curious but determined, Jake renewed his concentration but failed. Inevitably, he was drawn out of his office.

Denise bubbled with delight. Surprisingly, she blushed. Not only had the boss given her leave, but he arranged for her to greet and attend Dr. Pauling and his retinue for the duration of his visit. She'd just returned from escorting the man to his limo. Envious, as indeed was everyone in the department, Jake offered his congratulations and returned to his duties.

After a few minutes, there was a rapping on his doorframe. He scowled over the intrusion but moderated his attitude when he noticed Denise Davenport filling much of his office doorway. Concluding that turnabout was fair, he got to his feet and invited her in. If she suspected his remonstration over her snap to attention whenever he entered her domain, she failed to show it.

"There was a demonstration prior to the presentation of Dr. Pauling," she reported. "I thought you might want to know."

"Why might I like to know?"

"It was the Black Student Union," she announced. "There were a hundred or so who marched in and took over the podium before the guest was introduced."

"Anybody hurt?"

"No. Other than being inexcusably rude, there was no fuss."

Jake eyed her closely. She was very nice to look at despite her intimidating size, but she wasn't one of his players. She wasn't daunted by his glare—if, indeed, she bothered to notice it.

"The man speaking for the Union introduced himself. I remembered someone saying you were trying to contact him—or *them*. I jotted down some information."

This was no *jot*. In bold immaculate cursive was a name.

Jake accepted the paper. "As ever, Miss Davenport, you are a credit to the department. Thank you."

Had she initiated a bob curtsy, he'd have gagged. Instead, she smiled her thank-you and departed for her zone.

Milt Spurling

"Barbara, may I see your *Hall's*?"

It took only a moment.

"I apologize," Jake said. "I'll buy a copy of my own when I get a chance."

"Keep this one," she suggested. "My daughter can bring one in. We'll take it out of petty cash."

Jake thanked her, but he didn't give a damn how it was done so long as he had a copy when he wanted one.

Milt Spurling was listed as general studies, a university euphemism for anyone declining to declare a major. He had an off-campus address. Well, it would hardly require a detective to figure out that Milt was an agitator. Odds were good he was being paid by some parent group.

He took out a copy of the letter he'd previously put on ice. He placed it in a shotgun envelope together with a handwritten note and addressed it to the president's office. He did *not* call Barbara to do the leg work. He was capable of walking to the outer office counter and placing the document in the campus mail tray.

Thirty minutes later, when he heard the tray emptied by the campus courier, Jake picked up his phone and pushed the red button. Denise Davenport picked up. He was tempted to ask her if she was standing but suppressed the petty urge.

"Thanks again for the info," he stated. "Let me speak with the boss."

"One moment."

"I bet you say that to all the guys."

He was safe from her umbrage. He was on hold. He could disclose every military secret he possessed; they'd vanish into a void.

"This better be important, Jake," the AD announced. "I'm working on a baby slam."

Jake chuckled. His opinion of athletic directors in general was low. Nevertheless, he knew Ralph Preston did not play cards during work hours. Rather than trade silly quips, Jake reported his dispatch of his letter to the BSU via the president. He promised to avoid a face-to-face contact until he got the green light from the big guy. He also promised to keep Ralph in the loop.

"I think it's a good idea, Jake," Ralph repeated. "I'm backing you."

"Thanks, boss."

⎯⎯⎯•◆•⎯⎯⎯

"We got a tee time for tomorrow afternoon," Harry reported. "Charlie's coming. Want to make it a threesome?"

Jake gripped the phone until his knuckles blanched.

"Gosh, Harry, I was so looking forward to getting a root canal tomorrow afternoon."

The business manager laughed. "You're not that bad," he suggested insincerely.

"Harry, I can't think of anything I'd rather not do. If you and Charles want to pump me, let's meet for a drink after work."

"Lunch tomorrow? At Big Blue?"

Big Blue, where coeds in short skirts skated hither and yon to take and deliver drive-in orders.

Jake shuddered. "If we eat inside," he suggested.

"Done."

Okay, interrogation over sandwiches and coffee rather than a tedious round of golf. The burger joint was budget friendly as opposed to the overpriced drinks at the clubhouse. He counted on a satisfying meal devoid of alcohol. Further, he could return to his office and work rather than blow an entire afternoon.

Jake, 6; Suits, 0.

———•———

Charles wasn't satisfied with the biography gleaned from Jake between drives and putts. He had a bright if brand-new assistant. Better, he thought, to punch out Jake's biography himself. Chas's youth was misspent as a reporter for a small-city paper. Habits, however, die hard. He trusted primary sources rather than the I-heard-somebody-say-that-a-"friend"-saw-something brand of information.

Jake settled in behind a better-than-expected Rueben sandwich. Rather than respond to nickel-and-dime questions, he presented his audience with short blurbs between bites.

He joined the Marines days after Pearl Harbor. Guadalcanal, New Britain, busted leg, malaria that kept him off Peleliu where nearly all his surviving Canal buddies "bought it." Sent back to the States. Promoted to sergeant. Became a DI at Parris Island. Mustered out in 1946.

"You won a Silver Star," Charles reminded.

"Did I? I don't remember."

Message tacitly received. There'd be no more questions about his military service.

"Worked in Michigan, UP, as a longshoreman. I was asked to go to Iowa as an assistant coach. That was fifty or fifty-one. Got an offer and higher pay at Kansas. If I'd known Evy would be the new coach at Iowa, I'd have stayed on, but I met Betsy in Kansas, so that made the move worth it. After a year, I went to Texas Tech for two years. Betsy got a job there. We got married.

"One year at Nebraska, two at Indiana. To Illinois, and, well, two years—"

He didn't finish.

His first job as head coach.

He discovered Gus Avery in Indiana coaching a high school team to a long string of victories. They became friends. When Jake went to Illinois, he convinced his boss to hire Gus. When Jake got his first head job, he wanted Gus to come along. However, Avery lusted for a chance to coach in Canada where football was a bit more to his liking.

Two years as the head man. Jake brought with him a twelve-win, nine-loss, and one-tie record. No publicity man could make that look good. If Jake were the AD rather than Ralph Preston, he never would have interviewed a small-school coach with that record—never mind hiring him!

"Doesn't sound very impressive, does it, Charlie?" Jake asked, finishing his coffee.

"Prognosis?" Harry prodded.

"I've got a damned fine staff," Jake announced confidently. "We have to be reckless on defense and methodical on offense. We don't have the speed or the size to match up with the rest of the conference, so every game must be an alley fight. Messy, hard-nosed, bloody—"

"Like Guadalcanal."

Jake froze momentarily. He tried very hard *not* to think of Guadalcanal. When Charles threw it in his face, Jake remembered a myriad of horrific memories.

Reluctantly, he conceded the similarity. "Yes," he hissed through gritted teeth. "Like Guadalcanal."

——•—

Great! Just great!

There were days, sometimes entire weeks, when he blotted out his nightmare. When it came unbidden, he managed to suppress it with a few minutes of intense concentration on something else, usually football.

Thanks to Harry, Charles, and his golf game (without a spoiled walk), he was hauling Guadalcanal around as Jacob Marley dragged his chains.

Damn! Damn! Double damn!

To Brisbane, his body racked with malaria. Hell, the conditions and the mosquitoes in Brisbane were as hellish as the Solomons. Typical military snafu! Even the blockheads realized how malaria victims were better off in jungles surrounded by Japs. Some unknown official, with brains and compassion, ordered the malaria cases farther south. It came in the form of a direct order, perhaps from Admiral Halsey. Discussing the theater orders intelligently (and medically) was time wasted.

When Jake was strong enough to take care of his bodily functions again, boredom ravaged what was left. There was an edition of *War and Peace* used by the nurses to keep the ward door propped open. Jake began to read. He was scolded mercilessly until someone discovered that a brick served well enough as a doorstop. Better, in fact: no one was tempted to read a brick.

Jake read with little comprehension. The words and esoteric Russian names whirled in his brain, forcing his war memories out. When he finished the book, he turned back to the title page and began reading anew. As his mind and body grew stronger, the paragraphs and images settled into comprehensible form.

Jake never discussed literature. He felt like a dumbass whenever anyone launched into a literary critique. He didn't know *anadiplosis* from *verisimilitude*, but he could observe. The character of Countess Natasha captivated him. She was innocent, effervescent, optimistic, and filled with joie de vivre. Then she married Pierre and became a mind-numbed caricature.

He never discussed the book with any authority. He'd be embarrassed. Doubtless, he would be mocked or derided for his simplemindedness. Nevertheless, the transformation of Natasha was very real to him. It was a major part of his courtship.

When he met Betsy Ross, he was metaphorically bowled over. It wasn't exactly love at first sight, but he was impressed with her personality, magnified by her physical attributes. He wanted her for his wife, but he was reticent. He didn't want Betsy to suffer the fate visited upon Natasha. This fear blocked their union for a time.

Betsy earned Jake's trust. He trusted her enough to communicate his interpretation of a Russian novel. She did not laugh at him or attack his amateurish interpretation. Instead, she promised that she would not surrender her life to him or anyone else. On that basis, he proposed, and without any hesitation, she accepted. She married a football coach but refused to be a football widow. No matter how dark the clouds, win or lose or draw, Betsy remained the same. If he brooded over a loss or was drunk with the taste of victory, Betsy was his anchor. She kept his life "real."

Similarly, when he wallowed in his sordid wartime memories, she possessed the patience of Job. She lifted him out of the mire and horror. She led him back to reality. What's done was done. What was now demanded their attention. When Tami arrived, that became their principal focus. There was no room for selfishness, pity, or nightmares.

Well, Betsy wasn't with him. Still, their nightly phone exchange swept aside most of his morbid thoughts. After hanging up, Jake felt renewed. He picked up a book and read. When he got bored, he went to bed and slept like a baby.

Made Glorious Summer

The Thursday of dead week, Jake scheduled a team meeting. Most of the important classes met three times a week. The less-demanding courses (i.e., ballroom dance, math for morons, and boiling water at high altitudes) were scheduled for Tuesdays and Thursdays. Most were midmorning and afternoon classes. A team meeting set for nine o'clock roped in the entire squad.

Jake entered at exactly nine o'clock. Epps and Avery trailed in behind for no other reason than to display their loyalty.

The squad snapped to attention and stayed standing until Coach reached the podium and bid them to be seated. It did not escape his attention that Gino sat in the center of the front row.

"Men, I won't keep you long. I know some of you need to crack some books. You especially, Shumway."

There was a group chuckle as the team focused on the starting left tackle. He was smart and analytical. His skill in math and physics was exceptional. Philosophy and literature, however, were too "inexact" and "open ended" for him. He struggled with those required classes that could not be reduced to theorems and formulas.

"I know many of you have jobs. That's good. However, gentlemen, I want you to spend as much time as possible with your family. Hold them close, gentlemen. They're important—damned important. Don't wait until it's too late to realize that.

"Keep up with your conditioning. Eat smart. When you return, you'll get checked into the barracks."

There was subdued laughter over this term.

"Sorry, gentlemen. As soon as you are checked into the dorm, you will report to the track. You will run a mile. You must finish in less than six minutes thirty, or Coach Perry will have you running stadium steps until you choke on your own puke. We will face a top 10 ranked team right out of the chute. I don't want you to think about that. You've got something much more important to worry about: your grades. If you don't maintain your GPA, you don't play. It is exactly that simple. I understand, in the past, people have been allowed to slide. No more! I told you before, the NCAA has us under a microscope. They might put us on probation if they catch you jaywalking.

"Here's something else to worry about: your grades in the spring game. They were far from illustrious, gentlemen. We seem to have some vague idea of where the sidelines and the goal lines are, but your performance was *not* sit-up-and-take-notice. The coaches and I are grading every player on every play. This will determine your place in the depth chart when you return."

Jake cleared his throat.

"Dave Peck!"

"Here, sir."

"You're good pals with John Wagonblast."

It was not a question. They played together in high school. Peck to Wagonblast was a pass-catch combination that landed both on the all-state team. Wagonblast had a stellar sophomore year for the in-state rival. Peck sat out that year as a redshirt.

"Yes, sir. We live on the same block."

"Steal his playbook."

Another laugh. Even the least honorable among them knew the request was facetious.

"That's only fair," Peck responded. "He's got ours."

Even Jake joined in the laughter Peck's response initiated. His affection for the redshirt sophomore-to-be increased substantially. He reminded himself to be careful; one can get to like a player too much.

"I'm serious about this family thing, gentlemen. They are your best supporters and most ardent fans. Don't do or say anything to make them disappointed or ashamed. You play for this university and you play for me, but you play first, last, and always for your family.

"Study hard. Good luck on your finals. See you in August."

As he stepped from behind the podium, the team rose as one and remained standing until Jake exited the room.

It was a two-minute walk to his office.

"This young gentleman is here to see you." Barbara motioned to a bank of chairs beyond the counter.

Jake looked over his shoulder. "Mark!" He advanced back through the swinging gate and offered his hand the moment the former Marine got to his feet.

"Good to see you. Come into the office."

***

Jake felt jaunty when lunchtime came around. He eschewed wheels and invested seven minutes to walk up to the Union. The main hall was crowded with a couple hundred students gulping fries, swilling coffee, and reviewing notes and texts. The normal cacophony was missing. In its place was an eerie hush. Special interest groups abounded, each dedicated to a specific final. If he was recognized, his presence was ignored. Football was not on the exam docket.

He turned through a short corridor leading to a balustrade overlooking the ballroom. There below was a myriad of folding tables providing ample room for the additional study conclaves existing in a food-free environment. Many students enjoyed drinks, but these were procured from nearby vending machines.

Near the bookstore was a sandwich shop. Normally, it was crowded. Unless one preferred open-air seating, it was unlikely Jake would find a vacant table. It was, however, a social venue—a meeting place for a quick snack over coffee between classes. During dead week, however, it was sparsely populated.

Jake ordered a tuna sandwich, a green salad, and a coffee. He paid the cashier and retired to a table with a view. He enjoyed his lunch; he enjoyed the view. Spread out across the green of the university quad were more groups of young people. Some, he suspected, weren't even students. It was an assembly area for anyone seeking the outdoors on a balmy day.

He left satisfied. He was thankful to have a walk ahead of him before returning to "that damned desk." Jake took his time. Had there been a flower bed along the route, he'd have paused to smell the roses.

<hr>

Jake appreciated Barbara more each day. They felt they knew each other well enough to respect each other's abilities. Most secretaries would feel obliged to keep the boss briefed of any incidents during his absence. Barbara merely nodded as he passed. He returned it with one of his own.

There on his desk—in the center of his desk—was a yellow memo.

Coach Terry Called
Re: Kicker
12:46
Babs

In the lower right corner was a phone number with a Midwestern area code.

Jake knew no Coach Terry. It didn't matter. In the Fraternal Order of Football Coaches, everyone is a brother.

"Coach Oats returning a call from Coach Terry."

"Hold, please."

Jake held.

"Hey, Coach," a deep baritone voice greeted. "This is Al Terry from Central Valley College. I'm told we're not far from where you once coached years ago."

"Sure! I remember CVC."

In truth, Jake hadn't a clue. He'd coached in many places. There was always a small (*not* "smaller") school nearby. However, to admit ignorance was tantamount to authoring an insult. Central Valley College was an important part of somebody's life.

"We've got a young man here. He came out of the service and decided to use his GI Bill. He played ball for us last year. Now that he knows he can handle a college course load, he's transferring. I thought I'd give you a heads-up."

"He's coming here?"

"Yes, sir. He might get in touch with you. I advised him to, but he has confidence issues. He isn't sure he can handle big-time football *and* a full load."

"What position does he play?"

"Place kicker."

"Oh?"

Jake was interested. Kicking was a problem, but it hadn't yet made it onto his panic list.

"I can tell you aren't too excited," Terry noted. "What if I told you that he kicked a fifty-two-yard field goal in our last game?"

That got his attention.

"I don't know," Jake mused. "Do you think that's what you're going to tell me?"

The man laughed.

"His name is Gary Lynn. Pretty reserved. I think he experienced some messy things in the service. He was a medic, I understand. He doesn't talk about it—or himself—very much."

"He was Army?"

The Marines didn't have medics; they had Navy Corpsmen.

"Yeah. Low-key kind of guy, but he can put leather on the ball."

"I appreciate the call, Coach. I will be looking for him. Thanks."

Too late.

The story of Jake's life. He thought about essentials when it was too late.

He stood, prepared to walk down the hall to the AD's office. He hadn't yet taken a step toward the door when he froze. Pretty as she was, the impressive form of Denise Davenport filled most of the office doorway. She made a gesture begging entry. He nodded.

She was big, but she was graceful. Denise came through and casually closed the door behind her. If she'd worn ballet slippers, she couldn't have made such a mundane action more aesthetically pleasing.

"Mieko's father was a fisherman," she reported sotto voce. "He owned his own boat. He died six years ago. Cancer."

Jake nodded. "Thank you, Denise. That eases my mind considerably."

Did she notice he was standing? She wasn't stupid. However, would she understand the significance? He hadn't planned it, but he milked the situation. Instead of settling back into his chair, he remained on his feet.

"I was just on my way to see you."

She cocked an eyebrow.

"I saw some athletic scratch pads down your way. There's an image of the stadium on the front and the football schedule on the back. Do you still have some?"

"Only two boxes," she reported.

Did she suspect he wanted to send a pad to everybody in British Columbia?

"Could you send one, as a thank-you, to Coach Terry at Central Valley College? It will require a little detective work. It must be in the Midwest or Texas somewhere. Sorry, I can't be more specific. I didn't think to ask."

"No problem."

"Want me to write that down?"

"No, sir. I've got it. I'll let you know."

She opened the door and egressed with the same polish she displayed on her entry.

The furniture arrived sooner than expected. He got three volunteer players to help him get the furniture properly arrayed and boxes placed in the assigned rooms. Jake's tools and other related materials were stacked in the garage until he had the time and ambition to organize them.

A dozen players gladly volunteered their services, but Jake rejected all but the three who were finished with finals.

The phone rang. There was a wall phone in the kitchen, but Jake was nearer the den. He thought (hoped) it was Betsy.

"The memo pad has been mailed," Denise reported.

Jake was on the cusp of informing her that he was standing. Quickly, he realized it would be more rude than facetious.

"Thank you, Denise. Did you spend much time chasing it down?"

"I didn't spend any time," Denise replied. "Mieko found it in less than ten minutes. She'd make a great detective."

Mieko again! Well, Jake was no longer bothered by the possibility that he'd been the instrument of her father's death. It changed his attitude toward the eager import completely.

"Thanks to both of you. Is the boss there?"

"One moment."

He was on hold all of three seconds.

"Thought you were busy," Ralph announced.

"I'm on strike. Ralph, I don't know how this was handled before, but for home games, I want to take the team away somewhere. There's a motel about forty miles north at an intersection. There's no place around for miles."

"I know the place. It's a cheap motel. It couldn't possibly handle the team. No meals and no place to eat nearby."

"Just the traveling squad, Ralph. I wasn't suggesting *that* place, but you get the idea of what I'm thinking. I want the men away from parties, girlfriends, beer joints, and all other distractions. I just want them to get away from everything and concentrate on the game. It will help with team cohesion as well."

"I don't see how we can keep this a secret," Ralph warned.

"I suppose not, but we can post people in the lobby to keep out boosters and drunk alumni. In fact, I think the Booster Club might be willing to help."

The AD was thinking. "It will have to be out of town, for sure."

"Just a suggestion, Ralph. Still, I think it's a good idea."

"Let me see what I can do."

As he hung up, Jake wondered what else he'd left undone.

Jake took great care with Tami's room. His daughter loved to kneel on her bed and gaze out the window. She had an active imagination, and her imagination was triggered by looking out her window. It was a habit of long-standing. At first, Jake and Betsy were alarmed. They went so far as to consult a child psychologist.

"Other than an overactive imagination, there's nothing wrong with that child."

Despite the doctor's verdict, Betsy and Jake experienced unease when their daughter was silent for several minutes at a time. They took turns peeking into her room. They would find her kneeling on her bed and gaping through the window. She remained disturbingly silent, but her imagination was a veritable cornucopia of sensations, noises, and yes, visions. Frequently, she excitedly related her more joyous experiences. Other times, she'd make colored drawings; some were abstract and others consisted of recognizable forms. The only commonality in her visible renderings was color. All Tami's visions were recorded in bold primary colors.

Once upon a time, Tami's artistic presentations troubled her parents. They found them at times nightmarish and oppressive. When the child explained these renderings, however, they began to realize the joy, excitement, and votive qualities these creations engendered. Betsy collected them. Initially, she intended to keep them as evidence should they feel the need to call in a shrink. Ultimately, however, they became priceless works of art—at least in the eyes of mater and pater. Betsy, devoid of outside assistance, bound her daughter's collections. There were two volumes in the family bookcase.

Periodically, Tami leafed through them. Every visual representation unleashed a flood of memories.

"Remember the day when the rain was coming down sideways?"

Neither Betsy nor Jake need reply. The excited Tami would vociferously document the event in such precise and intricate detail to her parents who listened in awed silence.

Realizing that her sketches and watercolor and crayon creations were collected caused Tami to be more attentive. She studied drawings and paintings to learn techniques that might prove useful.

Jake positioned Tami's bed below the window looking out on the back lawn. There was a second window looking out on a low hedge and a neighboring yard featuring a mature cherry tree. He bought a wooden armchair and placed it at this second window. Once he found just the right cushion, Tami would have a second view port. Unfortunately, there was little room left for her rocking chair. It was designed for a child. Tami would be too big for it very soon, but she loved it.

"You figure it out," he mumbled to his absent daughter.

He did a load of bed linen, dried it, and prepared the beds for occupation. Betsy always ironed sheets and pillowcases. Jake would have none of that; indeed, he saw no purpose. Betsy, however, would strip the beds after their first night and redo them to her satisfaction.

Jake would sleep on the couch with a sofa cushion and a blanket. It was quite comfortable. Before the furniture arrived, he'd been sleeping on the floor. Some might find this needlessly spartan, but Jake once slept on the soggy ground of New Britain where it rained twenty-six hours a day! Compared to that, sleeping in a gravel pit would be luxurious.

He sorted the dishes and silverware to reflect the arrangement in their previous dwelling. If Betsy didn't like it, she'd rearrange things. Regardless, she'd know her husband had put forth an effort. She'd appreciate that.

"I thought you could only do blocking schemes," Betsy frequently commented.

If ever she was dissatisfied, she'd be no less generous.

"This is good, Jake," she'd say. "What if we did this [or that]? Wouldn't that be better?"

What kind of questions were those? Did Betsy expect him to veto her proposals? When had he ever done so?

"You take care of the punts," she'd say. "I'll take care of the pots."

How he missed her. He could be in a foul mood and contentious all day. Once home, however…

Whenever anyone asked him about his married life, Jake had a pat response.

"It's strictly fifty-fifty," he'd announce. "She cooks the food, I eat it. I track in the mud, she cleans it up. *And*, most important, *I* have the final say in every argument: *Yes, dear.*"

In truth, Betsy tolerated him far more than he deserved. Not a day passed without him realizing it. He realized it much more when they were apart.

"Let's eat out tonight," he often suggested.

"Why?"

"'Cause."

"You talked me into it!"

They always took Tami along. This was both a blessing and a damper. She was old enough now to be left alone for a couple hours. She no longer needed a sitter. She knew and observed the rules. In truth, she loved being alone to do *forbidden* things, such as singing at the top of her voice, watching TV shows or movies Mom and Dad objected to, fiddling with the radio (instead of leaving it on a single station), running around the house in her undies, leaving the light on in the bathroom, and violating a myriad of similar transgressions.

However, and without fail, she would cheerily welcome them home as if they'd been on a round-the-world tour.

Football was his vocation; he could hardly call it a profession. People like Joe Epps were career coaches. They would always be in demand; their lives were not dependent upon the boss. Should Jake be fired, Joe would find a new job under a new coach. There were rumors that he contemplated a move to the NFL. He'd had many offers, both pro and collegiate, and Jake considered securing his services was a conformation of divine intervention.

Jake would not be courted by the NFL. He was lucky to get a head job at a smaller school. He was double—nay, triple lucky to land his current post. Should he fail, he could return the assistant ranks again, but he didn't intend to fail. Well, neither had hundreds of others.

He was at a severe disadvantage. Nearly all head coaches lived and breathed football, even during the off season. Jake, however, made a sharp demarcation between work and family. When at home, football was seldom mentioned. He and Betsy agreed that *if* he *must* work at home, he he must retire to the den. Tami learned early on not to bother Daddy when he was in the den. In deference to his family, Jake established strict limits on his time in the office. He had a separate phone line on his desk. Whenever it rang, he would roll his eyes and go to work.

Tami, doubtless under Betsy's tutelage, respected the line between work and home. The loving parents assumed that their daughter of vivid imagination and an addiction for the tactile would take *some* interest in her father's work. Football, however, interested her hardly at all, though she did attend an occasional game.

"There's Daddy!"

Betsy was slightly embarrassed by her eight-year-old bouncing and waving at the sight of Jake on the sideline amid all those hulking players. To the precocious imp, there was no difference between winning and losing. For her, it was a medieval pageant. It was full of colors and noises and aromas and bursts of action for an imaginative girl to feast upon. She was amazed to see her father yelling and slapping players on the helmet or shoulder pads. He appeared as a sinister, vicious monster.

"Daddy's never like that at home," she observed, tears slithering down her face.

In time, Tami learned (through Betsy) that football was a highly competitive game and emotions ran high. Indeed, it was emotion that drove the players—and the coaches.

Tami beamed. "Oh! Daddy's *acting*—like that guy who plays Frankenstein."

Betsy howled as she related this precious anecdote. Jake enjoyed a hardy laugh. Over the years, the memory never failed to fetch a smile. Yet another line was drawn. No matter what happened at work, Daddy better not bring Frankenstein home. A somber Jake was one thing; outbursts of anger or morbid reflections, however, were strictly verboten!

Being a head coach during working hours was akin to running a race in iron boots. The best most successful head men worked twenty-eight to thirty-five hours a day, at least during the season. That was not Jake Oats. He required a refuge. For three or four hours a day, his refuge was wherever Betsy and Tami were.

The most glorious event Jake could imagine was their arrival.

He'd enjoy a full ten days with his family. He'd relish every moment. Betsy would direct him in getting their new home established according to her desires. Tami would have to explore the new environment and mentally catalogue every scent, every plant and tree, and every pet. If any readjustments to her new room were required, she'd manage them alone.

"There's a coaching clinic in Reno ten days after you arrive," Jake reported to his wife over the phone.

Betsy sighed. He'd done this several times before while an assistant. He'd lock himself away in his "office" for an hour or more every evening to prepare a presentation.

"I'm not presenting," he continued, reading her mind. "The AD is sending me, all expenses paid. Several coaches from the conference will be there. I guess the boss thinks I can spy on them. Either that, or he hopes I learn something he *assumed* I knew when he hired me."

Betsy laughed. She was good at laughing. It helped keep their relationship fresh.

"Confine your spying to the nickel slots," she ordered.

Jake laughed.

He didn't gamble. He figured that he'd used up his allotment of luck on Guadalcanal and New Britain. They never spoke openly of luck, but Betsy knew how he felt about it. As with most of the unseemly items in Jake's past, she respected his feelings. If he never talked about luck, she wouldn't ask.

Jake was the poorest secret keeper on the planet. Betsy and Tami *always* knew in advance what they would get on a birthday or Christmas. Once he decided on something, he could not keep it to himself.

He arranged for a woman to come in once a week to help Betsy with the cleaning.

He arranged for a man to clean the outside windows once a month until winter weather set in.

These were his housewarming gifts. As ever, Betsy knew weeks before the final move. She objected vociferously. Only she knew how to clean to her satisfaction. Similarly, the windows were strictly once in the spring and once in the summer. She scolded Jake for his extravagance.

"My head's made up," he announced over the phone, mimicking a radio comedian of earlier days.

In truth, he was hardly a spendthrift. All the coaches were accorded certain "discounts." The Chamber of Commerce encouraged local businesses to provide aid and comfort to the team mentors. They realized the university's athletic budget could not rival the salaries of the other conference schools. If the chamber wanted quality coaches and teams, it was obligated to offer certain benefits. The Booster Club supported this effort with money-raising events and activities. As a result, Jake's housekeeper and window washer expenses weren't budget busters.

Finally, the day arrived when he made the ninety-minute drive to the airport and his life became whole again. He paced for seemingly hours at the arrival gate. He perked up with the announcement that Betsy's plane had landed. Then he continued to pace for an additional eternity.

The plane braked, shut down its engines, and the large exit ramp was maneuvered into place.

More pacing

It took ages.

Jake imagined passengers jumping out of their seats to play the overhead-baggage-rack game. That would make for more congestion and another eight to ten hours before the aircraft could disgorge its passengers.

Jake paced as he did during practice or a game. His greatest hope was that he'd wear a path in the tiles and require the port authority to replace them. He was well on his way to accomplishing his mission when he caught sight of the only two other people on the planet.

"Daddy!"

Tami raced to him, deftly avoiding traffic and obstacles with the skill of an Olympic skier slashing through the gates on a slalom run. She launched herself high in the air and into his arms.

She wasn't seven years old anymore. She wasn't light as a feather anymore. He had to step back to avoid toppling over. Tami's arms tightened around his neck, making it difficult to breathe.

Jake could not remember a happier moment.

Betsy was strictly a skirt and dress woman. She'd often wear Bermudas around the house but never in public. For yard work, she had a "peasant's dress," a sack-like smock that covered anything she wore beneath. Similarly, Tami was a skirt and dress girl. Never would Betsy allow her daughter to venture beyond the hearth without proper clothing and hair brushed to a fare-thee-well.

Imagine Jake's surprise when the girl who threw herself into her father's arms was slovenly dressed. She wore cut-off blue jeans and a plaid lumberjack shirt that dropped halfway to her knees. He couldn't have cared less. His joy at seeing his little darlin' was so unalloyed that Tami could have deplaned in plastic trash bags. Nevertheless, he was owed an explanation.

"She's going through the tomboy phase," Betsy whispered.

They were at the baggage claim carousel. Tami was skipping about, jockeying for position. She was determined to reclaim their two small cases without requiring the aid of either parent.

Jake's arm around Betsy's waist drew her closer for the umpteenth time. His arms were empty for so long, he was anxious to feel her warmth to the greatest extent possible in a public venue. Her perfume, subtle though it was, made his nostrils prickle.

He refrained from comment. If Tami indeed entered a tomboy phase, she had Betsy's sanction. Jake possessed neither the will nor the desire to object. Anything that promoted Tami's happiness had his endorsement. Should the energetic imp stray out of bounds, Betsy would rein her in with a minimum of fuss and tears. Tami was hardly an obedient slave, but she knew the limits of her freedom. She'd suffer mightily rather than risk the umbrage of her mother. Even this possibility was superseded by the certainty that her father would be disappointed.

For reasons unfathomable, her father's frown was far worse than hours of her mother's creative oratory.

"God's been good to us," he muttered.

"Amen," Betsy replied.

They were hungry.

After collecting their modest travel cases, Betsy and Tami settled into Jake's rented van. The first order of business was to vacate the airport and the large sprawling metropolis it served. Betsy and Jake shared a dread of large population centers. Tami wasn't particularly fond of them either, but her stomach negated her antipathy. She made known her protests but did not press her complaints to the extreme.

Finding a roadside café along a rural byway, they enjoyed a light lunch while preparing an agenda. Jake and Betsy agreed long before that major purchases were arranged through mutual arrangement. Thus, the purchase of a new car headed their to-do list. Betsy arrived with a healthy check for the amount collected from selling their previous auto together with the sale of clothes, bric-a-bracs, and other sundry articles. Those items unsold were left with a charity shop.

Most of Betsy and Tami's clothes were sent along with the movers, but new togs would be among the first items on the docket. Since Jake and Betsy opened a joint account at a local bank during the Christmas break, dispersals would be made as needed.

"The Lodge," as Betsy and Jake called every new home since their marriage, was a three-bed, two-bath house of more square footage than they'd enjoyed to date. There was a den (or library) off the living room for Jake's office. The television in the living room might not promote felicity when he worked at home. They discussed placing the TV elsewhere. Perhaps they should sell their set and replace it with two smaller ones— one for Tami's room and the other to be positioned elsewhere.

Tami was enthused by this possibility, but the issue was set aside temporarily.

It was fun to speculate on such matters, but it was better to examine the Lodge rather than plan from memory.

Jake spent the bulk of the following day obeying Betsy's orders. He shifted items and rearranged carpets to fit her desires. It was, after all, her house. With recruiting, paper shuffling, equipment requests and requisitions, film study, playbook fine-tuning, etc., etc., etc., *and* etc., Jake's domicile habitation would be a fraction of the time Betsy and Tami spent there. Once the season began, Jake would be nearly invisible. If he were very lucky, he'd get to hug his daughter and kiss his wife before collapsing on the bed. He'd seldom see them in the mornings unless they got up at zero dark thirty—a rare event indeed.

Some husbands felt like a beast of burden in like circumstances. Jake, however, joyfully filled his wife's requests. He trusted her judgment implicitly. Even when she spotted furniture (seemingly) capriciously, he'd offer no objection. Experience taught him that he would eventually realize the wisdom of her placement. Once in a great while, Betsy would recognize folly. When she did, Jake would dutifully rearrange as directed. *Never* was he tempted to say, "I told you so." Their relationship was not a contest.

Much of Jake's time that first day was spent in watching, monitoring, and enjoying Tami's antics. She was a veteran of relocations. She seldom mourned the people and places she left. Indeed, she was always excited over a new home and a new room.

A new school!

She'd be starting junior high. That was an adventure all its own, but she habitually selected a new Estonian moniker when enrolling in a new school. She'd been Kaja until Jake got his first head coaching job. There, she became Rina. Now, her father was the head coach at a major conference university. She'd require a special name to fit the circumstances.

"Liisi!" she announced with glee.

It bothered her not that she was never anything but Tami at home. At school, however, she was a proud Estonian. Her parents were perplexed about her fetish, but they could find no real harm in it. So long as their daughter did not adopt haughty airs as part of her school identity, they reserved judgment.

"I'm part Russian," Betsy reminded.

"Aw! Everybody knows Russia. It's so big and so…yuck."

"Well, I'm from the Ukrainian part of Russia. That's not so well known."

Tami seriously contemplated this idea for a few moments. "No," she decided. "Estonia is small and special. I like the way it looks on the map. It's…I don't know, *cute*."

There was no reason to engage in serious debate over something Tami found *cute*. Jake had no knowledge of Estonia. He could recall no relatives who knew of anyone who had lived in the old country. Betsy was similarly ignorant of her family's origins. For Tami, however, Estonia was a product of her vivid imagination. It was so special to her because it was created to her exacting specifications.

Liisi would attract a lot of attention. That, Jake assumed, was the reason Tami selected it. His worst fear was that she would someday visit Estonia. She was bound to be disappointed. Reality could never live up to her castles-in-the-air image of that frozen land.

"Do we need a TV?" Jake asked of his wife. "Tami entertains herself—and us—quite sufficiently."

Betsy had previously pondered the issue for herself. Her instant rejoinder testified as much.

"Too much sugar isn't healthy," she announced. "We need a slug of vinegar now and then."

Jake grunted. If the football schedule were any indication, they would all be in for copious quantities of vinegar.

Carpe diem, Jake!

Let the Games Begin

Tami was up at the crack of dark. As always, she was enthused, energized, and full speed ahead. Jake and Betsy woke to the smell of frying bacon.

"Looks like the day has officially begun," Betsy mumbled.

Jake growled and forced himself out of a bed he seldom occupied. He hoped that this day might be a notable exception. However, he forgot about *Tami time* when making his calculations.

He entered the second bathroom, the one he and Tami would share. He'd lost the toss.

Tami's responsibility was to keep her bathroom neat and tidy. Often, she became careless or forgetful. Frequently, Betsy neglected to inspect until guests were invited. This resulted in a call to general quarters. Far safer, they decided, if an adult used Tami's bathroom to ensure she tended to her chores.

Jake shaved and cleaned up after himself. He had a quick scan. They'd only occupied the residence for a few hours. Not even Tami could create a tragedy in so short a time, but he took his job as inspector-general seriously. He made certain *he* hadn't left something amiss. Neither Tami nor Betsy would offer leniency should he falter.

"Must you go to work today?" Betsy asked. "I want to go car shopping."

"I have to put in an appearance," he replied. "If I don't, they'll wonder why they're paying me."

"It's summer," she reminded.

"There's no such thing in the football business," he reiterated.

"Bacon, toast, and soft-boiled eggs," Tami boasted.

The toast was whole wheat, and the eggs were scrambled. Jake preferred soft-boiled, but Tami hadn't the patience. Frying was her preferred means, so she rechristened the eggs in the unlikely event her father wouldn't notice the difference.

"If you won't dress before cooking, at least put on your robe," Betsy scolded.

Tami made a face. Barefooted and in her summer PJs was plenty good enough. Still, Mom's rules were not to be flaunted. She half stomped and half skipped to her bedroom.

"I'll get the coffee on," Betsy announced.

"Skip it," Jake insisted. "I'll have some at the office."

"At this hour?"

"Trust me. Holly will be there."

◆

He stopped at a twenty-four-hour café for coffee and a scan of the newspaper. Despite his assurances, Jake knew that Holly did not come in early. He had a key to the arena, but he saw no value in being the first in the building. He'd circulate, have a chat or two, check his messages, and fetch Betsy after the dealerships opened. He loved Tami dearly, but large doses of saccharine were bad for his mental health. The girl was wound up tighter than a shrinking hatband.

Betsy not only knew how to manage Tami, she also had infinite patience. Likely, the young Marine would learn how to stack the dishwasher and make her bed to exacting standards. When the morning brightened, the dervish would be busy exploring her new world. She made a bold reconnaissance during her Christmas visit, but she'd appreciate a more thorough study in milder temperatures.

As he pulled into the staff parking lot, he noticed Steve Thompson's dilapidated pickup in its reserved spot. Did that guy have any life at all?

Steve was one of the items on his to-do list.

The cigar clamped securely in his mouth was pointed at a helmet. One viselike hand secured it while the other gripped a screwdriver until his knuckles blanched. He grunted as he worked.

"This is important enough to get you here in the middle of the night."

"*Jesus,* Coach! You scared the crap outta me."

"What's up?" he pressed.

"Some big-shot photographer for *Huddle Magazine* is here to get a snap of Billy Morris. I gotta get him in pads and a uniform. *Jesus,* it will have to be a travel uniform. Our new home pants and jerseys ain't come in yet."

Jake nodded, but he remained puzzled. "You're taking that face mask off," he noted.

"You can't take a picture of one of our boys behind a face mask," Steve insisted. "That wouldn't look good at all. *Jesus,* Coach, ya gotta think of these things."

"Is Billy in town?"

"He's on his way."

"He won't be here for hours," Jake predicted. "You act like this is a rush job."

"Billy's a pilot," Steve reported. "He's renting or borrowing a plane. *Jesus,* I'm surprised you got here before he did."

Jake decided he'd had enough. Steve Thompson knew his business. He was a bit miffed, however. If some sport magazine wanted an action photo of one of his players, he should be notified. Perhaps he had. It mightn't be a bad time to look at his desk.

There were two messages.

Indeed, the photographer called the previous morning. Much more important, the boss wanted to see him. Barbara, looking as informal as she was likely to appear at work, passed him coming in as Jake left the office. They exchanged greetings. Holly predictably was getting the coffee on.

Denise didn't have to stand; she was on her feet inspecting something on the ticket manager's desk.

"Boss in?"

Denise looked disappointed. She couldn't get to her feet because she was already on them. As always, she looked fetching.

The Amazon wore only shifts, simple but attractive. Periodically, she put on a belt to provide an alternate look. She wore sleeves and heavier material in the fall and winter. As it was summer, Denise opted for a sleeveless light cotton print. Though Jake found her most attractive, he was diverted by a recurring thought.

I want her sons to play for me.

He'll burn in hell for that. If he confessed to Betsy, he might get a pass. However, he was in no hurry to seek absolution.

"He just came in," she reported. "Lots of early birds this morning."

Denise did not, as a rule, pass judgment or make observations. Suggesting Mieko would make a good detective was her first violation. Commenting on early arrival times suggested she was developing a habit. Jake didn't mind. Other than her irritating habit of standing whenever he entered, he doubted her tongue would ever strike a sour note.

"Maybe the poker game broke up late."

Deuce.

Denise withheld comment. Her silence was more suggestive than anything she could vocalize.

Not requiring an announcement, Jake made his way into the inner sanctum. Ralph, aware of his presence, settled down onto his throne wearing a dark tailor-made suit. Jake was envious, but not too much. He'd continue to buy off the rack because cultured duds would not make him look any less than the ex-Marine he was.

"Have a seat."

"Am I grounded?"

Ralph didn't smile.

Jake's antenna went up. He quickly reviewed his immediate past in search of a transgression.

"I got a letter from Dr. Burns."

A letter! A note or phone call was all Jake needed. A letter meant there'd be a copy on file. A copy, in turn, meant the epistle was *official.*

"I don't like the sound of that."

Rather than take a seat, Jake retraced his steps and quietly closed the door.

"I doubt this is top secret," the athletic director suggested.

"I might say something Denise shouldn't hear," Jake responded. "She probably thinks I'm an uncultured lout. No need for me to prove it. Is this in response to my proposed letter to the Black Student Union?"

"It is."

"It took him long enough to reply," Jake concluded. "I suppose he had to call in the entire Star Chamber to help him make up his mind."

"I don't know anything about that, Jake." Ralph sidestepped to avoid committing himself.

Jake forced himself to sit. He tried, and failed, to relax. "Give me the *Reader's Digest* version."

Ralph cleared his throat. This was a sign he suspected Jake wouldn't be receptive. "Dr. Burns feels that reaching out to the Black Student Union might exacerbate the situation."

Jake took a deep breath and let it out. "Translation: sit quietly and hope these people go away."

"I wouldn't put it quite like that."

Jake was beginning to burn. "Of course you won't. You prefer sitting on the fence. It's okay to smack *me* down, but you cannot upset the pope."

It was Ralph's turn to light a short fuse. "Don't bark at me, Jake. If we start butting heads, *I—will—win!*"

That was true.

"So I get to sit back and suffer the slings and arrows of outrageous criticism without so much as a whimper."

"The president will take the steps he feels are necessary." Ralph nodded.

"We both know what that's worth."

Ralph held Jake's demanding gaze for several seconds. "No comment," he said at last.

Jake started to get up, only to settle back in. "Level with me, boss," he pleaded. "Is there something more in play here?"

Ralph started to reply. He thought better of it. He leaned back in his chair. "No comment," he repeated.

"I'm going to draft a memo for you," Jake promised. "It will state that I recommended, *to you*, that I wrote a letter and attempted to get in front of this thing."

Ralph reflected for only a moment.

"I'll sign it, date it, and send it back," he promised.

Fine! Everybody's ass was covered. That, however, did not come within light-years of addressing the problem.

Jake decided to go home for lunch. He dallied longer than intended before going downstairs to exit via the equipment room. There was no reason for such silliness. He was beginning to feel a little paranoid. What if the BSU had a heckler or paid agitator posted just outside the northwest door?

He encountered Billy Morris in a T-shirt and jeans carrying a helmet in his right hand. Jake was impressed by the game films. Billy was a receiver and occasional running back. He ran good routes, had good hands, and had an uncanny ability to get open in clutch situations. As a ball carrier, he was a darter. His quickness at hitting the hole made him an asset in the Oats-Epps offensive scheme. He was medium in height and build. At first glance, Jake wouldn't have suspected he played football. He looked more like a swimmer or a track-and-field man. Regardless, he'd put up good numbers during the previous two seasons.

"Get your picture took?"

"Had to take a day off work," he informed solemnly.

"Well, think of the next issue of *Huddle*. There on the front cover, what will the nation see?"

"Dave Peck."

Jake grinned. He liked the taciturn young man from out of state. He followed him in as he returned his helmet to the cigar chewer.

"*Jesus*, that didn't take long."

"Hardly worth taking the mask off."

"Billy me boy, I'll have her back in fighting trim before you can sing the fight song."

"Careful what you ask for," Morris warned.

"How'd you get here from the airport?" Jake asked.

"One of the instructors drove me in."

"Need a ride back?"

Billy smiled. "I'd like that." He grinned.

This would give him one up on his teammates.

"Mind if we make a short detour?"

"No," Morris replied. "My workday is shot anyway."

Jake pointed his rented vehicle toward the south end of campus. Beyond the stadium, they crossed the highway and entered the area of married student housing. There were nearly thirty small units scattered through a housing project of long ago. Those residents who owned the properties dispersed, leaving the university to buy up lots and units. They rented out homes to students who paid rates *slightly* higher than the dorm rates.

"We're looking for 2614," Coach informed.

Most of the houses were numbered. The system was regular, so unnumbered houses were easily identified.

They cruised the street twice before stopping at what *should be* 2614. Billy Morris and Jake Oats looked out upon a neighborhood communal garden plot.

"I don't see no house," Billy volunteered.

"Not so much as a pup tent," Jake added.

"If somebody comes along and asks you about this, do you think you'd remember it?"

Billy looked at his coach as if he'd spoken in ancient Hebrew. "Do you expect someone to ask?"

Jake shook his head. "I can't imagine why. Still, would you remember?"

"I doubt I could forget."

Jake put the car in gear. "Let's get you to the airport."

⬥•⬥

Jake had no intention to stop for a chat. He was under strict orders from on high. He'd acted on a hunch—a hunch that turned out to be correct.

Mr. Milt Spurling, the spokesman for the Black Student Union, was enrolled under a bogus address. What struck Jake as queer in the AD's office was fast becoming sinister.

The mystery would have to wait. Betsy would be chomping at the bit.

Summer

Joe Epps and Jake were friends before they served together. Epps was the stuff of legend. He played with a gnarled right leg and was the starting guard for a national power. He studied engineering and held down an impressive grade point average for his entire playing career.

Fresh out of college, he was invited to coach at a small school in California. He was soon so enthused that he chucked a future in engineering for the emotional satisfaction of imparting his football skills and knowledge to young eager men. He was hired as an assistant in Los Angeles where he met Marion.

Jake had never met Marion until she and Joe moved into a home only a block away from the Lodge. He could easily imagine how she looked in her twenties because she remained a looker still. Tall and lithe, Marion once prepped for a modeling career. Warner Brothers lured her in for a screen test. It seemed Marion Turner was headed for many exciting and lucrative adventures. A former Rose Festival Princess and a society item, she met Joe during a Rose Bowl promo.

Just what happened or how remains secure in the Epps family vault. She was taller than Joe, and her looks had hundreds of men panting after her. However, after being with Joe for only a few minutes in full view of the public, Marion tossed in her chips.

They were married the following spring.

Betsy and Marion got on from the first moment. They shared only two things: they were married to coaches, and they were mothers of only children.

Little Joe was a bit of a brat. He and Tami got on well enough, but she was nearly four years older. Somehow, the boy's brattish behavior was blunted considerably when in the company of Jake's daughter. They played board games and enjoyed making use of the playground equipment of a nearby elementary school. They shared a marginal interest in college football. They were more interested in the tactile and in physical activities. Board gaming was as near intellectual as their mutual activities got. They much preferred climbing trees, running, jumping, digging, and exploring. They befriended every pet for blocks and attempted to befriend any bird, squirrels, and garter snakes they happened to meet.

It was difficult for the mothers to keep a close eye on their offspring, but there was one blessing they shared. Neither Tami nor Little Joe had any energy to spare at bedtime. The all too familiar "Do I have to?" was absent from the evening bedtime routine.

Because of their commonalities, strangers in the community, mothers, husbands who were coaches and often absent, Betsy and Marion were soon the best of friends. This was a boon to their husbands who could spare little time for domestic concerns.

———◆•◆———

Jake attended the Reno Clinic. He took copious notes. He ate, drank, socialized, and picked the brains of every presenter. They in turn were privy to techniques and tactics he'd developed over the seasons. Some of them were national celebrities. However, no coach worth his hire can resist learning about what other teams are doing. Similarly, they are willing to share information about what works for them and what does not.

"Ya know, men," one premiere head coach injected during his presentation, "when we scrimmage, we put the ball on the hash. We did a study years back and discovered that the ball is in the center of the field only a half-dozen times during the game. So we decided to practice on the hashes since that's where the ball will be spotted much of the game."

His was a high-powered passing attack. Much of his play-calling was predicated on where the ball was spotted. If you sent three receivers to the short side of the field, it had to be for a specific purpose because there was less room for maneuver.

Jake's offense would produce little beyond a low-powered passing attack. However, heeding good sense *made* good sense.

"When I get back," he informed the presenter over pre-dinner drinks, "I'm puttin' the ball on the hash."

That was the value of coaching clinics. Most of the presentations included tactics, drills, and techniques most coaches had used or were using. However, there were inevitably three or four little jewels that, if properly utilized, could give a coaching staff and a team just that little extra. Mostly, however, clinics were schmooze fests among people who shared a common passion. There was not a single coach who didn't have a prize-winning anecdote to relate; most were hilarious. Other accounts had the power to bring the most hard-nosed coaches to tears.

One of the presenters coached defensive ends at Iowa. Jake sought him out and introduced himself.

"Yeah, they warned me about you," he said, shaking Jake's hand.

Within seconds, Jake learned that the young future coach made the varsity squad two years after Iowa won the Rose Bowl. He had a myriad of Forest Evashevski stories from both a player's and a coach's point of view. He delighted in Jake's stories of his days as Evy's teammate.

"It's changed a lot since Evy took over as athletic director," the man reported. His body language suggested that he regretted Evy's retirement.

"Well, you come to our house the second week of the season," Jake thundered. "You tell Evy for me that I'll bonk his snoot for stealing Coach Agee from me."

"Yeah, Agee was the guy who warned me about you." The Iowa assistant grinned. "It wasn't Evy who stole him."

"Coach Lauterbur might have done the stealing, but it was Evy who put him up to it!" He barked like a rabid dog, but every coach within earshot knew it was empty bravado. All is fair in love, war, and football. Everyone recognized that. Ill will among former teammates and coaches was rare.

"None of my business," the assistant reminded. "After we kick your ass, you and Evy can settle this in the ring."

Jake laughed. "You're the ones who are gonna get your asses kicked!" he challenged.

"Save it. After Georgia gets done with you, the only people still standing will be your yell squad."

That sobered him up. The assistant realized he may have pushed too far. Some things just weren't funny.

"Yeah," Jake mused. "That one is gonna be tough."

"That's a hell of a nut to crack first thing out of the chute," the assistant concluded with no small dose of sympathy.

"It wouldn't surprise me if Evy was in charge of our scheduling."

That fetched a laugh, as intended.

"Evy speaks well of you," he offered.

"I'd be flattered if it weren't for the fact that Evy is a damned liar."

They both laughed and shook hands.

"See you in September, Coach."

"It's a date," Jake promised.

— • —

Betsy moved into a new house in a new city just in time to become a football widow. Jake spent hours watching films, meeting with his coaches (individually), conferencing with department officials, Steve Thompson, the team doctor, the "scholastic coach," and talking to young men who had yet to sign a letter of intent. He sat with high school coaches and quality players who wouldn't graduate until June. There was always something to tend.

From Betsy's perspective, a good week was any week when her husband got to sleep in his own house at least three nights.

The week prior to the team reporting was christened the athletic dead week. Save for the ultra-highest priority, every coach was expected to meet with Jake at eight in the morning and six in the evening. It wasn't enough to plan practices and revise the playbook; they must tend specific duties.

"Pink" Ostrander was in charge of dorm room assignments and bed checks (on the road as well as during camp).

Joe Epps oversaw the training table. He consulted with the department's dietician. He made out all the purchase orders, checked each delivery, and dispatched the paperwork to the people in charge of monetary dispersals. When the team was on the road, it was his job to coordinate with the host facilities for team meals.

Dave Thorne was responsible for coordinating with visiting teams. They'd require transportation to and from the stadium and arranging any special services the guests required.

This last was the subject of a thousand tired jokes, but girls and booze were never on the docket. Inevitably, someone required something (usually medical) that was perishable or couldn't travel with the team.

Church secured game films from future opponents. He was tasked with returning them in good condition. Similarly, he made certain to dispatch the legal number of films requested by their opponents and making double-damn certain they were returned in good condition.

The remaining coaches were tasked with petty concerns—*petty*, that is, until left untended.

The first morning's briefing began with a concern Jake harbored for some weeks. By the time his coaches were gathered, it was an obsession.

"Goal line offense and defense," he announced. "If the ball is on the hash, what formations and what plays will we use? Will we settle for a field goal? Must we score a TD? From the nine-yard line to the endzone, what plays do we use? Get on it, Joe."

"Yes, sir."

"Defense: we must assume that a TD will beat us. Assume a field goal will beat us. From the hash, against any formation they use, what sets and stunts do we run? From the nine-yard line to the end zone, how do we deploy? Gus, that's your baby."

"Okay."

"Men, this will be our first task in putting together our game plan," Jake said. "For every team we play, our first task is nine-and-in. Also, Wednesday practices will end with fifteen minutes of nine-and-in."

They nodded in unison.

"Pink, punting and punt return. Mike Perry, kickoff and kick return."

Both men nodded.

"Dave, offensive scouting. Everything from nervous ticks to what they eat for breakfast. Find us a cousin, someone who gets sloppy or dogs it."

"Right, Chief."

"Miller, defensive scouting. Slants, stunts, coverages, the whole deal. Find us a cousin, someone we can run at if we need two yards. Find another cousin we can slip by for a bomb and one who will let us throw short if we gotta have it."

"Can do."

"Check with me after lunch, say one o'clock in case I think of something else. Let's get to work."

Jake did not go out for coffee and a chin wag with Barbara and Holly. He went back to his desk to do battle with a mountain of paper. No matter who did what, he had to review and sign off on everything.

He counted it as a break when he got to the work/study women who waited table. The team would see them brining in meals. Jake looked behind the scenes. Tablecloths must be changed daily, place settings must be precise, fresh cloth napkins must be folded just so, pitchers of water must be spaced on each table. In the kitchen, potatoes must be peeled and sliced, dishes must be washed and stacked, silverware must be collected and segregated (and counted—there are kleptos in any organization, and silverware, apparently, is a prime target), tablecloths must be removed and stuffed in laundry bags together with napkins, aprons, and towels, pots must be scrubbed, and a myriad of other tasks. The work/study girls would be assigned tasks on a rotating basis. In short, the training table ladies were expected to do everything for the players and staff except tuck them in at night.

The university hired cooks and food handlers. Mieko, however, was charged with hiring and coordinating the training table crew. As expected, her written report was meticulous. She not only listed the names of the work/study crew, she included hometown, degree program, and campus residence.

Why would Jake be the least interested in any of those things? Confronted with bizarre data, his natural curiosity got the better of him.

One girl was from Georgia.

Jake chuckled. Perhaps Mieko suspected her of being a spy. Fat lot she'd learn at training table, but Mieko may have felt it was Jake's duty to be informed. Then, of course, it was odd. Students didn't often travel so far from home to attend school. Though Jake was curious to know the young woman's motivation, he realized it was none of his business.

When he had made an appreciable dent in the stacks of papers, he left his office to haunt the coaches' cubicles. He went first to Joe, who was making a list of offensive sets and plays.

"How's it goin'?" Jake asked, simply to announce his presence.

"Pull up a chair, Coach," Joe replied. "Let me show you something."

Jake obeyed. The chair was a metal-framed job with gray padding on the seat and back. It was the same type of chair one found onboard transport ships. Apparently, these items were standard issue on college campuses as well.

"Look at our fifty-two power," Joe requested as he drew up the onside line only. He sketched in a goal line set. "Instead of normal area blocking, we double down with the guard."

Jake grunted. "The linebacker has a clear shot."

"Hold on, Coach," Joe requested. "We only need a yard, maybe two. We create a crack right…here. Just enough for the fullback to squeeze into."

"Fifty," Jake pondered as his interest peaked.

"The lead back needs to get just a piece of the backer or the near lineman. Guard and center seal on the nose and, well, we should get our yard or two."

"We need to test it. It won't work against a gap eight."

Joe drew it up again. Jake grunted. It looked as if Joe was on to something. On paper, in the coaches' offices, it *would* work against a gap eight.

"How do we designate it? We've got fifty-two and fifty-two power."

"Call it fifty-two power, guard!"

Trust a former guard to come up with that nomenclature.

"Draw it up and get it in the playbook." Jake nodded. "We still have to test it."

Joe knew that. He figured Jake must be getting nervous. As a rule, he never stated the obvious.

Joe checked his watch. He left his cubicle and entered the conference room.

It was a small place with a chalkboard and a dining room table secured by a head coach three terms prior. Around the table was an array of battleship gray chairs. The staff could sit around the table with materials laid out in front of each and discuss whatever need be discussed. Similarly, they could gather on three sides of the table and watch a chalkboard or overhead presentation.

Four slovenly dressed young men sat nervously at the table. As with much else, the team managers were inherited from the previous regime. They'd served well enough during spring drills, but practice time was *the* most valuable commodity in the universe. Not a second could be spared. Equipment must be deployed prior to practice.

Jake peeked in and was greeted by eight bulging eyes. The managers hardly expected the big guy to be there. One of the kids gulped audibly.

Joe was in a hurry to get back to work. He snatched up a small piece of chalk and rapidly drew a rectangle. "Practice field," he announced. A vertical line was inserted running north-south. "Defense," he stated, writing the word in the assigned space. "Offense." He wrote as he spoke.

Jake withdrew. Personally, he'd have called in only the senior manager for the briefing. Joe, however, complained that the quartet lacked "cerebral acuity" (his diction). He felt if they all attended, they could do the musketeer bit and help each other out. One person could forget. Four people, however, better not forget! Joe could, and would, sack the whole lot and recruit his own people.

Mieko, Jake thought.

She mightn't be able to lug fifty-pound dummies and schlep blocking sleds hither and yon, but she could direct traffic. With the necessary bodies providing brawn, she'd ensure that everything was spotted correctly—likely hours before practice.

Jake called Betsy.

No answer.

She promised to take *Liisi* shopping for school clothes and scholastic accoutrements. When autumn drew near, Betsy missed working. To be more precise, she missed the additional income. She'd collected glowing recommendations, but firms—to include athletic departments—were loath to hire someone who mightn't last. If Jake got fired or got a better job, she and her acquired expertise would go away.

Betsy could do as good a job as Barbara, Holly, or Denise. Unfortunately, that trio was as good as Betsy—better indeed because they knew all the informal athletic and campus networks. Doubtless, there were openings in local businesses Betsy could fill. However, potential employers are reticent to hire a temp.

Recently, Betsy considered unskilled work. She could cashier or type (plenty of master's theses waiting to be typed). Unfortunately, people are reluctant to hire the head coach's wife. Too many were quick to assume it was a PR gimmick or, in the case of master's candidates, an attempt to impress the profs or curry favor.

Jake felt he stole a perfectly legitimate career from his wife. She never complained; that, of course, compounded his guilt. However, Jake's paychecks had wings. There was never quite enough to match Betsy and Tami's reasonable desires. Why, for example, did Tami's back-to-school duds have to be reduced to sale items and discount coupon availability?

He should have insisted on a more modest house. Even what he got was on discount. He could never afford the asking price. His family abode was made possible by a member of the Booster Club. If Jake weren't a football coach, he'd hardly enough chinks to rent space in the garage!

He found Mike Perry, his receiver's coach, bending over a yellow legal pad on his desk.

"Come up with something brilliant?" Jake asked, coming up from behind.

Mike straightened up and turned his head to bring Jake into his ken. "Huddle up with the kicker in front," he began. "When the kicker addresses the ball, the team spreads out to cover. If the blockers are counting, this might cause a slipup."

"We can't make a living with that," Jake growled.

"It's something to keep in your hip pocket," Mike insisted.

Jake nodded. "What else you got?"

"From the films, I noticed most conference teams use the end man on each side as the headhunter with the second or third man taking contain," Perry reported. "I say, use the sideline as contain. The end collapses when he's even with the ball. We use the second man on both sides as headhunters."

This was hardly new, but it demonstrated Mike had judiciously studied the previous year's films.

"Let's call them wild men," Jake announced. "We take as our theme alley fight. A wild man fits well in that context."

"No arguments from me," Perry announced.

"Returns?"

"Two deep," the young coach replied. "It's the same ol', same ol.' We could cross blockers and try to create a lane up the middle."

"No," Jake decided. "That would lead to clipping out that kazoo."

"Okay then, regular wedge with the second element."

Jake retreated. He went back to Joe's cubicle and wrote a note: *We need a quick kick!* Finally, he went back to his desk to deal with more paper. "Barbara, who will be at Maxwell tomorrow to check in the players?"

"Coach Churchill volunteered," she replied without looking up from her typing (though she did cease when speaking).

"Where the hell is he?" he muttered.

Other than himself, Jake didn't intend for anyone else to hear.

"He's in the offense meeting room," Barbara replied. "He's been camping there for two days."

He hoped she meant that in the figurative sense. Once he realized Barbara's hearing was so keen, he didn't dare talk to himself. He made a mental note to ask Betsy if he talked in his sleep. Though Jake and Betsy had no secrets from each other, he wasn't certain about his fantasies. She knew when he was back on the Canal or New Britain; she'd gently (and cautiously) prod him to bring him around. Nevertheless, fantasies could get him in hot water.

Jake avoided his desk and vacated the office. He could have (*should* have) thanked Barbara for knowing all, but he was miffed at her *hearing* all.

All but one curtain was drawn. Churchill sat scrunched over a clipboard crammed with papers. In his left hand was a control button to rewind the film. The projector he used looked ancient. There were more modern machines available.

The former running back scowled. He didn't like being interrupted. However, as the head man, Jake had a right to know what his coaches were doing.

"What are you doing behind my back?" he demanded.

"I've been watching last year's films," Churchill replied. "I've got a dossier on every returning player. I think you will find it interesting reading."

He and the staff had watched and rewatched the films so many times, they could ID the opponent, the down and distance, the score, and the time remaining simply by viewing any twelve consecutive frames. Yet here was Churchill breaking them down again.

"Take a break."

An order is an order. Churchill switched off the machine and gave his boss all his attention.

"Dorm assignments."

"The head manager will have the master key. He is responsible for bed checks, but they will all take turns, probably. If you want, I'll do it."

The poor guy had gone dopey. He'd been watching game films until his brain had turned to oatmeal. Jake appreciated his dedication but questioned his judgment.

"You're swinging after the bell, Brice. Take a second and clear your head."

The lowest of the low on the coaching staff grinned sheepishly. "Do I know you?" he asked.

Jake smiled. *That's better.* "I want to see Evans, Hackett, Black, Jordan, and Harris, and the two captains in the dorm lobby at five o'clock tomorrow. It will only take a minute or ten. We'll walk over to training table together. Have you got it?"

"All the black players and the captains. I got it, Skip."

"You want to be there too?"

"If you want me."

"You know what it's about?"

"I think I can figure it out."

Of course, Churchill was not stupid!

"The head manager gets a master key. Are there any others?"

"They'll issue us two. You want one?"

"Only for tomorrow afternoon. I may want to use the library. They do have libraries to keep copies of exams and stuff, don't they?"

"The one in Maxwell even has books. There are several on composition and grammar alone."

Jake took a deep breath. "Brice, you always amaze me."

The young coach smiled broadly. "You taught me, Coach. *Attention to detail.* If I only had a nickel for every time you yelled that in my ear, I'd own this campus."

"Church, I promise you, after this season, I'll get you on staff. More pay."

"And more stress headaches. Thanks."

"Of course, if it's too much for you—"

"I like stress headaches, Coach. Love 'em!"

For a moment, Jake opted to be serious. "You were my go-to guy on the field, Church. I always counted on you in a pinch. You delivered every time. I owe you, Brice."

The former player turned serious—and a bit maudlin.

"I hope I can measure up as an assistant," he stated.

"You're off to a hell of a start, Church. I look forward to reading this report when you're finished."

⬧•⬧

Jake unlocked the library just off the dormitory lobby. Indeed, there were many books crammed into two cheap erector-set bookcases, but very little additional furniture. Apparently, residents were discouraged from loitering. Pricked by curiosity, Jake pulled out a paperback math text. It was conspicuously stamped MAXWELL HALL. It contained a check-out card in a pouch on the inside cover. If taken from the room, the card would be left at the main desk.

Sloppy and Rube Goldberg, but *A* for good intentions.

The men entered casually.

Joe Hackett played behind Billy Morris at wingback. Leland Black was the undersized defensive guard who could leap over offensive blockers near the goal line and create havoc. Wesley Jordan was a hulking, muscle-bound linebacker with the speed and agility of a panther; Gus assigned him to play "swing" linebacker, playing head-up on the tight end on every play. Donte Harris didn't look like a football player. He played behind Ogle as a defensive back, but he was weak in man coverage. However, he could hit like a wounded gladiator! LeRoy Evans was the bruising, senior fullback. The previous coach used him as a lead blocker, but he got his share of carries. In the Oats regime, he'd pack the mail much more frequently. Built like a Sherman tank, he demonstrated he can carry the ball and run over people.

Zwetschke and Ogle brought up the rear as if embarrassed to be there.

Jake checked to make certain the lobby was empty before closing the door.

"Men, I'm not looking for trouble. I don't want trouble. I'll crawl on my belly over broken glass to avoid trouble, *but* I smell it. I'll tell you what I know about the Black Student Union. That group is upset that there are only you five on the team. I tried to find out from the registrar how many black students are enrolled and was told to pound sand. I wrote a letter to Milt Spurling who claims to be the leader of the BSU. The president will not allow me to send it. I complained to the athletic director. Apparently, he has orders to keep his mouth shut. He won't discuss it. Somebody, I don't know, knows more than he, or she, or *they* want us to know."

The entire assembly looked at him as if he spoke in Braille.

"One other thing: I looked up this Spurling guy in *Hall's Guide* and drove out to his off-campus address. There's no house there."

That got their attention.

"It could be nothing. It could be that people not affiliated with the university intend to make trouble. I don't know. You now know everything I know."

He let it settle in. When they realized he was finished, there was some shuffling of feet.

"What do you want us to do, Coach?"

It was Jordan, the man who stood aside for no one.

"What I *want* is to know if anybody claiming to be with the Black Student Union contacts you. I want to know what *they* want.

You're all men. You exercise your own judgment and come to your own conclusions. If you decide that it's none of my business, I won't order or coerce you. However, I want you to be aware that there is something fishy going on. Be careful. Don't do or say anything that might embarrass you or the team. I brought the captains in because they need to know everything that impacts the team. If you come across anything you want me to know, but for whatever reason you don't want me to know who you are, tell a captain. The captain will tell me. They will keep confidence, right, men?"

"Yes, sir," Ogle and Zwetschke said in unison.

"You can trust your captains, men. I trust you. If you are approached by the BSU, well, you associate with whomever you please. That's your right. If—and I emphasize *if*—you suspect that there is something screwy-louie, I want to know about it. We have a rough season ahead. We can't afford unnecessary distractions."

"You want us to keep a lid on this?" Harris asked.

"Use your discretion, Donte. I called you in because obviously, you are the people most directly concerned."

There was a thoughtful silence.

"Gentlemen, I told you all I know. I *suspect* there's something not right about all this…*stuff,* but I don't have enough information to judge. One thing, and I don't want to hit this one too hard, if you think you're getting negative attention in the classroom or on the practice field because of your skin color, I want to know about it. As far as I'm concerned, there are only two colors on our uniforms: blue and white. Personally, I think that combination stinks, but those are our colors, and that's what we play for."

That drew a nervous and reserved chuckle. It was obvious, to Jake at least, that no one in the room wanted a race war.

There was another thoughtful pause.

"Am I the only one here who is hungry?"

Ogle's face, for the first time, split into a smile. "No, sir."

"Well, let's get over to the Union."

Meeting adjourned.

The following morning, practice began in earnest. Everyone was rousted out of bed at six. The players were free to shower, shave, snack, play cribbage, or whatever they liked. They must be at the track at zero eight thirty (though his Marine days were behind him, Jake continued to use the twenty-four-hour clock).

Some players brought their cars to the dorm, but hardly any drove to the venue. Most of them walked. A more eclectic collection of rags cannot be imagined. The requirements were running shoes. What else the player selected for the Oats Mile was in accordance with the players' own (appalling) tastes.

A half dozen footballers opted for T-shirts and sweatpants. Some wore sweatshirts and gym shorts, Bermuda shorts, or cutoff jeans. One practical joker appeared in pink polka dot pajama bottoms.

The track coach was on hand. It was, after all, his domain. However, hope springs. He once discovered a track prospect among the football scholarship athletes and was about due to discover another.

First up were the defensive backs and linebackers.

"Don't know if I can make the cut-off time, Coach."

It was Mark Davidson. He wore blue gym shorts. His right leg was an ugly collection of scar tissue form midthigh to ankle.

"Why didn't you tell me you were wounded?"

"I said, 'A little.'"

"You passed your physical?"

"Oh yeah, but the leg isn't a part of that. I am to distance running what Twiggy is to sumo wrestling."

"Everybody runs," Coach reminded.

He couldn't start the season by issuing passes. A team is a team because they all endure the same pain. In this case, if a player did not make the prescribed time limit, he was automatically slated for extra conditioning. Translation: running stadium steps until Coach Thorne got tired of watching.

"Understood, Sergeant," Davidson replied. "I just don't want you to think I spent the summer in a hammock."

"Give it your best shot, son. Please, whatever else you do, don't walk!"

It was painful to watch. Ogle sprinted out into a substantial lead before shifting to cruise control. It inspired the others to see the team captain out front. Davidson, however, fought bravely to keep pace with the pack, but he dropped behind quickly. He wasn't alone. Schlosburg, the biggest, heaviest on the team, struggled even more.

"He works harder than anybody on weights and conditioning," Coach Miller assured. "He just can't run."

Jake nodded. His initial panic subsided. He could not afford to have a key member of his defense coming to camp out of shape.

"Anybody got a calendar?" Epps quipped.

The players, scattered through the bleachers awaiting their turn, got a chuckle out of that.

When at long overdue last Davidson and Schlos made the final turn, the big defensive guard fought like a champion to close the distance. When they crossed the finish line, the two-time letterman and the rookie were holding hands. This brought an appreciative roar from their teammates. This lifted Jake's spirits considerably. Though their times were far beyond the requirement, they finished as teammates—a gesture not lost on the others.

The second defensive group were up next. Most of them were either sophomores or had played behind someone previously. They made a better showing. Only two players failed to beat the clock, but they were obviously ready to suit up.

The first offensive group featured Billy Morris, who established an impressive pace and held it. His was the best time. Zwetschke finished a very respectable fifth place. These men were pumped.

The second offensive group produced only one slacker. Only five "extra duty" players out of fifty-one.

Jake was pleased.

After showering, they reported for brunch and unit meetings for an hour. Then to the dressing room to change into sweats and helmets, to the practice field for agility and conditioning drills, to special teams— punts, punt returns, kickoff, kickoff returns again, again, again, again, and again until the coaches' voices broke and the players were winded and drained. Finally, to the showers, save for the extra-duty crew.

There was a ninety-minute lapse before training table. Meetings until two.

"Get your feet up, men," Jake advised at training table. "Tomorrow, we suit up and go at it. We breakfast at six thirty, meetings at seven thirty, practice at nine. Get your rest."

Each player had a mimeographed copy of the following day's agenda. They didn't need Coach to read it to them, but Jake had to say something. He couldn't tell them that they'd worked hard and done well—not yet.

When he went home that evening, Jake had Churchill's completed report with him.

He made it a point to spend an hour, a non-football hour, with Betsy and Tami. It was his daughter's habit to sit in his lap as she related the day's events. On this evening, she didn't do that. This bothered Jake a little, but he realized she'd soon begin junior high. She was too old for sitting in Papa's lap.

This did not blunt her enthusiasm one iota. She bubbled with excitement because for nearly two hours, she got to look after Little Joe while Marion and Betsy teamed up to pay bills in person. The mothers wanted face time with local providers. It was good PR as well as a gesture of good will.

Little Joe was something of a hellion, but Tami was so proud of both her patience and her handling of her first weighty responsibility. The duo played together, snacked together, argued, made up, and played some more. No one was kidnapped or run over. Marion was pleased, and Mommy was pleased. Life was good.

Jake congratulated his daughter and let her know how proud he was. She hurried to her room by hop-skip-and-spring. She might be growing up, but Jake prayed Tami would retain her childlike energy for a few more years.

After a few moments of conversation, Betsy let Jake retire to his office where he studied Churchill's meticulous report.

It was the best damned scouting report he'd ever seen. The fact that it was the product of film study alone made it a monument to that much vaunted *attention to detail.*

Jake made copious notes, segregated by position. He would arrange special meetings during the week so he could go over Churchill's report with them. As an example, Zwetschke, a cocaptain and one of the best linemen he'd yet encountered (since Jake himself retired) tipped his trap blocks.

Jake had studied the films but hadn't noticed. He suspected that Joe Epps may have, but Coach wouldn't take the chance. They must break their star blocker from telegraphing plays. If Churchill noticed this anomaly, the folks in Georgia were certain to spot it.

The sounds of autumn. The sounds of football. The grunts, the pads popping, helmets banging, the huffing and puffing. The coaches screaming:

"Walk 'em up! Walk! Walk! Keep your base and walk!"

"You're not a receiver until you get your head around!"

"You can't block what you can't see!"

"Keep contain!"

"Attack the gap!"

"Go! Fifty-six power! Hate! Set! Go!"

"Paaaasssss!"

"Draw!"

"Keep your head on a swivel!"

"Don't get hooked! Don't!"

"Tighten up! A good play starts with a good huddle!"

"Run it again!"

These and similar scolds are dispensed on every practice field in the country. Jake reveled in it. This was his world. This was his reason for being.

He didn't miss the coaching tower. He'd not ask for one. If they poured money into such a structure, he'd be obligated to make use of it. That would make him just another spectator. He walked around from coach to coach, making mental notes as he went. If he saw something that needed correcting, he trusted his coaches to make on-the-spot adjustments. If they didn't, he'd be certain to admonish them at the next meeting. Every coach knew the more he was admonished, the shorter his tenure on staff.

Every coach had a watch. They were synchronized.

Every coach had a practice schedule. They were itemized by time, drill, and coaching points.

Jake had an air horn handy. If it were time to begin another drill or time to come together for group work, he'd instruct a manager to use the horn. He seldom gave the order. The coaches, managers, and players moved as if directed by a silent hand.

Joe spent eight minutes in the chutes ensuring his blockers kept low with backs straight as they fired into a block. There were wooden planks, ten inches wide, to remind the linemen to keep a wide base. If they attempted the *shove* rather than block, their cleats came down on the board; the offender would get no traction on wood and end up on his face. If the blocker rose, he'd be caught in the metal chute and laughed at.

After eight minutes, Epps, Miller, and Ostrander brought their charges to the pads laid out by the managers for the West Point drill. Both coaches and players sprinted to the venue.

Ten minutes—that's a very long time for the blocking and running-to-daylight drill, but everybody had to sell out as many times as possible in those ten minutes. Eleven blockers, six backs, and eight defensive linemen—they had to line up, run the drill, vacate the area, and allow the next group up. They had to get as many reps as possible to sharpen their skills. If Jake had his way, they would run three groups simultaneously for thirty minutes. Alas, the clock—in practice as in a game—was an enemy.

Jake watched the drill from start to finish. If the team were to beat the Georgia defense, mastery of this drill was vital!

The men had returned in good condition. Still, it took time and many bumps and bruises to get back into practice shape. They hadn't the time. They were forced to go full speed from the get-go. Mistakes were made. Blocks were missed. Backs cut into the wrong holes. There were fumbles, missed tackles, poor techniques.

This was unacceptable! If they had just three more days to relearn the game of football, improvement would be more pronounced. NCAA rules, however, would never allow extra time. So players made mistakes, and the drill was sloppy. Everybody, players and coaches, were frustrated. Tempers flared.

"Don't take it out on him when you're the one who screwed up!"

If Epps hadn't bellowed, Jake would have.

"That's holding," he observed.

He couldn't help it. No matter how hard he tried to keep his oar out, his experience as an assistant coach made his superfluous comments automatic.

"You just lost us yards!" Epps yelled.

Had he heard Jake? It shouldn't have made a difference. Joe was paid to see everything. He was paid to make certain the offending player would hear about it (again) in the next meeting.

Following the afternoon practice, the coaches' locker room was as silent as a tomb. It didn't matter that everyone realized the first days of practice were preordained to be next to worthless. Everyone focused on Georgia. There would be many prayers launched heavenward that evening.

"Please, God, don't let us embarrass ourselves."

Jake was the last out of the shower. He needed the extra time. He turned the hot water on full blast and reduced the cold water to a mere trickle. The scalding result forced his muscles to release their deathlike morbidity. When he reentered the silent locker room, his skin glowed red.

Poor Dave Thorne was a young eager man who didn't fall in love with football until he was a senior starter for Montana. He was, by nature, gregarious and optimistic. The silence grated on him.

"We're just a step away," he announced, shaking out his argyle socks.

His comment was sarcastic. He'd aimed for a laugh and failed. It was one thing for his comment to be left unappreciated, but it was far worse to be ignored. The grisly silence not only continued—it became oppressive.

Had Jake spoken, the mood might have shifted slightly. He had nothing to say, nothing that was fit for expression, nothing he'd wish repeated. All it took was a single comment or a single word to escape into the public forum. Loose lips sink ships, and coach's comments destroy team morale. Saying nothing was far worse than faint damns. In a few minutes, he'd be at training table. The team expected him to be honest. Honesty would not serve. He had to give his team and his coaches something to revitalize them.

There were the dirty half dozen running stadium steps as he toweled himself dry. They subjected themselves to unfair punishment because Coach Oats held firm to the time limit in the mile run. He didn't offer charity. Had he, the team would be conditioned to expect it. Georgia wouldn't offer charity. They would destroy anybody and anything that might impact the chance of a national championship.

Coach Dooley, Jake knew, was probably as depressed as he was. That was no comfort. If every team in America could skip the first week of practice and go straight into the second week, every heart would be young and gay.

Coach made certain everyone was in the dining room and on the dais before he entered. Everyone stood respectfully until he was seated. A moment later, a tallish moderately attractive young woman served him his steak, potatoes, and green salad.

Jake looked out at the long tables accommodating six players or managers each. There were two empty chairs. All the players were here. Anyone who was not would be "taken care of" before the next practice. A half dozen young work-study ladies scurried to and fro, either loaded with plates or rushing to secure more.

The head manager walked around with a clipboard, checking off the names of each player. Unnecessary and pointless since the manager did not yet know everyone, particularly the sophomores.

"St. John," a defensive end informed the manager. He spelled out his name. "S T P E R I O D J O H N."

The manager pretended not to notice. St. John looked across the table at a blondish teammate who was the other starting defensive end.

"Stone," St. John announced, pointing to his table mate. "S H I T."

No one laughed or cracked a smile.

No one, that is, except Jake.

These were young men he cared about. Realizing they maintained spirit and a sense of humor after a horrible day of practice was a balm to his soul. They may not be a college football team—yet. They were, however, young men. They had spirit and a life outside football.

"Joe," Jake said, leaning to the man on his right. "Tell the ladies to serve me last in future."

Epps nodded. He didn't need to speak.

There was light banter all around the room and on the coaches' dais when Jake stood. Chatter ceased and all eyes were on the boss.

"Men, I've seen considerable coordination and sense of purpose tonight watching these young ladies bring us our dinner. They didn't trip and fall, spill food in anybody's lap, or break any plates over anybody's head. In other words, they were proficient. How about you? Face it, men, our practices this day can best be described as pathetic. We must sell out, gentlemen. Every coach, every player, every manager, we must sell out and do our damnedest to get better with every drill, with every sprint, with everything we do on that practice field. You must give it a hundred percent in everything you do. If you make a mistake, make it full speed ahead. If you slack off, that's when you get hurt.

"We're going to do more sprints, gentlemen. No matter what happens, we will not get whipped because we weren't in condition. Some of you think you're in great shape. Some of you are. But you're going to get in even better shape. If we can't do anything else, we are going to be in the best condition of any team in this country. Make up your mind to that right now.

"Stay off your feet tonight. Get them up. Relax, get rested. You need to be at 100 percent tomorrow."

With this, he hurried out of the room.

The players, led by the coaches, stood while he exited. Well, at least they did that much. Jake realized he was not the best gung-ho speaker in the business. He knew all the clichés, but he wasn't convincing when he employed them. Maybe he wasn't cut out for this job.

When he got home, Jake feigned interest in Tami's recitation of her day's events. He wanted very much to be a part of her life, and if limited to her oral reports, he would never shut her down or send her away. He tried to make cogent comments, but he felt only the despair of powerlessness.

Not until Tami was in her room inventing unicorns and rainbows did Betsy have a chance to speak privately with her husband.

"How many of your players are married?" she asked.

"Four," he grunted.

Did she think he didn't know? As a former Marine DI, Jake made certain that he knew the men in his charge from A to Z. The habit carried over to coaching.

"Jeff Foster."

He eyed her curiously. Was this a test, or was there a reason for this interrogation? "Wife's name is Jean. They have a two-year-old girl, Kate."

"Three years old as of last Tuesday."

He cocked an eyebrow.

"Is there a reason for this?" he prodded.

"Their car broke down," Betsy reported. "They had to have it towed into the shop."

"And they need money to cover the tow and repairs," he concluded. "There's not a thing I can do, Bets. I told you the NCAA is on us like red on an apple."

Betsy shook her head. "They each have families," she reminded. "What Jean needs is a ride to and from the market and the bank and so and so and so. I could take her where she has to go."

"I know you can, but you won't."

Betsy sat. She didn't sit on the couch next to him. Instead, she opted for the easy chair canted toward the couch. "I overheard a comment yesterday," she continued. "Someone was complaining about you."

"Coaches are at the very top of every complain list," he reminded.

"Well, this one is a bit out of the ordinary," she continued. "The unknown somebody thinks you're too *virtuous*. That was the word used. He—or she—thinks you are bucking for martyrdom."

He chuckled. He couldn't help himself. Placed aside his troubles, this remark was comical.

"The coach's wife cannot be seen chauffeuring players' wives around. That would be the same as paying for their traveling expenses. I can't allow it, Betsy."

"Then allow me to talk with the church wives. They're always willing to do a good deed. It would only be for a few days. I've met Mrs. Foster. She doesn't strike me as a demanding sort of person, but she's a mother. Three-year-old kids need lots of consumables. You should know that."

"Talk to the women," he suggested. "I don't find fault with that. Just make certain that this is a charity case and *not* special favors for Jeff *or* me."

"Understood, chief."

She was making fun. He wasn't in the mood.

"How'd you find out about the Fosters' car?"

Betsy's answer was stifled just in time. "I don't think I should tell you."

Someone in the department, no doubt.

"How about the person who *heard* someone complaining about me?"

Always coy was Betsy. She cocked her head and grinned. "I can't recall."

Jake grunted.

After two minutes of silence, Jake retired to his office.

Selling Out

More days of meetings and practices before the players moved out. Many lived off campus, some of them shared an apartment, four lived in married-student housing, several lived in fraternity houses. Only three players lived in dorms. After Friday's double practice, team members would remove their property from Maxwell Hall and stash it in cars or with friends. Saturday morning, the campus dorms would bulge with early arrivals.

Practices were getting better. After the inauspicious start, there was no other possibility. Were they ready to meet Georgia? Jake doubted they were ready to meet the junior high team Tami would soon cheer for. Still, there were some successes.

Exhibit A: Despite being recruited as a drop-back passer, Save Peck took to Epps's rollout passing game with the eagerness of a child with a new puppy. "Come to run," Epps always reminded. So he did. He knew exactly where the line of scrimmage was. If he couldn't sprint for four or five yards, he'd snap the ball up field with remarkable accuracy. He could get the ball off his hip and in the air in an instant. It flummoxed the defenders and kept the receivers on constant alert.

Exhibit B: Epps's fifty-two power guard proved a reliable short-yardage weapon. No matter what Gus threw at it, the play always gained yards—never less than two. There were times when the big black fullback was met in the crease, but Evans refused to be denied. He'd move the rugby scrum up field fueled by sheer determination.

Exhibit C: The option plays were hit or miss, but the counter options shone. As with his passes, Peck refused to pitch the ball until the last possible nanosecond. Moreover, when the pitch man was covered, Peck would lower his head and get positive ground, even if it could be measured only in inches.

Exhibit D: Zwetschke no longer tipped his trap blocks. Therefore, he became more deadly.

Exhibit E: Gus's sixty-two had Epps in a tizzy. There was no way to know the coverage. Gus left the corners out on the field looking for a hurry-up while the rest of the defenders huddled up. When the safety broke the huddle, he'd signal to the corners the coverage call.

Exhibit F: The sixty-two confused the offense's line calls. The middle and swing linebackers played run with reckless abandon.

Exhibit G: "Scar Leg" Davidson was staking out a position as defensive end. Coach Thorne predicted the Marine would see action as reserve end and as a reserve swing linebacker.

Exhibit H: Gino lost his starting spot to Fred Shaw. Gino, however, was the best lead blocker on the team and excelled at making space for the ball carrier. Shaw ran better, particularly on trap plays, but his pass blocking and lead blocking lacked Gino's panache.

Exhibit I: Russ Capp, the team cut-up, started at split end for the second consecutive season. He ran good routes and, to the amazement of all, always managed to get open—if only for a split second. He and Peck were a great combination. ("I ain't got no speed," Capp reminded Coach Perry. "I gotta outslow 'em.")

Exhibit J: Jake's team was predicted to go three and eight and finish next to last in the conference. This negated much of the pre-season pressure. The men *knew* they'd win more than three games. That was a boost to team morale. They felt they could play with anyone and give a good account of themselves.

Exhibit K: Billy Morris was a fleet receiver, but he proved he could run the ball on options, counters, and traps. They had a reverse off the option. Instead of Peck pitching to the option man, he'd pitch to Billy coming around. Even when Gus knew it was coming, he had fits over the mass confusion Joe's option reverse created on the defensive side of the ball.

Exhibit L: Jeff Foote, the quarterback who wouldn't throw or run unless the temperature and humidity were perfect, the same player who worried about failing so much he'd never be more than mediocre, was fast turning into a ball player. They moved him to safety because there was nowhere else to put him. The staff didn't expect much, but Jeff the timid became a raging lion. He could play zone, he could play man (against tight ends particularly), and he could tackle. During one scrimmage, he went head-on with the bruising fullback who had sixty pounds on him. Foote stood him straight up and stopped him in his tracks! He couldn't bring him down, but once forward momentum was halted, his teammates came to the rescue. Jake insisted upon using Foote on both the kickoff and punt teams.

Then there were the innocuous signs most people would shrug off.

Jake learned of an encounter reported by Jack Dilley's wife.

Julie came by the dorm one evening for her husband's signature on their rental agreement. A lobby lounger promised to fetch Julie's husband. She settled into a mass-produced sofa and noticed a young man playing a stand-up piano. He had a toothbrush in his mouth during his entire performance. She was impressed by his musical prowess.

A much bigger man wandered in to investigate.

"How long you been playing?" he asked in a reserved tone.

"What time is it?" the pianist asked in return.

Julie thought the scene was surreal. It was a strange place for a piano. It was much stranger that a resident of the football dorm played so well.

It was Jeff Foote, former quarterback and current first-team safety.

When Jake heard about this anecdote, he took heart. These players had beat their brains out for nearly two weeks and were worked to exhaustion during every practice. Still, they had time and energy enough to relax of an evening. They (at least Jeff Foote) retained a sense of humor.

Jake was impressed. They, the coaches and players, were a team. If properly mentored and treated, they'd retain cohesiveness in the heat of battle and, more importantly, between battles.

Jake snuck away from the meetings. He liked to pop into the various rooms to monitor presentations. These special meetings were loosely scripted. If there was a new drill in the offing, the coaches drew them up and explained them to the relevant players. Otherwise, it was mostly down-and-distance discussions, most effective sets and plays, and a general review of the playbook, replete with oral spot quizzes.

Jake made it a habit to sit in for ten minutes or so as a reminder that the head coach did indeed exist. He never contributed. He was briefed by the several coaches about the content and purpose of each gathering. If Jake had any objections, the agenda was adjusted. If Jake objected to anything he saw or heard during his pop-in, he'd meet with that coach later.

He trusted his staff. If they strayed off the reservation, he refused to create an issue in front of the men. That could kill a program. Any issues Jake had with his staff was handled behind closed doors.

Jake felt he was shirking his duty in returning to his office, but there were matters only he could address. Details, details, details—most of them minor and most of them insufferable. However, his job was to do or die.

Normally, he shrugged off the trappings of his office, but on this day, he had a hankering for a nice cup of coffee. Rather than fetching the cup from his office, he'd save a minute or so by taking one of the supernumerary mugs Holly scrubbed every morning.

Passing the AD's office, he glanced in. He enjoyed catching an aesthetic glimpse of dark-haired Denise. He was shocked to find a long-haired blonde sitting at Denise's desk. Fearing an office coup, he detoured.

The attractive blonde eyed him warily.

She did *not* stand.

"Where's Miss Davenport?"

"You're looking at me," she responded playfully.

It wasn't possible. Denise Davenport might opt for a change of hair color, but she would hardly remain seated.

The young attractive woman was overflowing with self-confidence. However, the facial features were so familiar. There could be only one explanation.

"You're Vikki?"

She beamed.

"So I am," she replied. "And you are…?"

"Jake Oats."

If she was impressed, she disguised it well.

"Denise told me about *you*!"

"You expected me to have horns?"

She laughed. It was a gay, devil-may-care, undergraduate laugh. It was innocuous and enjoyable.

"I told her not to sit at my desk," a voice came from behind.

"Don't be an old poop," Vikki suggested. "I got tired of standing. Maybe you expect me to sit on the floor."

Denise appeared on Jake's right shoulder. "If we're going to lunch, get a move on. I'm a working girl."

"What am I, chopped liver?"

"Forgive her," Denise said to Jake, though her comment was aimed at Vikki. "She's a snooty sorority girl."

"I so enjoy going to lunch with sis," Vikki reported. "She pays."

Vikki pushed back and stood up.

Damn, Jake thought, *their parents must be eight feet tall.* Did someone tell him that Vikki was a shortstop? It would take a lot of agility and energy to move that tank chassis around.

"So hot dogs at the Union?"

Vikki rolled her eyes.

"Denny! Let's go to that English pub. I want to try fish and chips." Soon they were off.

"We can't dally," Denise scolded. "I only get an hour."

Vikki appeared disappointed. Apparently, the siblings were close friends. Jake admired that quality, but not without pronounced regret. Tami would be denied the opportunity to experience the exasperation and joys of having a sibling.

Jake couldn't dally. His quest for coffee was aborted. A pile of crap filled his in tray.

Monday was a holiday. Registration began the following day. This was Georgia week. The practice schedule was hashed out by nine o'clock, but there was no one to type and mimeograph it. While everyone, save Coach Thorne, could work a mimeograph machine like a pro, there wasn't a single person who could type worth a thimble full of dried peas.

Jake was on the cusp of picking up the phone and calling Betsy. He balked at the prospect. She'd do it with a smile on her face, but it would violate their punts-and-pots treaty. Moreover, she'd promised Tami to take her on a forest hike complete with a picnic lunch.

Mieko could do it. By this time, Jake was convinced the oriental could spit backward. Alas, she was busy changing apartments.

The head manager happened by.

"Hey, manage. Got a minute?"

"Yes, sir."

No matter what the senior had in mind, he knew better than to deny a request from the boss. However, he'd seen dozens of practice schedules. He knew the format. That would save considerable time.

"Can you type?"

"A little," he replied cautiously.

Better than not at all.

"I need you to type the practice schedule."

"Sure thing."

Jake handed him the printed schedule on two sheets of legal pad.

"Offense, left, defense on the right. Use that typewriter."

Barbara might kill him, but a hand-printed document was unthinkable.

The lanky young man settled down into the well-padded chair and inserted a mimeograph master with professional élan. Then he began to type.

Columbus method: discover and land!

Jake sighed. Any port in a storm.

He returned to his desk and pretended to be busy. He felt as if he were struggling to pass coconuts.

The coaches were viewing last year's Georgia films for the umpteenth time. He'd made his comments and observations known during the first three showings. Still, hope springs eternal. Perhaps the coaches would find that one hitherto overlooked key that would doom the Bulldogs. Nobody wanted that more than Jake, but he doubted they'd discover anything they hadn't already.

He glanced at the materials the Skywriters punched out. It was best described as *bland*. They were all aware that other "experts" had passed judgement. Jake's team would finish three and eight and be one step away from the conference cellar dweller. That suited Jake just fine. He wanted people looking past him at more formidable foes. The one truism he'd gleaned from his coaching career thus far is a weak sister that is prepared will triumph over "mighty Casey" if that careless opponent expects a scrimmage. One would think the superior club would shift into high and realize victory. For some reason, it seldom happened that way. If the big bullies lose the first five minutes of play, they seldom get their act together in time.

If Georgia was looking past Jake, they were focusing on Tulane. Hardly a powerhouse, but a conference team. Maybe…

Sure! The *Titanic* was buoyed up by weather reports from Fiji!

⬛▬▬●▬▬⬛

Wednesday of game week. Classes began on Monday, and most students were either in housing or would be in short order. Class schedules were in hand and the bookstore thronged with students in a desperate search for used texts.

The new cheer squad began workouts the previous week. They had two full weeks to get in shape and practice routines. They were arrayed behind the arena and on a corner of the practice field. It pleased Jake when his players hardly glanced at the assembly. Even in civilian clothes, the ladies were striking. It spoke volumes about the team's focus. (There were, of course, three males amid the lustrous ladies, but they were largely unnoticed.)

The rally ladies only were brought in near the conclusion of the evening meal. They introduced themselves and wished the team good luck in the season opener. They also brought gag gifts for the coaches. These were trite and amusing and based upon the only practice they'd witnessed. The team and the coaches were appreciative and entertained, but only one gift made it into the memory books.

"We heard Coach Epps yelling at the linemen," a sprite brunette with flowing tresses recounted. "He said instead of practice pants, they should wear pink pantyhose. So…"

From behind her back, she produced a pair of pink pantyhose. A red-faced Joe Epps had to walk around the dais and the team tables to accept his gift. The team applauded, which deepened his embarrassment. Returning to his seat at the coaches' table, he studied the manufacturer's tag.

"What's your waist size, Shumway?"

The resulting crescendo of laughter completely drowned Epps's discomfiture. No one paid much attention to the brawny offensive tackle, which was just as well. The reaction to the coach's barb indicated the team was not on the brink of panic.

By the time Jake got home that evening, he'd completely forgotten what his own gag gift was. His thoughts were elsewhere.

We Who Are About to Die

"How many coaches does it take to use a typewriter?"

Jake didn't hear the punch line, but he wasn't interested. Barbara obviously realized someone had accessed her machine. Just how was anyone's guess. It would have been better had she confronted Jake personally. She could yell and scold however much she pleased; he was used to brickbats—coaches either acquires an immunity or dies nervous wrecks.

"Tell me what to do?" he asked, taking the offensive. "We have a practice schedule to prepare and distribute and no one in the office."

Barbara was suddenly very meek. "Sorry, Coach," she replied. "If the issue comes up again, we will arrange something."

He thanked her, called Betsy, and asked her to bring in a modest bouquet as a peace offering. She promised to tend to the matter before the business day closed.

Jake didn't want to press his luck with Barbara further. He opened his door and exited. Barbara went about her business like the professional she was. She pretended not to notice his flight. She'd be suspicious over his sudden retreat, the momentary closing of his door, followed by Jake's sudden departure. Barbara Hicks was not stupid, but she was a team player. She allowed Jake to exercise his judgment as to which of his phone calls she would be privy.

He made the long walk down the hall. Denise got to her feet as always. Jake allowed himself to author a pun about Denise's habit of *long standing*. He might share it with Betsy someday, but he'd never share it with anyone else.

"Detective Mieko around?"

"She's in class, studying, or working," the secretary/receptionist informed.

"Classes haven't started," Jake replied, just to be pedantic.

"Then she's working on something."

"I want to meet Gary Lynn, an out-of-state student, as soon as we get back from Georgia," he announced.

Denise was anything but supercilious. She refused to state the obvious. Barbara was his appointments secretary.

"The case of the purloined typewriter," he added.

She smiled. Denise heard all and knew all. Elaboration was not required.

"How was your lunch?"

"Sis wanted me to join her in a beer," she said with disapproval.

"I hope you didn't have a tiff."

"We don't *tiff*. We'll, not since we got old enough to know better. Let's say I was disappointed. If I come into this office with beer on my breath, it will be a banner headline in every paper this side of the Mississippi."

If ever Denise ran for Director of Hyperbole, she'd get Jake's vote.

"Do you want me to write it down?"

"Gary Lynn. I'll remember."

"Could you do me a favor?"

She too was suspicious.

"That depends."

"Make a date with sis to have a beer after work."

She smiled appreciatively. "I think I might just do that," she stated playfully.

There was only one offensive meeting on Thursday. It was Pink and the quarterbacks to review the play list and the coaches' battle plan. Since Joe would call most every play, Jake questioned the need to have this meeting. However, it wouldn't hurt to keep the quarterbacks in the loop.

Gus called his own meeting with those he felt should be there. He'd brief Jake *after*. Perhaps he thought Jake would betray him to the enemy. Perhaps it was Gus's way of underlining the contention that the defense belonged to him alone.

If it ain't broke, don't fix it. That was Jake's position. If he felt the need to stick his nose in, he'd not hesitate. Until then, laissez-faire, or as he'd overheard one player say, *lazy fairy.*

They had a down-and-dirty eighty-minute practice with limited contact. They concluded with eight minutes of nine-and-in, which was a ripsnorter. The team was ready. They were chomping at the bit. It didn't matter if they were going up against the Georgia Bulldogs or the local Pop Warner eleven—these young men wanted to play!

Prior to training table, as the players lounged in the Union concourse waiting for the doors to open, the managers handed an itinerary to each player. Personal information was attached, so every itinerary bore the name of the player to whom it belonged. This created embarrassment to the managers who hadn't yet fixed names and faces.

The reserve fullback initiated a tradition. While waiting for the team meal, he'd tarry at the unabridged dictionary mounted atop an impressive stand near a drinking fountain. He'd turn a page, arbitrarily, and find a word he didn't recognize; he committed the word and its definition to memory. By the Thursday before the big game, the fullback had a squad of six following his example. Donte Harris sat in one of the overstuffed chairs with a copy of the local bugle; he was particularly attentive to the movie announcements and movie reviews.

"Didja see this movie?" he would ask of any casual passerby. "It's a boss flick, man."

Others studied the sports pages of three regional papers. What happened to the other sections of these publications was known but to God. Of course, football was of prime interest, but any sport rated attention.

Jake studied the itinerary. It included, of course, a long, long flight. There was nothing he could do about that. What he found most interesting was the details of their Georgia sojourn. They would not stay in Athens or even Atlanta. Mieko booked them into a resort in Commerce (wherever that is).

"This better be good," he muttered to himself.

He pictured a Bate's Motel in Resume Speed, Georgia, where snipe hunting was the chief recreation. They'd need to dine together—that was the prime directive. There must be no more than two to a shared room. Only the head manager and one assistant would travel. The coaches also doubled up, except for Jake.

Fred Shaw hated to fly. To keep him stuffed in a coffin for hours and hours violated the Constitution—the part concerning cruel and unusual punishment. They couldn't dope him up for obvious reasons. It was a charter flight. The AD, doubtless with the aid of Denise and Mieko, allowed Mrs. Shaw a place on the plane. She must pay her way to and from the airport and could not stay at the team's residence. Nevertheless, having her on the flight to and fro would lessen Fred's anxiety no little.

Jake feared he should inform the team about this arrangement. He notified the team captains and urged them to spread the word. He didn't want his starting halfback hazed because Mommy had to come along. It was totally unnecessary. Similar situations arose before Jake arrived. If any snarky remarks were made, publicly or otherwise, Zwetschke and Ogle were unaware of them. They suspected they harbored other acrophobics who, if anything, would be envious of Shaw's not-so-secret weapon.

Fear of flying aside, it would be grueling.

The team must get aboard the bus early the following morning. They must wear their team blazers and ties and black slacks. They must board the aircraft in the state's second international airport (the first, a residual of World War II, was a dirt strip in the middle of nowhere—some joker labeled it an *international airport,* and it survived as such). They would fly forever, dismount, check into the motel, change into sweats and helmets, bus to tiny rural high school, work out on the school's field, return to the motel.

Jake didn't want to think about it. If he got where he was supposed to be, the team would get to where it was supposed to be. The arrangements were made. Two overnights in Georgia.

What did they expect? Was he supposed to whip them into a fury and turn them loose to destroy the banquet room and burn down the Union? What possible good would that do? They had to be up for the game. They were. Just before kickoff was the time to put fire into the berserkers. Prior to that, there were practical concerns.

He stood up and waited for the conversation to subside. He didn't have long to wait.

"Gentlemen, we're as ready as we can make you. Get a good night's rest. Don't stay up half the night thinking you can sleep on the plane. You may sleep, but you won't get rested.

"I'm proud of you men. You've done everything we asked—though not always the way we wanted it done."

There was subdued merriment at this comment.

"I've been hearing whispers, gentlemen. There are people in this town and perhaps in this room who think I'm pretending to be a saint or something. Well, I am and I ain't. We leave on a chartered plane tomorrow. Only people from this university will be aboard."

He realized Mrs. Shaw was coming along, but he'd not bring that up. In a real sense, she was a part of the university.

"There will be stewardesses and a few wives of university officials on that plane. No touchy-touchy or feely-feely. There will be no off-color remarks. We play like hoodlums on the turf, but we behave like gentlemen and representatives of this school when not on the field. If anybody does or says something to bring shame upon me or this school, I will yank his scholarship. I do not repeat myself! Any time you are in public, on or off campus, you represent this team—and *me*."

He let that sink in. Judging by the visages turned his way, he'd convinced a clear majority. Hopefully, the few who weren't impressed would be influenced by the many who were.

"Gentlemen, despite the odds, we are not going all the way to Georgia to lose. Keep your mind on what you must do. I don't want anyone bitching about somebody else not packing the freight. If you're watching your teammates, you're not doing your job. If you want to watch your teammates, you can do it from the sidelines. No mental mistakes, gentlemen. That starts here. Think about your assignments, your keys, your techniques, and your scouting reports. If you play the game in your head, if you dream about it tonight, then your mind is where it should be.

"Breakfast at six thirty. If you ain't on that bus, you'll be left. It is exactly that simple, gentlemen. Get your rest."

He strode boldly from the room. There was no noise or commotion as he exited.

It was near two hours to the airport. The bus drove out onto the tarmac, and the men boarded via the old-fashioned roller steps. The AD and other dignitaries were already aboard. Thanks to the airline (and Mieko), each player's itinerary included a row and seat number. The head manager and Pink double-checked to make certain everyone who boarded the bus had also boarded the aircraft.

Twenty minutes later, they were airborne. Fred Shaw's grip on his armrests may have helped lift the machine from the runway. Now began the endless flight across the nation.

Jake was invited to join the card tournament in the rear of the plane. He lied and said he didn't know the game.

"We'll teach you," Ralph insisted.

"At the moment, I have other things on my mind."

It was a rude rebuff, but Jake didn't want to be tied down to obligatory card games on these tedious flights. He'd played and brawled over cards as a Marine. His penchant for gaming had long ago been satisfied.

He ambled down the aisle for brief snippets of conversation with his players. He avoided football; he'd preached enough sermons on that. He wanted his players to relax and not be submitted to cross-examinations.

Jake paused at Fred Shaw. He had an aisle seat because he preferred *not* to look out the window. Mrs. Shaw, a slim woman who carried her years well, sat relaxed in a simple print dress. She wore an attractive bracelet and modest earrings. The window shade was drawn three-quarters down so she could surreptitiously peek out onto the landscape. She spoke casually to her son and patted his arm from time to time.

Fred seemed calm enough, but he gripped the armrests tightly at the slightest turbulence.

"Not like when I played," Jake volunteered. "We usually bussed to games. For the long trips, we took the train."

"The train?" Fred asked, as if being introduced to an unknown.

"If we played Georgia," Jake continued, "we'd have maybe two practices—if we were lucky. The rest of the time we'd be on the train."

Shaw's eyes grew wide with wonder.

"We loved to play visiting teams from far away," Jake continued. "We could practice right up to game time. The other guys couldn't practice on the train. It gave us a big advantage."

"I've never been on a train," he said.

"I didn't much care for it. Long rides with little to do but sit and eat and be bored. I tried to study, but reading on the train gave me headaches, so I just waited for the trip to end. A lot of guys played cards, read magazines, or talked about whatever was topical. I wasn't much of a talker."

Fred Shaw was pondering life in a world before reliable air travel. "I think I'd go crazy if I couldn't get out and run or at least play some catch."

"Then be thankful you only have to be cooped up in this cocktail shaker for a few hours."

He nodded. "Yeah, but it's a long, long few hours."

"Mrs. Shaw, can I get you anything?"

"I'm fine, thank you."

He had no intention of fetching anything. There was nothing he could bring. He simply wanted to acknowledge her existence. He was happy to have her along.

After a brief patrol, Jake settled into the seat beside Gus.

Good old Gus!

As an assistant, Jake would be chewing his nails down to his knuckles fretting about what he may have neglected to practice or discuss. Gus was as calm as anyone had a right to be. He was digesting a newspaper—not just the sports page, but the modern living section and the financial reports. Though Gus held only modest investments, he kept a close eye on the markets. He was interested in gardening, though he seldom had time to grow anything other than weeds.

"How many defensive coaches does it take to change a light bulb?" Gus asked the boss.

"Eleven?"

Gus shook his head and turned to the comics. "It doesn't take any. Coaches don't change."

Jake enjoyed a chuckle. Levity had become a rare commodity of late.

They had a snack on the plane an hour before landing. Jake made clear his feelings about gorging on airline food the day before a game. They had sandwiches, chips, and salad—just enough to keep hunger pangs away until after practice.

From the plane onto another bus. Jake was pleased to see Shaw hug his mother before they parted. She had a ticket to the game, complements of the university, but she was nervous about watching her son play in a hostile stadium.

"Coach Dooley told me I'm ta drive you'uns around and get you tired out," the bus driver announced over the intercom. "So before we head out, I'll show you some of the sights here in Atlanta."

Pucker time for Jake. He had perhaps ninety minutes to fret over the motel. He had visions of players wandering about town unsupervised. So nervous was he that he would recall very little of the "*Gone with the Wind*" tour. He'd never been to Atlanta before. If pressed, he'd have to admit he didn't recall a thing about it. Well, maybe Stone Mountain.

And that's not in Atlanta. Or is it?

Finally, they arrived in Commerce.

The motel was located at the intersection of two busy highways. Blessedly, from Jake's perspective, there wasn't a population center within sight—there was the "resort" and the highways. Unfortunately, there was a very large pool.

Memo to Mieko: no swimming pools!

Save for this worst of all mistakes, Jake could not object to the lodging. It was comfortable, remote, clean, and the staff was hospitable.

While the team got the deluxe tour of Atlanta, Thompson loaded up a truck and, with local hires, got the equipment to the locker room in Athens. Somehow, he transported helmets, cleats, and sweats to the resort during the same interval.

One hour after check-in, the team was back on the bus wearing their gear. It was twenty minutes to the high school. The school year hadn't started; there was no one to greet them, but they hardly needed a guide. The football field was not fenced. The driver parked near the south goal posts, and the team poured out onto the newly mown grass. Doubtless, it had been manicured so Jake and his team could practice there.

The men ran and frolicked for a few minutes before called in for calisthenics. Following this, they lined up to practice kickoffs and returns. They concluded by practicing punts and returns. When everyone was sweaty, they reboarded the bus for the trip back to the resort.

"Coach!" someone yelled from the back of the bus.

As the vehicle pulled away, two men wearing red and white shirts and carrying clipboards walked out of a nearby tree line.

Jake laughed. He wasn't the only one.

If the Georgia scouts expected to learn anything substantial about the team, they were disappointed. True, they were clueless about Jake's offense and defense—it was his one great advantage. However, they must have secured films from his previous school. That couldn't be very satisfying. Jake had new offensive and defensive coordinators. Coach Dooley would enter the contest blind.

Jake thought very little about his pretend advantage. Dooley was a quality coach with a quality staff and an experienced team. They'd make the necessary adjustments as the game progressed. Jake's edge would be short-lived.

———— ••• ————

There was a diminutive Georgia peach who apparently accepted the mission of ensuring the comfort and needs of perhaps the last group visitation of that summer season. She must have been of voting age, but she looked sixteen. She was hardly a Southern belle in accordance with the *Gone with the Wind* archetype. Jake classified her as *cute* in accordance with the Andy-Hardy motif. During key dispersals, she looked over staff members' shoulders (metaphorically speaking) and constantly referred to her master list. Thereafter, Jake noticed her scurrying hither and yon to make certain the public areas were properly policed and ready for the guests. During the team meal, she monitored the liquid consumables (water, milk, and sodas) to ensure all pitchers and ewers were refreshed as needed and all empty soda bottles were quickly removed. She also monitored the three women and two men who brought out the blue-plate meals.

Jake wondered if she was a supervisory trainee. He struck her as astute and persnickety—a younger more personable Mieko Takada.

"After tomorrow, gentlemen, you can swim as you please, provided you remember there are *other* guests. Until the game is over, the pool is off-limits. Quiet hours begin at ten. This ain't the dorm. A manager ain't gonna come round to beat on your door. It will be an employee. If you get tossed out, you can sleep under the trees with the copperheads and racoons. You better be too busy thinking of the game to raise hell.

"Coach Ostrander will call us together here for cocoa and cookies at nine o'clock."

There followed a few snickers at the thought of a kindergarten snack before lights out.

"Now you know why Coach Ostrander was such a terror on the field in his playing days. Cocoa and cookies: Attila the Hun insisted his army feast on them before going into battle. Oh, I don't share my cocoa, so don't bother to ask."

There were few courtesy cackles, but broad grins were copious.

"Bring your scouting reports. They will be collected at that time."

He asked the staff if they had any announcements.

They did not.

"Go to your rooms or lounge around the facility. I want you to relax but look over your scouting reports one last time and think about what you're going to do tomorrow afternoon. Save your energy. Don't be horsing around. See you here at nine."

Thompson arrived to load the sweats, helmets, and cleats. He and a manager worked before absconding unnoticed. The cleats and helmets would be in their proper places when the team entered the following day. The sweats, meanwhile, would be laundered, dried, folded, and stowed in preparation for transport with the rest of the equipment on the return flight.

Jake wondered if Thompson ever slept.

Coach Ostrander was as nervous as a Georgia hound dog passing peach seeds. He'd guesstimated how much cocoa the staff must prepare. Not surprisingly, the Georgia peach was in attendance, taking in everything and saying very little. She was there at nine to make certain everything was orderly and properly prepared.

The players filed by to get a cup and saucer and helped themselves to as much (or as little) as they liked from a huge urn. One at a time, they took a seat in the horseshoe table arrangement. There were four assorted cookies at each place setting. Jake and Pink made certain there was no cookie snatching; too much sugar mightn't facilitate a peaceful slumber.

Ostrander conferred with the Georgia peach at the conclusion of the ceremony. He wanted to know exactly how much cocoa was prepared and how much remained. He was informed *exactly* within three minutes of his request. Jake was impressed when Pink reported this. Obviously, the Georgia peach was more than "cute." Her similarity to Mieko was further enhanced.

—■•■—

The next morning, a hearty brunch was served at ten. Immediately following, two busses arrived. The players, neatly attired in their team blazers and ties, boarded. The Georgia peach stood stoically at the resort office entrance and watched the team pull away.

Tradition dictates that the visiting team stroll across the field of play. Some insisted that this offered them the opportunity to examine the condition of the field. Jake never paid much heed. Both teams would play on the same turf, so in his mind, field condition was moot. He felt the "stroll" was little more than a reminder of why they were there.

The vast stadium was beginning to stir. The ground crew was adding a few touches in the end zones, and the hawkers were setting up under the bleachers. They could be heard, but they were not seen.

Once in the locker room, it was time for Jake to kick it up a notch.

"Get your head on, men! You've practiced, you've studied films, you've gone over the scouting report. This is where we make it pay off. Think, men. Get it in your head that you are going out to an alley fight. Be reckless! If you make a mistake, make it full speed. Don't pay attention to the cheerleaders or the band or the refs. You pay attention only to your job and that Georgia Bulldog who is out to make you look like a fool. Don't let him. Make that man a believer. Let him know that you have a job to do, and you won't allow him to get in the way of your doing that job. If you get busted in the chops, you bust *him* back on the next play. I'm not talking dirty, gents. I'm talking within the rules of the game: hit *him* harder, make *him* hurt. Make up your mind to do that."

Now he would retire to a neutral corner and experience the tiny, malevolent beings gnawing at his insides. It was always like this—as a player, as an assistant, as a head coach. This was the worst part, the waiting. Not unlike that day on Cactus when you were waiting in that damned Higgins boat ramp to drop. Realizing that when it did, you and everyone with you could be murdered by Jap fire.

When they hit the beach, hardly a shot was fired. They walked up onto the shore and sat down and waited for something to happen, *but* that gnawing feeling wouldn't go away. There would be a brawl. Sooner or later, there would be a brawl!

The waiting.

That damned endless waiting!

————•————

They exchanged punts. They exchanged fumbles. Georgia ran back a punt for a touchdown—that hurt. More punts. An option play for a TD, and Jake was down by two scores.

Big bad Evans rumbled for a good gain. Shaw racked up several yards on a middle trap. A screen pass to Billy Morris and another to

Evans and the pin-their-ears-back pass rush was blunted temporarily. A pass interference call put the ball on the two-and-a-half-yard line.

Fifty-two power guard and a kick. Fourteen to seven, as close as Jake would get.

That touchdown was scored by Jake's black fullback. Not until the ref's hands signaled the score did Jake realize that a black man scoring against the Bulldogs in their house might not make for a salubrious reaction. However, if there was any outrage, it did not manifest itself in any noticeable or audible means.

It was a story of throwing more times than the coaches intended. It was a story of dropped and errant passes. Peck was put down only once, but many of his passes were hurried.

Epps began most of the first quarter with flanker and slot formations but shifted them in before the snap. The bulk of the plays were from a full-house T, which caused only minor and limited confusion on defense.

Georgia tried a fake field goal that was drawn up perfectly, but Gus didn't fall for it. His swarming defense shut it down.

It was embarrassing. Two punts returned for touchdowns. The Georgia quarterback gobbled up yards on the option and planned sweeps. The vaunted Georgia backfield made little or no headway through the line, so they ran and threw for acres on the edges.

"We got our asses handed to us, men," Jake told them in the locker room. "We just got a good ol' down-home whoopin'. *But* we *were not* beaten. We played hard the whole way. Only you, every man of you, knows if you gave it your all, but I didn't see anybody quit. I'll take the blame, gentlemen. I didn't prepare you properly. If you play as hard as you did today and you get buried alive, then *I* take the rap."

He had their attention. He saw many angry faces, but he did not see anyone hanging his head. They were upset, they were embarrassed—they were *not* ashamed!

"Now, let's make a choice, gentlemen," Jake continued. "We can cruise through the rest of the season, collect our three assigned victories, and wait for next year. That will make practices easier and game day easier. The alternative is that we take our whippin' like men and commit ourselves to win as many games as possible. You're not the most talented bunch I've ever been around, but you showed yourselves this day to have both heart and guts. That's very important."

The score was 56 to 25. That would haunt them for the rest of their lives. Unlike Cactus and New Britain, however, none of your buddies got killed.

"Okay," Jake continued, "we all know what we did wrong. Let me tell you what I saw that was right. Schlosberg, Noelle, and Black: their backs got by you once—only once during the entire game. Gianelli, I never saw one man defend the whole field the way you did this day. Foote, you didn't blow your coverage once, and you made excellent tackles.

"Offensively, Shaw, you ran well and you blocked better. Gino, when you were in there, you really gave an account of yourself. How did it feel to knock that big linebacker on his butt? He looked stunned, a pathetic sight sitting there like a kid in a sandbox. Did that make you feel like you got beat, Gino? Peck, the passing stats won't look so good, but you were under pressure. You made smart decisions. You didn't force a pass. If you were beat, you'd wing-and-a-prayer it. That speaks well for your first game. Helfrich, great punts—every one of them. Dilley, every long snap was perfect, and your blocking was excellent.

"I'm sure the film will show us many more things you men did well. I feel we have plenty to build on. Anyone here feel like taking out your anger on Iowa?"

For a moment, Jake thought the stadium might crumble and bury them in the locker room. He was convinced that the team could put the ball down where it was whistled dead and play for another hour. Glad he was that the Georgia team wouldn't agree to continue.

They were tired and humiliated, but they put up a proud front. This was the first game, not the last. There was plenty of time to give an account of themselves.

The post-game meal was subdued, but nobody looked or acted defeated. There were a few guarded laughs. The players who did so glanced at the coaches' table, expecting withering glares. Jake didn't mind. If they could laugh, their spirit remained intact.

The Georgia peach hovered over the staff. She did not appear to gloat over the home team's emphatic statement that afternoon. However, she didn't show signs of pity for the vanquished.

"We just blew up our summer recruiting," Jake mumbled as he joined Joe and Pink in the capacious lobby.

Nobody wants to be part of a team that gets blistered like they did that afternoon.

There were nearly a dozen players at the pool. They were not boisterous or obnoxious. They didn't want to call attention to themselves. When you get beat 56 to 25, you don't strut like a rooster. One player floated, spread-eagle, on his back. Several others sat with their legs dangling in the pool. Still others just lounged on the pool furniture.

No one thought to pack bathing garb in their carry-on bags. Who would suspect the university would billet the team in an establishment with a pool? The determined, however, wore pajama bottoms. There were few other guests residing. The few who opted to splash about to relieve the heat and humidity did not object to the muscle men's bathing attire.

"I never saw much of our vaunted rollout we've been practicing," Jake observed.

By this time Joe and Jake had a tacit understanding. If Jake disagreed with the play calling or the way Joe ran the offense, he'd state his objections clearly and without reserve. Therefore, Joe Epps failed to bristle when his boss launched a remark that, by someone other, would be viewed as critical or openly hostile.

"We gotta keep something up our sleeve," Joe replied sedately. "Besides, did you notice our pass blocking? I'm proud of the way the line blocked. Even when they knew we'd be throwing on every down, they gave Peck the time he needed."

"The backs weren't quite so good," Pink volunteered to redirect Joe's progression.

Epps shook his head reservedly. "They did a good job," he insisted. "Yes, they missed their blocks here and there, but they did pretty damned well."

"Two dropped passes by men in the open," Pink reminded.

"Yeah," Jake injected. "Mike will have to get on them. I never thought I'd see Capp drop that slant."

Joe shook his head vigorously this time. "Dave audibled to that," he stated while reviewing the game in his mind. "It was there. That was a golden opportunity gone up the spout."

"Mr. Oats, sir?"

He looked up to find the Georgia peach approaching.

Mister Oats? Had he been fired already?

"Mrs. Oats is on the phone," she reported. "You can pick up over there. We'll connect you."

He thanked her and headed for the wall-mounted courtesy phone. "Bets?"

"You didn't call. I just wanted to know if you were okay."

"I've had my head in a burlap sack since the game," he said.

She didn't laugh. "Tami was in tears most of the afternoon."

"I never expected her to get so excited about a game," he admitted.

"She didn't care about the game. She was feeling horrible for you."

"Well, you remind her that I'll survive. Give her a hug. I'll see you tomorrow afternoon."

Betsy knew. Sure, five minutes while he shaved and changed, she'd see him. Well, a coach's wife is to do or die.

Renaissance
(Cheap Imitation)

As the bus pulled out, the only figure seen was the Georgia peach. Was she gloating over the team's humiliation? She didn't look it. Was she watching the departure of her first major assignment as an apprentice? Was she mourning the end of the vacation season?

Jake gave her the benefit of the doubt. He raised his hand. She raised hers. A moment later, the facility and its Georgia peach were left behind.

He was not invited to play cards in the back of the plane. He would have begged off anyway, but he wasn't given the chance. Ralph and his group were playing cards before Jake arrived; they'd be playing cards long after he was sent packing.

Mieko met the team when it deplaned. She handed the game film to Jake as he mounted the bus for the trip homeward.

The film was flown by air express the evening before. Mieko picked it up and escorted it to a local TV station and the subterranean film-processing facility. She studied her texts in the lobby for over two hours. Shortly after midnight, she and the film left in a state car provided by the university motor pool. Where did she spend the night? Jake didn't ask, despite being curious.

"You didn't have to wait for us," Jake scolded.

"I wanted to be sure it got into the proper hands."

Did she suspect saboteurs in the athletic department, or was she merely overscrupulous? Had she driven home, the woman could have grabbed a few hours' sleep. She could have met the busses on campus, but she opted to meet them at the airport.

This would be hell day.

The team endured airline food. The moment they got back, it was into sweats and onto the practice field to loosen up preparatory to running ten twenty-yard sprints and six forty-yard sprints. After showering, they'd meet in the squad room to watch the films. Each player graded himself. The score cards were collected by their respective coaches. Finally, they enjoyed training table prior to a well-deserved rest.

After training table, the coaches returned to the facility and watched the game again, grading players and making notes as they went.

Jake did not arrive home until after one in the morning.

Betsy was waiting.

⬛◆⬛

"Welcome back," Barbara said, taking a second-and-a-half break from typing.

"Still talking to me?" Jake asked.

"Oops. I slipped. You won't tell on me, will you?"

"Your secret is safe with me."

In the center of his desk was a yellow sheet of thin inter-office memo paper. It announced that Gary Lynn had a nine o'clock class. He promised to come by the arena after.

That was very inexact. Jake assumed it was a fifty-minute class, but where? If he had to walk from the far end of campus, well, he couldn't sit around waiting.

He went into the coaches' nest. Gus and Miller were in a spirited conclave. Similarly, Joe, Pink, and Mike Perry were going over blocking rules and making an Iowa ready list. Jake wasn't too concerned about that. The offense played well for the first game. It was the defense that surrendered forty-four points and the punt team (an adjunct of the defense) that allowed Georgia the remaining twelve.

"The Hawks will put the ball in the air more than Georgia," Jake informed.

"We're working on a rush-and-cover package," Gus informed, looking as if he resented the interruption. "I want pressure in the face. We'll send an end to on-side action. I want the quarterback to see him coming. He's only taken a few snaps before this season. He'll be sweating backside pressure. We can make arrangements for that too."

Jake thought for several seconds. "I don't like it," he announced. "You're going to have to sell me on it. It's only fair to tell you that I doubt you can. Save that fight for later. Let's settle the depth chart."

Gus and Miller shuffled through a stack of material.

"Move St. John up," Miller suggested. "Brown didn't play well. Let's make him earn the spot back."

Dave Thorne must be consulted, but Jake was in favor of the move.

"Let Black have a series or two," Miller continued. "He's earned a shot. Don't move him up just yet, but let's spell Schlosberg for a few downs now and again."

Jake nodded. He recalled reviewing the previous year's films and how Black impressed him, particularly on the goal line. "How about Davidson?" Jake asked.

"He's coming on strong," Miller observed. "He ain't there yet."

"I want him on kickoffs and punts," Oats demanded. "Anybody got heartburn with that?"

Both men shook their heads.

———•◦•———

Iowa got their ears pierced by Ohio State in the opener. It was 52 to 21. Both teams were buried by ranked teams. Both teams featured an offense that moved the ball against top-flight defenses. Both teams experienced special teams problems. Both teams were spotty on defense. It was a battle of losers. Jake didn't like the terminology, but facts speak louder than words.

He moved a few paces to look over Joe's shoulder.

"Twenty-eight and twenty-nine," he pontificated. "I want to see them Saturday."

They'd been so intimidated by Georgia that they omitted the counter option from the ready list. Despite Iowa hiring a defensive "genius" for their new head coach, his defenders were nowhere near Georgia's quality. Jake could test the counter options against the Hawks and evaluate the results. If they proved satisfactory, they'd make them a staple. If they bombed, opponents down the line must prepare to defend against them regardless. Every moment the opposition spent on defensing weaknesses made the stronger plays more effective.

"Depth chart?"

As the senior man, Epps went first. "Shumway and Swofford had a good game. Zwetschke had a great game! Dilley made all the right line calls. Smith didn't show well. We could move Materie over because Dolan is not ready to move up. That will take more than three practice days."

"Move him," Jake decided. "We may need him as the season goes on."

"Peck is our man," Pink stated. "Gino and Shaw are neck-and-neck. Joe likes to use them to shuttle plays in. Billy and Evans are solid. Black works hard. Let's give him a few carries."

"Can Black block as well as Evans did Saturday?"

Pink calculated for a moment. "I'll answer that after Tuesday's practice."

"Mike?"

"I know Capp dropped an easy pass—"

"So did Billy and Rush," Epps observed.

"Capp's still our man. Billy, for certain. I like Parks, but his blocking isn't as good as Rush."

"So no changes there," Jake concluded.

"Keep an eye on Hackett," Joe suggested. "I have a feeling after Billy graduates, Hackett might be even better. He runs good routes."

"I'm naming Dilley the *hustler* unless there are any objections."

Jake initiated awards for the best offensive and defensive players for each game. The awards were cheap mass-produced trophies with the engraved player's name and opponent. The offensive player was the week's hustler. The defensive player, Jeff Foster, was designated the hard rock.

None of the offensive coaches objected to Jake's selection of the senior center as the Georgia hustler. His blocking was textbook, his long snaps were perfect, and his attitude throughout the massacre was exemplary.

Jake wondered why he'd not been selected as team captain. Of course, Zwetschke was hardly a charity case.

———•—•———

Gary Lynn would never be identified as a football player. He was short, stocky, and wore thick glasses. Jake found him amiable. His vocabulary was extensive, and his articulation was worthy of a stage actor. Nevertheless, he was the caricature of a wimpy brainiac.

Jake arranged an audition for the following afternoon *after* practice. If it proved satisfactory, he'd need a physical before he could report to Thompson and be fitted for his kit. Lynn suspected something; he brought his kicking cleat to his new school.

Jake had only a few minutes before practice to meet with the incoming freshman. Brice nodded to Jake when the troops were assembled.

The moment Jake entered the room, thirty-eight young men got to their feet. Of that number, he could expect only a dozen would survive the riggers and move on to varsity.

He mounted the rostrum and drew up to the podium. Immediately, he spied a familiar face. He pretended not to be fazed, but he was.

"Gentlemen, some of you might have heard about what happened in Georgia."

There was a nervous titter.

"To be frank, we got our asses handed to us. Why? We got our asses kicked because, gentlemen, *you weren't there!* We've got a great team. We need you men to make it better. Every varsity player is looking over his shoulder wondering which of you is going to take his job. Gentlemen, it's up to you. The harder you work, the harder the man in front of you must work to keep his spot. As freshmen, you can't play varsity, but you can stake your claim. You can put your stamp on your territory.

"Coach Churchill here was a great running back, a great receiver, and as a tackler, he could bring down King Kong. I know him. More importantly, he knows me. He knows what I want. He knows what I expect. He knows his job. He has three graduate assistants who played here last year. They know what it takes to play here. They will get you ready *if* you stick it out.

"I guarantee, Coach Churchill will have you all stepping on your tongues. You will hurt and ache like never before. When you finish your season, however, you will have earned the right to call yourselves football players. I only hope we can schedule Georgia again so you can hand them *their* asses. You have the talent. If you didn't have talent, you wouldn't be here. Now, you must go out and make yourself a hundred times better. Every drill, every sprint, every scrimmage, every game: you must make yourself better. That goes for your schoolwork as well. I don't care if you're the *greatest* player who ever lived. If you don't make it in the classroom, you're no more use to me than the *worst* player that ever lived.

"Mel Manning, report to my office and make an appointment to see me tomorrow!

"Coach Churchill, they're all yours."

———•———

Why Mike Perry? Who else was there? Joe was hip deep in scouting and game planning. Pink had to oversee his normal duties. Gus was putting together a rush-and-cover package (and preparing his effort to lobby Jake into accepting his pass rush from the edge), Miller and Thorne were memorizing every detail of Iowa's loss to Ohio State.

The report lay on Jake's desk waiting for him.

Mike Perry's forty-five-minute post-practice tryout evaluation was terse.

Kickoff: goal line.

FG from 35 yards: 10 of 10 middle, 9 of 10 left hash, 7 of 10 right hash

Longest: 45 yards middle (three tries)

PAT: 10 of 10

———•———

Tuesday was booster day. The conference room of the premier Chinese restaurant could handle one hundred people. There was less than half that number attending after Georgia. There was a buffet set up for the attendees at six dollars a head. That seemed excessive to Jake, but he assumed the owners and manager of the establishment knew the business.

In a break with tradition, Jake served himself. He hadn't an appreciable appetite and dodged the embarrassment of speaking from behind a pile of unconsumed food.

When the buffet line was reduced to those boosters seeking seconds, Jake stood up.

"Gentlemen, I bet you didn't expect to see me today."

There was a polite smattering of laughter.

"I didn't come here to be ridiculed and abused, but I forgot where I usually go."

More laughter. This was less reserved. The assembly was coming around.

He held up a six-inch length of movie camera film.

"To save time, I brought with me the highlights of the Georgia film. I'll pass it around so everyone can enjoy it."

More laughter and a smattering of tentative applause.

"The bottom line is this, gentlemen. We ain't quitting. The team lost by a ton, but they don't feel they were beaten. Oh, we *lost*, make no mistake, but we weren't *beaten*. The team is anxious to regain its pride. Georgia is a closed book. We learned a lot. We will build on that, but we ain't gonna cry over it. We're looking ahead, not behind.

"If we could dim the lights a little and start the film, I'll show you my favorite play from last Saturday."

The assistant manager flipped the switch, and the projector threw an image of Jake leading his team out onto the field.

"That's it, gentlemen. My favorite play."

Laughter and applause.

From this point on, Jake did the play-by-play *and* the color commentary. He related interesting facts about his players and a few anecdotes so the boosters would know more about individual players than a number on a jersey. He was quick to point out those who made a brilliant play or who put forth tremendous effort. He knew because he'd seen the film, backward and forward, several times.

"Now, I want you to watch Gino on this play. Fake handoff to Gino, watch the linebacker run it back, manage. Okay…right…*here*! He knows Gino don't have the ball. He's chasing Billy and watch…*BOOM*! That, gentlemen, is one hell of a block! Just about now, that linebacker is figuring out what day of the week it is. Losers don't block like that."

On it went until both the film and Jake's commentary were finished.

He had to stay for a few more minutes for silly chatter and a round of introductions. At the first opportunity, he was in his car and pointed for the facility.

———•◦•———

He shook Mel's hand warmly and directed him to the chair. He did not sit down behind his desk until Mel was comfortable. He didn't close the door. Had he done so, Barbara would conclude he was chewing out the diminutive black freshman. She'd not broadcast this, of course, but she'd reach the logical conclusion. Jake didn't want that.

"Mel, I told you before, I just don't think I can use you."

"And I tol' you before, I don' wanna play for nobody else."

"How can you afford it?"

"The ol' man put 'side enough fo this year. He think I, maybe, get a schol'ship."

Jake leaned back and studied the young man carefully. "What are you studying?"

Mel shrugged. "Nuffin' really. I'm takin' required classes."

"What required classes?"

"Bi'logy, algbra, English comp, West Civ, and ROTC-Navy."

Jake did a quick calculation. Mel was carrying a full load.

"ROTC is not required," Jake reminded.

"Yeah, but I wanna take it. Maybe I be a Marine after all."

Jake's heart was bleeding. "Son, I admire your ambition. I'm flattered by your dedication to me. What if you can't play football…for whatever reason?"

"Coach, you believed in me. I believe in you. The ol' man works hard to get me here. I believe in him too, but I don' wanna be a truck driver. I don' know what I wanna be, but not a truck driver. I wanna play football, but if I can't, I'll try the Marines like we talk 'bout befo'."

"Let's put football aside for the moment. Coach Churchill will take care of football for now. Let's talk Marines. Let's talk *not* being a truck driver. In other words, let's *talk*. That's the first thing. Learn to speak proper English. *Ol' man*, just as an example. When you use that phrase, it sounds disrespectful."

"Oh, no! I respects my ol' man plenty. I wouldn't be here if he didn't wants it."

"Nevertheless, you give people the wrong idea when you say *ol' man*. If you're going to be a Marine, you must look like a Marine. You must wear the uniform just so, you must walk just so, you must do your tasks just so. It's how you are judged. A Marine who says 'ol' man' and 'nuffin'' and 'algbra' sounds ignorant. Mel, I know you aren't ignorant—not even close. Don't advertise yourself as ignorant."

"It's how we talk at home."

"And you always will. That's a great thing about home. *But* you're not at home here. Coach Churchill talks exactly like you do—at home and sometimes around me. You listen to him. See if you can talk the way he does—only without the swear words. Will you do that?"

"I can try for certain."

"Good man. I'll be wanting to talk with you often. Right now, I got a lot of work to do."

"Thanks, Coach. I wanna—um, I want to make you proud of me."

"You're off to a good start, Mel."

They shook hands again.

⬥

The Black Student Union was very quiet. Jake expected a great to-do from the bunch. They'd insist that if an all-black coaching staff had taken an all-black team to Georgia, they would have sent the segregationist bastards to hell.

Silence

Perhaps the organization's planned narrative was knocked askew when the team's first touchdown was scored by the bruising black fullback. Regardless, as on Cactus and New Britain, silence was the greatest generator of fear.

Likely, the BSU was run by agitators and off-campus underground conspiracies. If so, it might take a few weeks to gather student forces and issue orders. Regardless, Jake was irked by President Burns and his insistence on *not* getting ahead of the issue. Perhaps he knew there were powerful political forces behind the group, and he wanted to keep his head down. It made no sense to Jake. If the BSU went after the football program and the athletic program in general, how long would it take before the BSU confronted the president and the Board of Regents?

Be thankful for the respite, Jake told himself.

He put all his energy into preparing the staff for the Hawks. He was more hands-on than he'd been with Georgia. He had an accurate gauge on his players, their limitations, and their strengths. He would make certain those strengths were brought to the fore.

"I want Lynn as soon as we can bring him up to speed," he announced.

The staff looked at him as if he'd spoken in Portuguese.

"Smith is better on the line than Dolan or Materie or Williams. That's where I want him on PATs and field goals. If he's where he belongs, someone else must kick. Dig up somebody to work with him. We've got all the gas we're allotted with Church. Find someone who is willing to help the program gratis. How about a manager? Send them down onto the field while we're on the practice field. He's got to be in shape in case he takes a hit. That means sprints. He also needs someone to hold the ball when he kicks. Joe, make this happen."

Epps didn't like it. He didn't like this at all, but he nodded his head. An order is an order.

"I want Peck and Murray to practice pooch punts. When we're in the plus part of the field, we'll punt high and short. Helfrich can't do that. He has one speed: forty yards or bust. He's got no touch. Let's see if our quarterbacks can keep punts out of the end zone. Joe, that's you again."

"Right, chief." Joe could see the logic behind this order. "Are we changing anything else?"

"More cover one," Gus piped up. "They've thrown deep only twice. Their pass protection isn't real good. Their receivers are faster than our d-backs, but we can play 'em tight on the short stuff. Foote will be on his own, but he's got good vision and instincts. He can handle it."

"Let's do it. Anything else?"

"On 28 and 29," Joe suggested. "Change the offside blocking rule. Let's reach block and see if we can cut the backer. No line call. Whoever is uncovered must reach."

Jake nodded. "Anything else?"

There was a quick scan around the room by everyone.

"Scouting reports?"

"They hired this guy because he has a reputation for tough defenses. He went twenty-two and zero or twenty-one and one at his previous school."

That was Joe. How he found time to look up all this stuff was beyond Jake. Perhaps he had a secret research assistant. Regardless, his information wasn't good news. Still, coaching division 2 is way different than coaching division 1. Jake could testify to that!

"They're loaded for right-handed teams," Miller volunteered. "If we run to the left, we might find soft spots."

"Boss," Joe inserted, "we normally put the tight end to the short side of the field. I want to put him to the wide side now and again."

Jake nodded. "Anything else?"

Silence.

"Okay, let's get them ready."

Since Iowa was making the long trip out, the pre-game routine was easier and on familiar ground. Mieko located a nice motel (with no swimming pool) in a neighboring burg. It had conference rooms and a ballroom. Frat dances and high school proms were often booked there.

Mieko coordinated with the Iowa people and recommended a neighboring establishment. Jake wasn't thrilled. The opposing teams would be billeted within three blocks of each other. There was no reason to assume the players would desire to fraternize, but there was a very real possibility that an unintended spark might result in damning publicity. He advised the department to keep a lid on the proximity of the two gladiatorial contingents during the evening prior to the contest. On the other hand, Jake might be able to steal away long enough for a drink and a chat with Evy.

Fortunately or unfortunately, Evy didn't travel with the squad. He was busy with his job and sent his regrets. Coach Agee was scouting the Hawkeyes' next opponent. He did meet with one of the assistant coaches and a publicity man, but they had nothing in common. Jake walked back to his team's quarters in plenty of time for cocoa and cookies.

The game was never in doubt. Joe's offense shone. The rollouts and the counter options ticked like a jeweled watch. They had few long gainers, but they ate up the yards methodically. The punting game reflected the time and effort Jake's players put into their practices. The longest Iowa punt return was seven yards.

Gus called a great game, and the defense held the Iowa offense in check. They were far from perfect, but they did not commit the egregious errors that plagued them the previous week.

Jake expected a much tougher contest than he got, but he wouldn't complain.

The offense put up thirty-three points, but that wasn't surprising. Joe's offense performed well in Georgia. The difference was that the defense and the punt team refused to allow the opposition an undeserved score.

Jake met with the press to make the obligatory comments and answer the standard questions with the standard answers. He liked this part of the job the least. He was euphoric over his first victory in division one, but he kept his head. He didn't want to say anything the next opponent might interpret as a boast or, worse, disrespectful.

When he entered the coaches' room, Joe Epps sat in front of his locker in his street clothes. He was tying his shoes and making ready to go upstairs.

"Got a second, Joe?"

"Of course."

Gus and Dave Thorne entered. They had yet to shower and change. Doubtless, they had to schmooze with the press box gaggle before making their escape. They congratulated Jake and Joe. In return, the boss and his first sergeant lobbed a few plaudits of their own.

Jake shared a selected anecdote about Evy before coming to the point. Joe, who might be encouraged to pen a tome, *Coaches I Have Known*, had previously regaled his boss with stories both poignant and humorous of his encounters.

"Let me run this by you," Jake began, turning to business. "Fourteen and fifteen."

"Oh?"

Joe's curiosity was piqued. These were the simplest plays in the repertory, a straight-ahead dive to the halfback (or wingback) into the guard-tackle gap. It demanded adroitness of the quarterback who must reverse pivot and tuck the ball into the stomach of a ball carrier shooting out of his stance like an Olympic sprinter. They seldom ran the play in practice and had yet to attempt it during a game. Baring a mishap, it would net a yard or two. Chances were excellent that it would be stuffed at the line. Unless Joe was facing a junior high team, this basic dive play had no legitimate place in his battle plan.

"Suppose the quarterback doesn't reverse out?" Jake asked. "Suppose he reads the tackle or end. If he comes, Peck keeps the ball and rides the tackle's far hip?"

Joe made a thoughtful noise. They had triple options in seventy-four and seventy-five, but those were based on riding the fullback. In fourteen, just as an example, constituted riding the halfback and optioning off the end—with the fullback as a lead blocker on the edge. Evans was a reliable pass blocker, but his ability to lead was untested.

"Let me think about it."

Jake didn't push. Evy would push. Likely, Evy would rant and ride roughshod until Joe submitted—or quit. Well, Evy would always be Evy.

Jake, however, could never be Evy. To begin with, Evy would travel in the back of the plane holding a fist full of cards.

"We've scored fifty-eight points in two games, Joe," Jake reminded. "That's a great start, but we must continue to build."

"Agreed." Joe nodded.

That was noncommittal.

The Monday following, Joe nudged his boss and commented that his suggestion was the basis of the Houston veer that Bill Yeoman used (with great success).

Jake grunted. "I thought I was being groundbreaking original," he replied, only partly in jest.

"We'd have to recruit a different kind of animal to run the veer," Joe pontificated.

"Well," Jake decided, "let's pocket it for now. Maybe we can kick it around a little when the season's over."

"I'm intrigued, Jake," Joe insisted. "You got me thinking."

"Joe, it's best if we think only about what we're doing right now."

The offensive coordinator nodded his head. The matter was tabled.

For now.

Rumblings

Jeff Foote, former timid quarterback, was a tiger at safety. His pass coverage was hardly stellar, but his tackling was sure and, in desperate situations, innovative. In the Iowa contest, he netted four solo tackles, six assists, and was in or near the action a dozen additional times. He was the runaway choice for hard rock honors. Jake decided alone, Evy style. However, he had the tacit support of the entire staff.

The hustler award was not so clear cut. As a former lineman, Jake felt Shumway had a career game. He buried the Iowa tackle on every on-side play and got three impressive downfield blocks. Capp, who dropped crucial passes in Athens, caught all four passes aimed at him—one of those a highlight-reel catch. Shaw swivel-hipped to sixty-seven yards, Evans scored two touchdowns, and Billy Morris scored one on the ground and one on a pass reception.

It was tough. Jake stepped back and allowed the offensive staff to argue the matter. Eventually, they compromised and selected Dave Peck, the quarterback who played above his sophomore status. Jake growled. He thought Shumway should be rewarded. He compensated by complementing the big tackle several times during the team's self-grading session.

Jake asked to see Shumway's score card. He was not surprised to see the man had evaluated himself with more minuses than plusses. The big guy was not being modest, he was being honest. Line play is not an art; it's brutal. If the line were flawless, there'd be a touchdown on nearly every play, and the sport would be, in Jake's estimation, pointless.

It was well past midnight when Jake got home. As always, Betsy was there to greet him with a hug and a kiss. Jake tiptoed into Tami's room to look upon the young girl he seldom saw. She lay atop the covers in a pair of gaudy yellow print pajamas, but she looked healthy. Asleep, she was precious. Awake, of course, she was a pest.

"She wrote out a summary of her first week in junior high," Betsy whispered. "You can look at them after you get some rest."

He shook his head. "Now," he insisted.

There were five sheets of notebook paper with her precise cursive adorning both sides. She related, in lyric prose, her impressions of each day's highlights. At the bottom, in bold, artistic letters was her name: *Liisi.*

Jake's mind was fatigued, and his blurry eyes slowed his reading speed, but he devoured every word, including those Liisi misspelled. The events she recorded were important only to an impressionable young girl, but her presentation was special. They hardly had a chance to speak while awake, so her writing was a valued treasure. He vowed to scribble a few words in reply whenever he had a few free seconds. He reckoned that by day's end, he could leave two or three hundred words for her perusal.

His brief missives mightn't be important to Liisi as hers were to him. However, responding to her priceless mini histories would do him a world of good.

❖

Jake found six sheets of paper on his desk when he entered his office. It was Churchill's handwritten summary of the frosh practices. The last page was a summation of his impressions. Mel Manning was mentioned frequently. The little runt was a dynamo.

During rush drill, Manning throws his hip at the defender's Adam's apple. Effective!

Jake reflected. None of his running backs, except for his hulking fullbacks, were big enough or skilled enough to take on a linebacker or end in a chicken fight. If they tried to cut them and missed, or if they charged and didn't hit the big men square…

However, if you came in neck high and perpendicular, the defender must duck or risk being bowled over. Either way, he'd be neutralized.

Mel believed in throwing his body around. How neatly that fit with Jake's offensive philosophy.

Joe would be informed of this.

———•———

"Coach Agee on line two."

Jake thanked Barbara and picked up his phone. He punched the correct button. "You damned pirate! I missed seeing you Saturday."

"They had me scouting. Congratulations, by the way. How much did you have to pay the refs to hand you the game?"

Jake laughed. Agee habitually made allegations in jest. However, it would not be beyond some zealous scum bucket in the NCAA to tap his phone. It would be both illegal and preposterous, but Jake would take no chances. He wanted to tell his friend and former assistant that the officials sold out for two turnips and a dozen rare baseball cards. Instead, he denied bribery just to be safe.

"Evy is everything you told me, Jake. He's a character, but he's a straight shooter. He thinks we're in for a long, long season. I think we're going to have to suck it up. We need a half dozen quality recruits and a lot of time to adjust to this new system."

"We're facing the same problems, Gee," Jake responded. "We're running an offense tailor-made for the personnel we inherited. The same with our defense—especially the defense. Nobody knows what the hell they're doing, including the coaches. All we can do is plug holes until we stumble onto something we can live with. Headaches, Gee. One damn headache after another."

"That's why we make the big bucks, Jake. Dollars for headaches."

"One thing is for certain, Gee: we're grossly underpaid."

"God bless us, everyone. Gotta meeting, Jake. Good luck, buddy."

"Good luck to you, Gee. Let's try and arrange a meet after the season ends. I'll buy you a drink."

"Look forward to it, boss."

He put the phone back where it belonged. The few seconds he had with an old friend were precious. What he wouldn't give to have Agee in one of the cubicles just beyond his office. Well, there was nothing to do but put his dreams away and get back to work with the staff he had.

Barbara stuck her head in his office just as he was about to dispatch his latest pile of correspondence. "Leroy Evans to see you," she announced.

It was established procedure to remain seated and say, "Send him in." Jake eschewed that. People who assumed imperious airs should, in his estimation, possess imperious positions. Jake was a plebeian, born and raised. He pushed back his chair and went into the secretarial sanctum.

There he found Leroy Evans, all six-three, 236 pounds in modish slacks and a solid yellow shirt with a button-down collar. Jake shook the young man's hand and escorted him into his office. On the practice field, Leroy Evans was one of many under his command. In his office, he was an honored guest. He was, therefore, motioned into the comfortable armchair facing the coach's desk.

Jake pointed to the door. Leroy nodded his head. Jake closed it silently and returned to his chair.

"The Black Student Union," the burly fullback announced.

"They contacted you?"

"Thursday night." Leroy nodded. "I didn't say anything because we were thinking about the game. I didn't want to upset the routine."

Jake nodded. Evans had done the right thing. "What did they want?"

"Me. Well, maybe. What they really want is my skin color."

Jake pondered that. He suspected this BSU was more of a publicity campaign than a group dedicated to societal readjustment.

"They want to showcase me at an event next month."

"You up for it?"

"Well, yes *and* no. I mean, I understand why they think black students should be recognized as a part of the university, but I get a little, well, *nervous* when they demand special treatment for black students.

That kind of, well, it pisses me off. I don't want to skate on privilege. I want to be judged for myself—just like my teammates."

Jake cleared his throat. "I'm not certain I understand, Lee."

Jake was ever attentive to his team members and how they responded to each other. He noticed, during spring and fall practices, how his fellow players addressed the big-bull fullback.

"Hey, Lee!"

"Great job, Lee!"

"Watch out for Lee!"

Thus, in Jake's office, he deferred to the team members and addressed him as did they.

Leroy Evans squirmed in the chair. For a single bone-chilling moment, Jake feared he'd made a serious error. Thankfully, it wasn't his mode of address that bothered the powerful running back.

The young man cleared his throat. "When I was a sophomore, my English prof assigned us *Black Boy*. I guess it's part of the propaganda program, I don't know. Have you ever read it?"

Jake shook his head.

"I recommend it, Coach. Anyways, the prof takes me aside after class and says that I probably don't need to read the book. He said my own experience as a black person was enough. That's when the alarm bells started going off, Coach.

"I grew up in a nearly all-white town and went to a nearly all-white school. I do not recall skin color ever being an issue. I don't know what was said behind my back, but there was never a problem behind my front. The first slurs directed at me were by a couple of those Georgia boys. They didn't amount to much, really, and I wasn't bothered. I've said a few things myself during games.

"Well, like I started to say, I read *Black Boy* just to find out what that butthead prof thought of me. Let's see, it begins with hanging a cat and burning down a house—that's just in the first couple pages. I couldn't put it down, Coach. Well, this Richard Wright guy grew up on a completely different planet than I did. I had no idea, Coach. I guess, maybe, I should have known, but..."

Jake sat silently. He had a million things to do, but Leroy Evans was more important than all the other things put together. He was not his starting fullback; he was a young man with issues. He needed to talk. More importantly, he needed to be heard.

"Well, the author gets wooed by the Communist Party. He's got a pile of chips on his shoulder, and he thinks the Commies are on his side. He joins up. It wasn't long before he realized they didn't give a damn about him. They only wanted his skin color. When he figured that out, he dropped them like a ton of rotten, putrid fish. So when these guys come to me and start kissing my ass, I wonder if they want me as, I don't know, a kind of trophy."

After a thoughtful pause, Jake spoke. "Wes is a starter on defense," Jake observed. "Have they tapped him?"

"I don't know, Coach. You're the first person I've talked to about this."

"I appreciate your telling me, Lee. I can't advise you on what you should do. You must wrestle with this on your own. Maybe Wes and the others can help. It certainly can't hurt to talk with them about it. Keep me in the loop."

"I will, Coach. I promise I won't be doing anything behind your back."

How Jake appreciated those words!

<hr>

Jake needed to talk with Wesley Jordan, the swing linebacker. This made him uncomfortable. Wes was the Gary Cooper type; he knew his job and did it well. He was hardly an All-American linebacker, but he was reliable and a sure tackler. He didn't talk much, even with his teammates. Wes was hardly a recluse; he got along with everyone, but he had no close friends. He had piercing eyes that looked right through you when a coach or another player spoke to him. His replies were generally monosyllabic if he spoke at all. Often, he'd simply grunt.

Wes was an excellent listener but taciturn to the extreme.

To aid his understanding, Jake had Barbara pull Wesley's file and bring it in. Of necessity, it went to the bottom of the stack while Jake went to war with the myriad of junk on his desk.

Not until after practice did he have an opportunity to peek into Wesley's scholastic records. He was majoring in chemical engineering and maintained a 3.28 in his electives. His GPA in required classes was not impressive. That spoke volumes. His father was a minister.

"I'd like to meet him," Jake muttered to himself.

He'd had a soft spot in his heart for ministers since his New Britain days.

Every day, he'd pull out his wallet to scrape the slimy green mold off. He did all he could to keep the moisture from getting to it, but the relentless rain and humid air defeated his every attempt. After three weeks, the seams rotted away, and the only bit of his personal property was reduced to disarticulated leather.

He had no money, of course, but he had his military ID and a picture of his girlfriend.

Her name was Nancy Ripley, a perky blonde coed who enjoyed dancing to Miller, Jimmy, Tommy, and especially Goodman. Jake, on his *best* days, danced like a wounded moose. Fortunately, Nancy liked him for himself and not his rhythmic dexterity. She made him laugh. She made him feel special. He thought (and hoped) he did the same for her.

Her picture disintegrated in the hellish New Britain environment. The pieces were scattered on the jungle floor together with what remained of his rotted wallet. His only remaining ID were his dog tags.

By the time Jake could write and send a letter, he was presumed dead—swallowed by the mud and muck of New Britain. Then there was that bone-rattling bout with malaria. He did write from the Australian hospital. If Nancy replied, the letter never caught up with him.

When he was transferred to Parris Island, Nancy had disappeared. He found out, years later, that she married an accountant and lived somewhere in Ohio.

Ministers, ah, yes! Jake refocused.

On New Britain, in Australia, and on the troop ship home, the one constant was the clergy he consulted. They provided for the men's spiritual needs, of course, but they were the only officers Jake could talk to about anything. They discussed *War and Peace*, for example. They commiserated about the loss of personal property (wallets and photos), griped about chow (what little there was), and the futility of jungle fighting. These men of the cloth never betrayed his confidence.

Occasionally, they touched on spiritual matters, but until he met Betsy, his religious beliefs were, well, confused. However, ministers *ministered*. They didn't belittle or criticize. Even during his DI days, when he was yelling with the best of them and literally kicking brainless kids in the ass, he turned to the only officers in whom he could confide. They did him a world of good.

In fact, Jake would rather speak with the Reverend Jordan than the man's son. Wes, when shorn of his football talent, was an unknown. If he resented Jake's prying into his personal affairs, the Black Student Union problem could blow up in his face. On the other hand, nosing around among his teammates for information about Jordan was spying, the very thing he promised *not* to do.

Jake Oats felt very alone and very vulnerable.

On the Road *Again*

It took two games for the staff to settle the issue of sideline phones.

Jake had only been on phones two seasons. Both were high above the action in the coaches' booth. He didn't feel comfortable giving advice to the troops from so far above the cacophony on the sidelines. As a head coach, he refused to have anyone yelling in his ear or, worse, informing him of things he observed for himself. Therefore, he remained aloof from the staff's struggle. They were too professional to argue or bicker, but plenary sessions frequently became spirited.

The matter was resolved without Jake being forced to lower the proverbial boom.

Gus wanted to be in the box where he could get a good view of the coverage packages of both teams. He allowed Coach Thorne to call the defensive coverages and stunts unless Gus gave a direct order from on high. If he observed a weakness in the opposition's deployment, he'd nudge Pink, sitting beside him, who would pass the word along.

Pink would attend the opponent's defense, but he observed only. Joe would be on the sidelines. He was the coordinator. It was Joe's job to call the play. Pink would make suggestions only when he noticed something exploitable.

Joe, wearing a headset, would follow the line of scrimmage from the box. There were limits beyond which coaches and players were not allowed to wander, though this was seldom *strictly* enforced. As a career line coach, he preferred to bully his way up and down field. He *almost* never called a pass play on first down, holding that ace up his sleeve until exactly the right opportunity.

Jake would position himself near Joe when on offense and near Dave Thorne when the opponents had the ball. He'd stand stoic and remain aloof while his coaches called the game. He had the power to overrule them, but he resisted the temptation—mostly. There is nothing more demoralizing to a team than the coaches bickering among themselves. If he thought either Joe or Dave botched a call, he'd make a mental note and bring it up at a coaches' meeting.

He hired his staff as much for their judgment as for their training skills. There's more than one way to skin a pigskin. Just because it wasn't Jake's way did not ipso facto make it a "bungle."

One thing that was *not* subject to debate was the scouting duties.

Since the staff would have, at least, three game films from their opponents, there was little need for a scout to take copious notes or make tedious drawings of formations. However, a scout could measure certain intangibles: the team spirit, the level of discipline, clock management, and obvious "tells" in formations, stunts, and shifts.

When Churchill was available (the first four games of the season), he scouted the opponent three weeks ahead. Mike Perry attended the game of the opponent two weeks out. Miller, the want-to-be coach of all positions, was dispatched to watch the next opponent. They got transportation, lodging, and one meal a day. It was like a mini vacation. The young men got to travel and see a game gratis. If it rained, snowed, or gusted, they'd be in the press box.

"It's a tough job," Churchill pontificated. "Somebody's gotta do it." The huge grin on his face betrayed his true sentiment.

Jake looked back fondly on those early days when, as junior man on the totem pole, he was dispatched to an opponent's bailiwick. There was no pressure, no stress, and no one barking orders.

Churchill and Thorne had seen Michigan State play. Churchill got to see State's opener against Illinois. Thorne flew back to Georgia to watch the Spartans take on Tech. Whenever those two crossed paths in or around the coaches' cubicles, they'd slowly shake their heads. They never exchanged a word. They didn't have to. The films of both games spoke loudly enough.

Michigan State sputtered and stumbled their first two games, but they won because they had superior speed, talent, and team unity. They also had a top-of-the-line coaching staff.

Duffy Daugherty had four national championships under his belt. He had *eight* assistant coaches. Additionally, he had a deep talent pool. This contest might be as embarrassing as—don't even think about—Georgia!

⎯⎯⎯•⎯⎯⎯

The team was staying near enough East Lansing to be considered "in town." There was no pool. In fact, the team was booked in the same hotel as transplanted alumni who were unfortunate enough to live within driving distance. These loyal fans, ranging in age from late twenties to retirement age, were undoubtedly booked into the team's hotel by Mieko. Jake suspected she'd cut some package deal with the hostelry so the team wouldn't be forced to sleep in enemy territory. He was curious but decided the matter was best left uninvestigated.

Fred Shaw was a real trooper. This was his second long flight in three weeks. He was a nervous Nellie still, but he kept himself diverted unless the aircraft encountered turbulence. There were episodes during the flight when Shaw was left alone in his seat for three or four minutes at a time. Jake kept an eye on him, but the young man never freaked out.

Michigan State had a practice field. Jake and the gang were allowed the use of it. Unlike Georgia, where spies were sent out to monitor the team workout, MSU officials needn't bother. Had they the inclination, they could sit back on the modest bleachers on either side of the fifty-yard line and spy openly. As in Georgia, there was nothing to see other than a team running around in sweats and practicing punts, kickoffs, and kick returns. If any scout discovered anything they hadn't learned from the game films, they were prized dumbasses.

The bus disgorged the team. They rushed out onto the field for calisthenics and several minutes of stretching and pitch-and-catch. The

Spartans, also in sweats and helmets, were leaving the field as Jake's team entered. From around the far side of the field came a man in a green windbreaker and cap. Even from a distance, Jake had no problem recognizing Duffy "Four National Championships" Daugherty. He looked like Farmer John strolling across a wheat field. This man needn't put on airs. His accomplishments did all his boasting for him.

He waved to Jake, whose heart skipped a beat—maybe two. Here was one of the greatest coaches who ever lived; he waved as if they were long-lost war buddies. Jake remained where he was. There was a slender chance Duffy would stop for a chat. Jake wasn't about to throw away a chance at a scrapbook moment.

A bevy of young women, some in shorts and some in sweatpants, appeared from parts unknown and began jogging after Coach Duffy. They didn't brandish pom-poms, but their function was betrayed by their gait. These were athletes. They were nimble, spry, and they trotted with a purposeful spring.

Duffy won the race by several seconds. He firmly shook Jake's hand and greeted him. "Welcome, Coach. Is this like you remember it?"

Jake, slightly stunned by the informality of an icon, shook his head. "It's all changed since the war, Coach," he informed. "I don't recognize anything."

"Yeah. No more leather helmets, no more high-top shoes, no more watermelon-shaped footballs. The game has grown up so much. It's a damned shame."

Before Jake could articulate a response, the cheer squad surrounded them. They pretended to want to say hello. Well, why not? Duffy may not be Tom Jones, but in football circles, he was infinitely more famous.

The ambush didn't surprise Coach Daugherty one iota. He was a people person. Jake imagined him as the quiet, unassuming Elwood P. Dowd, a man pleased to be with whomever he was.

"Ladies, be good hosts and welcome Coach Oats."

Eight shining faces focused on Jake. He was treated to a collection of salutations, all of them friendly.

"Oats is a Wolverine," Daugherty announced.

There was a low chorus of boos, but the expressions on the young women's faces lacked any sign of hostility.

"Careful, ladies. Coach Oats is a very dangerous man. He's come all the way out here to show us how they play football back in his territory. It ain't pretty."

"Certainly not as pretty as the present company," Jake inserted.

"See that?" Duffy chuckled. "He's trying to turn you against us, and the game ain't even started. Want to help settle his hash?"

"Sure!"

It was a tallish brunette who spoke. None of her teammates lodged an objection.

"Well, when Coach leads his team onto the field tomorrow, you all rush over and hug him and kiss him. His wife will hear about it. The poor man won't dare go home. We can keep him here and make a *real* coach out of him."

This did not fetch a roar of approval, but it initiated an innocuous little laugh. Jake felt his face redden. Duffy and his entourage either didn't notice or pretended not to notice. He was grateful for that.

They exchanged a few more pleasantries before Duffy and Jake parted with another firm handshake.

Despite himself, Jake could not help but feel blessed. *If only the boys on New Britain could see this!*

Jake gained a precious memory. It was enough to erase a few of those New Britain recollections. Two minutes with Duffy was worth the trip. It was best not to dwell on the game. The morrow would arrive soon enough.

Later at the hotel, Jake realized Duffy arranged for the yell squad to join him in a plot to deliberately embarrass the neophyte. There was no advantage to be gained by it. If Duffy thought he could put an entire team off by needling their coach, he was an idiot. Duffy Daugherty was *not* an idiot! If Jake was used as a foil, a means of amusement, he took no offense. Four national championships afforded a person liberties that, when practiced by lesser men, would be an inexcusable affront.

The game took the regulation sixty minutes. The contest lasted for less than half that time. Jake's team was tenacious for twenty minutes, but the edge was lost under the relentless onslaught of superior players and superior execution. The offense, hitherto Jake's pride, sputtered and coughed like an old steam-powered automobile. It mounted only one sustained drive, which failed to produce points.

The defense was subjected to a remorseless pounding by bigger, faster, stronger combatants. Duffy's run game was a study in precision, and the expert passes of the quarterback defied textbook coverage through pinpoint accuracy. Jake, Gus, and Dave shouted, screamed, and cursed. However, one cannot ridicule one's team when the opposing team was perfect. The coaches could only curse the darkness.

They accounted for fourteen anemic points. One TD came after a Spartan fumble on their own thirty-two-yard line. The other was the result of a botched punt, an alert Jeff Foote scarfed up just before it dribbled out of bounds. The Spartans, expecting the ball to go out of play, were surprised when the former quarterback ran, unmolested, for an eighteen-yard return to the Michigan State twenty-four. From there it was Evans right and Evans left until, against all the football gods, Billy Morris ran it in from seven yards out on a middle trap. Defenses don't get trapped near their own goal line! However, Joe was paying close attention. When he detected a flaw, he kept it in his pocket until just the right moment.

Doubtless, it was Duffy's turn to be embarrassed. However, he could afford it.

Michigan State won, 31 to 14. It could have been (perhaps should have been) much worse.

Mason Greig, the left defensive tackle, had tears in his eyes when he met Jake and Gus just outside the locker room door.

"Coach, I…I couldn't have played any harder!"

"I know, son," Gus replied, grabbing him by the shoulder pads. "I appreciate that. We all do."

"You did all you could," Jake seconded. "We've no right to demand more than that."

Greig, defeated but partially consoled, hid his face to mask his tears.

***

It was a somber group that gathered for brunch the following morning. The conversations were whispered, even among the coaches at the head table. There was no detectable tension, but a solemn quiet had descended, and everyone was loathe to break it.

From brunch to the bus, to the airport, and aboard the charter plane. The cabin crew were flummoxed. The two women and one young man were familiar enough with team charters, but there was something not quite right about this one. It was as if one of their number had died, and his remains were assigned to the cargo hold.

Jake didn't like it.

They'd been outplayed and outcoached, but young players were resilient. They mourned a loss, but they didn't carry their sorrow to extremes. Jake wondered if a coach had ever been fired after only three games. It may have happened. Still, being trapped in a mausoleum was beyond his endurance. His main concern was for the team. Would they be able to finish the season, or would it dissolve? Teams had been destroyed by tragic accidents, but he knew of none that simply evaporated.

He wasn't concerned about Betsy and Liisi. They'd stand by him and support him, emotionally at least, no matter what lay ahead. His heart ached, however, for these young men he'd come to love.

Gary Black, the second-string fullback, had played only on the extra-point team. Therefore, he was on the field but twice in East Lansing. He occupied an aisle seat and looked as crestfallen as any of his teammates. He shifted in his seat in a struggle to find any posture that would afford a modicum of comfort. He wore a perpetual scowl. The reserve defensive back, Herb Okino, leaned against the window trying to sleep and attempting to keep aloof from Black's thrashing around.

One of the stewardesses trotted up the aisle. She might have been on an errand. Just as likely, she intended to shelter in the galley as a relief from the eerie silence of the cabin. Gary Black felt her approach and turned to confirm his suspicions. As she passed him, he touched her tentatively on the elbow. She halted her march and attended him.

"Ma'am, I'm sorry," he said in his best Oliver Twist impersonation. "I'm really hungry."

Those within earshot scoffed at the notion. They'd eaten a copious meal only two hours before. Gary Black was not a boat rocker. He was being either grossly fatuous or inexcusably malicious. Both possibilities were beyond his character. Therefore, the reserve fullback had a small but intensely curious audience.

"We don't have any food on the plane," the young woman informed. "Peanuts? Coffee creamer? Anything?"

There was a quality in his facial expression and the tone of his voice that communicated genuine desperation.

The airline employee's maternal instincts were instantly accessed. "I'll look, but I don't think there's anything. I can bring you coffee, tea, a soda. There might be some milk. I'll be right back."

There followed some elbow nudging and similar tacit communications. Suddenly, in the disturbing quiet of the cabin, several eyes were on Gary Black, who remained oblivious to the audience.

The stewardess returned with a small carton of milk. "We only have a few jars of baby food," she stated quietly.

He took the carton and looked at it as if he'd never seen one. "I'm hungry," he repeated.

The unfortunate airline employee was struck with pity. She hurried forward, leaving Gary to look at the item in his hand as if it were a dead puppy while curiosity among his fellow passengers spiked.

The woman returned carrying a jar of baby food and a spoon. The audience increased. There wasn't a single person on the aircraft below the age of nineteen, and team curiosity swelled. The moderately attractive young woman strode with purpose and urgency. Heads turned. No few stood to get a better view.

When the woman sat on Gary's armrest and spoonfed him, they were the focus of all attention. Even the card players in back, playing more from form than skill, paused to have a peek. Gary didn't give a rat's patoot! He was hungry, and it mattered not how ridiculous the scene appeared.

Suddenly, the mood shifted. A surge flowed through the entire assembly. The hitherto despondent team was resurrected. They'd watch the film, they'd grade their performance, they'd suffer the slings and arrows of their campus chums. They'd show up the following day and practice as if they had a purpose. Well, they did. They wanted to show themselves and their institution that they were *not* dead.

Jake smiled. He wished he had a camera.

He started to make a note, only to renege. Mieko should warn future charters to have a few morsels aboard, just in case. Why compose a memo? Mieko would hear of this episode and probably from the AD himself. She was smart enough to reach a conclusion on her own.

Again, Jake arrived home after midnight. Again, Betsy waited up for him. Again, he wanted to look in on Tami before undressing.

"Is she getting any static at school?" he wanted to know.

"She doesn't say."

Once upon a time (he couldn't be precise), Tami was taunted by some mindless twerp who repeated something a father spouted about "piss-poor coaches." It was not a personal attack, but Tami considered it as such.

"You don't know my father," she scolded. "I know him very well. Don't talk about people you don't know."

Tit for tat, of course. Tami was repeating the sentiment of someone else, likely a teacher.

After relating details of this altercation, Jake and Betsy encouraged her to pay no heed to future criticisms.

"The greatest coaches in the world never coached," Jake informed her. "If people think they can do better, let them think so. You can't change their minds. You worry about Tami. I can take care of myself."

Now, of course, Tami took care of Liisi. However, she was mature above her years in her ability to suffer the slings and arrows of others. She might take exception to a personal attack, but generic complaints about "stupid coaches" were left untended.

"Did she leave me another book to read?" he asked.

Betsy snickered. "You get off easy this week," she whispered. "She left you three drawings to admire."

Homecoming

Jacob Oats had a life of football, save for a brief stint in the Marines. However, he never got a handle on the concept of homecoming, its activities, or its origins. He'd never returned to Ann Arbor; he never felt the inclination. There was nothing that could lure him back to Guadalcanal, New Britain, or Parris Island. However, he knew something about the accepted format. Specifically, homecoming games were traditionally slated a midseason or late-season contest. Finding himself confronted with early season hoopla was one more hurdle for a program struggling to find itself.

No one could explain how an early home game was selected or by whom. Perhaps the opener was the only home game Jake was expected to win. Faced with a disastrous season and the basketball team facing equally bleak prospects, the powers decided to schedule all the pageantry and silliness on the one week when a happy ending was likely.

The Black Student Union lingered on the fringes. Jake looked up Milt Spurling in the newly published *Hall's Guide* to discover that enigmatic personage lived in a *real* residence—well, his mailing address at least was real. This made the BSU slightly less sinister, but he feared Spurling's crew might be organizing a splash. During homecoming week, any disturbance would be guaranteed acres of publicity. On the other hand, if they played their cards too soon and their exhibition was lost in the myriad of festive displays and activities, the BSU would lose both face and luster.

Well, whatever happened would happen. Jake, his coaches, and his team had a more pressing agenda. Speaking from experience, Jake enjoyed spoiling another team's homecoming. From accumulated evidence over the years, he knew most coaches enjoyed a special surge of energy from "pooping in someone else's punchbowl." It was petty and childish, but it was both real and pronounced. Jake and his team must be alert to avoid ambush.

"Is Lynn ready?"

Joe looked at Pink, who, in turn, looked at Mike Perry. It was as if Jake spoke in Urdu. In that pregnant pause, Jake made a command decision.

"When we practice field goals and PATs, Lynn will do the kicking. Capp will handle kickoffs still—for the time being."

No one made any comment.

"Davidson?"

Jake's question was directed at Gus, who did not defer to either Miller or Thorne.

"He's solid. Make him a wild man."

Gus liked to have different wild men for each game just to confound the scouts. Davidson would line up as always, but he'd fly to the ball rather than run a lane. There was a second wild man on the other side of the kicker. Being designated a wild man was an honor.

Jake nodded. "Hustler?"

Tough choice. This selection must be based on effort alone since no offensive player excelled in anything against the Spartans.

"Dilley," Joe announced.

No one objected.

The center had proved as constant as the North Star. He didn't bury anyone or roll a mighty linebacker, but he'd worked like fury on his blocking assignments. He'd made no obvious mistakes.

"Hard rock?"

"Black," Thorne piped up.

The man hadn't been at the game, but he'd seen the films.

Miller may have had another candidate, but he hung fire. Leland Black (not to be confused with the baby food addict), didn't play the entire game, but he caused confusion in inverse proportion to his size. It was Black who first caught Jake's attention with his goal line antics. He was quick and fearless.

Jake sensed a discussion was about to break out. He stifled it.

"Moving on, I want to add fifty-four and fifty-five to the list this week. I want them on short yardage especially. That gives us two lead blockers."

Normally, he hated these plays. They took forever to develop, and the line must hold their blocks forever. In practice, however, and against the scout defense, the holes were *huge*!

"Cover three is a disaster, Gus. The guys aren't quick enough to react, and we don't have the speed. Use cover five instead. I know what you're going to say, but no more cover three unless we can do it properly. If you need to tweak your packages, do it."

That left it up to Gus. If they worked hard in practice and brought cover three back to respectability, they'd put it back into the game plan. Jake, however, didn't expect miracles. However, he would not bet against Gus making a silk purse.

⬤•⬤

"Like basketball, gentlemen," Gus reminded during film study. "Stay with your man!"

It was so simple. Of course, there was nothing simple about it. The whole idea behind multiple and whack-a-doodle offensive sets was to confuse the defense, to catch someone out of position and exploit the weakness. These poor fellows, inheritors of a proud football pedigree, were little more than a sandlot team. NCAA probation and poor recruiting coupled with lackluster coaching left Jake's next opponent with little more than gimmicks and the gridiron equivalent of sleight of hand. They were dangerous because of their unpredictability.

Evy could have molded them into a fighting force. The current staff had neither Evy's guts, daring, nor his imagination. Despite unbalanced lines, tackle (even guard) eligible, empty backfield, double wings, trips formations, and general free-for-all, this team (or *any* team) would run, pass, or kick. The job of Gus and his underlings was to thwart them.

After forty-five minutes of watching their opponent's offensive circus, Gus turned off the projector and marched to the light switch. There was a stunned silence. The myriad of offensive sets and plays had them wired. The defenders were bewildered and slightly panicky. Digesting the endless supply of variations, the defenders felt like they were cramming for an examination for a course they weren't enrolled.

"When in doubt," Gus reiterated, "stay with the man you've been butting heads with. These guys lined up in punt formation on first down. We will assume they will not punt. If anybody drops back to receive, I'll have you running laps until graduation. If they do punt, we will all gather around the ball until it stops rolling and the ref whistles it dead, but don't make plans. Their entire offense is designed to confuse you. Tackle the guy with the ball, rush the passer, cover the receivers—just as you always do."

This simple dictum was the bulk of their defensive preparation.

Jake called it the KISS formula: Keep It Simple, Stupid. Staying with your man was as simple as a thing could be.

Gus and Dave worked hard to produce an offensive playbook for the scout team. They used grease pencils to draw up formations and plays. There were only a dozen plays in the enemy's repertoire, but they were run from two dozen formations.

The most oft repeated plays were drawn up on document protectors and placed in a large ringed binder. Dave Thorne would select a play, flip to that page, and hold it up so the members of the scout team knew their assignments. The quarterback announced the snap count; the scouts would sprint up to the line and run the play. This was a three-quarter speed drill. The purpose was to recognize and react. Full-speed tackling and pursuit were consigned to the drills leading up to the mock scrimmage.

Gus and Dave threw every piece of garbage they could draw up at the starting D. By the close of practice Wednesday, the defense was no longer baffled or nervous. The "stay with your man" doctrine provided a solid base. From there it was read and react—just as it always was.

For Joe and his assistants, it was polish, polish, polish. If the offense botched a play, run it again—and again and again. Blocking was always and ever the key to a successful play. As the line coach, Joe focused on his starting five (six, counting the tight end).

During a spirited scrimmage against the starting defense, Joe's offense broke the huddle and sprinted to the line. Gus called a defensive set requiring the offense to employ alternate blocking rules.

"Red Bluff," Dennis Swofford, the strong-side tackle, announced in a conversational tone.

Joe blew the whistle and sprinted to Mr. Casual. "What the hell was that? Swofford, do you know how many people will be in the stands Saturday?"

"Yeah, I was just telling Rush."

For want of a conjunction, an argument was lost. However, a spirited scrimmage was interrupted when the offensive and defensive units shook with laughter. Even the furious Joe Epps could not suppress a smile. He bellowed like a wounded buffalo, but he couldn't make his countenance match his words.

"Yell out the line call! Don't whisper it. Your tight end must hear you! Huddle up and call it again."

When Swofford and Rush, the tight end, approached the line of scrimmage, they were confronted with the same defensive alignment.

"*Red bluff!*"

Swofford's bellow could be heard on the tennis courts a quarter of a mile away.

Even the perennial fault-finding Joe Epps could find no fault with that line call.

———•◦•———

Betsy was ecstatic. She procured two tickets to the Dionne Warwick concert on homecoming Saturday evening. She knew her husband was a fan. She also knew her husband was *never* placid after a game—even after a win. Hope springs eternal, however, and Betsy had high hopes.

Jake genuinely wanted to attend the performance. It would be held in the basketball arena, just a few dozen steps from Jake's lair. However, the duties of office beckoned.

Betsy was momentarily despondent.

"Tami, would you like to go?"

Tami (Liisi at school only) was excited in the extreme. To see Dionne Warwick in person *and* to hear her perform! It was rare, baring illness, for Tami not to eat. At the dinner table that evening, however, her indefatigable babbling was so intense that most of her meal was consigned to the fridge. She might regain her appetite over time. Betsy hoped she would, but Tami was, well, *Tami*.

———•·•———

"Line 3," Barbara announced.

Jake groaned. His standing order that morning was no calls unless they were "super" important. Barbara had exercised excellent judgment so far. If she slipped this time, there would be words.

"Oats!" he barked into his receiver.

"It ain't Oats, it's Ots, and you're a damned hard man to get hold of."

"And who the hell are you?" Jake demanded.

"Harman, you sorry bastard. Got so big in your britches you can't remember a teammate?"

Jake was momentarily flummoxed. He hardly recognized the voice, but Tom's personality was instantly identified. "Tom! Great to hear from you. I ain't heard about you since you got shot down."

There was a warning sound on the other end of the line.

"The less said about that, the better. I just wanted to have a quick chat. I don't know if I'll have the chance to visit when I'm up there."

"You…you're coming to town? If I'd known, I'd roll out the red carpet."

"Get with the program, Jake. I'm announcing the game. Don't tell me you didn't know about my gig."

It was an "oh, damn" moment. Of course, Jake knew his former teammate was the radio voice of this week's opponent. In all the fuss and worry, it never entered his thick head.

"I don't want to insult you, ol' buddy, but it slipped my mind in all the excitement."

Tom laughed. "Well, I wish you luck, Jake. It's treason, I know, but this team is in a rebuilding phase. I'm rooting for them, of course, but I'm not stupid. Congratulations on the job, fella. Your school hired a good man. Whatever happens Saturday, I'm pulling for you."

"Thanks, Tom. I appreciate that. I hope I'll have chance to see you. I'd like to buy you a drink—or two."

"May have to take a rain check, pal. Still, I'll hold you to it whenever we do get together."

There were a few other exchange of sentiments before they were both forced to conclude.

"Do you know who that was?" he asked of Barbara.

"You bet I did," she responded, not looking up from her work. "Do you think I'd bother you for a mere peasant?"

— • —

Jake stepped out for a surreptitious, post-game meal. He didn't need much. He didn't expect much. Not much was exactly what he got. One really had to know where to go after a homecoming game if one intended to remain incognito.

Doubtless he was recognized, but the girl behind the counter and the two people seated near the cash register apparently considered him either an apparition or a look-alike. His anonymity was further advanced by being "escorted" by a member of the homecoming court. It was JoDell Lessing (the third spelling of the name he'd encountered *and*, this time, the correct one). So long as she was near him, no one paid attention to Jake.

They were kindred spirits—refugees more like. JoDell was enticed to the school by a scholarship offer as a cheerleader. It offered her a full year's tuition, so she attended summer school to get greatest advantage.

After her stint in rah-rah, she stayed on to study pharmacy while dabbling in pastels and oil painting. She came from Resume Speed, a pioneer agricultural town several miles up the valley. It was, once upon a time, a boom town. The Depression left it a mere shadow of its former glory. Currently, the population consisted of three Lessing families and a dozen other families loosely related to each other that settled in after World War II.

Being selected for the homecoming court was "an honor she dreamed not of," to quote someone famous. She didn't mind the cheering and the acrobatics of the yell squad because she was earning room, board, and "free" classes. Riding around the field during halftime in an open-air Caddy with another princess was blissfully short and, therefore, tolerable. The fuss and feathers of the homecoming activities, however, proved too daunting for a small-town girl. She had a date for the homecoming dance and the concert, but her beau, a sociology student, learned a brutal botany lesson after wrestling with poison oak one afternoon.

No concert and dance for him—or much else for several additional days.

Because of Dionne Warwick, the homecoming dance was Friday night. Jake's players were bussed to their out-of-town hideaway at ten thirty. Well, they enjoyed part of the dance. Instead of their travel uniforms, the players checked in to the motel in suits and ties. For cocoa, they discarded their ties and jackets.

JoDell turned down an alternative dance invitation because she was wading through a mountain of organic chemistry. She and a sorority sister planned to attend the concert in mufti. Meanwhile, she opted to slip away during the post-game hoopla.

She was lurking about the parking lot when Jake attempted his breakout. All she wanted was a light meal and a few minutes of relative calm.

She recognized Jake. They were two people who shared a single thought.

Thus, Jake and JoDell, both fashionably attired, sauntered into a hole-in-the-wall deli. Jake, despite the young woman's protests, offered to buy. JoDell ordered a ham on rye. Jake opted for chopped liver on rye.

"Have you tasted our chopped liver?" the coed hire asked.

"No."

"Would you like to taste it before you order?"

"No."

The flustered attendant motioned to JoDell. "Would you like her to taste it? She can tell you."

"No."

If Jake didn't have a conference with Joe Epps in the offing, he'd have laughed. Well, he and Betsy would laugh about it later. For the moment, he wanted to eat and move on.

They sat together and consumed their sandwiches and coffee.

"I understand why she tried to warn me off," Jake admitted.

They enjoyed a muted conversation lasting nearly twenty minutes. He drove her by the sorority house and dropped her off. He wondered if there'd be rumors about the coach and a homecoming princess. Doubtless, the school paper would make hay if word got out. Jake didn't give a rat's patoot. Betsy knew him too well to put stock in campus scandalmongering. JoDell, however, might suffer. Well, she didn't seem worried. Typically, small-town girls were resilient and able to look after themselves.

When he returned to the arena, the reserved parking lot was nearly empty.

He was worried about the meeting with Joe. He was the man who replaced Agee when Evy "stole" him away. It mattered not that Joe Epps was possibly the premier line coach in the country. Jake was lucky to get him. Agee was a close friend and a good coach. He regretted not seeing him when Iowa came to town.

Jake heard rumors that Agee was not happy at Iowa.

Damn!

On his desk were three sheets of neatly typed paper. Barbara didn't work on Saturday. Jake hoped that whoever typed these pages hadn't used Barbara's machine. He didn't want to go through that again!

He examined them quickly.

54 power

	Attempts	yards gained
Shaw	5	42
Gino	2	11

55 power

Morris	3	14
Hackett	1	17

He flipped the page.

56 Pass

Rush	2	22
Shaw	2	18
Gino	1	12

52 Pass

Capp	3	47
Morris	3	58

He flipped the page and found the complete game stats, offense and defense.

There could be no doubt, the offense clicked. The defense needed fine-tuning and perhaps some major adjustments. However, it was a very satisfactory win. The euphoria, however, was tempered by the quality of the competition.

Joe arrived stripped for action. He wore a yellow shirt, tan slacks, and black shoes. By community standards, he was casually togged. By post-game standards, he was formal. He didn't offer a salutation; he took the hot seat. Joe did not cross his legs. Instead, he leaned forward as if confronting a high wind.

"Is there a coup attempt afoot, Joe?"

"Coach, you can't believe that. This was not planned. I should have consulted with you, but, well, in the heat of battle, things happen."

"Peck is a sophomore," Jake reminded.

"He's smart, Coach," Joe responded. "He made two obvious errors—"

"Don't I know!"

"Damn it, Coach. Three-year starters will make two mistakes a game. Sometimes they make more."

"When you cooked this up, you didn't see the need to keep me in the loop."

There it was. Jake's team had three audibles: 90 (split end), 70 (tight end), and 80 (slot or flanker). Each was a quick inside slant called only when the defensive alignments were exactly wrong. Peck called 90 against Georgia, the one Capp dropped. Since then, no similar situation presented itself.

"It was field expediency," Joe responded.

A military term. Momentarily, Jake's mind snapped back to the knee-deep mud of New Britain.

"Keep talking," Jake commanded.

"Dave was upset because they lined up to defend the play I sent in. My fault, I'm sure. They scouted us well. They threw down-and-distance up against what I've been calling."

Jake looked at the stat sheet again. "Evans gained a hundred and twenty yards," he observed. "Doesn't look like it did them much good."

"It rattled Peck," Joe announced. "He doesn't like running plays against a stacked defense."

Jake said nothing. This was Joe's doing; it was his job to explain.

Joe cleared his throat. "We agreed that I'd send in the play, as always. Dave would do *check with me* in the huddle. If it was there, he'd run the play. If not, he'd check off."

Jake took a deep breath. In the heat of battle, the sidelines were chaotic at the best of times. It's possible that the offensive coordinator and the quarterback might initiate an on-the-spot correction, but damn! Jake was the coach; he had a right to know what his team was doing.

"I don't want a sophomore calling plays!"

Joe did not say, "Read you loud and clear." His facial expression left no doubt he was not a mutineer.

"Dave, Fred, and I meet twice a week," Joe began, pushing his luck. "We cover everything from A to Zed, Coach. I encourage them to discuss things, make suggestions."

"New coaches, new system, new ideas. Joe, until we *all* have the *same* amount of experience, we stay on book."

Joe nodded. He didn't like it, but he knew who was boss. He'd do things by the book. He would, at least, until the *next* time. When that next time arrived, he'd make certain Jake knew immediately. Jake must maintain veto power.

They were satisfied with this tacit compromise.

After Joe left, Jake breathed a sigh of relief.

He called Betsy. She and Tami were excitedly preparing for the concert.

"Have you eaten?"

"I grabbed a bite at a deli with one of the homecoming court."

"Careful, Jake."

"I was," he promised. "She sat in my lap, but I made her behave herself."

Betsy laughed. A solid victory at home was uplifting. It was far better than the funk that followed a home loss. Betsy and Jake liked exchanging jests.

"Enjoy the show," Jake said.

"We'll come by your office after," Betsy promised. "If you're not in, we will see you here. Of course, if we meet a couple good-looking boys…"

Jake smiled.

❖

Mieko was sitting in the lobby of a TV station waiting for the film to be developed. She'd miss the concert. Jake felt bad about that. Doubtless, Mieko could have asked someone else to take the film up and bring it back. However, responsibility was her defining characteristic. It was *her* job. She considered it a betrayal of her culture and upbringing to leave *her* job to someone else.

Gus was watching film of their next opponent. Jake sat with him and watched in silence as Gus dissected the other team frame by frame. He made a few mental notes. He'd expect to see or hear these items later in the scouting report. If he didn't, he and Gus would have a chat.

Joe and Pink were studying a second film. Churchill was with them. He could hear him making salient comments from time to time. Joe and Pink also exchanged comments, but their voices were softer and indecipherable from a distance. Jake was tempted to go in and look over their shoulders but opted out. He'd leaned on Joe enough. He didn't want his offensive coordinator to think he was being evaluated.

When Jake returned to his desk to draw up a tentative agenda for the Tuesday practice, he found one of the lights on his phone flashing. It was the AD's line. Some fan or prank caller likely. No sane person would call the AD or the ticket office after business hours *and* on a Saturday. He paid it no attention.

They worked and studied. The amplified sound from the stage was more a serenade than a distraction. The whispered comments in the film rooms graduated to nudges and nods. The staff was listening to the concert as they worked. It wasn't as satisfying as being in the audience, but their auditory receptors were well satiated.

Jake would pop in, stay a few minutes, move on to the other film group, stay a few minutes, and return to his desk. The concert, including intermission, lasted a shade over ninety minutes. As the packed arena emptied, Jake made a command decision.

"Let's break this up," he announced.

"Almost finished," Ostrander reported.

"Enough for tonight, Pink. I want you fresh and alert when we view the film tomorrow."

"Round the horn?" Joe suggested.

Jake braced only momentarily. If it would ease Joe's mind, there could be no harm. Additionally, it would take only a moment.

"Okay," he agreed.

"Church?"

"Lynn: four for four PATs and two for two field-goals, one from thirty-seven yards."

"Pink?"

"The backfield performed well, both rushing and blocking."

"Joe?"

"Fifty-eight pass was tight. Peck came to run and made positive yards when he didn't have a receiver."

Only positive comments were allowed during an all-hands meeting. The rollout to the left needed work. Peck had problems getting his shoulders square, making both his passes and running less effective. Jake made a note earlier. This issue must be addressed.

"Dave?"

"Our coverage packages were much better. We're getting much stronger there."

The "bad guests" still scored fourteen points. Pass coverage, despite improvements, remained spotty.

"Gus?"

"They expected us to call a time-out when they shifted into that double spread," he gloated. "The stay-with-your-man rule negated that. The defense reacted instantly, and we shut that trick play down cold."

"Davidson as a wild man worked well," Jake contributed. "Let's keep him there for next week."

"Okay," Joe said, clapping his hands schoolmarm fashion. "Clean up your trash and go home."

Jake did not go home. He waited for Betsy and Tami. They each gave Jake a congratulatory hug before gushing about the concert.

"I heard most of it," Jake informed. "It sounded great."

Betsy drove them home. Jake had misgivings about leaving his car at the arena overnight, but the joy of returning home together cancelled his concerns. It was as near normal as he was likely to experience during the season.

Stale Beer

Betsy was more than happy to drive her husband to work. Indeed, she initiated a hat trick. She and Tami dressed for church. After dropping Jake off, mother and daughter enjoyed a leisurely breakfast at the premier pancake house before attending services. Those few schoolmates who attended Lutheran services were flummoxed by Tami's double identity. They accepted her as an eccentric, and they refrained from mocking or ostracizing her.

There was work, correspondence, chalk talks, and plotting out a tentative Tuesday practice schedule. When the team arrived, they reviewed and graded the film. They did their traditional workout in sweats and helmets. The players were excited about the one o'clock dispersal. It was the first afternoon and evening the men enjoyed since the season began. Most retired to apartments, dorms, or fraternities to watch pro football and college football highlights. A few headed for beer joints, aware that they were recognized by all and sundry. This took a considerable edge off any boisterousness or rowdy tendencies. It also moderated their alcohol consumption. They knew Jake was a man of his word. He promised to lower the boom should anyone violate social or civil expectations. No one was anxious to experience the lowering of the boom.

The coaches adjourned to a bar and grill where they enjoyed a light lunch and even lighter conversation. By the terms of a tacit treaty, they avoided any mention of football. Even the most dedicated coach needs a break, however brief. Off-color topics and language were discouraged. Nevertheless, the conversation around a large table was muted. Any casual observer might find these quiet conclaves reeking with conspiracy.

Back at base, the coaches put together a five-page scouting report. Jake reviewed all the submissions, edited them as needed, "neatenized" them (Holly speak), and placed them on Barbara's desk. She'd type it up, mimeograph it, collate the pages, and staple them.

Jake discovered, weeks later, that any diagrams included with the text were meticulously drawn by Mieko. For her, the term *work-study* was highly abused. Eventually, Jake would lobby for a modest stipend on her behalf, without caring what the NCAA had to say.

⎯⎯⎯•⎯⎯⎯

Jake arrived during the traditional morning break. He met briefly with the Athletic Council and, even more briefly, the Academic Board. Every player maintained acceptable academic performance, though a couple were flirting with a warning. It was early in the term, but Jake made certain his players, particularly sophomores, got extra help when needed.

He headed first for the coffee room. The AD, Steve Thompson, Barbara, and a few other employees Jake recognized by sight were gathered around a large round table enjoying a midmorning boost. Denise was immersed in a recitation. As per custom, she stood when Jake entered.

"At ease," he said, half in jest and half in admonishment.

She did not "at ease." She remained standing while Jake took a clean mug and filled it.

"I came by the office, I don't know why, and the phone was ringing," she reported. "I was here for the concert, but the phone kept ringing. I thought that was weird."

"I wondered about that too," Jake volunteered. "I was in my office and saw the light flashing."

Denise was put off only momentarily. "Well, I had my key with me. So I went in. I was really curious why anyone would be calling in the middle of the night."

She let it hang there. She was watching Jake. He intended to take his coffee to his office, but he got the feeling Denise was waiting for him to make a comment. He eased her mind by taking a seat next to Ralph.

"I picked up the phone. It was Dionne Warwick's mother. She wanted to know if her daughter got here safely."

"*Jesus!*"

Immediately, Jake's mind thought that someone *claiming* to be the star's mother had called. A moment later, he considered what action he'd employ if Tami were roaming in faraway places. Betsy, well, all bets were off with her.

"Dr. Pauling and Dionne Warwick," he said. "You're becoming quite a celebrity magnet."

He killed the conversation. He realized it too late.

"Where's Mieko?" he asked in self-defense.

"In class," Denise reported.

"When does she have time for classes?"

"When does she have time for sleep?" Barbara wondered.

Jake rose and set off for work. "I thought I was the only insomniac around here," he said upon parting.

"*Jesus!*"

Steve Thompson, Jake decided, was due for vocabulary enhancement.

⸺•⸺

They flew down for the second conference game. It looked like a toss-up until the teams took to the field. Jake noticed it even before the kickoff. There was no *there* there. The grammatical gymnastics of the previous sentence is predicated by the dearth of tangible (or even spiritual) resources. As Jake paced the sidelines, he grew more and more dissatisfied. If he'd paid to see the game, he'd demand his money back.

What did the team do wrong? Outside of the infrequent bonehead mistakes, there was nothing out of place. The blockers blocked, the running backs ran, the defense pursued and made tackles and defended passes. Nevertheless, it was like ordering strong coffee and getting green tea. There's nothing tragic about it, but when a person wants coffee, green tea won't do.

Jake stoked momentarily when the team scored the go-ahead TD late in the contest. Peck connected with Capp on a rollout. The team comic fell backward into the end zone holding the ball in the air as if it were a beacon.

"This could do it," Jake muttered to himself.

His euphoria turned to terror when he noticed a tepid sideline demonstration. It was eerie!

Jake stood as stoic as a statue, watching the opposition march down the field. They scored with only seconds remaining.

30 to 27.

Jake had to face the press.

"We didn't have any schmaltz today," Jake reported.

Of course, no one, especially Jake, knew what the hell *schmaltz* was. It was, however, decidedly missing.

"I'm the coach. It's my job to diagnose the problem and fix it. I felt like I was watching a plane crash. The wings are on, the motors are running, the weather's good, the controls work, but the damn thing won't fly."

The press insisted on pinning him down. Jake entrenched himself in ambiguity.

The post-game meal was as ever. There were the normal muted conversations. The bulk of the exchanges concerned the tightening pennant races. There were a few other topics introduced and dispatched quickly. However, football, as a topic, was conspicuously missing.

Even after a loss, players exchanged anecdotes. There was always a takeaway, even if it was merely a comment made to or by an opponent. Players were ever ready to relate a particularly satisfying moment, or an embarrassing blunder, or especially a memorable hit. Jake fully expected Russ Capp to make a hyperbolic monument of his TD catch. "Mr. Nonsense," however, confined his dinner conversation to frat house high jinks.

The bus ride to the airport was normal. The boarding and takeoff were normal.

Gary Black may have been hungry, but he reclined his seat and went to sleep.

Jake was making the rounds. He talked with players, coaches, cabin attendants, Ralph, and members of his entourage. He even sat with and listened to Steve Thompson and his never-ending tales of woe. Some passengers were morose, others were taciturn, but none provided Jake with a clue. It was as if the game never happened, or if it did, it had nothing to do with them.

Alone and afraid, he wandered up the aisle toward his seat in what would have been the first-class section on a scheduled flight. He turned around to gaze upon a scene that, like the game and the meal following, radiated the day's entire atmosphere: flat as last night's beer.

It was dusk when they took off. The sky had turned black. The cabin lights were on.

Jake caught Mark Davidson's eyes. He was a fellow Marine. Why was that important? Any port in a storm perhaps?

He gestured. Mark unsnapped his seat belt and started forward. Jake proceeded up the aisle, trusting Davidson to follow.

"Coffee on?" he asked of the stewardess leaning against the counter in the galley.

In reply, she took up a paper cup and poured from a polished pot.

"Cuppa joe?" Jake asked of Davidson, who'd caught up with him.

"Yeah, I guess."

His response fit right in with the theme of the day.

"Sugar?" the stewardess asked. "Cream?"

"No thanks."

"Not for me," Mark echoed.

"Ma'am, may we squeeze in here for just a couple of minutes? I'd like to speak in private with this young man."

On a charter, FAA rules were iffy at best. Dave Peck and Billy Morris, for example, spent part of every flight in the cockpit chatting with the flight crew. Likely, there existed some officious regulation about passengers in the in-flight galley, but no FAA button poppers were aboard. The not-so-young woman respected their privacy. What could they do? Spike the coffee? Steal the creamer? Regardless, they'd hardly step outside for a chat.

She smiled, squeezed out of the closet, and trotted down the length of the mausoleum.

"Ever experienced this before?" Jake asked without preamble.

"In Nam—twice."

Apparently, Mark Davidson was all too aware of the "stale beer syndrome."

"I saw it on Guadalcanal twice." Jake nodded. "What is it?"

Davidson shrugged. "Damned if I know what to do about it. Morale seems solid enough. They played…okay."

Davidson was careful in his choice of words.

"We played like it was a practice," Davidson corrected. "It was a team polish. We did what we were supposed to, but there was no sense of urgency."

"If this hangs on, we might as well hang up our cleats and cancel the rest of the season."

Davidson sipped his coffee. It wasn't his place to give advice to the commanding officer. "Coach, whatever it is, it doesn't linger," he announced. "At least, it didn't in my experience."

"Nor mine," Jake seconded.

"It sure would be nice to win two games back-to-back," Mark said, taking a chance.

Jake grunted. "I just hope that whatever this is, it gets off our asses soon. Mark, if you hear anything—I mean, well—"

"I know what you mean, Coach. If I hear anything to explain this, I'll come see you."

"Thanks, Mark. I appreciate it."

The conversation may have ended. Mark may have returned to his seat. Jake may have put all his attention into drinking coffee without spilling it. However, one disturbing thought remained.

We should have won that game!

Resurrection

The bus from the airport pulled into the arena before eleven o'clock. That was earlier than anyone had a right to expect. Jake and his staff adjourned to the offices for a quick postmortem and to get a jump on the following week.

Their next opponent was noted for team speed. They were perennial powers, frequently listed in the top twenty teams nationwide, except for their off years when they sagged down among the top twenty-five. They'd be out for hair. For five consecutive years, this mighty program lost to the university Jake represented. They and their fans vowed to show no mercy. If they asked for the film of the game just concluded, they might as well get a head start on organizing their victory parties.

"Two hours," Jake decreed.

He was with Joe and Pink when the projector was threaded. They fast-forwarded through the initial offensive series (their upcoming foe scored quickly) to scrutinize the defense.

In an instant, Jake's lethargy evaporated. "Run that back!"

Joe obeyed.

They continued viewing until the offense was forced to punt.

"How's Dave Peck for grit?" Jake demanded.

"The only thing he fears is letting the team down," Joe assured.

Jake went to the chalkboard and drew up the offense. He used Vs for defenders. His expert fingers marked the blocking of the offensive line.

"Direct snap to Evans, right through Peck's legs. Dilley blocks the backer here, Peck blocks the backer here, and Evans has a free ride into the secondary."

"Peck ain't no blocker," Pink protested.

"He doesn't have to be," Joe assured, warming to the idea. "All he has to do is get in the way. Evans hits the hole quickly. By the time the backer sheds Peck, he's out of the play."

Pink rubbed his chin thoughtfully. "It will make them break their package," he concluded. "They might be forced to do something they don't want to."

"And," Jake added emphatically, "take them out of their game plan."

"What do we call it?" Pink asked.

"Ten," Jake replied.

"Make it a live call," Joe suggested.

He and Jake glared at each other for a long while.

"Okay," Jake agreed.

"Not *ten*," Joe objected. "If they suspect it's a live call, they'll shift into the zero hole."

"Betsy," Jake suggested.

They turned and eyed him closely.

"Any objections?" Jake challenged.

There were no objections.

After two hours, Jake asked for a few minutes more. By the time Oliver Twist got home, it was after two in the morning. As always, Betsy was up.

———•◦•———

The Black Student Union organized a demonstration in the quad with hints that it threatened a student strike day later in the term. Evans refused to allow himself to be showcased. If Wesley Jordan was approached, he declined as well. Apparently, without militant black athletes, the BSU was not ready to take on the athletic department. However, it was, as Jake well knew, only a matter of time.

Jake was petrified that the studied ennui would carry forward to the next game. He was heartened to witness a spirited practice on Tuesday. When they finished up with nine-and-in, there were two near riots. Jake thought they should use a referee to avoid future temper tantrums. It would have to be volunteer since the athletic budget was committed. Perhaps Perry and Miller, the scouting crew, could officiate. Jake dismissed this because both would be biased in favor of their respective players.

"Don't waste practice time!" Jake bellowed in one of his very few addresses during practice. "If you want to settle differences, we'll fit you with gloves and have you duke it out on the wrestling mats *after* practice!"

Even the belligerents knew tempers would cool long before a grudge match was organized. Still, to discover his players vehement about their goal line scrimmage gave Jake a much-needed injection.

Practices were technically closed. However, curious students and any passersby would stand at the open entrance of the practice field and watch for a few minutes before going about their business. Zeke Bratkowski strolled in one afternoon on his way to scout prospects elsewhere. He didn't think to inform people of his presence. He leaned against the break in the fence surrounding the practice acre in casual clothes with his hands in his pockets.

Pink, who was nearest, turned to order him away until he recognized him. "If you're spying for your alma mater, you're over a month late!" he shouted.

The former All-American and NFL quarterback laughed. He was a pro scout, not a spy.

During the nine-and-in, when everyone was in a fever pitch bordering on enmity, Joe Epps noticed the profile of a car idling in the parking lot. Two people sat in the front seats and were studying the action. Joe dispatched a manager to remind the occupants that the practice was closed. They replied with a single-digit salute accompanied by matching words.

Joe was instantly in a state of passion. Before he could get himself in trouble, the interlopers' car squealed out of the parking lot. When cooler heads prevailed, Joe suggested at training table that campus police be encouraged to monitor the practice area more frequently on Tuesday, Wednesday, and Thursday afternoons.

The suggestion was forwarded. However, no one thought to follow through.

When Jake did the play-by-play at the Tuesday Booster Club luncheon, he made a series of critical observations about everything *not* related to uninspired play. He did not approve of Free-Loader Hill where people watched the game while enjoying picnic lunches that could put a JJ Astor outing to shame. He cracked wise about locker facilities and their hotel. Much of his talk was pure fiction and not intended as slander. Anyone taking him seriously would, in his estimation, be much too stupid to run a local business.

He had to fill the void with something, or insipid blather would rule the day. As a stand-up comedian, he was less than brilliant, but the assembly found his comments amusing enough to applaud him—well, twice anyway. Save for comments about himself, he was careful to keep real people out of his recitations.

Once a year, each of the state's two major universities played a "home game" at the facilities located in the urban population center. Jake and his players would bus up to the Hilton Hotel to overnight prior to the season's only night game. They'd bus back home and arrive well into Sunday morning. Jake suggested they bus to the game and overnight *after* when everyone would be banged up and weary. The department vetoed the suggestion.

Back at base, he stepped into the AD's office to get Denise on her feet. That was a tertiary purpose. His main goal was to talk Ralph into putting Mieko up in the Hilton where the team would stay prior to the away home game.

"She can have a nice time-out. She won't have to make a round trip to bring back the film at some ungodly hour Sunday morning."

Ralph let out a sigh. "We're strapped," he insisted.

He knew better. The AD and his court enjoyed green fees paid for out of the public till.

Denise probably overheard. Ralph possibly changed his mind. Mieko may have fiddled with the itinerary (highly unlikely), but she was assigned a room (at the reduced group rate) for Friday evening.

It was pass-the-hat time. Jake was not an instigator (he suspected Denise was), but he pitched in twenty bucks without qualm. He avoided the appearance of pressuring his staff. He made no mention of either the hat passing or his own contribution. Perhaps they all pitched in. Perhaps none did. Mieko's reputation as an organizer, proxy innkeeper, and rabid team fan, however, influenced no few in the sport complex. She alone had a single room in the big city. Normally, Jake and Steve Thompson were the only solos, but Jake would be joined by his family on this trip.

Ralph's green fees remained sacrosanct.

Friday afternoon was the first frosh game. Jake wanted to be there. He wanted to see his future players (the few that remained after the weeding out). He suspected Churchill might think he was checking up on him. It never became an issue. There was no way he could attend. He had a job to do.

Only one team member had a three o'clock class. Jake warned him if he did not attend his class on Friday, there would be many stadium steps in his future. He needn't have threatened. Larry Benson was majoring in forest management, and his required three o'clock class was too important to skip.

The team bus lurched forward out of the arena parking lot at a whisker past four fifteen. They arrived at the downtown Hilton just shy of seven o'clock. A team meal was scheduled for seven thirty and a team meeting at nine, so there was little chance for the adventurous to wander far. There would be a bed check at ten thirty.

Betsy and Tami did not dine with the team. They ate in the hotel dining room and ordered from a menu. They crossed paths with Mieko, who was overwhelmed by an upscale Western hotel. Betsy invited her to eat with them, and Mieko jumped at the opportunity.

Betsy had no opportunity to speak with Tami. She wanted to remind her that any reference to the war should be avoided. Predictably, it was the first item on the agenda.

"My dad was in the Marines," Tami announced with pride.

"My father was conscripted," Mieko responded. "Since he was a seaman, they put him in the army. He married my mother, and four days later, he was a soldier."

"My dad was on Guadalcanal," Tami boasted. "He doesn't talk about it."

"My father served in Japan only. He didn't talk about it either."

That, blissfully, was the extent of the "war talk."

Some months passed before the Oats family learned Mieko knew nothing of Guadalcanal or anything beyond the two bombs. Her father was trained for use in the expected invasion of the homeland. He was not subjected to any fighting, but life as a Japanese enlisted man was brutal. He strove to block out his memories. A vital part of that program was to keep his military experiences from his family.

Betsy was curious as to how and why Mieko opted to finish her education in America. Of course, she was very tactful.

Mieko never saw Americans except in the movies and on TV. She considered their informality a sign of barbarism at first, but her revulsion dissolved into curiosity. They didn't seem evil or backward, but in manners and customs, they were decidedly "different." When confronted with the opportunity of study in America, she jumped at it. For her first several weeks, she was petrified. She didn't know how to act or the proper way to speak. Slang words and phrases made her think she was incredibly stupid. However, she realized that most Americans were friendly, receptive, and eager to help her.

Tami reciprocated by expounding upon her infatuation with Estonia. Mieko's radar picked up all the excitement and every nuance of what the young girl brought to the table. Before they left the dining room, Mieko was calling her Liisi, much to Tami's delight. That was fine, but after her Estonian dissertation, Tami thirsted to know all there was to know about Japan and Mieko's life there.

Betsy hadn't the strength to deny her daughter's adjournment to Mieko's room. She made her promise not to be a pest (good luck with that!) and to mind her manners (a much sounder bet).

After ninety minutes, she went to the solo room to check. Liisi and Mieko were joined-at-the-hip friends. They wanted to chat a while longer. After another ninety minutes, Betsy called the room and ordered Tami to come down. It took her thirty-three minutes more to make the three-minute journey.

A hotel room in the big city was as alien to Mieko as an adventure in a Japanese public bath would be for most Americans. She phoned Betsy near midnight. She pleaded for Liisi to sleep in her room because she didn't want to be alone in that huge building. Betsy was naturally reticent, but Mieko's pleading was formidable.

Tami, not the least modest, trundled down the hall to the elevator in her pajamas and slippers.

There was only one bed in the single room. Tami slept there. Mieko spread her coat out on the capacious window ledge, wrapped a blanket around her, and slept there. Of course, no one would know of this bizarre arrangement until much later.

Jake stumbled into the room shortly after midnight. He looked tired and worn. He wasn't too dull to inquire about Tami. He wasn't surprised that she and Mieko had bonded. Indeed, he would have been surprised had they not. As for her decamping, Jake trusted Betsy's judgment implicitly.

"How was the cocoa?" she asked.

That was long past.

"I needed the boost," he reported.

"You look exhausted."

"Damned night games!"

"You're still looking for the Aladdin's lamp?"

"Gotta keep looking. There's always something we've missed."

"What can you do now, even if you find it?"

"I can't answer that unless we find it."

Betsy sighed. "This would be so much less taxing if the boys could just go out and play," she concluded.

"Then they wouldn't need me. I could sell cars or tires, I suppose, and make more money."

"You wouldn't be happy selling cars or tires."

Jake sighed. "Right now, it's looking pretty good."

"Oh, stop! You love it. Get some sleep. You'll feel better in the morning."

———•———

Jake was up at six. He shaved, got dressed, and left the room. There was more room to pace in the lobby and more pacing room on the lower level. He'd meet with Gus and Joe for breakfast at eight. Meanwhile, he reviewed everything he knew about football and every detail of the playbook.

Tami knocked loudly a little after seven. Betsy was just beginning to stir. She forced herself to get up and put on her robe.

"We're going to breakfast," Tami announced. "Come on!"

"I'm not dressed," Betsy replied, stating the obvious.

Tami bounced on her toes with impatience. "Can I have some money? Mieko will be down in a minute. She's hungry, and I want to have breakfast with her."

"If you promise to come back, take a shower, and change your clothes."

At this juncture, Tami would have agreed to wash all the linen in the hotel. It was well that Betsy was not yet aware of the sleeping arrangements in Mieko's room, or severe penalties would have been initiated.

"You come right back after breakfast," Betsy reminded.

"Promise. Promise. Promise."

One Dionne Warwick concert, and Tami assumed she could sing.

◄●◄

Finally, the teams took to the field. It was a warm evening, but there was a hint of an approaching dip in temperature. The opposition was wild. This was the year the team would overcome their curse. There was a movement underway to get the school out of its current conference and into the one Jake haunted. A victory would not only advance the lobbying, it would go down in history as their "first new-conference win."

Jake didn't give a damn about conference politics. He noticed that his team was emotionally charged. The players wanted to make a statement. They wanted to prove to the world that they were a force. More importantly, the wanted to show themselves.

Jake was uncomfortable with Davidson being a wild man again. He was a known quantity and a marked man. Someone would be assigned to take him out. Undoubtedly. However, the back who handled the kickoff at the eight-yard line considered it a head start in his race for the opposite goal line. As he made a cut at the twenty-two-yard line, he was crushed.

The capacity crowd let out a collective groan of sympathy for the poor creature who'd taken the fiercest hit of the season.

When Davidson came off the field, he was pounding a fist into his other hand. The former Marine had become a savage.

"You may want to get him in for a few plays tonight," Jake muttered to Thorne.

He mightn't have heard. Gus was expressing the same sentiment from the press box. From on high and from his side, the defensive coach got the word.

For a quarter and a half, Jake waited for *Betsy*. Several times, the defense gave the look, but they'd shift into a different alignment. He thought of those two kids in the car during practice, the ones Joe was ready to assault. Had they? But how? "Betsy" was not a goal line play, and they'd been practicing nine-and-in. Of course, they may have been spying at other times.

Perhaps Betsy needn't be a factor. Despite its speed, the opposing defense was being overpowered by Joe's big offensive line. The power plays were gaining yards. The middle traps were gaining yards. The rollout passes were gaining yards.

It was 14 to 0 at the half. It should have been twice that. Save for fumbles and incomplete passes, it *would* have been twice that.

Finally, there it was!

"Go!" Peck barked. "Betsy!"

The audible! The next sound from the quarterback's lips would be the snap count.

"Go!"

The ball sailed through Peck's legs. Evans plucked it out of the air as he initiated his charge. The center sealed left, as planned. Peck, nearly fifty pounds lighter than the man he was assigned, didn't bother to rooster fight. He dropped down onto the man's knees and cut him as neatly as Jake often had before he retired.

It gained eight easy yards. It sent the opposing sidelines into a fit. *What the hell was that?*

Dave Peck, the quiet sophomore, went back to the huddle as calmly as a three-year starter. In that short period of time, Jake saw his friend and former teammate, Forest Evashevski. Many years and two and a half wars previously, Evy was moved from tackle to quarterback. It was his job to call plays and block for the money man, Tom Harman. On that night, for that one play, Dave Peck was Evy's successor.

Prior to game's end, they ran the play again for twelve yards and sent the defense into another seizure. There were serious adjustments made, quickly and to Jake's advantage. They could not allow the fullback to run at will up the gut, so they took measures. At this juncture, the halfback and wingback started piling up yards. Joe was using the offense like a precision surgical instrument.

Jake, who had authority over the special teams, sent Gary Lynn into the game on kickoffs. His first boot went to the two-yard line. His second was downed eight yards deep in the end zone.

The guests, primed for revenge, were forced to play catch-up.

Jake turned to find Jeff Foote, last year's quarterback and currently the starting safety, sitting ashamed and despondent on the bench, his helmet off and his head down. Gus had "fired" him. Jeff made a big mistake, blew his coverage, and allowed some pipsqueak to catch a pass and shuffle into the end zone unimpeded. Sid Parks would play the rest of the game. He wasn't nearly as good, but he knew the coverage assignments.

Mieko watched the game. It was the first she'd seen. Tami excitedly explained what was happening and why. The young Japanese woman didn't understand much, but she grew excited just listening to Tami's play-by-play.

When she fetched the film directly from the cameraman, she fled to the state car, only to get caught in the post-game traffic jam on her way to the TV studio.

Jake made a mental note to send Gary Lynn's former coach a more substantial thanks for calling him. Lynn was *almost* perfect in point-after touchdowns and had hit every field goal attempt thus far.

The final score was 24 to 18 over the hotshot conference wannabe.

The score did not tell the tale. It wasn't that close.

The Desert

The following week was the disaster in the north. A very powerful team made Jake's team look foolish. Due to fumbles and an interception, the powerhouse scored twenty-one easy points. They didn't need them. The defense, despite courageous play, surrendered seventeen hard-earned points. Jake's crew managed only fourteen.

These fourteen were "honest," as tabulated through Joe's play-calling and the team's prodigious effort. They were bloody points, scored through grit, determination, and ferocity. The team was proud of them. Few mourned the drubbing, but everyone was proud of their reward, meager though it was.

During the early stages of the battle, Dave Peck looked awful. He made a bad decision on an option play resulting in a fumble and loss of possession. He threw three passes that missed the intended receiver by miles. He put a man in motion but forgot his own snap count, causing a collision and an illegal-motion penalty.

"Might wanna get Peck outta there," Jake mumbled as he passed Joe.

Joe was tenacious. He chewed Peck out on the sideline, but his confidence in him remained solid.

"Joe, you better put Murray in," Jake ordered during the next set of downs.

Joe pretended not to hear.

After another gaff, Jake rushed over to Joe and grabbed his arm. "This time, *I'm telling you.* Put Murray in there!"

They both knew the substitution wouldn't be made prior to the next punt, but Joe resisted telling Fred Murray to warm up.

Peck began regaining control. He was the key in two large gains. It was clear he'd found his stride.

"Still wanna yank him, Coach?"

In the heat of battle, emotions ran high. Joe would never throw an in-your-face comment at Jake during a game, but he did that afternoon.

It was Jake's turn to pretend he hadn't heard. Half the team did, however. He and Joe would exchange words later and in private.

The following week was at home on Halloween. The conference favorite came to town expecting an easy victory on their way to a certain bowl appearance. They were ambushed. It was twenty-one to six at halftime. Jake's proud warriors were making a mockery of their opponents' vaunted defense while Gus's crew held a leading Heisman candidate and his group of highly publicized receivers to only five first downs. On offense, Evans, Gino, Shaw, and Billy Morris accounted for a hundred and a half yards while Peck fired two TD passes, one to Capp and one to Billy.

In second half, the sleeping giant awoke and left town with a 31 to 24 victory.

Fans and players were deflated by a last-minute spurt, which fell just short of tying the score. That evening, on all the sports shows, the primary topic of discussion was how a group of moderately talented upstarts came so close to a David-and-Goliath moment.

The next away game was played in the desert heat. It was laundry night. Jake's banshees played well but were plagued by penalties—most of them on successful third-down conversions.

Only two of their second chances resulted in a first down.

Jake had scores of run-ins with officials both as a player and as a coach. However, this was the first time he ever accused a crew of deliberately conspiring against a team. He regretted it immediately, but he'd made the accusation, and there was no taking it back. The officials were from outside the conference. However, if Jake ever faced that crew again, they'd make him pay.

The 34-to-22 loss was devastating. It meant that Jake was doomed to a losing season. With the two teams remaining, the chances were excellent that he'd end the campaign with only the three victories the "experts" allowed in the preseason prognostications. That was unacceptable! His team was better than that—much better!

When they loaded the projector, Joe pulled out his pencil. "Let's see how many of those penalties were *really* penalties."

"Like hell!" Jake scoffed. "We owe it to the team to do as we always do. If we spend time studying the officials, we'll be here until the Fourth of July!"

Gus admitted his defense hadn't lived up to either his expectations or his demands. He wanted to make changes—major changes.

"The defense will have to learn an entirely new system," Jake reminded. "You can't expect them to do that in a week or even three. They'll make a ton of mistakes, which will result in unearned touchdowns. Sorry, Gus, I'm putting my foot down."

Gus nodded. He knew the boss was right, but he desperately wanted to go down swinging.

"Shelve this stuff for now," Jake ordered. "When the season is over, we'll spend time on it. We can introduce it in spring ball."

"Okay, chief," Gus acquiesced. "I guess this gutsy defense has some fight left in it."

Denise continued to stand whenever Jake walked into the office. She was not motivated by habit alone. She recognized the pressure being applied to Jake and admired his courage. She wanted to make her respect and admiration for his tenacity manifest. The habit continued to irritate Jake, but not so much as before. He concluded that Denise Davenport was a person of habit, and her habits were based on a sense of honor.

He saw Mieko infrequently, but Mieko and Liisi were together on game days.

Betsy was mortified when she learned of the Hilton sleeping arrangements. It was Mieko's room, and by rights, the bed was hers. She was also upset over anyone sleeping on the window ledge. True, it was designed to double as a bench. Furthermore, it would take a determined maniac with a stuffed toolbox to egress via the window, but the idea of anyone sleeping next to a hundred-foot plunge caused Betsy's hair to stand up.

Perhaps, to make amends, Betsy made Mieko's game-day visits special. She cleaned the house judiciously, cooked up a storm, and treated her guest as royalty.

"I thought you'd want to be at the game," Mieko commented during the only home stand of the "deadly three."

"I only watch football when Jake and I can watch together," she replied. "He keeps me informed about what's going on, and I keep him calm. If I were in the stadium, I'd bite my nails to the knuckles. Better to listen to the radio."

Mieko remained stoic, but she wasn't convinced. "Don't you like to go to the games?" she asked Liisi.

"Football! Yuck!"

Betsy enjoyed the laugh she got from that.

If she had a day off school or at least an afternoon off, Tami would head for the practice field. She'd go to see her dad and amuse herself by playing games only she understood. After a few minutes, she'd give her father a hug. He'd kiss her hand. She'd disappear into the arena for a few minutes prior to setting off for home.

She was getting a bit old for girlish indulgences. She was, unfortunately, filling out as well as growing up. Twice, she'd been mistaken for a precocious coed. That didn't rest well with Betsy. Having Mieko around kept Tami occupied in and around the house.

Tami wanted to know *everything* about Japan. Mieko agreed, with Betsy's permission, to cook a Japanese meal. To make things more authentic, she brought along certain implements, including chopsticks (*not* the dime-a-gross variety so common in Asian restaurants, but the implements used by her family).

In many ways, Tami was becoming more mature and urbane. Nevertheless, she remained a little girl. She sampled Mieko's offerings eagerly. If she didn't like something, however, she made it clear. Betsy was again mortified. Mieko, however, laughed—not at Tami's honesty, but the childlike way she expressed it.

Estonia remained a forbidden area on the maps. Japan, however, was not. Predictably, Tami began her laborious campaign for a Japanese vacation. "Just two weeks. Ten days? A weekend? Can't we visit Mieko when she goes home? Can I go alone?"

Whenever Jake thought he would experience peace on the home front, Tami would begin pestering him about Japan. She was impervious to logical arguments.

⬤▶•◀⬤

Churchill was good at checking in periodically on his progress with the frosh team. These reports lasted no more than fifteen minutes a week, though Jake spent a lot of time at home (he had very little time at home) pouring through Church's practice and game reports.

He gained valuable insight into the players he'd inherit in the spring. They were *not* his. They were recruited by the previous staff. Only four "walk-ons" survived. Mel Manning was one of them.

Church won two games and lost one. His next opponent was the cross-state rival. Many of Church's players had been wooed by that "other" school. Those who committed found themselves with a coach they'd never met and a system they knew nothing about. Jake expected that some, perhaps many, would transfer. He'd be forced to scout junior college players or face the prospect of a team devoid of underclassmen.

BSU had Jake stymied. He was certain they would move, and they did. They called for a student strike, held rallies in the quad, passed out propaganda fliers, posted signs, and found effective ways of getting the attention of both the campus and city newspapers. However, the athletic department avoided direct assault—so far. Evans not agreeing to be the poster child for the black athletes apparently left the BSU in a quandary.

Jake oversaw a losing season. An unsuccessful program was a vulnerable program. Though Ralph assured Jake that the board was certain to retain him for three more years, Jake knew such promises weren't worth the paper they were *not* written on. If the Black Student

Union really kicked up a fuss, Jake could be flushed down the drain without advance notice.

"Tell Church I want to meet with him tomorrow at eight," he told Barbara, who relayed the message to the frosh coach's office.

Eight was an ungodly hour for a person blurry-eyed from watching films and studying scouting reports. However, nearly every minute of his day from ten in the morning to ten at night was spoken for. He hoped he could be up and in the office by eight. With luck, Churchill would be there as well.

———⋗•⋖———

"I see Mel has gained a hundred yards or more in every game," he stated.

Churchill squirmed furtively, but not unnoticed, in his chair. "Yes, sir."

"How does a halfback in a fullback-oriented offense gain so many yards?"

Brice cleared his throat and shifted his posture. "Well, ah, sir, we don't exactly run our offense as you do up here."

"Relax, Church. I'm not upset, and I'm not out to kick your ass. I just want some information. Your reports are all I could ask for. Now, I want to know about a few things not in your reports."

The trusted assistant was visibly relieved. He shifted his posture again. This time, his object was to make himself comfortable.

"Our middle traps work very well," Churchill began. "We run 58 and 59 quite a lot. Once Mel takes the pitch, he's got moves that can best be described as superhuman. No one, so far, gets a clear shot at him. Even if they do, he can take it. He blocks like a charging bull. He doesn't shy away from anybody."

"He's very small."

"Yes, sir. That works well, especially with the middle traps. The linebackers can't find him."

That was an angle Jake hadn't considered. "You think he can do the job up here?"

"Yes, sir."

The response was devoid of hesitation. It was also emphatic.

"How's his talking?"

Brice smiled. "He told me what you said to him. Kinda puts me on the spot, being an elocution teacher."

"That was not my intent," Jake snapped with early morning petulance.

"No, sir. I didn't mean—well, he is slow to talk because he wants it to be…I don't know, *more correcter*?"

"I'll pretend I didn't hear that, Church. I recommend your manner of speaking, and you throw that in my face."

Churchill didn't know if he was being teased or scolded.

"He didn't have any problems talking to those BSU guys—oh, and they're all *guys* by the way. Those coeds that turn out are not students here. Several of them come from, well, that *other* school, the one neither of us cares to mention."

"You said he talked to the Black Student Union?" Jake asked, dragging him back to the topic most important to him.

"Yes, sir. They were piqued about being turned down by Evans—"

"*Piqued*?"

Brice grinned.

"I are a college grad-u-ate."

"Sorry. Evans told me he'd not represent them. How about Wes Jordan?"

"I don't think they even approached him. The big silent types probably scare them a little."

Wes Jordan would scare anybody.

"Go on."

"Well, the cadre—you know, the great organizers, the officers, whatever you want to call them—they spoke with him one morning after class. It might have looked like a scene from an old movie. Three big mean-looking guys calling him aside after class. They started talking the talk and made the mistake of letting slip a snide or disrespectful remark about you. He really went to bat for you, sir. He said you were the only person who took him seriously enough to recruit him. He told how he followed you out here because you were the only coach he'd play for."

It was Jake's turn to clear his throat. "How do you know this?"

"Not every black student on this campus is a member of BSU. One of Mel's chums was in the same class. He saw all and heard all. The three guys started talking, you know, like inner-city thugs. Mel scolded them for it. He said the least they could do to get people to take them seriously was to talk like educated people. Oh, by the way, Coach, I've heard him use that word around me. He doesn't say *edge-u-cated*. He says *ED-u-cated*. That's a freebie for you under the heading of language. It is a lot different than it was two months ago."

"Thanks, Church. You're doing a hell of a job. Beat those bastards Friday."

Churchill grinned.

Meeting adjourned.

⸺•⸺

Jake knew he was in the hot seat. His staff knew that they were in the hot seat with him. Somehow, they avoided panic or anxiety. They had confidence in themselves and in their team. The players sensed this business-as-usual attitude. They were hungry, they worked hard, and they responded to every adjustment and new wrinkle with enthusiasm. Team spirit remained high.

One morning, Jake accepted Barbara's offer to make a sandwich run. He slipped her some money with a request for tuna salad. This allowed him to linger at his desk and catch up with his correspondence.

He heard familiar voices from the coaches' den.

Jake did not hesitate to leave his desk. He found Churchill and Mel Manning, both standing, discussing (what else?) football. They weren't reviewing the playbook or the practice agenda. Instead, they were discussing *the* "big game" in the Southwestern Conference scheduled for that weekend.

"Sorry, Coach," Mel said, surprised to see the big guy coming through. "Were we talking too loud?"

"A few weeks ago, you'd ask, 'Was we talkin' too loud?'"

"I can still talk like that. Wanna hear?"

"Up to you, son. How are you doing in your courses?"

"I think I'll get a C in algebra. I'm doing better in my other classes."

"You know how to get help if you need it."

242

"Yes, sir. I've been assigned a tutor from the department. I listen to him talk, and I listen to Coach Churchill here talk—you'd be surprised how fast you can learn a new language when you listen careful."

"Carefully," Jake corrected.

"Yes, sir. *Carefully*. Next year, I take a speech class. It's one of the requirements. I'm not as afraid as I was before."

"Great. Nothing like confidence, huh?"

"Yes, sir."

"Coach here tells me you work your butt off in practice, and your game stats speak volumes."

Mel nodded.

This was the moment of truth.

"Still think you can't use me?"

That was blunt—and bold.

"You keep your grades up, Mel. You got heart and a good work ethic. There's always a place for someone who has the tools."

Mel grinned. "Thanks, Coach."

"Don't thank me, Mel. You still have a long way to go."

He nodded. "I'm packed and ready, Coach."

Jake returned to his desk and wrote a memo to himself.

Must get Mel a scholarship!!!!!!

Rebound

Jake recognized the analogous nature of his next opponent. Both schools were the smaller of the state institutions. Not only were they similar in student enrollment, but they were also parked in areas best described as rustic. Both schools featured strong agricultural programs. Both teams were struggling. The signature difference, however, resided in the fact that the campus stadium was the smallest in the conference. Tradition dictated that when the southern neighbor came for a visit, the game would be played in the nearest population center, similar to the "away from home" home game that showcased Jake's "greatest upset" (thus far).

Thankfully, it wouldn't be a night game. The team would fly to and fro in two small prop jets (one of the schools broke the bus-travel agreement, so Ralph and Mieko arranged air transport on short notice). They'd play, shower, have a box lunch, and fly home shortly after dark.

This opponent was as limited as Jake's team because of personnel problems. They attempted to overcome their lack of size and skill by employing a ground-based option attack. On defense, they ran an endless array of stunts. The only thing Jake's offensive line could know for certain was that they'd seldom block the person nearest. They must block area, no matter what the play call. This stripped Jake of half the playbook.

Both teams had poor records. Experience taught Jake that such teams fought like wounded wildcats to salvage pride. It mattered no little that they were struggling to stay out of the conference cellar.

"This game will be an alley fight, men," Jake warned. "There are a lot of people out there, people who do *not* suit up and play, who insist that we are both patsies, that we should be playing in diapers and in a play pen. If you listen to that or read that crap, and if you believe it, you'll get slaughtered. These guys will be coming at you like Indians at the Little Big Horn. They will *not* take prisoners. You better be ready, men. These guys are not fooling around."

That night in the hotel, Jake decided he needed a cup of coffee—perhaps two. He'd been a coffee glutton on Guadalcanal and New Britain. It did not inhibit sleep; a Marine can sleep upside down while hanging from a tree branch. Rule number one: sleep whenever you can, even if it's only for a few seconds. Rule number two: coffee keeps you alert, even when your energy level is below zero.

Since the war, Jake kept alert on office coffee. Holly made Marine Joe strong enough to suit up and play smash-mouth football. However, for enjoyment, nothing could beat a nice leisurely cup of freshly brewed coffee. The team's hotel was hardly the Hilton, but it had a quality reputation. It had a coffee shop situated near a full restaurant.

Jake wandered in. There were few customers. The card-playing contingent were in Ralph's suite since the small aircraft could not facilitate their traditional tournament. One of the customers, however, was a striker.

Regina Davis was tall and muscular. Jake assumed she was an athlete, but discovered she had little interest in sports. She was attractive, studious, and personable. Jake knew her as Mark Davidson's girlfriend. She sat as prim and demure as a character in an Andy Hardy film. Clad in black slacks, red long-sleeved sweater, and a yellow and black scarf, she enjoyed sipping a milkshake from an old-fashioned glass tumbler.

"Sit over here if you like," she invited.

He didn't hesitate. "Are you staying here?"

She wrinkled her nose. The idea appeared to displease her. "I can't afford it," she admitted. "I'm staying at the Motel 6 just outside town. Mark just left, by the way."

He checked his watch. It was two minutes past curfew. "I didn't know you were a fan."

"I'm not," she admitted. "I don't know a first down from an infield single."

Obviously, she knew much more than she'd admit to.

"Black coffee, please."

The stealth waitress nodded and moved away.

"I came to support Mark," Regina continued. "Well, I had the weekend free. I'm all caught up with my studies, and I've never been here before. Mark got two tickets for me, but my roommate couldn't come."

"What are you studying?"

"Marketing." She wrinkled her nose again. "It's starting to sour on me," she confessed. "I don't think business and I will play well together. I've been thinking about switching to accounting."

Jake grunted. Accounting sounded like business to him. Regina, however, struck him as a person with a cool, intelligent head on her shoulders; she probably knew a lot more about career options than he did.

"How does Mark feel about the game? Has he said?"

"He's chomping at the bit," she assured. "He told me he was not too excited about playing—I mean, trying out for the team. Now, he's pumped. He likes the guys, he likes the challenges. He speaks highly of you."

"I appreciate your telling me that."

He did indeed, but he wished she hadn't. However, she'd opened a door.

"Does he...I mean, does he ever get morose?"

Clearly, she wasn't eager to address the issue. She took a sip of her drink and stabbed at it daintily with her straw. "He tells me...things. Not about the war, but about, well, nightmares, regrets, guys he knew who... aren't around anymore."

Jake wasn't certain he should probe further, but he liked Regina. Maybe he liked this near stranger too much.

"My wife has put up with that since I've known her, since before we were married. She's been a big help. That's all I dare say. I guess I felt I had to say something."

She played with her thick milkshake a bit longer. Jake's coffee arrived, and he took a tentative sip. It was hot, and it was good. It was not Marine coffee.

"I like Mark a lot," she confessed in a tentative voice. "I want to help. That's one reason why I'm here. That means more to both of us than the game. I guess I shouldn't have said that."

"Why not?"

She couldn't look at him anymore. She shrugged her shoulders and studied the molecular structure of her drink.

"Mark doesn't need you or anyone else to mother him. If he likes you, and if you like him, the two of you will figure out how to deal with it. You should know this: he will never get past it—whatever it is. It will never go away, not completely."

She said nothing.

"I'm sorry you invited me over. I can't keep my mouth shut."

She sighed, took a sip, but didn't enjoy it. "I don't know if this… thing between us will ever amount to much," she began. "I do like him. He's been nothing but nice and supportive. There are times…well, it frightens me. Sometimes, when we're just sitting and talking, when… when he isn't *there*. I mean—"

"He isn't," he interrupted. "That's why it is doubly important that you're with him. When he comes back, it's your presence that means more than anything else."

She eyed him cautiously.

"When I'm away from my wife or my daughter and I experience… an episode—" He drank some more coffee. He couldn't finish that sentence. He didn't want to finish it.

She stared vacantly into what was left of her shake for some while.

"He started talking nonsense one afternoon in the Union. He'd forgotten I was there, I guess. He rambled on for a few seconds. I…I was too stunned to say anything. When it—when he came back, he was really embarrassed. I was pretty scared."

"You did the right thing. If he starts talking, just let him get through it. Has he ever done anything violent?"

She snorted. "Of course not! I wouldn't be here if he—well, I wouldn't be here."

"Just let him talk. The best thing you can do. Just listen. No, that's wrong. The best thing you can do is be there. My wife's done that for years. She's my best medicine."

Regina Davis possessed a highly enigmatic expression as she continued to poke at the milkshake she no longer wanted. She studied the billowing white concoction that was beginning to congeal.

Jake felt he'd stuck his foot in his mouth once again. "I'm sorry," he began. "I'm always sticking my nose in where it isn't wanted."

If Regina threw Mark over because of his chuntering on about life lessons, he'd never forgive himself.

"I like Mark a lot," she said, reading his mind. "His stock went up considerably when I found out he'd served. I live with a girl who lost a husband…over there, and I know another whose fiancé is missing. At least with Mark, I don't have to dread his being called up."

Jake groped around for something both cogent and germane. Not surprisingly, he failed miserably.

"He's going to play tomorrow," he promised. "Not as much as he will next season if he comes back, but I trust him. His position coach trusts him. Mark isn't one to lose his head."

She smiled, put down her drink, and leaned back. "That's good to know," she concluded.

"Let me get that," he said, pointing to her abandoned treat. "It's the least I can do for horning in."

"You weren't horning in," she asserted while standing and reaching for her jacket draped over the back of her chair. "I invited you to join me, remember?"

Ah! Come the dawn! If Jake hadn't blabbed his head off, she'd have pumped him. Jake didn't recall the coeds of his day being so resourceful. Regina Davis struck him as a woman who was much more than a pretty face.

"Good luck tomorrow," she added, putting on the jacket.

"I don't believe in luck," he replied. "However, I appreciate the sentiment."

He didn't believe in luck. When it came to football, it was preparation, execution, and knowing one's opponent. That's what mattered. Luck played a miniscule part.

On Guadalcanal and New Britain, luck was practically the *only* thing that mattered.

———◄●►———

The game was indeed an alley fight. Both teams were determined to win, and neither team budged an inch. The option game was run with skill and daring while Joe and the offensive line punished the defense with a bruising power attack. Both defenses were ferocious and determined.

Tied at halftime, the two squads retired to their respective locker rooms exhausted.

"This is where you find out who you are," Jake reminded them. "You've played a brutal first half. So have they. You're worn out. So are they. You must find it, men. Somewhere, buried inside you, there's more. You must dig it out and use it. When there's nothing left and your back's against the wall, you must find it and use it—that's the part of yourself that won't allow you to fail. I can't get it for you. It's up to you to find it."

Jake wasn't much for clichés. He'd experienced total exhaustion on Guadalcanal. More than once, he was satisfied to lie down and let some Japanese bullet or grenade put him out of his misery. Somehow, he found the energy and the will to go on just a little longer. He was not unique. He knew many men who confronted death and defeat, but they survived. Maybe many of the dead "found it" and failed anyway. Who can know? The dead cannot tell us.

It was a brutal second half. Neither team would quit or slack off. There was only one touchdown scored in the second half, and Billy Morris scored it.

In retrospect, it was one of the best games Jake ever witnessed. No one, certainly none of the players or coaches, would have suspected they were playing for next-to-last place in the conference. Judging by the ferocity and the energy levels, the fans might have thought they were watching a battle for the national championship. Jake was excited about winning, but he felt empathy for the losers. They played inspired football.

This was one time when Jake's victory celebration was conspicuous in its reserve.

Showdown

That Tuesday at the booster meeting, Jake was confronted by nominal attendance. The local big shots were happy with the win, but the atmosphere was riddled with resentment. A seven-point win was not acceptable. Jake, already on a short fuse, tried to remain civil.

"This, gentlemen, was a game in the great tradition of days gone by. Two teams with little to play for took to the field and played as if a championship was at stake. Neither team would surrender an inch. Both teams had to fight ferociously for every inch. I'm proud of my men. They were full gas from start to finish. During the flight back, there was no celebration. There was dead silence except for the moaning of the engines. Those heroic players had no energy left to celebrate. They left everything on the field. They were drained. Make no mistake, they were happy and cocky during our Sunday afternoon workout, but Saturday afternoon and that night, they were all in.

"I know that other team was in the same state as we were. I sent a telegram to Coach Jenkins telling him that I was proud to share the field with him that day. It was the toughest, hardest-hitting, most ferocious four quarters I've ever experienced. You will see it in the film, gentlemen. Not a single personal foul the whole game. It was a clean game, but it was a battle. If any of you have cardiac problems, I urge you to leave now. The film you are about to see is not for the meek."

He must learn to keep his big mouth shut. The film spoke more vividly than anything Jake could invent. Several times during the screening, the audience reacted audibly. There were groans and gasps mingled with whispered exclamations. At the conclusion, their applause was as ruckus as any Jake had experienced to date.

After showing the boosters what a football game *should* be, he returned to the arena.

Jake was the disgraced owner of a losing season. There was nothing he could do to change that. However, the final game of the year would be against the cross-state rival. There was little more than fifty miles separating the two largest schools in the state, and their rivalry went back to the days of the flying wedge. It made the Michigan-Michigan State game pale by comparison. This was a game even football phobics followed—the one sporting contest that roused the entire state.

A victory in the rivalry game could overcome a multitude of sins.

The newspapers, from the regional and state-wide press along with the county-wide publications and the small-town weeklies, were devoting scores of column inches to the impending contest. There were publicity photos of Dave Peck and John Wagonblast, both All-State. Both were starters for their respective teams. The two conquers and shining stars of the state-champion high school team just three seasons prior were to face off against each other in *the* game of the season.

No motivational speeches were required. The enemy had been buried by the conference leader, the team Jake and his *men* came so near beating. They also lost (by an embarrassing margin) to the team that defeated Jake's in the *Lethargy Bowl*. Notably, they lost to the noble inspired team that Regina Davis watched the previous week. Still, if they beat Jake, they would obtain that coveted prize of a winning season.

For Jake's crew, defeating their archrival would soften the pain of so many lost opportunities.

Jake did not initiate the fervor of the interstate rivalry, but he was inundated soon enough. It wasn't just students and campus organizations that wore team paraphernalia and erected signs demanding victory; it spilled out into the community. Local businesses, to include those who weren't members of the booster club, were draped in school colors and displayed spirit signs. A newspaper with a state-wide circulation found a small rural burg that was literally split down the middle by team allegiance.

There were clashes across the state. The overwhelming majority were limited to exchanges of good-natured insults, and many communities organized segregated functions. People who never attended either school, including people who never finished high school, got caught up in rivalry fever.

Denise Davenport, who insisted that blue and white were "not her colors," came to work in gaudy scarfs and shifts that hurt the eye. Jake never did warm to the color combination. He soon found himself operating—or attempting to operate—in a state of perpetual nausea.

"Don't think we will require many pep talks this week," he mumbled to Joe.

As a reward for his keen observation, Jake was awarded the offer of one of Joe's cigars. As Jake gratefully accepted, he noticed the brand-name product had acquired a blue and white band. The head coach was poised to make a sarcastic remark but hung fire. He should be thankful, he reminded himself, that the cigar itself was not dyed blue and white.

He seldom got home before midnight, but he knew Betsy would always be up. He took a moment to call her from his office. Twice, she was out. The third time he was lucky.

"If we have anything blue and white in the house, would you please put it away?"

She laughed, but she was aware of the communal insanity whenever she left the abode. Tami felt obligated to wear something blue and white to school, as did her peers. Thanks to Betsy, the girl opted to keep such items stashed out of sight when her father was at home. She was seldom awake when he roamed the house, but Betsy made certain to remind her about leaving "certain items" where her father might see them.

"I'm looking forward to two weeks of vacation," he said to Betsy at midnight thirty Tuesday morning. "I wish we could take them beginning the Sunday after this game."

Betsy, as ever, was curious. "What do you want to do?"

"Two nights," he replied. "Camping away from everyone and everything. I'd lay out on the ground and just look up at the stars and maybe watch a moon rise."

"It will get very cold," Betsy warned.

"Yeah. We'd have to go to the southern hemisphere. Not practical."

Betsy considered for a moment and decided to forge ahead. "You get two weeks during summer."

"I'll be out of the mood by then—probably."

"Could I give you something to think about?"

He went to the fridge to pour himself a small glass of milk. That was his mission, but he didn't want Betsy to think he was ignoring her. He gave her an interrogative grunt.

"Mieko invited Tami to visit her this summer—in Japan. I guess we're invited as well."

"We might be able to go to Japan," he informed. "We might be able to stay a few days. However, there's no way we can afford both the trip *and* lodging."

Betsy cleared her throat. It was a habit she picked up from her husband. They both knew the portent of a throat clearing. "Mieko says we can stay with her and her mother. There's plenty of room, she says."

Jake took his empty glass to the sink and rinsed it out preparatory to putting it in the dishwasher. His attitude and facial expression made clear his feelings about the matter.

"They don't live in the city, Jake," she hurried on before he could render a verdict. "Their house is in a little fishing village on the inland sea. No nightclubs, no sports arenas, no tourist spots, no commotion—unless of course you want to help with the fishing fleet."

He put his hands on his hips and exercised his aching neck. Betsy surmised that he was considering this unexpected offer.

"I don't know, Bets."

"Your daughter would love you for it."

"I thought she loves me now."

"Well, yes, but—"

"I'm not comfortable about it," he confessed.

That was the cue Betsy had prayed for.

"This would be good for you, Jake. It would settle something for once and good."

"Settle what?"

"It would prove that the war is over."

They glared at each other for several seconds. Finally, he grunted.

That grunt communicated volumes. Among the most important items was his assurance that he would give the matter proper attention—later! There was a big, big, *big* game Saturday.

Joe puffed away on his blue-and-white–band cigar and printed in his bold precise hand on a yellow legal pad.

"Trick plays?" he growled.

"Quick kick," Jake stated for the eleventh time in eleven weeks.

"Ain't used it yet," Pink noted.

"If we need it, we will want it ready to go," Jake scolded. "Any requests, Mike?"

Mike Perry was seldom asked for his input. He coached the ends and receivers. His job was important but limited. He'd been deployed as a scout all season long. Now, however, there were no opponents to scout. He would be on the sidelines for the big, big, *big* game, shoulder to shoulder with the rest of the staff.

"A suggestion," he announced timidly.

"Suggest away," Jake ordered.

"We've been running the face pattern all season. The enemy is getting wise. The last three games, the backers are jumping on Morris when he comes out. They know Peck likes to throw to him, but he isn't getting the yards he was earlier in the season."

Jake grunted. This must be going somewhere. He wasn't very patient with people who state the obvious. Joe, Pink, and Jake were aware of the drop in Billy's reception stats.

"How about a face and up?"

The archrivals had a linebacker they were promoting as an All-American. If this monster sniffed pass, he'd be on Billy Morris like red on an apple. He wasn't likely to bite on a fake, but Billy was adroit and a good actor. If he looked back at Peck and got his up-field shoulder past the linebacker, he could break free for an instant. That instant could turn a three- or four-yard gain into a twelve- or twenty-yard gain. If the linebacker was as nimble and smart as they advertised him, it could be an interception and touchdown for the bad guys."

"Put it in, Joe. Let's see how it works in practice."

Joe's pencil rapidly recorded the "new" route.

"Anyone, other than me, noticed how Smith is improving?" Jake asked.

"And I thought I was the only smart one," Joe muttered.

If Joe spoke like that, he had noticed. If there was any doubt, he removed it by his subsequent remarks.

"We've been using Zwetschke and Dilley for short yardage gotta-haves," he began. "I think Dilley and Smith can serve just as well. Better, in fact, since you can bet they've scouted us down to the pimples on our butts."

Gus was reading through Churchill's reports to the boss. He was salivating over the certainty that two linebackers were only a few months away. Of course, they'd require seasoning, but they were on the way. Mark Davidson would return. He looked good as an end, but he could play linebacker in a pinch.

After Churchill's season ended with a convincing win over their cross-state rivals, Gus brought him into the defensive powwow. He was there when Jake entered.

"They come out in split backs a lot," Gus informed Jake unnecessarily. "They like that quick hitter between guard and tackle. I want Gianelli to call it when they split. Tackles squeeze down with the call."

"How do you call it?" Jake asked.

"*Split!*"

"They do shift out of it, you know."

"*Off!*"

Jake liked it. It adhered to that marvelous KISS doctrine. The defensive line was smart. They could adjust and readjust mentally without having to think it through for twenty minutes. Of course, stopping the run was a priority, but the enemy liked to pass from split backs. Wagonblast was the preferred receiver, but the enemy quarterback threw a lot of passes to the backs coming out of the backfield. He was no slouch. The pro scouts had been in that quarterback's pocket for two seasons.

Because Jake was getting caught up in the pre-game hysteria, he was concerned that the team treated the Tuesday practice as just another day at the office. They worked hard on drills and at the eight-minute scrimmage, but the team didn't appear properly motivated. Half the team members knew many of their cross-state foes personally. A dozen or more had either played with the opposition or knew them from social venues around the state.

"This is for bragging rights for the next twelve months," he reminded them.

They knew that. Somehow, it didn't make an impact. Jake feared a midseason redux that cost them a game they could have, and should have, won. Jake expressed his concern to Gus, who was busy putting together a more comprehensive coverage package.

"These guys have a hell of a passing attack," he stated with trepidation. "Their receivers drop the ball a lot, but we can't count on them to keep doing that. Wagonblast is the money man. What if we keep Eberhart man on and play cover two and three behind him?"

"Ogle's the captain," Jake reminded. "What will that do to morale when we send him away from their best receiver? Do you really think anybody can go man with him?"

"Nah," Gus admitted. "Still, I'd feel better if he was double covered—man on with zone reaction. Might getta pick."

"Can we compromise? How about we do your man/zone on third and long."

Gus pumped his knee anxiously for several seconds. "I can live with that."

Jake was far more concerned about the rushing game. Those guys ran a lot of quick openers out of the split backs. All the ball carriers needed was a crease, and they were good for eight to ten yards—if not more. Rather than talk to Gus about team ennui, he made several pointed remarks about the running backs' speed and agility.

"Taken care of," Gus replied with a dismissive wave. "I'll have it ready for you in the morning meeting."

It better be bloody good! Jake thought it but did not verbalize it. He had to trust his defensive coordinator. If he didn't like his defensive game plan, there was still time to adjust.

Joe was left deep in cerebral exercises.

"Coach, these guys are ready to explode. Don't get too rah-rah with them. They don't need hokum or pep talks. A nudge here and a nudge there. Before the game, get 'em pumped up. Believe me, this team is ready to bust out."

"Not a moment too soon," Jake replied.

He left unconvinced, but his assistants were the hands-on people. They could see and sense things that the boss couldn't.

———•———

"What do you think, Dave?" he asked of his starting quarterback.

"I hope John has a good game," he replied.

"Loyalty to a former classmate and teammate is an admirable thing," Jake acknowledged. "In this case, it strikes me as misplaced."

"I can't help it, Coach. We've been best friends since the fourth grade. The only argument we ever had was over what college we'd commit to. I want to win this game. I do not want to see my friend humiliated."

Jake hesitated. "Well," he concluded. "At least you won't be on the field at the same time."

"If we were, I'd do everything I could to kick his ass."

That drew a smile. Friends are the fiercest competitors. Neither wants the other to suspect they balked.

———•———

Jake woke early. In truth, he woke a dozen times that night from a sleep so near consciousness that there was little appreciable difference. Betsy, disturbed by her husband's restlessness, jumped up to get the coffee on.

When Jake finished shaving, he found Betsy *and* Tami at the breakfast table. It wasn't unusual for Tami to be up in the early bright on a Saturday. However, sitting quietly behind a cup of cocoa wasn't her habit.

"Still cloudy," Jake noted.

"They expect a shower or two," Betsy added.

She had the radio on at low volume. She repeated the latest weather report. Tami sipped at her drink and twitched noticeably.

A shower wasn't a problem. Rain, however, could kill a game plan. Well, maybe not. Joe was in a bully mood. He planned to beat down the defense with the power game. On a wet field, that might constitute a slight advantage.

"Coffee?"

"Better not," Jake replied. "I'll have a cup at breakfast and call it good."

"Good luck today, Daddy! Kick 'em in the knee."

He chuckled.

Two years before, Tami introduced a vapid doggerel.

Rah-rah Rhee, kick 'em in the knee.
Rah-rah rass, kick 'em in the other knee.

He doubted she was the author, but it became a family tradition. Betsy was reaching for the soap, figuratively, during Tami's initial recitation. She laughed with both glee and relief. After that, she considered it old hat. Jake, however, enjoyed it still.

Breakfast was quiet. *Too* quiet, in accordance with the universal B-movie cliché. It was early, to be sure, but not that early.

The ladies, including the Georgia girl, marched hurriedly to deliver the steak, eggs, and potato breakfasts. They habitually hustled to and fro with little or no comment. This morning, however, their rapid steps echoed like an elephant stampede. There was no casual chatter, no joshing, no rehashing of a recent athletic contest. Every member of the team was deep in thought. Jake hoped they were occupied with high-octane concentration.

The serving girls were put off by the quiet. It was unnerving. Normally, they were barely noticed, save for occasional flirtatious grins. On this morning, the final training table of the season, they were the star attraction—the only animation in the entire room.

"Good luck today," one of the girls whispered as she served.

Moments later, the sentiment was being whispered by all the girls with each plate they set down. It was eerie and bizarre. Nonetheless, it was appreciated.

Jake made a note to show his appreciation later. This same crew would serve the multitude at the end of the season banquet, so he was certain they'd receive his thanks before being transferred to their next work-study task.

They boarded the bus. They filed on silently, sat silently, and waited for the trip to be over silently. Thompson drove the equipment truck over the evening before. He knew the way from many previous journeys. He drove the equipment personally. The man had collected helmets and cleats from the locker room in the dead of night so the players needn't worry about anything other than getting their butts on the bus. Everything would be laid out in the stadium visitor's locker room well before the team's arrival.

Jake saw no need to disrupt the silence.

When they arrived, Jake and Joe led the players off the bus. They wandered about the field for several minutes. The new stadium replaced a previous one five years before. It was big, but it was designed to allow for expansion if (when) needed. The field itself was artificial turf. It was the only conference school so equipped. The manufacturers put it down for a very nice price. It would serve both as a test site and a huge advertisement.

"Think it'll rain?" Jake asked, just to make conversation.

"I got more important things on my mind at the moment, Coach."

Joe Epps could be a grade-A grouch. At that juncture, however, he probably stated truth. He must call a heck of a game. There'd be little margin for error.

* * *

Crisis!

There was no response to Joe's repeated banging on the locker room door.

"Manage, find a security person and bring him down here!"

Damn! This could really break concentration. The team didn't need to be standing in the tunnel scratching their asses, waiting for someone to unlock the changing room. Jake was about to blast off, but he was as helpless as everyone else. There was nothing he could do that wasn't being done.

After seven minutes, the manager returned with a uniformed person.

"We need the key," Joe explained brusquely.

"I don't have a key," the bewildered person responded.

"Our equipment man is elderly," Joe barked. "He could have had a stroke or a heart attack. If we can't unlock this door, we'll break it in!"

Jake took one look at the door and realized Joe was dreaming. It might be possible to break *out*, but there was little chance of forcing entry. Still, with a couple tons of testosterone behind him, Joe and the team could do serious damage.

"*Jesus!*"

The name echoed through the tunnel. Moments later, Steve Thompson, cigar in his mouth and key in his hand, broke through the assembly. "Ya have to walk two miles just to grab a cup of coffee!"

As Steve unlocked the door, Joe glanced over the shoulder and grinned at the security guy. Both were palpably relieved. Thompson might be an eccentric old buzzard, but it would put a serious rupture in team morale had the old man been in trouble. Joe was much relieved. It made Jake feel better and more confident.

Team warm-ups and the lack of enthusiasm ate away at the pit of Jake's stomach. The stadium was filling rapidly. School colors were evenly divided. Many families were divided in their showing individual allegiances, but they sat together. Over the years, these familial groups found ways to maintain unity despite the highly charged partisan atmosphere. Jake's players, however, went through their pregame routine as if this were just another day at the office. Jake's unease was allayed only slightly when he noticed the opposing players similarly stoic.

This could be a pretty bland game, Jake told himself.

He'd expected an uncontrollable display of emotion. Most games were preceded by an electric charge or a subdued if palpable expression of rage. Being confronted by two teams seemingly going through the motions made him wish he were elsewhere.

For a moment, he was stepping into a landing craft. At Guadalcanal and later at New Britain, Jake was folded into an eerie calm. The motors roared, the covering fire boomed, the air cover zoomed. In the craft, however, the Marines huddled in silence. When someone spoke, it was a whisper—a whisper swept away by the ubiquitous cacophony of impending battle.

Jake was unused to this calm on the gridiron. He'd never experienced it before. Players were nervous before a game. They masked their nervousness with noise: grunts, growls, roars, and an occasional burst of blue invective. On this cool, overcast day, two teams kicked, passed, caught, and ran as if trapped in a silent film.

Spooky!

The word was given, and the teams sprinted for their respective locker rooms. Jake and Gus brought up the rear.

"Are these kids ready?" Jake asked.

"They're wound up tighter than a hay bale," Gus replied in his Southern "aw shucks" baritone.

Jake took some comfort in that. "Best of luck, Gus."

"We're ready, Coach. It's a matter of getting it done."

"Well," Jake replied, "help us get it done."

Gus slapped his boss on the back and veered away. He'd climb the stadium steps to get to the press box on the south end of the stadium. A small room and headset awaited him. One of the managers had deposited a Polaroid camera, a clipboard, several pencils, and several sheets of scrap paper. Normally, the coaches in the booth took along a copy of the game plan. Gus, however, played it by ear. He knew what must be done and by whom. It was only a matter of tweaking, that and informing Miller of anything the opposing offense exhibited that didn't appear in the scouting report.

Jake didn't bother to tell the men what this game meant. They knew. He kept his pep talk short. If they weren't charged up, his words would mean nothing. If the players were ready, his words would add nothing.

They listened in silence as the schools' combined bands played the anthem. As the muted notes leaked into the room, a few players were seen praying. Jake didn't know about the personal beliefs of some, but

Jeff Foote was a staunch Catholic; he always said a quiet Our Father before and *after* every game.

"Okay, men. Hook up, and let's head for the beach!"

Why Jake employed that mode of expression was a mystery even to him. The team, however, reacted as if he was George Patton. They were up, loud and eager. If Steve Thompson had locked them in, the team would have torn through the locker room door as if it were paper.

Gary Lynn kicked off. A future All-Pro quarterback brought his team out. Ogle, all 180 pounds of him, was assigned to away from the future All-Pro receiver. Even when he wasn't playing man-to-man, Ogle was aware of the offensive deployment. Luke Eberhardt, the other corner, kept the captain aware of any anomalies; together, they made certain Gus was apprised of anything they hadn't seen in the scouting report. Gus hadn't experienced this before. He normally picked up on surprises very quickly, but it was a boon to realize his players were as astute as he was.

The opposition quarterback was disturbed. Why? His star receiver was faster than anybody Jake had. If the defense intended to play man, the long ball would kill them. Jake's defensive backs inexplicitly shifted from time to time.

Jake sensed this perplexity from the sideline. When you have the advantage, why be flummoxed by a shift in the defense? It was unexpected. Quarterbacks, especially, hate anything unexpected.

Perhaps the much-vaunted quarterback suspected. If he didn't, the opposing staff must have a projected suspicion. Mr. Brilliant would be double covered all day. Underneath, the onside end would help Ogle. Over the top, the safety's priority was to help Eberhardt. The back who averaged eight catches a game would manage only three on this day. He might have gotten five had he not dropped two. Wagonblast was forced to carry the water. He was capable, but Gus had an answer for him as well.

Ogle played the game of his life. He'd studied the film. He knew his opponent's every pattern and how he ran them. He and Gus broke down everything about the wide receivers except for nervous ticks. There were several subtle "tells." The way they came off the ball, the way they used head fakes when changing direction, the way they cut—if he cut on the right foot, it presented an entirely different set of options than cutting on the left.

The slower Ogle knocked down one pass and intercepted another because he was *prepared.*

John Wagonblast killed them on the short routes that day, but he could not break away for the long ball. Gus sacrificed the short game to keep his defense from surrendering the quicker, more deadly long gainer.

The third leading conference rusher gained over a hundred yards, mostly on that quick hitter. Jake quickly deduced that the man was among the conference rushing leaders because he got credit for YAF (yards after fumble). Early in the game, he bolted for twelve yards, fumbled, and Jeff Foote recovered twenty-two yards up field. Thirty-four rushing yards in the books, but Jake's offense had the ball.

The slow-developing 54 and 55 powers chewed up yards like a harvester. Jake thought it was like watching plays in slow motion. It took Shaw and Gino and Billy *days* to turn up field, but when they (finally) did, they made good gains. Evans punished people on the fullback powers. Capp scored a touchdown on a rollout. Peck waited until the last second and zipped the ball to Capp, who turned his body toward the sideline while his feet went the other way. The defensive back flew harmlessly by, and Capp gobbled eighteen additional yards for the score.

Gary Lynn kicked three field goals. He missed another from forty yards out—his first miss of the season.

With three minutes remaining, Jake's squad was up thirty to twenty-nine. Joe didn't dare try to run out the clock. The opposing offense was too potent. The best defense was to keep the ball out of the hands of the bad guys.

It was fourth down and a yard from the minus forty-eight-yard line.

As the chain gang hustled back to the sideline after the measurement, Jake turned to Miller who was in contact with Gus in the booth. "Can the defense hold?" Jake demanded.

Miller conferred with the boss through his headset. A moment later, he nodded. (Later, he claimed he hadn't nodded; he'd *swallowed* very hard.)

Jake turned to Joe and repeated the nod.

Joe held Peck close by one finger wrapped around the quarterback's face mask.

"Left opposite, 52 power guard."

The moment his finger dropped from the face guard, Peck sprinted back to the huddle.

Gut-for-garters time. The formation was strong to the left. Dilley and Zwetschke were the best blocking combo. Evans *must* attempt to crash through that hole. The entire defense knew what was coming. The middle linebacker cheated—ever so slightly—to the strength of the formation.

The crowd arose as one, and the noise was deafening. When Peck broke the huddle, the noise increased. The young quarterback had a single goal: to get that clock ticking again. He hustled his squad to the line and made certain everyone was set.

The defense put ten men on the line. The safety was deep. That is, he was four yards behind his teammates. Russ Capp was split wide right. Peck held his gaze until the split end went into his three-point stance.

Peck squatted down behind the center.

"Go!"

The quick count.

Joe was right, the sophomore was smart. The defense could not afford to be drawn offsides and, doubtless, dug in to wait out a long count. Peck's men knew they were going on the quick count. Normally, at the first *go*, the linemen and backs flexed—a surefire way to draw the impatient players offside. The defense knew about the flex. They'd seen it every play since the kickoff. They'd be double sure not to get suckered. This gave the offense the tiniest advantage, but a drowning man clutches at straws.

The line fired out like a herd of raging bulls.

The defense clawed up field, determined to move the line of scrimmage backward. Peck turned and handed the ball to Evans a fraction of a second before some kamikaze linebacker could leap over the mass of humanity to knock him to the turf.

Not one of the thousands of fans would notice Russ Capp. Only when they viewed the film would anyone notice.

The moment the ball was snapped, Capp stood up and extended his left hand as if gesturing at a museum exhibit. The defensive back, hardly two feet away, was mesmerized. He looked at Capp, looked at his left hand, looked at the heaving pile of humanity, and looked back at Capp as if expecting him to run a delayed route.

Evans hit the only crease between Dilley and Smith and made the first down with ease. The hulking fullback was suddenly confronted with nothing but grass and yard lines. The man was near exhaustion. He'd gained eighty-one hard-fought yards; he'd blocked like Satan for nearly four quarters. His tank was empty.

It was pathetic.

The slowest running back in the conference was in the clear and desperately looking around.

"Won't somebody tackle me? *Please!*"

He didn't say a word, of course, but his body language was unmistakable.

The defensive line fired out and lay, together with the offensive linemen, in a pile. The linebackers shot every gap (except one) and lost their footing trying to catch up with the line plunge. It was the defensive back on Capp who eventually reacted. He took one last look at the split end and realized that the man with the ball, not the statue, was his prime concern. He left his post and easily chased down the winded fullback. However, Evans, by force of habit, kept chugging stubbornly for an additional eight yards. He might have been good for an additional ten, but the struggling d-back got help from two additional tardy teammates.

The crowd was absolutely insane.

Evans gained twenty-nine yards.

First and ten from the twenty-three-yard line.

Jake turned to find Gary Lynn stretching out. His foot could put the game out of kicking distance. John Wagonblast and company would have to drive all the way down the field to pull this one out. They were quite capable of doing so. "Those people," as Jake called them a la Robert E. Lee, were as dangerous as a wounded grizzly. They still had a lot of strength and a lot of weapons—and they were pissed!

He turned to Joe. He was on the cusp of telling him to run the clock as much as possible. He stifled the urge. Joe knew the score, and he knew his business.

Joe gripped Gino by his shoulder pads at the base of his neck. "Right opposite, forty-one," Joe barked. "Fumble the ball, and you won't get on the bus—you'll be under it!"

Quick count again. Get that clock running. Gino fought like a demon for three yards. Six seconds ticked by, and the defense called their last time-out.

"Right opposite, fifty-four power."

Joe shoved Shaw out onto the field.

Jake took a deep breath. That damned play that took forever and ever to develop. This was exactly the play to drain the clock. He hoped Billy Morris had sense enough to run like hell if the hole wasn't there. Jake would gladly give up ten yards if his men could eat up twenty seconds.

Billy hit the hole and could have gained five yards easily, but he cut and headed for the sideline. It cost precious time to head him off.

"Don't go out of bounds," Jake growled.

He muttered. He did not yell. Billy couldn't hear over all that noise. Additionally, he was a senior. He should know what to do.

One bold linebacker breathing fire was determined to shove Billy off the playing field. The back caught him with peripheral vision, turned, and ran directly at the closing tackler. It was like a semi plowing into a Volkswagen. The collision was tumultuous, but Billy went down inside the painted white lines.

Another two yards, and precious seconds more drained away.

Everyone looked up at the clock. Peck looked to the bench. Gino and Shaw alternated plays, carrying Joe's calls in with them. These two luminaries were on the sidelines with Joe, impersonating a statue. A referee approached the conclave. Fearing some obscure rule might work to his detriment, Joe clutched Gino.

"Tell 'em to call a play, any play, go up to the line, and let the clock run."

Gino rushed out onto the field, but he didn't bother to snap his chin strap. He spoke to Peck. The huddled assembly heard and understood.

Later, Jake would get a report from Dilley, the center. Peck called *right opposite, sneeze.*

In the retelling, it got a chuckle. At the time, however, no one found the call the least amusing. They broke the huddle, walked to the line of scrimmage, and stood, most with arms akimbo, as if waiting further orders.

The yellow flag flew. Delay of game. Five yards stepped off.

From the nineteen-yard line, fourth down with twenty-two seconds remaining.

"Twinkle Toes!" Joe bellowed. "You're up!"

Normally, the pejorative would sound offensive. However, Gary Lynn's foot had contributed to their slim lead. The kicker jogged out onto the field, but Joe kept Peck close.

"Stay on the field," he cautioned.

The quarterback avoided controversy by remaining two long steps from the sideline.

"If they block this kick, we're in deep doo-doo," he reminded the young quarterback. "If they block it and run it back, we lose. If we miss, they start from the twenty with their entire playbook open. They're still very dangerous, Dave."

The young man nodded.

The moment Joe motioned the quarterback back into the game, Jake took up station behind him. "Why didn't you just tell him?" he demanded.

"I want him to think it's his idea," Joe replied placidly.

The ball was snapped. Lynn approached the pad to find the ball missing. When he looked up, he saw Dave Peck running like a scalded dog for the sideline. He didn't fool anyone. The defenders converged and cornered him quickly. Peck, following Billy's example, lowered his head and ran straight into some very angry opponents.

The ball was turned over on downs, and there were twelve pathetic fleeting seconds remaining.

Well, "those people" went down fighting.

They attempted a hook-and-ladder, but the ball was overthrown. John Wagonblast made a valiant if futile attempt to snag the pig skin, but he required a trampoline to reach it—he had none.

The insane crowd spilled out onto the field, and it was impossible to navigate. Jake was ushered out onto the field. He remembered shaking hands with the opposing coach. They exchanged words, but they were impossible to decipher amid the thunder and chaos.

The last thing Jake saw before nearing the tunnel was John Wagonblast and Dave Peck standing near the twenty-yard line. They held their helmets by the face mask and were hugging each other. They were bawling like three-year-old kids.

⎯⎯⎯◆⎯⎯⎯

Jake met with the press. He avoided saying anything inflammatory. He'd face this team again next year, and he didn't want to stir the pot.

"Nobody really won this game," he concluded. "The clock ran out before this thing was settled. I guess that's why we keep playing each other."

Mark Davidson broke away from the locker room celebration to greet Jake after his escape from the press.

"It was a long wait," he said with amazing stoicism. "We won two games in a row."

Jake shook his hand. Mark hadn't made any tackles on kickoffs, but he disrupted the return package twice. He also got a few downs as defensive end but had no chance to make a play. Regardless, he was as much a part of the victory as those few who played every down.

"Talk to me again after you help us win eight in a row."

"I'll do that."

Eight victories total appeared an impossibility. However, Jake and his staff would do their damnedest to improve the odds.

Poor Mieko! No one thought to tell her that there'd be no Sunday team meeting and, therefore, no rush to get the film developed. Likely, it wouldn't have made any difference. She took her work seriously and wouldn't dally because of some fatuous break in routine.

She picked up the film directly from the cameraman, raced down to the parking area, jumped in the state car, and wove her way through the post-game traffic before it became too intense.

The good and faithful servant was perplexed to find the arena locked when she delivered the film. It was nearly two o'clock in the morning, but there was always someone on hand (usually Coach Churchill) to accept the artifact. She let herself in with her key.

Yes, she was trusted to have her own key.

When Jake arrived at the office Sunday after church, he found the game film on his desk.

He muttered to himself. "Someone should have told her."

What the hell?

He eschewed the work on his desk. He took up the container and headed for the nearest projector.

Downhill

He met with Ralph about the team's awards banquet. It was his job to get the ballots from the team members for most team spirit and most valuable player. Jake and his staff took care of the rest, save one. The team trainer, who fancied himself an Ogden Nash, always presented an award for the player who consumed the most tape during the season. It was an empty tape cannister with a red cross attached to the top. Prior to announcing the winner, he would deliver, from memory, a three- or four-minute speech in doggerel. In recent years, it proved the most popular antic of the evening. Jake hadn't taken the job to throw out established tradition; when Ralph asked to put the trainer on the rostrum with the coaches and invited speakers, it was the easiest decision Jake made all season.

On his way to meet with the boss, Denise stood to attention as always. This practice continued to grate on him, but he refused to scold.

"By the end of the day, I'd like your nominations for All-Conference players," Ralph reminded.

It was one of the many things Jake shoved onto his to-do pile. He'd given the matter some thought, but realized time was ticking away, and he needed to focus. Ralph was scheduled to leave for the conference AD get together (and cash bar) the following afternoon. Two conference games remained to be played, but Jake declined to turn pedantic. If (a very tenuous *if*) he ever became an athletic director, he'd throw a champion fit over such sloppy conference practices.

"Miss Davenport appears handicapped. Can she still lift that hand?"

"She's getting married in the spring. Her husband-to-be works in the state capital. I have plenty of time to find someone, but damn!"

Jake nodded his head. He'd have put in a good word for Mieko.

Later that day, he bumped into her in the coffee room.

"Can you take shorthand?"

"No," she replied, nonplussed.

"Can you type?

"Not very well."

"Good."

He did not explain. The wily oriental fell back on centuries of cultural tradition and stifled her curiosity. However, she'd become Americanized enough to display a queer visage when Jake departed without further comment.

If Mieko had been eligible to fill Davenport's place, she'd become a full-time employee, but she could hardly be expected to perform Denise's duties and continue as his team's travel agent and film fetcher. Keeping her as a work-study for perhaps another year was hardly likely. There were several university departments to vie for her intelligence and work ethic, but there was a chance (no matter how slim) that she'd return as Jake's indefatigable and reliable go-to person.

Jake kept an eye on the Black Student Union through the *Spectator*. There was very little to track. The organization was, for whatever reason, keeping a low profile. Jake was dissatisfied with the fourth estate as a whole and seldom believed the accuracy of any reporting and, especially, the transient and nonprofessional journalism students who put out the campus bugle. He could hardly snoop on his own. Someone would get wind of it; his activities would be announced in the *Spectator*, picked up by the city daily, and would circulate state-wide within a week. The college president and the athletic director would be dancing on Jake's desk wearing track spikes. They'd demand to know why he dared defy their orders. Jake daren't call in Evans, Mel, or any of the other "colored" players. That would come under the heading of "unauthorized" conduct.

If *they* came to *him*, that was acceptable. However, the AD and the president would *not* be happy.

As a coach, Jake had rubbed too many people the wrong way. He could hardly afford to earn the ire of his superiors.

He deduced that the Black Student Union was the product of a larger off-campus agitation organization. He had reason to believe that outside money was used in their promotions and (thus far) small-scale demonstrations.

Jake wanted to deal with the group in a civilized manner. If his overtures were shunned, he'd appeal to the public with logic, reason, and perhaps evidence on his side. He remained convinced that the ostrich head-in-the-sand strategy would exacerbate the situation and result in an emotional explosion that would make any resolution a hundred times more difficult.

Jake knew his recruiting efforts would be examined under an electron microscope. He hated having school and NCAA big shots looking over his shoulder. Adding an outside agitation group sticking their big fat nose into his work was intolerable.

What, he wondered, would have happened if the Marines on Guadalcanal waited for the Japanese Army to go away and bother them no further? How he and his buddies (both survivors and deceased) wished the Japanese Navy would never have sent fourteen-inch shells down on them for an eternity one dark overcast night. It did, of course, and nearly a thousand rounds left the island and everything on it a smoking ruin.

"Oh, they went away. Big whoop! Let's put out the fires and bury the dead."

Well, Jake's notion of addressing the problem before it became a major issue was *officially* rebuffed. Jake was not allowed to control his own fate.

<hr>

Jake was juggling recruiting, BSU, Steve Thompson, and domestic problems (Liisi had decided she wanted to take piano lessons—how to practice without a piano at home? Buy one. With what?) He stumbled upon Gus Avery and Dave Thorne reviewing a series against their bitter enemy.

"They shouldn't have scored twenty-nine points against us," he muttered.

Gus stood up like a grizzly preparing for dinner. "You don't like my work, I'll pack my bags!"

Jake realized the imbecility of making such a bitter and thoughtless comment. This was no time to be meek and mild. Gus would blow a gasket for certain.

"Easy, Gus. I know your heart is with Canadian football, but you're the best damned defensive coordinator this side of the Mississippi, and…I don't know, most of the other side of the Mississippi as well. If I've got a beef, I'll get in your face. I'm not criticizing your game plan. I'm bemoaning sloppy play of a few players who didn't have their heads on right. Do you want to tell me that all those points were earned?"

It was a clear challenge. Gus was not a prevaricator. He shot from the hip. It only took a couple of seconds to realize the truth of Jake's comment.

"They shouldn't have scored all those points," he admitted.

"I need you, Gus. I want to move Church up, but hell, I can't afford to lose you. Next season, we'll have a couple linebackers—"

"And Davidson," Thorne reminded.

"*And* Davidson," Jake acknowledged.

Gus was cooling down. "That gives us more scope," he announced.

"Crap!" Jake inserted. "They'll be green as grass. Who will get them ready? Dave here, of course, but we need you to design the defense and crack the whip."

Gus was thinking. He loved challenges. There was nowhere in America *or* Canada where he'd find a greater one.

"Going for it on fourth down," Jake injected. "If you told me to punt, we'd have punted. I trust your judgment, Gus."

"Okay, Coach," Gus sighed. "I think the CFL can survive without me for another season or two."

"Good man, Gus. Now, give me a defense."

"With twelve men, can do." He grinned.

"American rules, Gus. American rules."

Gus grinned again and resumed his seat. "Punctilious bastard," he muttered to Thorne.

Jake heard him. He knew that Gus knew he'd heard.

Jake wasn't much of a theater student, but he recognized a great exit line when he heard one. Since Gus refused to exit, Jake decided it was his cue.

It's a sin to ruin a good exit line.

⸻ ◆ ⸻

The snows came early, but they didn't amount to much. Jake and Tami shoveled the driveway and the sidewalk themselves with minimal effort. In truth, they needn't have bothered. The temperature seldom dipped below freezing, and the neighbors, save for Jake and the family Epps, didn't bother with the niggardly accumulation. Given a couple hours, the white substance would have melted on its own.

Once upon a time, Tami enjoyed making snowmen. She aided Little Joe in his effort, but he was disappointed by the tiny lawn ornament. It failed to survive the day. The young boy was disappointed, but Tami felt no remorse when their snow art was reduced to a pathetic lump of slush on an otherwise bare lawn.

As with everything she took on, Tami was obsessed with piano. She made a keyboard out of three sheets of art paper and practiced her fingering by commandeering the coffee table. Occasionally, she would vocalize the notes. Lacking a singing aptitude, Tami relied on her mother's voice to redress any "clinkers" she produced. As with her artwork and literary endeavors, the paper piano bothered Jake in his office hardly at all.

On Sunday mornings, the family would leave early for church so Tami could practice on the instrument therein. Mrs. Workman, jealous of her position as *the* volunteer accompanist, would loiter after service to provide the girl a few minutes of supervised practice.

Jake, observing a tacit treaty with Betsy, allowed himself only one football game a week. He had no use for either the network play-by-play or the endless stream of commercials. The sound remained muted. He watched and from time to time made a quick note of items (particularly blocking schemes) that piqued his interest. In short, he watched and observed without any noise other than Tami and her virtual piano.

He watched as the team they beat in the away-from-home home game cruised to an easy bowl victory. They were ranked sixth in the national polls. That highly publicized team suffered only one defeat: a 24 to 18 loss at the hands of Jake and company.

He didn't watch the upset bowl appearance of the conference champs. He was glad he didn't. It would have hurt too much to watch the team Jake *nearly* beat. The pain was compounded enough by their upset win over Jake's alma mater. That really hurt. Watching it happen would be unendurable.

Later, neither he nor any of his staff made mention of either bowl game. They, like Jake, could only sigh.

We coulda been a contender!

Spilt milk.

Georgia also won their bowl game. They were knocked out of the national championship picture by a loss to Auburn late in the season. There were no wistful sighs wasted on that result. Jake and his team were soundly crushed by the Bulldogs. Chances were excellent that the result would prove nearly as bad had they played them last rather than first.

It took three weeks to tie up all the ends and officially close the football program until February when the run-up-to-spring ball began. He spent enough time with Steve Thompson that he unconsciously began using the word *Jesus* as a conversational filler. Betsy put the kybosh on that at home. He became self-conscious and began monitoring his language even beyond Betsy's hearing.

Traditionally, the head coach got December off. He was expected to come into the office and check in with the AD periodically, but he essentially had the rest of the calendar year off.

Neither Jake nor any previous coach had problems touching base. There were plenty of things to keep him occupied.

Jake was the guest speaker for three organizations around the state. He preferred to take his family on these outings, but Tami's school and piano lessons forced him to travel solo. He found himself talking football, but he didn't enjoy it. Fans, no matter how dedicated, cannot (or will not) understand either the limitations of practice time or the nuances of the game. However, he had a bevy of anecdotes about Michigan football in the pre-war years. Even the grumps and growlers perked up when he trotted out a few choice stories from the "long ago."

He experienced loneliness. He'd spend his evenings on the phone with Betsy and Tami. If he were near a prospect, either coming or going, he'd arrange for a home visit. He was always provided a state car for such extracurricular activities. It was the university's clever way of chaining him to the office. He didn't like the arrangement. Mieko was dispatched to fetch his vehicle from the motor pool and deliver it to Jake's parking space. When he returned, she'd drive it back to the motor pool.

"I can fetch the car and do all the paperwork myself," he objected. "Mieko has enough work to do without running my errands for me."

Such objections were either ignored or shrugged off.

"This is how it's done," he was repeatedly told.

That, Jake vowed, would change! However, this involved memos, meetings, and amending office policies. A simple seemingly innocuous change required an inordinate amount of time, but Jake vowed to stick it out. If he were lucky, he'd fetch his own car the following winter.

One afternoon, he returned to his office early.

Barbara was not at her desk.

"Her daughter was in a car accident this morning," Holly informed.

"Is she okay?"

He caught himself in time. He did not say *Jesus.*

Holly nodded. "Only a fender bender," Holly replied. "However, a mother worries. She shouldn't be away much longer."

Jake wasn't reassured, but he recognized Holly was void of concern. He'd have to accept her report until Barbara showed up.

"Mel Manning will be here at three," she added.

"Good."

He didn't want to hang around until three, but this was important. He had a scholarship to award. Mel was the front runner, but Jake continued to entertain doubts. Despite the kid's performance in the frosh games, despite the numbers he put up, there remained the problem of his diminutive stature.

Barbara stuck her head in his office to find Jake wading through his correspondence. Judging from her visage, she was not pleased.

"Mr. Manning is here," she announced softly.

"Is your daughter okay?"

He was slightly miffed. She neglected to report to him the moment she returned.

"Sadder but wiser," Barbara replied.

That was totally unsatisfactory. He assumed the girl was in deep poo at home. Had she sustained an injury, Barbara's response wouldn't be so dismissively callous.

"Send him in."

Jake was standing with his arm outstretched when Mel appeared. He wore a sweater and a heavy coat, but he shook Jake's hand firmly.

"Hang up that coat and have a seat."

Mel was eager to comply. Before sitting down in the overstuffed leather chair, he extracted something from his coat pocket. Proudly, he set it down on Jake's desk. It was his first quarter grade report.

"You got a C in algebra," Jake observed.

"I think the prof cut me some slack," he admitted. "I have to take a math sequence or a lab science. I signed up again, but I signed up for biology too. If I can't hack the math, I'll drop it."

"You have to carry sixteen hours," Jake reminded.

"Math is only two hours. If I drop it, I'll still have sixteen."

Jake grunted.

"How do they teach you to appreciate literature?"

Mel grinned. "The prof don't know either," he replied. "Uhm, *doesn't* know either. The first class he asked us what we wanted to do. He wasn't anxious to meet three days a week. I said that *he* was the man. If he didn't know what we should do, maybe I'd better find someone who does."

"And you still got a C?"

"My composition needs a lot of work."

"Are you getting help?"

"Yes, sir. Prof said I had a lots of good stuff to say, but he understood me better when I talk than when I write."

Jake grunted again. "Your speech had improved, Mel. That's important. Writing is important too. Could you make a copy of some of your work this next quarter and let me see it?"

"Yes, sir. I will make that happen."

Jake smiled and nodded. "There's a theater prof here I've gotten to know. He teaches Voice and Articulation. I'd like for you to take it this spring."

"I ain't no actor, sir."

Jake leaned back in his chair.

"I'm not an actor, sir," Mel corrected.

"This class isn't for theater majors, it's for everybody. You'd please me, no end, if you sign up for it."

Mel grinned and nodded. "Consider it done, sir."

"Western Civ is required?"

"Yes, sir."

"You got a B. That's impressive. I had problems with required classes. I thought they were a waste of time."

Mel was getting comfortable. He put his arms on the rests and grinned. "I thought it was interesting. Well, I thought his lectures were interesting. The textbook was, well, it helped me get plenty of sleep."

Jake chuckled. Mel joined in.

"Do you think you can play here, Mel?"

"Yes, sir. I do think that."

Jake was calculating. He'd need a lead blocker clearing the way for Mel. They would use the *I* formation more often—lead blocker, pulling guards. It would be tough getting him to the corners, but if they did… Mel's time in the forty was eye-popping.

"Coach Churchill speaks well of you, Mel. This grade card speaks well of you. You're learning to talk like a college man. I'm offering you an athletic scholarship, son."

Mel sat quietly for a long while. The tears forming in his eyes communicated everything important.